Has Anyone Seen Mavis?

Lucy Scott

For JPB

Prologue

Dear Father – I don't know why I call you father, you are anything but, but in a world so obsessed with identity I feel I must give you a name. I can't tell you this in person; you'd only laugh and sneer and mock me so I must write it down.

I remember the first time that I knew childhood was fading fast and young womanhood was approaching. It had crept up on me unawares as I turned from a shy child with my teddy bears and toys into a young woman on the verge of adolescence. I looked at myself in the mirror and saw for the first time my blossoming breast buds and curving figure. That was the day my childhood disappeared forever.

Fate is so cruel. I look back on that day, only six months ago, with a cold grief that has settled on my soul. I thought you cared for me, the nurture I thought you wanted for me so clear in your words and actions. How bitterly I was to be betrayed. I was away from home, my parents far away and I went to you for solace and companionship. For a while, our time together was good. We talked together, we laughed together and we read together. I felt happy and content. But then it changed. The day it happened is branded so deeply in my consciousness that it will remain there for ever.

The man I knew as a friend had turned into a monster. That look in your eyes frightened me beyond measure. You said, "You're a woman now, you're mine."
At first I didn't understand you but your intent soon became clear. I couldn't fight you, I wasn't strong enough. I just laid there, mind and body frozen as my breath and my purity were stolen from me as your body lay on me. It didn't take long. In a few short minutes you destroyed everything there had even been between us. I fought

but you were stronger. You left leaving me blooded and defiled. I knew exactly what had happened – any childish innocence that I possessed, had vanished in those few disgusting minutes. I felt sick, humiliated, dirty and violated. I had no choice in the matter or did I? Had I encouraged you? Was it my fault? I am wracked with guilt.

You came again and again, the months a torture. There was no escape. To escape I would have to expose you but in doing that I would expose myself. Who would believe me against you? No one, I fear. I can tell no one, I have to carry this pain alone.

Now there are two of us. I have another to care for. It is a gift I didn't ask for but one I have to accept. You can do no more to me. This has to end. I don't know how but I will find a way.

Chapter One

Alexis sat on an old fallen log with her back to the late November sun, huddled in a thick winter's jacket against the chill of the day. The waters of the River Teigne slowly trickled by in front of her, nibbling at the pebbles which lay next to the river's edge. The river wasn't full, the autumn had been unseasonably dry, but the water was sufficient to disturb the hanging branches of willow trees, which dipped, bare and leafless, into the shallows. This was a place of peace for her, a peace she so badly needed. It was also a place where grief was stored, but a grief tempered by time. As the late afternoon sunlight filled the small haven she had created for herself, Alexis thought back to the day she had had. The call had come out of the blue, and although quickly realising that it was a recognition of her abilities as a detective and not a punishment, as she had at first feared, it had completely floored her and now she needed time to think.

Earlier that morning, Detective Sergeant Alexis Longbow had been happily detecting crime in the busy city of Hereford. She loved her work and had fought hard for her position, but now in her early thirties she was feeling slightly adrift and directionless. She often felt that being a woman in what was still really a man's world, gave her little chance of promotion, even though she had passed the inspector's exam, so her mind and body were restless and eager for change. Happy enough to carry on with her CID work in the city for the time being, she had nevertheless been toying with the idea of moving to another town, or even another force, anything for a change and a breath of fresh air. Then, when the phone rang on her desk earlier that morning, that change would seem to have come sooner than she could ever have expected. Alexis had been ordered to report to the Assistant Chief Constable at nine the following day at Police Headquarters in Hereford to discuss the possibility of a secondment to Scotland Yard in London, to work on the Anti-

Terrorist Squad. As she replaced the receiver she felt sick, her mind numb and her thoughts in freefall. She had thought of making a change but this? Could she do it? Was she ready for the challenge? She caught her breath and tried to steady her heart beat. 'Be careful what you wish for', she mused as she thought through the conversation she'd just had. This would be a dangerous and demanding role but even in her shock she felt gratified that someone at Headquarters obviously thought she was up for the challenge. Now sitting by the sparkling waters of the River Teigne in the small village of Culliston, Alexis spoke to her father. This was no ordinary conversation but one that was private and so very special. Richard Longbow, Alexis' father, had suddenly passed away after a brief illness, exactly two years ago to the day. The coincidence hadn't been missed by his daughter, and at the exact place where a few weeks later she and her sister Georgia had scattered his ashes, a favourite spot of her father's where he'd fished for trout, she now pondered her future and just wanted his advice.

"What shall I do, Dad? I need your help."

She often chatted away in her mind to her unseen father, sometimes there was nothing but silence but other times she heard his words as clear as if he'd actually been sitting next to her. Today was one of those occasions, and as the birds sang in the trees and the rippling waters slowly flowed past her, she heard him. It didn't come as conversation, it was an impression in her mind, but she heard his thoughts just the same. Her whole body relaxed, and her mind cleared. Her eyes moistened with gentle tears and she felt them cool as the breeze lifted her blonde hair from her shoulders and rustled the long grasses beside her. She looked across to the far bank, where the countryside stretched up towards the hills she loved so much, and knew what she had to do. The sun disappeared behind a cloud and she shivered as the illusion of warmth vanished in an instant. It was a brief moment but enough to shake Alexis out of her thoughtful mood. She gathered her coat round her shoulders and headed back to the car. The lane took her down to the main road, following the river, and after crossing the little bridge further down, she turned north for Teigneford where her mother lived. Alexis herself lived in a small stone cottage in Moreton, another small village just south of the main town. It meant a bit of a commute every day into the city, but its benefits were legion. The closeness to the hills and forests which surrounded her and where she could walk to her heart's content, was balm to her soul and where she could cleanse her mind whenever she wanted to.

After a brief visit to the local supermarket to stock up on a few provisions, Alexis pulled up outside her mother's house, a Victorian house built in a quieter part of the town, a genteel road lined with ancient oak trees and full of characterful houses and bungalows. Alexis loved this house; she had been born in it and had grown up knowing every nook and cranny and it felt so familiar. Although a large house, and one that Alexis had thought her mother might have wanted to sell after her father's death, she had been so relieved when Mrs Longbow had decided to stay.
"It's my home, our home, Alexis. Your father is still here with me. I can't leave him."
She could still remember her mother's words and been so grateful for them. They hadn't been morbid thoughts; her mother had grieved and still grieved, but she had moved on, making a new life for herself in the community. Now as Alexis walked up the front path, and round to the back, she felt she had come home. Mrs Patricia Longbow heard her daughter's footsteps and recognised them and was ready with a smile as Alexis rounded the corner into the back garden, where she was sitting in the conservatory at the back of the house, the doors open as she enjoyed the late afternoon's sunshine.
"Alexis! How lovely to see you. What brings you here?"
"I've got something to tell you, Mum," came the enigmatic reply.
"Not bad news, I hope," she countered, her smile abating a little.
"No, just something important I need to chat about."

"Come on in then. Want a cuppa or a cold drink? I've got some fresh lemonade I've just made."

"A coffee would be just the thing. Thanks, Mum."

With the drinks duly produced, and her mother settled opposite, Alexis poured out the day's events and what they would mean. She detailed the two options, refuse or accept, and the dangers with either decision. Mrs Longbow listened in silence, her face grave as she looked at her eldest daughter. She saw the slim figure perched on the edge of the seat, her blonde hair curling just as it touched her shoulders, cradling her now half empty mug. Naturally, a mother's love kicked in first and she was horrified at what Alexis was considering. But, she had a sensible head on her and bit her tongue at the comments which came readily to her lips, so forcing herself to relax, she listened as Alexis outlined what could lie ahead.

"You've already decided, haven't you dear?" her mother said when Alexis had finished.

"I think so," she replied.

"And you've already told your father, haven't you?"

Alexis didn't even blink at this rather unconventional question. Her mother knew her too well.

"Yes Mum, I have. I stopped off at the river on my way here from work."

"And what did he say?" replied her mother with a smile.

"Nothing specific, but you know…" Alexis tailed off. "I just felt though, that he was with me. I felt relaxed. Yes, a bit tearful, but I think he gave me his blessing."

"Then go with it. You know what's involved; it won't be a walk in the park, although I hope you get the chance to do a few of those," finished Mrs Longbow with a smile.

Alexis wasn't fooled. She knew that the separation would be hard, albeit for only a few months and her mother was bound to worry, but she had her blessing and now her mind was clear.

"What will it mean for your job at the police station?" asked Mrs Longbow, momentarily concerned.

"Haven't got a clue. The kudos of the appointment won't do me any harm, I s'pose. Just have to wait and see. I bet they'll be surprised in the office, though."

"What will Archie say?"

"Haven't told him yet. Was going to wait until after I've seen the ACC tomorrow."

"He'll miss you."

"I'll miss him."

Detective Constable Gabriel Dax, known to his friends as Archie, a diminutive nickname from the Archangel Gabriel, and Alexis had known each other for a long time, ever since Dax had appeared fresh from police training college eight years previously and delivered into the safe arms of Police Constable Longbow, who then had been asked to tutor the fledgling constable, having completed her probation a year before. The two had become firm friends and quickly discovered a shared taste and skill for detective work. They had both applied to CID in Hereford and once accepted, quickly established themselves as successful investigators, notching up many solved crimes as time went on. Inevitably, being the elder, promotion had come a little sooner to Alexis, and they had gone from strength to strength. When Dax had married Claire, two years ago, Alexis was pleased. Her friendship with both Claire and Dax was now both firm and strong but nothing more than that, so without the ties of love, their professional life and working relationship were everything they should be.

Alexis stayed with her mother for a bit longer as each discussed the way ahead but as the sun eventually sank behind the tall trees at the end of the garden, Alexis made a move.

"I'll get going, Mum. I need to get home. Got some thinking to do."

Mrs Longbow had been going to offer her daughter some dinner, but recognising Alexis' needed to be alone for the evening, she satisfied herself with a hug as she kissed Alexis goodbye.

"Let me know how you get on tomorrow," she said as Alexis walked back with her mother up the path and round to the front of the house.

"Will do, Mum. Love you."

Mrs Longbow watched as her daughter drove off up the road, a pensive expression on her face. She too spoke to her late husband.

"Keep an eye on her, Richard my love. That daughter of ours is going to need all the help she can get."

The following morning, Alexis sat in the office of the Assistant Chief Constable and now that the decision was truly upon her, her mind was again in a whirl. Last night, after talking to her mother, she had gone home, had a quick bite to eat then walked up on to the hill behind her cottage. The sky was clear, the air chilling in the twilight and in the distance, the slopes of Cleeve Hill stood silhouetted against the pale sky. It had been a restful scene and Alexis' mind was still, her decision had been made but now, in the cold clear light of another day, reality threatened to undo her calm. On the one hand she was being handed a boost to her career, to be much envied by her fellows, but on the other it would mean uprooting herself from her home and her friends for six months, maybe longer if the need arose, and subjecting herself to unimaginable horrors. London had been quiet for a long while, the terrors of the bombing campaigns of the seventies were thankfully long past, but now a new threat had inveigled itself into London society, a malicious interloper from the East, and London, once again, was riven with terror and bloodshed.

"Sergeant Longbow," said Assistant Chief Constable David Grainger. "I appreciate this has come out of the blue. I am aware that you will need some time to think, but time is of the essence. If I could have your decision by the end of today, I would be grateful."

"Yes sir. I think my decision is made but if you could let me have an hour or two, just to take in the details that you've given me, now that I have them, that would be good."

"That's agreed, Sergeant. Say, by four this afternoon?"
"Yes sir. Thank you."

She thought about it on the drive back from Headquarters to the police station. She had made up her mind, but just wanted the chance to talk freely to her colleagues, in particular Archie. She hadn't been given much time to think about the new posting, just a few hours in fact, but it was an opportunity not to be turned down lightly. The risks in accepting were only too obvious; leave a safe and secure posting in the shires and swap it for an unpredictable life in the capital, with all its inherent disadvantages and dangers. Hardly a day went past without some new horror being visited on the British public, so far away but now so close to Alexis, if she chose. The risks in declining were there too. Alexis was only too aware that a woman in what was still a very masculine world had few choices and chances and to say no would inhibit her career, probably for ever. She had been given a very rare opportunity; then self-doubt kicked in and she asked herself, why? Was it because she was a very good detective, or was it because she was a woman and they could get rid of her in the Met for a while.
'Stop it!' she told herself. 'You're being stupid'.

The conversation back in the office had been predictable. The less charitable had exclaimed their doubts in no uncertain terms.
"Why you? Why are you so special?"
This had hurt Alexis, particularly as one of the most negatively opinionated had been her own detective inspector.
"You'll never make the grade, girl. London? You'll drown on the first day," he had finished disdainfully.
Other comments had been more complimentary and congratulatory.
"Well done, Lexi. You deserve this. We'll miss you."
Alexis had seen Dax leaning against the wall at the back of the office. His face gave nothing away. She dreaded his contribution to the office chat. Tears threatened to well up in her eyes as she contemplated the future. Her decision was truly made, she was

13

going but first she needed to chat to her friend. He watched her, seeing the conflicting emotions chasing themselves across her face, mirroring his own conflict.

"Fancy a bit of lunch?" he asked quietly as he walked to stand beside her.

"Thanks, Archie. Canteen?"

"No, let's get out of this shithole for a while. You need to unwind."

Alexis' shoulders sagged with an emotional exhaustion and he led her gently out of the office and into the city. The place was busy; traffic clogged the streets, taxis and buses came and went adding to the noise and nuisance, but in a back street, known to them both, he found a table in a small bistro. It was quiet and secluded and the perfect place for a chat. He sat her down and went to order a coffee and a baguette and then returned to the table. Alexis looked grey and his heart filled with compassion.

"So, what are you going to do?" he asked, his voice quiet and solemn.

"I've got no choice, Archie, have I?" she cried. "If I don't go, I'm stuck here for ever. No one will give me another look. If I do go, I've got to leave my family, my friends and my job for a very uncertain future. London's a dangerous place to be at the moment."

"Of course you've got to go. Once you get there, you'll enjoy every minute."

Dax tried to infuse his voice with as much feeling as he could manage.

"D'you reckon?"

"Of course you will," he said simply. "It's a marvellous opportunity. I'm quite envious really."

"Claire would never let you go," said Alexis with a smile.

"Probably not."

The two officers paused to eat their lunch, then Dax went on.

"What happens next?"

"I've got to let the ACC know by four, then all systems go, I expect."

"When will you leave?"

"Monday, I think he said."

"Blimey, that's only four days."

"Doesn't give me much chance to think, but perhaps that's a good thing."

"Right, let's get back to the nick. Ignore all the doomsayers. You're a great detective and an excellent police officer. You'll sail through this."

"I really hope you're right, Archie."

Once back in the office, which had thankfully emptied, giving Alexis a chance to breathe and ring the ACC in private, she made the call. Now that her decision had been made, arrangements for board and lodging were swiftly arranged and the logistics of the secondment laid out in detail. Late, on the following Sunday afternoon, off to London she had gone.

Christmas had come and gone, always a busy time in the Church, and now Bishop Anthony was enjoying the relative peace and calm of the New Year. Spring was just on the doorstep and as he welcomed Stephen, his successor, into his private study at the Bishop's Palace in Hereford, snowdrops and crocuses danced in the early spring sunlight that played on his garden. He sighed as he looked across the lawn; he would miss this beautiful place, but the time was right to retire. He had done his bit and now it was time to hand the reins to a younger man. Coffee and biscuits had been served and the two men sat chatting as Anthony ran through a brief history of the diocese. Talk turned away from religious affairs and turned towards more mundane duties that the new Bishop might be expected to come across.

"Whatever you do, don't get involved with Graham Harper," said Bishop Anthony. Anthony was not an uncharitable man by any means; he was a good and kindly priest and was held in very high regard. He had enormous patience and time for even the smallest thing, but he could read a man like a book, and the headmaster of Coates Norton School was as transparent as a very clean pane of glass. The two men sat companionably in Bishop Anthony's study.

The air smelled of books, some dusty tomes long since abandoned to library shelves, others well-thumbed and marked from long and affectionate use. The sun shone through the stained glass windows of the Bishop's Palace, lighting up dust motes as they danced in the air. It was a warm and comfortable room, and in the winter made especially cosy by a log fire which always greeted the Bishop's visitors. Today, the window was slightly open and the sounds of a busy cloister filtered in on the spring breeze. Bishop Anthony loved this room, and he'd be sorry to leave it, but the time had come. He had reached the age when retirement had become a necessity but he felt he was leaving it in capable hands, as the morning had given him the opportunity to size up his successor. The impressions he had gained heartened him. His flock was in good hands.

The air also smelt of coffee, little tendrils of steam rising to greet the dust motes. The two men sipped their scalding brew as they discussed the handover, necessitated by Bishop Anthony's imminent retirement. The outgoing Bishop had spent the last two hours going through a long list of things with which to acquaint the yet to be installed Bishop Stephen, and the subject of Graham Harper had just been reached.

"Who's Graham Harper," replied Stephen innocently, taking a sip from his cup as he relaxed further into the deep padded cushions of a worn, but very comfortable leather chair.

"He's the headmaster of that small private school out at the Coates estate, a few miles north of here, up near the Mynden Hills. If you let him grab on to your coattails, he'll never let go."

"Why's that then," replied the new Bishop, puzzled by the edge to his predecessor's tone.

"He's always inviting dignitaries out to his confounded school for something or other, Prize Giving, Music competitions, lunch, or as he calls it luncheon, the list is endless."

"What's he like then?" went on the new Bishop, curiously.

"The man is an insufferable prig, a social climber and his grovel is unseemly. He also has no regard for his staff and every time I do go there, I pick up a sense of ill ease and extreme dislike. I can't stand the man, so watch out," finished Bishop Anthony.

Bishop Stephen had met the outgoing Bishop before, on a few social occasions, and in his previous post as Dean of Worcester, at various synods held around the country. He had come to know Anthony as a good man; one with a sharp academic mind and a good head for business nonetheless. Management of a diocese wasn't just about going to church and taking the odd service now and then. It required good leadership and a sharp business acumen, something which Stephen was yet to try out in his new post, but felt eager and up to the task. Bishop Anthony had seemed to Stephen to be a kind man and one whose heart was genuine. This odd outburst was out of character, but seemed to be heartfelt, nevertheless. Stephen shifted uncomfortably in his chair and put his now empty coffee cup back gently down on the leather coaster protecting the highly polished coffee table, wondering how to respond without embarrassing his host.

"Thanks for the warning. I'll try to steer clear of him, then. He sounds an odious man." Stephen replied.

Bishop Anthony sat back in his chair, slightly flustered by his outburst; perhaps he shouldn't have been so direct.

"I am sorry, I shouldn't have spoken thus … not very charitable I know, but the man has been a constant thorn in my side. I thought you deserved this timely warning."

"Thank you. I appreciate the advice. I will try and keep the man at arm's length."

"You have been warned," finished Anthony with a wry grin.

The two men relaxed and moved onto subjects more interesting. Diocesan matters again took over, and the nitty gritty of the new responsibilities which now faced Bishop Stephen filled his mind. Graham Harper was forgotten in a moment.

Six months after her move to London, Detective Sergeant Alexis Longbow sat at her desk in the offices of the Anti-Terrorist Squad at Scotland Yard, re-reading a report that she had just written and drinking from a mug of coffee, and as a gentle spring breeze through the open window disturbed papers on a nearby desk, her concentration was broken. Now emptied from other officers, the silence of the room was peaceful and Alexis allowed herself a moment to relax. She stood up and walked across to the window. The same slight breeze which had disturbed the papers now ruffled the fresh green leaves on the lime trees which grew alongside the street. From her vantage point, four floors up, Alexis watched as the busy London scene bustled below. Cars, vans and red London buses along with the familiar black cab tussled for space on the congested street. Pedestrians came and went and even in the busyness below, a kind of calm prevailed. Alexis heard birdsong in the trees, and a workman whistled as he cleaned windows on the high Victorian tenements opposite. This was so different to the torment that had ripped another London street only the other day.

The last six months had proved to be both exhilarating and life changing. She had faced personal danger and seen sights that would haunt her for a long time. The memories of the day when that London bus had been blown up would stay in her mind's eye for ever, but the experience and the friendship she had encountered from both her London colleagues and members of the public had humbled her. It had taught her new detection techniques, a different way of looking at things which she knew would stand her in good stead for the future. She was a changed woman but, she hoped, for the better. A door banged behind her, making her jump and bringing her out of her mental wanderings.

"Morning, Lexi, you still here? Thought you were off home?"

Alexis grinned as her fellow sergeant, Colin Mason, hurtled into the room, cheeks suffused from his usual lunchtime tipple.

"No, not just yet, a week or two to go. Sounds as if you've had enough of me" retorted Alexis with humour.

Mason laughed.

"No, you've been great. Sorry to see you go, mate, even if I did have to wash up your coffee mug!"

18

Alexis smiled, remembering the day she'd first walked into the office.

"It'll be nice to get home, back to some sort of normality, but despite the horrors I've seen, I wouldn't have missed this opportunity for the world. Made some good friends, too, I hope"

"Absolutely, we'll miss you when you do go," agreed Mason, sincerity in his voice. "See you in the pub later?"

Without giving Alexis any time to answer, Colin Mason grabbed a pile of files, dropping one on the floor in his hurry, and left the office as violently as he had entered it. Alexis smiled and walked across the room to retrieve the fallen papers. Her colleagues had been a great bunch of blokes, initially suspicious with this interloper from the other side of the country, particularly a female one – she'd been the only woman on the squad - but she had worked hard and gained their trust. Yes, she would be sad to leave them but how she longed for the peace and tranquillity of her home town once more. She returned to her desk and sat down, pushing the almost finished report to one side. Her mind was still full of memories and Colin's entrance had brought another back. She grinned, remembering the first day on the squad. She'd reported, as requested, to the desk sergeant downstairs, introduced herself and informed him of her appointment with Commander Nevern.

The look on the officer's face had been a picture.

"You sure, miss?" he'd asked suspiciously.

"As sure as I'm standing in front of you," she replied.

"But… you're a …" he stopped himself just in time.

"A woman, is that what you were going to say?"

Alexis mischievously looked down at her chest. "Yup, I was last time I looked. Still am, it appears."

The desk sergeant had the grace to blush.

"Sorry, miss, er, Sergeant Longbow. I think there's been something lost in translation. We were expecting a Sergeant Alex Longbow. There's going to be some head scratching upstairs. Just be warned."

Alexis' heart sank. This was all she needed. Had there been a genuine mix up or had the Marches Police ACC been a little economical with the truth, trying to pass off a woman where a man had been expected. With a heavy heart, she followed the desk sergeant's instructions and made her way upstairs. To his credit, Commander Nevern had quickly summed up the situation, seen Alexis' obvious discomfort and done his best to make the best of a bad job.

"I can assure you, Alexis," he'd said. "When I asked your force for an officer to be seconded to the squad, I was most certainly not gender specific. I read the opening paragraph of the accompanying letter to this file, and went from there. I meant to read the file itself, but unfortunately events took over."

He pulled a green covered file towards himself and opened it, then turned it towards Alexis and pointed to the letter. There, in bold letters was the name Detective Sergeant Alex Longbow but as Alexis looked at the front sheet of the file itself, it was obvious that her true gender had most definitely not been hidden. There was even a photo.

"My sincere apologies. I should have read the file."

Alexis grinned.

"They're all expecting a bloke in there?" she asked, pointing to the main office door."

"They are," agreed the Commander.

"This should be fun. Will you introduce me, sir?" she asked mischievously, her humour restored now she'd realised that this was just a typo and an oversight in the Commander's concentration.

The outer office was packed and the noise level was high. People shouted across the room, a telephone buzzed incessantly on a desk over towards the window, and someone's mobile phone aggressively announced with a very discordant ring tone, that the caller was not to be put off. It was bedlam but as she and the Commander walked into the main office, the noise ceased abruptly, even the phones went quiet and everyone stared at her. Alexis looked round at the faces turned towards her, not sure what she would see. She held her ground, eyes raised, looking all around her with a confidence she didn't really feel. She knew that if she looked down, all was lost. She had just walked into a very male environment. The next few minutes would configure the rest of her secondment.

"Let me introduce you to Detective Sergeant Alexis Longbow. She'll be joining us for the next six months." Commander Nevern didn't even blink, his poise was absolute and somehow this went Alexis' way. She noticed a raised eyebrow, a mouth opened to speak then closed as quickly, even a grunt from someone at the back of the room, but there had to be one.

"You any good at making coffee?" a disembodied voice rang from the corner.

"You any good at doing the washing up afterwards?" she countered with a grin.

The tension eased as a laugh filtered through the office. With that simple remark, Alexis had stood her ground, but without rancour. The next twenty minutes had involved introductions, handshakes, what experience did she have, where had she worked. It had been tough but by the end of the day, Alexis had made her mark, shown she was capable and willing to learn, become part of the team. There was still a small feeling of dissension floating around, she could feel it, she hadn't convinced everyone, but there was still time. At least they were being polite. That was a start and that evening she'd shown them she was quite capable of downing a pint, not to mention a dram or two. The following morning had been easier, even Colin who had made the coffee remark had apologised, although she could have done without the slight hangover.

Alexis reverie ceased suddenly, as the office began to fill as officers returned after various investigations. She finished reading through her own papers, her thoughts of a pint in the pub with Colin Mason filed for the time being as she concentrated her mind on the dawn raid she'd participated in that morning. The suspects had been holed up in flats south of the River Thames and the raid had proved to be ultimately successful but not without its risks. Shots had been fired, an officer wounded, but the suspects were now in safe custody, awaiting interrogation. The flat had turned out to be a bomb factory and the evidence they had recovered, not to mention the disaster that had been averted, had been well worth the early start at four that morning. Just as she put the finalised report into a neat folder, the phone on her desk rang. She picked up the receiver and was startled to hear a familiar voice.

"Good morning, Sergeant Longbow, Assistant Chief Constable Grainger here."

"Oh, good morning sir," replied Alexis, recognising the dulcet tones of her commander back home. "How are things?"

"Fine thanks, Sergeant. How are things with you?"

"OK, busy, but no doubt you've seen in the press what's been going on up here."

"Yes, quite, no doubt difficult times for you all."

"Yes, sir," replied Alexis, now becoming puzzled as to the intention of the call.

ACC Grainger wasn't one usually given to general chit chat, so there had to be a purpose. Alexis wasn't long left in doubt.

"We originally agreed for six months on the squad, with an option for longer...?"

Grainger paused and Alexis' heart sank as she guessed the reason for the Assistant Chief Constable's call. She was two weeks from the end of her stint on the squad and was looking forward to going home. She was tired, physically and mentally, and needed some fresh air to rid her soul of the things she'd witnessed. Now it seemed the time was to be extended.

"Yes sir," she replied wearily.

"But," went on Grainger, "we need you back here."

In an instant, Alexis' spirits soared and the image of soft, rolling countryside and sweet smelling hay strewn meadows flitted through her tired brain.

"Yes, sir," replied Alexis, now considerably brightened.

"Yes. You will report to me at Headquarters tomorrow at midday."

"Yes, sir. Thank you."

With that the call was abruptly concluded and as Alexis replaced the phone, her mind did a dance. She was actually going home. Thank God for that. She paused in her mental rejoicing as she suddenly realised she would be leaving her friends and colleagues without much time to say goodbye. She rose from her desk and headed for the commander's office. She knocked gently and received a 'come in' in reply. Commander James Nevern, a tall, distinguished looking man, greying at the temples but otherwise showing no sign of the years of service he had under his belt, waved her to a seat.

"Come in, Alexis. Have a seat. Coffee?" he said, almost before she had shut the door behind her."

"Er, no thanks, sir," replied Alexis. "Just had a cup, thanks."

"Righto," replied Nevern as he poured himself a mug from the jug on the simmer at the back of his office."

Nevern seated himself back at his desk, neat and tidy and everything in its place, just like the man, and leant back in his chair and relaxed.

"Thanks for your help on the raid this morning. Got some useful bodies in custody."

"You're welcome, sir," replied Alexis. "It was a dodgy exercise, but well worth the risks. I think Jim will be OK, just a flesh wound in his arm. He was at A&E for a while, but he's been discharged. Back home, I think, now. My report is ready."

"Nasty business with Jim. Those flak jackets are all very well but they don't protect arms and legs. I'm glad he'll be OK. Must pop in and see him at home."

Nevern paused and seemed to relapse into deep thought. A fly buzzed impotently at the closed window, dangerously close to a cobweb, its spider lurking menacingly within. The clock ticked the seconds as the commander remained silent, suddenly oblivious to Alexis' presence. She waited patiently, her own thoughts taking over, then visibly jumped as Nevern suddenly came to life.

"Give it to Inspector Childs when he comes in."

"Oh, er, yes, my report. Will do. Er, sir…"

Alexis paused, unsure how to inform the Commander of her impending departure, when she was interrupted.

"Oh, it's all planned, by the way," said the Commander.

"Er, what is, sir?" replied Alexis, momentarily nonplussed.

"Your leaving do, tonight. Stag and Beetle, 7.30pm."

Alexis smiled and relaxed. The squad grapevine was as healthy as ever. She suddenly realised that she was the last to know, as usual.

"The ACC has obviously been in touch," said Alexis ruefully.

"Yes, he rang me this morning, while you were still out on the raid."

"Does everyone know?"

"More or less," Nevern grinned, then, more seriously, he went on.

"We'll miss you, Lexi," said Nevern, slipping into the friendlier form of Alexis' name. "You've been a great asset to the team. You've brought in some valuable information, and gleaned some useful contacts. We'll be able to capitalise on this as time goes on."

"Thank you, sir," replied Alexis. "It's been tough, and I've seen some pretty awful things, but I wouldn't have missed the opportunity for the world."

The Commander smiled thoughtfully. Then dismissing his thoughts, he went on more brusquely.

"Right, Stag and Beetle tonight and be prepared for a heavy head in the morning."

Alexis had experienced a squad drinking bout before, holding her own with fortitude. They were not for the faint hearted. She grimaced as she remembered the stonking great headache she had woken up with after the last one.

"I'll have to try and keep a clear head. I've got an interview with the ACC at midday so I'll have to be up early."

"I'm sure you'll do you best, Lexi," replied the Commander with a smile. "See you tonight."

Alexis was dismissed from the commander's office with a wave of his hand. Returning to her desk, she ruefully surveyed the piles of paper still stacked on one side. The coffee dregs in her mug were now stone cold, so putting it to one side, Alexis sat down, realising she still had a fair bit of tidying up to do, let alone pack up her stuff back at her digs. With a sigh, but with a light heart, she got down to her tasks.

Chapter Two

The following morning, at six a.m., Alexis was awoken by the shrill insistence of her alarm clock. Blearily, she turned over and grappled with the offending instrument, managing to silence it at last. She lay quietly for a few minutes collecting her thoughts, and tried to rid her head of a persistent nagging pain around her temples. Although she'd tried hard last night to limit the alcohol intake, she had nevertheless drunk more than she should, and the promised heavy head was upon her. She'd overdone it last night, she knew she would, but it had been a great evening all the same. Her mates had done her proud - they'd even had a quick whip round and bought her some beautiful pearl earrings - and the friendships she'd forged were worth all the horrors of the last six months, but they'd been a little too generous with their spirits, under both kinds, last night and her head was now paying the price. Now the day of her departure had dawned so, groaning, she reluctantly threw back the duvet and swung her legs over the side of the bed. All she needed to think about at the moment, was getting up and getting dressed. The train left just before eight, so she didn't have much time. The hot water of a power shower brought her round quickly, and the heavy head abated a little. She still had a niggle in her temples but she hoped a strong coffee and fresh air would see to that.

She looked at herself in the mirror as she towelled himself down. She was still a young woman and her blonde hair, curling damply across her forehead showed no signs of grey. Her hazel eyes looked back at her from the mirror, and the few worry lines etched around them, showed the effects of the last few months. Anyone who'd lived through those sorts of experiences without showing some scar, was a very lucky person but she hoped that with a bit of luck, these would fade under the tender loving care of the English countryside. With little time for deep thought, Alexis rapidly got herself sorted, and after grabbing a quick breakfast of toast, hot coffee and paracetamol, she said goodbye to her landlady for the last time and hot footed it to the station. Half an hour later, with her headache abating gradually, Alexis closed her eyes and relaxed as the train pulled out from the station. The scenery changed from built up urban landscapes to little back to back Victorian terraced houses. Gardens, backing on to the raised railway line, raced by as the train picked up speed out of London. Grim and grey industrial estates, filled with early morning traffic, vanished in a blur as the train headed for the suburbs. Now that the time was here, Alexis was glad to be leaving the city and heading home for the less frantic life she would have in the shires. She rested her head and slept.

The refreshment trolley came through, rousing Alexis with its rattle and the cheerful tones of the woman who trundled it along. She treated himself to a coffee. The scenery had changed during her short nap as the city was left behind. It wasn't the fastest of trains, stopping at a few stations on the way, but as it headed for Worcester, Alexis sat back contentedly in her seat, coffee cup nursed carefully in her hand as the countryside sped by. The night before had been uncharacteristically stormy for May, but now the weather was clear and as the train got close to Worcester, the distant slopes of the Malvern Hills, with the distinctive Worcestershire beacon on the top, glimpsed into view and Alexis' heart sang. She was nearly home. Oh, how she had missed the hills around her home, some topped with green forest, some pointed with sharp rocks which once graced the depths of a primordial sea, the song of the lark and the purple heather. Her future was uncertain, a return to Hereford she supposed, but she would be home and back with her family and friends. The distant horizon disappeared as the train approached the city, and soon it trundled into the station, pulling up with a jerk. It had arrived at its destination in good time. After scrambling for her bags, which had somehow found their way to the depths of a huge pile of luggage on top, Alexis left the train, carefully avoiding the large gap between train and platform. A careless move would at the very least leave some nasty bruises, and at worst a broken leg. Now was not the time for accidents, especially after surviving all the dangers of terrorist ridden London. Her journey necessitated a short delay as she had to change trains, but within a few minutes the Hereford train arrived and she settled once again into her seat and as the familiar tops of the Malvern Hills disappeared behind her, it wasn't long before the magnificent cathedral of Hereford hoved into view. She had arrived.

Alexis had just under an hour before her appointment with the Assistant Chief Constable; it would take twenty minutes to walk to Headquarters from the station, so judging that there was just time to spare she headed for the buffet, her nose guiding her to the delicious smells of fried food which wafted gently from the open door. After buying a newspaper and a freshly prepared and piping hot bacon sandwich and this time a cup of tea, Alexis settled at a table in the corner for a short but very welcome rest. The news headlines proclaimed that London had yet again been hit by a bomb, three people dead and many more injured. For a brief moment Alexis felt left out. She should have been there, helping her London colleagues, but as she lifted her head and viewed the hustle and bustle of the station, her momentary frustration dissipated and she felt glad to be alive and nearly home.

An arriving train jerked her out of her thoughts and looking at her watch, realised she only had thirty minutes to leg it up the hill and make her way to Police Headquarters. She would just make it if she hurried. Leaving her bags in storage at the station, she ran and with just three minutes to spare, she walked up the last few steps to the imposing red brick Marches Police Headquarters building, and hurried inside. She was glad she knew where she was going, having been to the Assistant Chief Constable's office those six months previously. Her late night and early morning, and the effects of the headache and the journey, were beginning to tell and she was glad to slump down in a chair outside the ACC's office. However, her respite didn't last long. The phone on the ACC's secretary's desk buzzed and as she listened to the call, her eyes looked towards Alexis.

"Detective Sergeant Longbow," she piped merrily. "The Assistant Chief Constable will see you now."

Alexis stood wearily, her legs giving way slightly after the exertion of the mad dash from the railway station. She'd only had four hours sleep last night and with hardly a chance to breathe over the last forty eight hours, now felt shattered. She still didn't know why she was here. In her tiredness, she felt irritable. Why couldn't she just go home and get on with the job? She didn't need a debriefing, did she? She'd done her job, and she knew that any report requested on her conduct from Commander Nevern should be favourable. Wasn't that enough? Alexis walked the short distance from her chair to the closed door of the Assistant Chief Constable's office, straightening her jacket as she went. She tapped smartly on the door and after a muffled 'come in', entered ACC Grainger's office. It was an elegant room, obviously a place of work but a beautiful room, nonetheless. The large marble fireplace dominated the room at one end, and huge bay windows overlooked the garden outside. The walls were lined with bookshelves, each heaving with generous tomes of police law and procedure. Alexis caught sight of Archbold on the shelf nearest to her; the criminal law reference book which had been her constant companion during her studies for the Inspector's examination. In that instant, she idly wondered if all the hard work had been worthwhile. Would she ever get promotion? It was something to hope for, one day perhaps? The ACC waved Alexis to a chair in front of him.

"Please be seated. I hope you had a good journey," opened Grainger immediately and rather pompously.

"Yes, sir, thank you. It went well."

"You look tired, Sergeant. Not overdoing it, I hope?"

"It's been a hard few days and I haven't really caught up with myself yet," admitted Alexis ruefully.

"Tell me what you've been up to?" went on Grainger more gently. The two officers chatted comfortably for about half an hour about London and its difficulties with terrorism, and what Alexis had been expected to do. They discussed the London bombings, and the latest dawn raid of yesterday. Alexis didn't hold back, the Assistant Chief Constable had a right to know, but all the same she really didn't want to talk about it. The memories were so fresh. She could still hear the cacophony of noise that came with a huge bomb blast and even in the silence that followed for a minute or two after the explosion, she could hear sounds in the unearthly and deathly quiet; the tinkling of glass, the wind rustling in the trees and the gentle sighs of the dying. She could still smell and even taste the odours of spilt blood mixed with diesel fuel and the sweet scents of a London spring. It was like nothing else she had ever experienced and, although she would bear the psychological scars for the rest of her life, she had sensibly just started to file them away in her mind. This recollection was painful, but Grainger was giving her no choice.

At last, she came to a stop; there was simply no more to say. Grainger watched as Alexis closed her eyes for an instant. He allowed her a brief respite, realising just how tired she was and how difficult the résumé had been for her. The sun shone in through the open window and the smell of late spring flowers wafted in on a slight breeze. A lamb bleated in the distance and a blackbird announced its presence in the garden, in its own very distinctive way. A heavy almost uncontrollable drowsiness threatened to overwhelm Alexis; her eyelids heavy, the lack of sleep was beginning to take its toll and her temples throbbed. A slight smell of lavender furniture polish infused the air and the effect was soporific. She forced open her eyes in an effort to stay awake and looked around at the room. It was a comfortable room, a room she would be happy to have at home. She loved her books, and this room was full of them. Alexis shook herself, physically and mentally, and shifted in her seat. It had only been a few seconds, half a minute at the most, but this briefest of interludes had helped her to come round. Grainger stood up, acknowledging that Alexis had mentally returned, and went to the tray at the back of the room. He poured two cups of steaming black coffee from the flask on the tray and handed one to Alexis.

"Thank you for your account. It's been very informative, and I appreciate your feedback … Inspector Longbow."

Alexis was tired and only half listening but as the heat of the coffee cup struck her hand, the penny dropped as the Assistant Chief Constable's words hit home. Alexis' hand shook and the coffee cup rattled in its saucer. She had heard correctly, hadn't she? She steadied herself and put her cup down on Grainger's desk in front of her.

"Excuse me, sir?" replied Alexis taken aback.

The Assistant Chief hadn't got her rank wrong before. The man must be going senile.

"It's OK, I haven't lost it," grinned Grainger.

Alexis reddened, realising that her thoughts had been exposed. Grainger continued.

"I've had a report from Commander Nevern. I am hugely impressed which, together with your detailed report to me this morning, has made up my mind for me."

Alexis spluttered.

"Oh my God! Oh sorry sir, I really didn't expect this. I thought you just wanted a debrief – that's why you called me to see you…., wasn't it?"

"Yes and no," replied Grainger, with good humour.

"So, am I to replace my inspector at Hereford? Where's he going? Is he retiring? I thought he was way off retirement. Do you want me back in uniform …?" Alexis tailed off in confusion. Her tired brain was racing, teeming with questions to which, as yet, she had no answers.

"No, Alexis," replied Grainger, smiling. "I have other plans for you."

"Oh." Alexis was now lost for words. All she could do was wait and let the ACC spell out his plans.

"You will be aware that the county is expanding, not size wise of course, but in population. What used to be sleepy towns and villages are growing and I am responding to the current trends."

Alexis said nothing. She had nothing to say. Her puzzlement was growing, however. Where was this going?

"At the moment, there is a very small police presence in Teigneford. I am increasing its importance. Currently, there is a nine to five uniform presence, and a small CID unit consisting of one Detective Constable and one Detective Inspector. The Detective Sergeant, who left a year ago, was never replaced. The town deserves more and that's where you come in."

Teigneford! Alexis' heart jumped with excitement. She truly was going home.

"Can I ask what is expected of me?" asked Alexis, her voice tired and strained but now armed with a growing vitality.

"You are to head a new Criminal Investigation Department. Teigneford will be the police centre in the county, covering all the hamlets, villages and small towns, in fact everything that isn't covered by Hereford or Shrewsbury. Detective Inspector Colin Redway, the current DI there, has taken early retirement, so that vacancy is now yours. I have appointed a new DS, who has already started, and I will add two extra DCs to the team. That number may grow – I'll see how things pan out. I will also be adding to the uniform contingent, but that's not your problem. So how say you?"

Alexis paused, for what seemed an eternity; she just couldn't get her mind to work. Her thoughts ran riot, the confusion shredding her mind. Her tired brain was having great difficulty in assimilating all this. She panicked and for a brief moment she felt sick. Was she really ready to become a Detective Inspector? She flushed with a momentary anxiety that became all but overwhelming. The

Assistant Chief Constable just sat back and watched the play unfolding across Alexis' face.

"Well?" asked Grainger kindly, after a short interlude.

Alexis pulled herself together, literally and physically. She sat up straight in her chair, and dabbed at her mouth with a tissue pulled from her sleeve. The man needed a decision, and apparently right away. Alexis, in that instant, made up her mind.

"Well, thank you very much, sir. I'm delighted to accept. Thank you."

"You're expected at Teigneford Police Station for the start of shift at two this afternoon. You'd better get a move on," said Grainger, looking at the elegant clock on the mantelpiece above the fireplace.

"Do they know at Hereford nick and Teigneford for that matter?" asked Alexis, already suspecting the answer.

"I've informed both senior officers, so probably, yes, the cat is out of the bag," Grainger finished with a knowing smile. "I have to warn you, however, that Superintendent Barnes at Teigneford didn't take too kindly to the news. He's old school and change will not come easy to him, so you may have to tread gently for a while, but I'm sure you're more than capable of dealing with that."

With that slightly ominous warning hanging in the air, the two officers stood, and the Assistant Chief Constable shook Alexis' hand.

"Congratulations, Detective Inspector Longbow. I expect good results."

"Yes, sir, thank you," replied Alexis again, her mind in a whirl.

Alexis left the office and said a cheery goodbye to the receptionist. She headed for the sunshine and the fresh air, and once outside, breathed in deeply, all irritability gone. Her body still felt exhausted but her brain was invigorated. The surprise had been absolute and so unexpected and now she needed a little time to think. The newly promoted Detective Inspective Alexis Longbow stood briefly on the steps of Malton House, the Headquarters of The Marches Police, and blinked in the bright sunlight. The weathered red brick of the old house glowed in the late spring sunshine and Alexis could feel the warmth reflected off the walls. She stood for a minute and savoured the birdsong and the breeze, relaxing after what had been for her a nerve wracking interview over the last hour, despite the Assistant Chief Constable's efforts to make it otherwise. She could hardly believe what had happened. Promotion had been the last thing on her mind; it was totally unexpected. She was only just in her thirties, so promotion had come early, but the last six months' secondment to the Anti-Terrorist Squad in London had obviously helped to bolster her chances. There had been icing on the cake, too. Alexis was going to Teigneford, a town she had known and loved all her life, as the new Detective Inspector. Although Alexis had never been posted to Teigneford, the town was so familiar to her. She felt as if she was going home. Alexis realised that the posting had probably been the only reason for the promotion, although she hoped that her abilities and accomplishments were also contributory factors. It didn't appear that her gender had interfered with the decision for which she was grateful. She'd done it on her own merits. Grainger could easily have posted her without a promotion to a different police station, away from her old haunts, but instead he had gone further. The vacancy had come up at Teigneford and Alexis had been in the right place at the right time.

The Detective Inspector she would be replacing hadn't been a popular man. Alexis had worked with him on one case in the past, a series of burglaries which had overlapped Teigneford and Hereford, but had been frustrated by his lack of vision. So often Alexis had directed cases towards a successful conclusion by her lateral thinking and ability to see things where others couldn't and the blinkered inspector had been no different. But the man had now had the good sense to take early retirement. As she thought about her predecessor, she remembered a small incident that had made the office laugh at the time. Redway's brother had rung, asking to speak to the detective inspector. At that moment, DI Redway had gone to the hospital on an enquiry and his brother had been told he was there. The response had made the office laugh at the time.

"Having his mouth stitched up, I hope."

Obviously, Redway's shortcomings were well known amongst his family as well as colleagues. As a smile played on her lips at the memory, Alexis briefly wondered what had made the man go early. He'd seemed to be such a fixture and fitting at the CID office at Teigneford, lording it over them, that nobody thought he would ever go but something must have happened to shift him.

Alexis ran down the steps of the Headquarters building, and walked away, heading for a seat in the grounds of Malton House. She didn't want to go just yet. She'd been told to report at the nick for two o clock, so she had time, time she wanted and needed for herself. As she sat, she remembered when she had first come to Malton House, as a raw recruit, facing the process of enrolment. She had been a nervous twenty one year old, fresh from a law degree at university. Her parents had been a little disappointed when she hadn't turned that degree into a career at the bar, but the police had been her first choice. She had set her eyes early on a career in CID and her promotion to sergeant had made her parents proud. But now she was a detective inspector, all within eleven years, and the new responsibilities excited her. The sunshine seemed to have brought everyone outside and the area became busy as people crossed from the training suite to the main house. Alexis needed a little more time to collect her thoughts, so she got up from her seat and wandered along the path down to a small wooded area. Here she sat on a bench under the trees and watched as birds busied themselves with nest building. The air was alive with the sounds of bird song and buzzing insects, and the gentle ripple of a nearby stream rested her mind. She thought back over the last six months. When the call had come through to take the secondment with the Metropolitan Police, she had, at first, faltered. Was she ready for the upheaval? She was happy at work, a detective sergeant at Hereford police station. She was part of a good team, apart from the DI, who really was a waste of space, but she was also very ambitious. Alexis had quickly recognised that the secondment would not only give her good experience, but also a certain cachet, which wouldn't harm her promotion prospects in the slightest. Other than her mother, and a younger sister who was happily married with children, she had no other close family to worry about, so she had accepted and moved to London for six months. The work had been hard, at times physically dangerous and mentally exhausting, but nonetheless rewarding. She had got on well with her colleagues there and had made a lasting contribution. It had brought her up against an aspect of life which she had never thought to see. The bombings were brutal and indiscriminate, the injuries and devastation catastrophic, but the goodness that came from the victims involved, one to another, had made a lasting impression. It had been a very stressful time, to say the least and she was glad she had been recalled home. She'd missed her friends and the gentler pace of life in the shires, but the experiences had changed her, honed her and sharpened her wits. She was ready for the next step.

Just then, a police car hurtled past on the road behind, blue lights flashing, and the noisy siren shook Alexis out of her mild day-dreaming. She stood up, startling a large blackbird busy in the process of pulling a long, fat worm from the soft ground. The sounds of the stream and the busy birds receded into the background. Detective Inspector Alexis Longbow had work to do so she hot-footed it back to the railway station, collected her bags and hopped on the next train to Teigneford. The familiar countryside sped past as she travelled north, small villages and hamlets that she knew so well. The ruins of an old medieval castle came into view and Alexis remembered with fondness the times she had played amongst the old stones with her sister when they were children. She breathed happily at the memory and the comfort that such familiarity engendered in her mind. She relaxed, stretched out her legs and watched the world race by outside. All too soon, the train pulled up at Teigneford railway station and came to a halt. Doors flew open and after grabbing her bags, Alexis began the walk down the hill towards the police station, lugging her bags along with her. As she walked, she wondered how she would be received. For some reason, the ACC had been vague about her new colleagues, just saying a new detective sergeant was already in post and he'd appointed another couple of DCs. Her thoughts turned to Archie and her heart lurched. She missed him; missed his sensible head and clear thinking. They'd made a good team in Hereford. Resolving to give him a buzz for a catch up as soon as she could, she walked the final few steps up to the front door of Teigneford police station.

Mavis was not where she should be. Normally, she would be busy, doing what she was paid to do; the dining room floor, still slightly sticky from breakfast, definitely needed her attention and as for the staff toilets, well she really didn't fancy those after a busy break time in the staff room. None of these unwholesome tasks appealed right now because today her mind was on other things. There was still an hour to go before she would have to present herself in the kitchen to help serve lunch to two hundred and fifty hungry school children so now she had time to herself, to think about what to do next. Mavis sat on the edge of the table and swung her thin legs gently as she munched on a chocolate biscuit. A mug of coffee sat untouched next to her, gently cooling as its steam tendrils wove their way upwards to meet the cobwebs hiding in the dusty corners of the storeroom. She looked around, seeing the carefully stacked packets of dried food and rows of bottles of squash, and sighed. She'd been feeling a bit unsettled lately. Home life left a lot to be desired living as she did with a boring husband and her demanding mother but otherwise things were jogging along OK. But, for some reason she felt as if something was going to go wrong; as if her own control was weakening. She'd woken from a bad dream that morning and it had left her feeling uneasy and bothered. As the morning had moved on, this feeling had slipped away slightly, but ghostly fingers of misremembered thoughts still played at the edge of her consciousness. In a brief moment of unusual foresight, she wondered if this was an omen; was she trying too hard in her greed, but in her usual arrogance, this thought vanished as quickly as it had come. She shook her shoulders and took another bite of her biscuit, resolving all the same to be just that little bit more careful.

Mavis Greene worked as a domestic employee at the school. She had been there for a couple of years, two years which had seemed like a lifetime. It was not a role she would have chosen for herself, she was still in her twenties and had ambition, but it would do for now. Her wages were on the minimum pay threshold but the perks, all of which she had found for herself, were financially quite good and not something to give up easily. The storeroom in which she now sat had been the source of a few good things. Her weekly shopping bill in the local supermarket had been kept to a minimum as her light fingers collected the odd bottle of washing up liquid here or a bag of sugar or flour there from the well-stocked store room. From time to time, Mavis had even appropriated toilet rolls and boxes of cereal and helped them on their way homewards, hidden in her voluminous bags which she always brought to work. She was nothing if not prepared. Mavis wasn't altogether a very nice person; secretive, sometimes mean and slightly dishonest. She wasn't generally lazy, but could make herself missing if a particularly unpleasant task presented itself, most recently the staff toilets and the dining room floor. Mavis had also found other ways of supplementing her monthly income. She had an uncanny knack of always being in the right place at the right time; the things she'd discovered whilst hiding in the tiny kitchen off the staff room were legion. There was little which had been discussed in confidence between colleague or friend that had by-passed Mavis' ears. Suspicion was rife and people tended to avoid her; nothing had been proven but the little gifts which always seemed to come her way spoke volumes about how she used this information.

Now she sat alone in the store room, savouring the melted chocolate and the oaty biscuit crumbs in her mouth, and her feelings of unease finally began to dissipate in the dusty air along with the steamy tendrils of coffee. She felt smug and self-important, as her thoughts turned to her latest project and how she could bring it to fruition. It held a lot of promise and would have to be handled very carefully. She thought back to only the other day when she had been working overtime one evening, preparing supper for a few school pupils coming back from a late night theatre visit. Laziness could always go on the back seat where the promise of extra money was concerned. Some staff members had been milling around in the quad as the returning children either greeted their waiting parents or, being boarders, began to make their way to the dining room for a late supper, but she'd watched eagle-eyed from the dining room window as two staff members broke off from the group. Her eyes followed their retreating backs as they disappeared around the front wall of the school, presumably heading for the back of the building. Their body language spoke volumes and it fascinated her; her interest was piqued and Mavis realised with satisfaction that this was well worth investigating. She had a shrewd idea as to where they were heading, so leaving the freshly prepared pile of sandwiches on the table, ready for the children, she carefully made her way outside and along the side wall to the back of the main building, following at a distance the backs of the retreating couple. She hovered in the shadows of a large tree, watching as they finally disappeared back into the building. Now she knew exactly where they were going, so standing patiently outside one of the larger rooms on the ground floor, where windows overlooked a small neat garden, she waited for events to unfold.

She didn't have long to wait as, after a brief pause, lights were lit in the room and curtains were pulled against the twilight, and her patience was rewarded. Whoever had pulled the curtains together had been careless and as the weight of the heavy drapes pulled back on themselves, a small gap appeared. It was enough and Mavis' excitement rose. Keeping low, she edged closer to the window and raised her head and peered carefully through the gap. She watched, both fascinated and disgusted as the two began to undress then fumbled with each other's buttons and hooks. Her eyes became glued to the scene with a kind of morbid attraction as two half naked bodies, neither particularly pretty in themselves, writhed together in some primeval act of union. Mavis' heart began to beat with a strange excitement; this was true gold, a gift of the gods, and one she could milk for a very long time. The evening had now darkened considerably and the brightly lit room held no secrets to anyone watching. Mavis had no difficulty in seeing the unfolding drama so she held up her phone and without flash, as none was needed with the light streaming from the room, took one picture which said it all. It was perfect. The two involved in their own adulterous activities saw nothing of their peeping tom, they were oblivious to anyone but themselves. Mavis slipped away in the encroaching darkness, highly satisfied with her evening's work.

Now, two days later, she sat in the store room, thinking about how best to further this wonderful information to her advantage. The people in question would not take easily to her advances. There would be bluff, anger and embarrassment but with the threat of ultimate humiliation, Mavis held a strong hand, a hand which would have to be shown carefully. There was no rush, she could bide her time, but the moment would come when she'd find herself in the best position to play her cards. She reached into her pocket for her cigarettes, the biscuit having long gone, but the little flashing red light of the smoke alarm high in the ceiling above her, warned her to put them away. Time enough later. She looked at her watch, she'd have to make an appearance in the kitchen sooner or later, so with the coffee now cooled sufficiently, she lifted the mug for her first sip.

Chapter Three

"Has anyone seen Mavis?"

Mr Graham Harper, headmaster of Coates Norton School, swung the door open between his office and that of his secretary, and bristled in, red in the face and obviously in short temper. Sarah Dixon, his long suffering secretary, looked up at her boss from a pile of paperwork, which she was sure had got larger since she had arrived that morning, and distractedly asked,

"Mavis?"

Sarah knew perfectly well who Mavis was but irritated by the Headmaster's tone of voice, she deliberately prevaricated.

"Yes, you know, my office domestic," he replied irritably. "She hasn't brought my coffee and it should be here on my desk waiting for when I return from teaching. Pay attention, woman."

"No, Headmaster, I haven't," replied Sarah wearily. The headmaster was usually in one of his moods after a lesson and she was usually the recipient of such a mood. Today was no exception.

"Would you like me to find her?" asked Sarah patiently, summoning up a reluctant smile.

"No, just get me a coffee!"

The headmaster turned on his heel and without a please or thank you, went back into his office, slamming the door behind him. The room shook, the windows rattled and Sarah grabbed a small pile of envelopes, disturbed in the draught, before they cascaded to the floor.

Graham sat down at his desk, his temper inflamed, and angrily contemplated the pile of exercise books piled up in one corner. He had just returned from teaching a History lesson, and had been looking forward to a few quiet minutes over his coffee, as he prepared himself for a meeting with some prospective parents who were due to visit the school. He felt flustered; the lesson had not gone well. He had been caught out, not knowing the answer to a question he had been asked. He had been made to look a fool and Graham Harper did not like being made to look a fool. He was the least suitable person to become a teacher. He hated children and had no patience with them whatsoever, especially if they asked questions he couldn't answer. He remembered with grim satisfaction, however, that the child wouldn't ask that question again as Graham had covered his embarrassment with the bald statement that they should know the answer to that and that the headmaster would expect a five hundred word essay on the topic by nightfall. The class had groaned and Graham had enjoyed their discomfiture at the time but the feeling brought about by the small victory had soon worn off and left him feeling angry and irritable. He snatched a pen from the pot on the corner of his desk and grabbing the first exercise book from the pile, got to work marking Year Seven's history homework, the red pen in his hand and the anger in his head making the task a short one.

Sarah sat quietly for a minute or two collecting her thoughts and tried to calm her rising temper. How much more of this could she take? It had been OK to start with, but as the years had gone on with this new headmaster, her life at school had become more and more stressed. Her own particular workload hadn't particularly increased, but the time she spent picking up the pieces from a man who was inefficient, and who usually blamed her for his mistakes, was increasing, and thereby inevitably digging into her own precious work time. He was becoming more and more paranoid, even suggesting once that she was in cahoots with the staff room, and planning things behind his back. This was nonsense, of course, but could she convince him? Much more of this behaviour and she would seriously have to consider her position. With a heartfelt sigh, she pushed her work aside and stood up from her desk. Straightening a picture dislodged by the headmaster's door slamming fit, she left her office and headed for Reception, on her way to the staff room, to make the headmaster a cup of coffee.

'At least it will keep him in his office for a bit longer and out of my way,' she thought to herself as she walked.

As she passed out of the inner Hall into Reception, through the ornately carved oak doors, she noticed Frances Smythe, the school's receptionist, sitting at her desk. Frances was an excellent front to the school – her appearance exuded charm and elegance, her voice soft and seductively low and wonderful when it came to charming parents out of several thousands of pounds for their children's education. This very nearly justified her existence as when it came to doing the rest of her job, her interest waned considerably and she preferred, instead, to use her time for her own ends. Frances was devious, adept at hiding what she was really up to. Sarah tolerated Frances, knowing there was little she could do about the woman's laziness, just glad that she at least managed to answer the phone when it rang, thus relieving that particular burden from Sarah herself.

"Have you seen Mavis?" Sarah asked, as she came up to the table.

Frances looked up guilty and rapidly clicked her mouse to hide the page she was reading on her computer. Sarah wasn't fooled.

"Who's Mavis?"

Sarah was just about to explain when Frances interrupted.

"That woman's a pest," answered Frances abruptly, negating her first question.

"Why a pest?" asked Sarah, curious at this odd response.

"The woman's a bloody nuisance. She's always tidying up and picking things up she shouldn't. Can't even leave a cup of coffee lying round without her picking it up."

"Perhaps you ought to tidy up for yourself," Sarah replied tartly, annoyed at Frances' attitude.

Sarah had a good working relationship with the domestic staff. She knew how hard they worked, often for scant recognition, and took it personally if one of them was criticised unfairly.

"You do know there's a kitchen in the staff room," Sarah finished, her voice tinged with a hint of sarcasm.

Frances looked up, her face reddening with annoyance. Sniffing angrily and with a toss of her blonde curls, she stood up from her seat. Gathering some papers together, she abruptly announced, "I will be in the headmaster's office if you need me. I have some papers for him to sign."

"He's busy at the moment. He won't want you to interrupt. He's working on some history homework," replied Sarah with asperity.

"He has just called me in," replied Frances with smug satisfaction.

"Fine, but don't forget those prospective parents will be here in twenty minutes."

Sarah stood back, allowing Frances to come out from behind her table, and watched as the woman walked off with her nose in the air. She grinned as Frances' cardigan snagged on the handle of the door and as the door closed behind the receptionist, Sarah idly wondered who the secretary in the school really was. She shrugged. She knew exactly what Frances had meant, papers indeed. It was no secret in the staff room that the headmaster had long been captivated by the wriggle of Frances' curvaceous bottom and the flash of her ample pink cleavage. It was a bit of amusing gossip that passed the time of day nicely in the staff room. Vaguely wondering if Mrs Barbara Harper also knew of her husband's amorous wanderings, or indeed if Frances and the headmaster were aware that their secret was common knowledge, Sarah left Reception and headed for the staff room.

She found the room full, being break time and the air was full of the buzz of conversation. Sarah smiled. She loved this room. In its heyday it had been beautiful with high ceilings and a magnificent tiled fireplace, redolent of past glories, but now tired and sadly in need of, at the very least, a good coat of paint, it gave off a faint aroma of mild neglect, mixed with the smell of abandoned football boots, sweaty towels and stale coffee. Although the room was large, it felt small when full of teachers and their associated baggage. Rudimentary shelves had been fixed into the alcove at one side of the fireplace, and they sagged with books, old catalogues and paperwork. Sarah determined that if she ever got a spare moment, as if she sighed, she'd tackle the out of date catalogues and at least make some space for more books and paperwork. The teachers were sorely pressed for room in which to work away from the classroom so a little housekeeping might come in handy. An old white painted cupboard, which had probably once housed linen, had been requisitioned to act as some sort of extra storage, but that too overflowed with all and sundry. The room was inadequate for the purpose but Sarah realised that Graham Harper would never countenance an upgrade for his hard working and sorely pressed staff, however much they deserved it. The staff room was also a place where she had friends and those friendships she treasured. The headmaster's paranoia about collusion in the staff room, and his offhand threat to ban her from the room had deeply upset Sarah. Without her friends, her job would be misery itself. If that ever happened, she promised herself she really would walk. The large bay windows looked out over the front quad and children, released from their educational chores, thronged round and about as their pent up energies stifled in the classroom, were released in a gloriously happy cacophony. The campus teemed with young life and Sarah revelled in the noise. She watched idly as a battered old four wheel drive negotiated the bends in the driveway carefully and at a very low speed. She vaguely wondered if they were the new parents.

"Hello, Sarah, what're you doing in here?"

Her reverie was broken as James Picton, the music master, spoke from his chair in the corner and her consciousness once again registered the friendly buzz of conversation in the staff room.

"Oh, hi James. Mavis forgot to deliver his lordship's coffee, so I'm making him one."

"You're too good to him," James went on. "Why can't the lazy bugger get one for himself?"

"Oh, you know..." Sarah tailed off.

"Oh, yes, we know. Anyway, who's Mavis?"

"She's the domestic allocated to his office. Any idea where she is?" went on Sarah. "She seems to have done a disappearing act."

"Nope, haven't a clue," said James, as he subsided happily in his chair, nursing his own coffee, his nose once more nestled in a magazine, the fate of missing domestics far from his mind.

"Sarah?"

Sarah turned to face Denise Grant, the English teacher. "Oh, hi Denise, can't stop," she replied in a hurry.

"No probs. Just wanted to know if you'll make up a foursome with me and my brother and sister at the local pub's quiz night, next week?"

"Oh, I'd love to," answered Sarah with pleasure. "Thanks for asking."

"I'll give you the details when you've got a minute. Seems you're a lady on a mission at the moment."

"Got to make his nibs some coffee."

"Can't he make it himself? Anyway, thought he had his delivered. Not like us poor sods, got to make our own."

"His milk monitor has gone missing, Mavis, one of the domestics. You haven't seen her by any chance?"

"Not recently. I expect she's in the kitchen getting lunch ready. Need any help?"

"No, thanks, Denise. It's only a cup. I'd better get on with it."

"Right you are."

Sarah headed to the little kitchen, which had been made out of an old, but very large, pantry adjacent to the staff room. It was small but served its purpose well. As she prepared the coffee, she determined to have a chat with Brenda. Mavis had an uncanny knack of going missing when she should have been working. It wasn't really good enough and it made her life difficult when the headmaster got into one of his moods. Anything to keep the man appeased was something to be welcomed.

With the coffee quickly made in the best cup she could find, and bearing it on a small tray with a couple of biscuits rescued from the depths of a now almost empty tin, she returned to her office, and knocked lightly on the adjoining door. Hearing nothing at first, she tapped again. This time, she heard a brief scuffle, a light cough and a giggle inside. She waited, visualising the scene. It brought a smile to her lips. After a short pause, a peremptory 'Come in!' filtered through the heavy oak door. Suppressing the smile on her lips, Sarah entered, knowing exactly what she would find. She wasn't disappointed. Frances and Graham Harper sat on the brown upholstered sofa in his office, a respectable distance between them but both looking flushed and slightly dishevelled. Keeping her face as expressionless as possible and avoiding eye contact with the headmaster, she placed the coffee down on the table. Frances, the top two buttons of her blouse undone and red finger marks on her soft skin, wriggled uncomfortably, her face red with embarrassment. Sarah caught her eye and out of sight of the headmaster, Frances pouted with anger and humiliation. Graham Harper merely grunted but the lipstick smearing his chin told the full story. Sarah returned to her own office, shutting the door gently behind her and laughed quietly to herself. Fools, utter fools, the pair of them, she thought, as she sat back at her desk. It was a bright moment in an otherwise stressful morning.

As she sat down, the front door bell rang. Presuming, rightly as it happened, that this would be Mr and Mrs St James, the prospective parents who were expected, and also presuming, again correctly, that Frances hadn't yet returned to her desk, Sarah rose from her seat and with a sigh, headed for Reception. She greeted the two newcomers, introduced herself and invited them to take a seat, telling them that she would notify the headmaster of their arrival. They thanked her warmly, and sat down on the polished boards of a large wooden settle, placed to one side of the fireplace. There seemed to be no child with them. Sarah presumed that they were just on a fishing trip and would bring their cherished offspring on a later visit if they had been hooked by the headmaster. His powers of persuasion were quite strong and it took a strong will to say no, but it had been known.

Reception had been decorated to impress visitors, being the first inside sight of the school that any new parent would see. Today it smelled of new lavender polish, carefully laid by Ella, one of the team of domestics, and a beautiful floral arrangement of lilac and greenery adorned the large hearth, the weather being just too warm for a fire. The fine stucco ceiling had at one time been decorated with gold leaf but this had long been replaced with gold paint, and the effect didn't seem quite as effective. Overall, the entrance hall was a beautiful opener to the school but the effect was somewhat marred by a chipped panel in the wall, dirty fingerprints on the plaster next to the door and the untidy nature of Frances' desk, but Sarah hoped that Mr and Mrs St James wouldn't notice these failings. Leaving them with a copy of the new glossy prospectus, which promised much and looked very impressive, Sarah returned to her office and again knocked on the interconnecting door between her office and the headmaster's. This time the 'come' was rather more immediate. As she entered the room, the outer door from the headmaster's study closed. Frances had disappeared, hopefully back to her desk, thought Sarah. Sarah informed her boss of the new arrivals and left him to it.

Graham Harper, having drunk his coffee and with Frances dismissed from his office, stood up and straightened his jacket, brushing biscuit crumbs from his shirt front as he did so. He was aware that parents were waiting to see him but he walked across the plush dark green carpet of his office and looked out through the tall windows, instead. A boy was wandering, obviously lost, across the grass so Graham hurriedly opened the window and shouted.
"Boy, where do you think you are going?"
The child skidded to a halt at the edge of the grass and froze, colouring up in embarrassment. He was new and wasn't sure where he was going or what he was doing.

"Sir?" he whimpered, a question in his voice.

"Don't you know you're not supposed to be on the lawn? Get off this minute and come to see me after lunch."

"Sorry, sir, I didn't …" his voice trailed off into a dumb misery.

"Don't answer me back – I'll hear no more. See me at two-o-clock."

Graham slammed the window shut, turning his back on the outside, leaving the little boy staring miserably up at the closed window. Today, the Bishop was coming to luncheon - Graham didn't do lunch – and this gave him a chance to preen his feathers. He looked at his watch. He had twenty minutes to see the parents in his office, then leave the rest to Frances, after all that was part of her job. The Bishop was due in half an hour so with recalcitrant boys and missing domestics summarily dismissed from his mind, he invited Mr and Mrs St James into his office. There followed an uncomfortable interlude for the poor parents as they came up against the unstoppable force that was Graham Harper. He proceeded to regale them with exam results, statistics, finances and everything to do with how wonderful the school was. He flattered their choice, choosing to ignore the fact that they hadn't actually made a decision yet. Fifteen minutes later, and blinded with facts, but still ignorant as to how the school worked and what it could do for their little boy, Mr and Mrs St James were shown from the headmaster's office and left with Frances for her to give them a tour of the school. They thanked the headmaster and turned to Frances, eager to see a pretty face and enjoy the rest of the school. The headmaster's study had felt stuffy, whiffs of stale perfume and old sweat mixed with the atmosphere in the room, and they were keen for some fresh air.

Brenda Jarvis, the Catering Manager of the school, was annoyed. It was getting on for lunchtime, and Mavis still hadn't turned up to start serving the two hundred and fifty hungry mouths, not to mention the teaching staff, all of whom would soon appear in the school dining room. She angrily stirred the gravy, now bubbling nicely on the hob and thought dire thoughts about her missing maid. Brenda's life was a busy one and she rarely had a moment to herself, so having to worry about missing staff made her job more stressful than it should have been. With the gravy now simmering gently, Brenda looked up, wiping her hands down her apron. Her face glistened with gentle perspiration from the heat of the stove, and her cheeks were reddened with the effects of heat and stress.

"Has anyone seen Mavis?" she asked in a loud voice to her fellow domestics in the canteen as they, too, busied themselves with last minute preparations for lunch.

"Last I saw, she was in the staff room, washing up after assembly this morning. Those teachers always leave the room in such a mess," replied Jane Milling with a sniff.

"Yes, quite," replied Brenda shortly, "but we'll worry about that another time. Right now, my concern is getting everyone in place to dish up dinner and Mavis is nowhere to be seen."

"Would you like me to stay on and give you a hand," asked Ella, who having fulfilled her cleaning duties was now helping the kitchen staff, but had been due to go home. "I can help out for another hour if you want."

"Oh, thanks, Ella," said Brenda. "Would you mind? Could you keep an eye on this gravy? That girl will be the death of me."

Ella was what one might call, 'the salt of the earth'. She had been at the school for ten years, and had become Brenda's right hand woman and unofficial deputy in the kitchen. She had also become a good friend to Sarah, whose office she cleaned. Sarah treasured the few moments they had each day when Ella came to her office. Sometimes, she bought a coffee with her and the two women took a short breather together, spending a minute or two putting the world to rights.

Brenda had been at the school for thirty years and had become somewhat of a fixture. Never married, and consequently childless, the school with its staff and children was her home and family. She worked hard, usually unappreciated by the headmaster, but it was a job she loved nonetheless. She was a practised manager and an extremely good cook. Often faced with tight budgets and increasing demands from Graham Harper, she had never failed to perform and her celebration meals were legendary amongst parents and children alike. Right now, she was harassed and irritable. The school at lunchtime was a busy place, particularly as there was also a special lunch to prepare. Typically, the headmaster had landed that particular meal on her at the last minute. He had known for some time that the Bishop had agreed to visit today for lunch, but he had neglected to tell her until yesterday. She had then had a last minute panic getting in supplies, ensuring there was a good stock of the right wines, cheeses, fruits and a nice plump chicken for dinner, and making sure the table linen was laundered and presented properly. She had spent some time early that morning laying the table in the headmaster's own private dining room, polishing the cutlery, setting out dishes on the sideboard which would later accommodate a selection of cheeses and water biscuits, and laying pristine dinner plates on top of a snow white table cloth. That had taken some considerable time out of her already busy day, so Mavis' non-appearance rankled more than it might otherwise have done. Leaving the kitchen in Ella's care, she decided to have one last look for Mavis. Hanging up her apron on the hook by the kitchen door, and wiping her damp cheeks on a kitchen towel, she headed for the staff room, where Mavis had last been spotted. She left the steamy heat of the school's kitchen behind and went outside where her cheeks cooled and her good humour returned. Brenda breathed in the gently warm late spring air and felt a moment of ease. It felt balm to her troubled mind and the brief interlude calmed her spirits. She crossed the quad, now empty and quiet as the children had returned to their classes after break time and not yet reappeared for dinner. Going back inside the building at the other side of the quad, she pushed open the staff room door and looked round. She sniffed irritably as the room bore no obvious trace of the missing domestic. Dr George Lowe, the history professor and sole occupant of the room at that time, looked up airily from the marking he was busily engaged in as Brenda buzzed in.

"Can I help you?" he asked pleasantly?"

"Have you seen Mavis?" Brenda asked quickly, anxious not to hang around. The gravy would be ready now, she fleetingly thought as she was perforced to stop in her tracks.

"That's Mavis, your kitchen lady, is it?"

Brenda, slightly mollified that he knew who she was talking about, nodded.

"No, I'm afraid I haven't, not since first thing this morning that is," George replied. "She's usually in here just before break time making coffee. I have a free lesson then so I'm usually in here too, but she wasn't here then. I assumed she'd been and gone. Is she missing?" he finished politely.

"Yes, she's disappeared. God knows where she's got to."

"She'll turn up, they usually do," finished George, and with an airy, dismissive wave of his ink stained hand, he returned to the papers on his lap.

Brenda carried on through to the little kitchen. Momentarily impressed at the tidy nature of the room, every cup and spoon washed and back in its place, even the sugar canister was clean which normally sat minus its lid with a wet spoon in it, she quickly ascertained that Mavis was nowhere to be seen there either. She poked her head round the staff room toilet door and found that room empty too, although desperately in need of a good sort out. Brenda momentarily caught sight of her face in the small round mirror on the wall and sighed at her reflection. Her grey curls looked dishevelled and her cheeks were red with exertion. Her weight added to her physical discomfort and not for the first time wished she was several sizes smaller. She shrugged her large shoulders with impatience and with her double chin wobbling dangerously as she walked, she left the staff room, leaving George to his marking, and carried on out through to Reception. George never even saw her go.

As Brenda walked through, on her way back to the dining room, Frances, now back at her desk, the prospective parents successfully toured and now departed, looked up.

"Oh, Brenda, please could you get me a cup of coffee?" she asked sweetly. "The one I had on my desk seems to have disappeared."

Brenda was also under no illusion as to Frances' behaviour and already vexed with the missing domestic problem, and anxious to get back to the kitchen, retorted angrily with impatience.

"Get it yourself, I'm busy."

Brenda stormed off, feeling slightly guilt at her own response. She wasn't given to rudeness, and her response had been very abrupt, but she had better things to worry about than a lazy receptionist. Frances wisely said nothing but turned back to her computer, an angry red tint suffusing her pretty cheeks.

Graham looked at his watch and decided that he had just enough time for a short walk around the campus to get a breath of fresh air. He donned his gown and left his office. Frances was still at her desk, and as Graham walked through Reception and out to the front of the building, she looked up as he passed and smiled. James Picton, strolling through Reception at the same time, wondered if they realised how loudly their body language spoke volumes. Love maybe blind, but a school full of two hundred and fifty children, forty teachers and thirty other staff most certainly was not! He grinned as he watched Frances' eyes follow the headmaster's back as Graham walked through the front door. She had the grace to blush as she realised she was being watched. The music master wondered if Frances was intelligent enough to realise that she had been found out as well.

The building which housed Coates Norton School had stood on the hallowed grounds of the Coates estate for over two hundred years. The estate itself had been in the Coates family since the early thirteenth century, a gift from the King, but with the burgeoning industrialisation of the country at the turn of the twentieth century, the family realised the need for good schooling and with the huge financial assistance of Charles Norton, a successful mill owner, one of the large houses on the estate had been converted over a hundred and fifty years ago, thus giving birth to Coates Norton School. It had seen mixed fortunes, particularly during the Second World War when an influx of evacuees had impacted on the finances of the school, but generally it had flourished and academically had done very well. Its initial establishment of fourteen boy scholars had given way to more boys, gradually increasing in number over the years, who had come and gone and then replaced with more boys, and for the last ten years, girls as well. It was a truly co-educational modern independent school and, until its new headmaster had taken over, five years previously, a successful and thriving one. Graham Harper walked through the thick oak front door, oblivious to the thoughts of his music master, and down the stone steps, worn smooth by generations of schoolchildren and their parents as they had come and gone over the last century and a half. The newly gravelled driveway spread out in front of him and gleamed in the spring sunshine, its new pristine surface channelled with the comings and goings of cars and school buses that morning. He vaguely wondered what sort of car Mr and Mrs St James had; hopefully not some tatty old Chelsea tractor, which seemed to be the car of choice these days. His practised but jaundiced eye roved across the parked cars, all bar one a Chelsea tractor, some better looking than others admittedly, and the one on its own was a battered old Ford. He knew whose car that was, one of the domestic staff. He would have words – this wasn't the sort of vehicle he wanted on show. She had been told to park it round the back before.

The school had been a happy and thriving place but after five years under the headship of Graham Harper, it now looked tired and ill at ease with itself. What was obvious to those with perception was seemingly invisible to the man himself. He either had chosen to ignore it or was simply oblivious to its parlous state. Today particularly, the state of the building and its imperfections were far from his thoughts as Graham pondered on things that would exalt him to higher status, or so he thought. He was not a confident man, but as such men do, he hid it well in bluster and egotism. He would not countenance arguments or another man's honest opinion, frightened that if he gave way he could be made to look weak. This made him a bully and whenever possible, people just kept out of his way and hoped they wouldn't be noticed. This didn't help the smooth running of the school, and things were beginning to suffer. The teaching staff knew what was happening, but even with their best efforts, were powerless to do anything about it. They satisfied themselves that eventually something would happen, but for the time being they just had to make the best of it. Rebellion simmered in the staff room, but for now that was where it stayed. Graham looked up at the building's façade and sighed contentedly. He chose to ignore the perilous state of its lofty chimneys, twisted and turned in glorious echoes of a distant past, but now sooted and black and leaning dangerously. The roof, a tile hanging precariously from the edge, was topped with a row of intricately carved ridge tiles which stood proud against the clear blue sky. The mellow golden stone of the main school building glowed in the warm midday sunshine, the appearance of dirty and crumbling mortar seemingly disappearing into the shadows. Tall windows, with bull's eye roundels at their tops, were set into each wall and gave glimpses of the oak panelling and delicate plaster cornices within, echoes of a worthy past. The golden weathercock, which topped the roof, swung very gently in the light spring breeze, the wind direction auguring well for a glorious afternoon.

Graham Harper was tall and thin, giving the appearance of quite an imposing man. He liked to think he was distinguished whereas, in fact, white hair which crowned a rather small head, black bushy eyebrows and a thin aquiline nose all gave him the look of a frightened owl. He was clean shaven, but a weak receding chin and mottled cheeks which were unbecomingly flushed, did nothing to improve his appearance. He walked across the quad, staff and children alike scattering to the four winds as they saw him coming. His gown billowed out behind him, making him look like one of the crows which nested on top of the school's chimneys. His presence usually meant trouble for someone, and people soon learned to make themselves scarce. The grounds were beginning to fill as morning lessons came to an end. Teachers and children alike emptied classrooms and the route to the school's large dining room became filled with chattering, hungry voices. Michael Shepperton, the Biology teacher, paused as he closed the laboratory door and sniffed the air, appreciatively. It smelled like a roast dinner today, his favourite. The morning's lesson had been challenging and he was really ready for his lunch. He suddenly espied Graham, who hadn't seen him, and he skirted round the corner quickly, anxious to avoid the headmaster's roving and critical eyes. Graham had paused in his wanderings as, in the distance, he had caught sight of his Finance Manager, Gerald Leigh, who was making his way into the school canteen. Graham grinned. Now, here was a man he could work with and just now he wanted a quick word.

"Gerald, just the man", the headmaster shouted across the quad, his stentorian tones disturbing a flock of sparrows which had injudiciously stopped to peck at a misplaced crust which had found its way onto the playground.

"Could you spare a moment or two after lunch? There are things I need to discuss."

Gerald groaned inwardly, or maybe it was just his empty stomach calling restlessly for lunch. He stopped in his tracks and turned reluctantly to the headmaster.

"Headmaster?" he said as Graham caught up with him. If only he hadn't taken that last call, he'd have made it into the dining room. Gerald sighed as the headmaster approached.

"Gerald, my dear man. I have some expense claims I need to discuss with you. You know the usual sort of thing."

Gerald knew very well what the 'usual sort of thing' meant. Expenses claimed in the execution of the headmaster's duty they

56

most certainly were not. He knew the headmaster had been away for the weekend, and not where he said he was, he was sure. He was pretty sure that Frances had accompanied him. The Headmaster's Conference to where he had said he was going had been cancelled, so goodness only knows where the pair had disappeared to. Gerald was used to this and didn't ask too many questions but creative accounting, which wasn't in his CV, had become a useful skill, acquired since he had begun in post at Coates Norton. Gerald always feared that all this would catch up with him one day, and always meant to make some sort of reparation, at least lessen the damage, but somehow he could never quite get round to it. He loathed the danger that the headmaster's peccadilloes placed him in, but he had never had the courage to confront the man. He managed to keep the ordinary accounts on an even keel, he was a very good accountant, but he had to rob Peter to pay Paul on too many occasions, and he doubted how long he'd be able to keep the subterfuge going. Graham smiled warmly. Gerald and he seemed to understand each other – singing from the same hymn sheet was his favourite phrase. He cared not a jot if the finances were in such a mess as long as he had some showy buildings, a few clever children to keep the examination statistics high and some gullible Governors who did what they were told. Gerald had by now collected his thoughts and grovelled appropriately to his boss.

"Headmaster", Gerald crooned. "Of course, it would be a pleasure."

"Would you join me for luncheon, my dear man? I'd like you to meet the Bishop," Graham added as an afterthought.

Gerald wasn't sure about this. He was a basic sort of chap and he enjoyed his pie and chips for lunch, usually with lashings of tomato ketchup. He knew that Brenda always cooked a good meal, but the fancy fare that he knew would be offered to the Bishop wouldn't be his cup of tea at all. Still, he sighed and replied.

"Of course, Headmaster," he unctuously declared. "I can think of nothing better." Gerald kept his fingers crossed behind his back and hoped that his lies would go unnoticed.

"Perhaps you could join us in the dining room in ten minutes. So glad you could make it," finished Graham, his attention suddenly diverted by an unfortunate pupil he'd seen climbing on the tennis court wall.

"Boy!" roared Graham, making everyone jump around him, not the least of whom was Gerald.

"Get down from that wall at once."

The boy jumped dexterously down and away from the headmaster, before his identity could be established. Graham sniffed with deep annoyance, angry at being outwitted and denied his prey. Gerald had taken the opportunity presented by the diversion to escape. He was not best pleased. He hated formality of any kind and had been planning a quick lunch, then some quiet time poring over his beloved spreadsheets. It was time for the monthly round up of the school's cash accounts and, as usual, there were those few small discrepancies that the headmaster had supplied, which he knew would take up most of the afternoon.

"Oh, well," he sighed to himself. "Just have to wait."

He turned and went back to his office to smarten himself up a bit for the forthcoming lunch. As luck would have it, he'd brought a reasonable jacket to wear today. Just as well he'd decided against the threadbare jumper, which had become his trademark. He changed from his sweater to the said jacket, but was suddenly overwhelmed with an acute weariness and sat down suddenly in his office chair. Life had become quite burdensome lately, he thought, as he contemplated the papers on his desk. He had previously looked forward to going over these accounts but now all enthusiasm had evaporated. He sat for a few minutes, trying to collect his thoughts and attempting to put himself in the mood for a posh lunch and some academic chit chat, which he knew without doubt, would ensue. Perhaps he'd be able to keep a low profile, and let the headmaster do all the talking. With a humourless grin,

Gerald realised that the headmaster was very good at talking, not so good at doing and producing the goods. He realised, too, that the headmaster's wife would be at the lunch. She was always at these sorts of occasions. He knew quite well that Mrs Harper would hate the occasion as much as he would; she was never the life and soul of any party, always finding such events difficult. She was a shy woman by nature but this was made even worse by her husband's overbearing nature. Perhaps they could commiserate together. Gerald always exuded a cool, calm, practised exterior in public, the man who dealt with the school's intricate finances. Most people, having no idea of accounts and book-keeping thought he did a brilliant job, and so he did. However, in the privacy of his own office his efficient demeanour vanished and although good at his job, sometimes wondered in what direction it was going. His stomach fluttered with mild panic as he contemplated the time ahead of him: an uncomfortable hour with a pompous headmaster and an honourable cleric, then hours spent unwinding the headmaster's tricky and somewhat dubious receipts. Time was ticking on, so with a sigh Gerald lifted himself out of his seat and his gloom, locked the office and headed for the headmaster's private dining room. If he was late, he'd be late. Tough, he thought with a moment of rare courage.

Graham looked at his watch and grunted in annoyance. The Bishop was late. Graham expected punctuality from everyone, whoever it was, even the Bishop. It would never have occurred to him that the poor man might have a valid excuse. Mind you, there was late and there was late. The Bishop had been invited for lunch at one, and it was only five past. Graham never allowed for fallibility in others despite the fact that he was full of it. Just then, he saw a car pull onto the driveway from the main road and negotiate carefully the deep gravel. Ah, the Bishop at last. Graham's good temper was restored as he headed for the front steps to welcome his eminent visitor.

A month after his conversation with Bishop Anthony, Stephen pondered on his predecessor's words as they came home to roost with that morning's post. A large ostentatious pale blue envelope, bearing a rather flamboyant crest, had landed on his desk, demanding to be opened. Never having seen such an envelope before, Stephen picked up his letter knife and slit the envelope with curiosity. He soon wished this particular epistle had got lost in the post. His heart sank as he recognised the school's name at the top of the letter and with his heart sinking further as he did so, he read the formal invitation contained within.

"My Lord Bishop. I would deem it a great and enormous pleasure if you would grace us with your presence at luncheon next Monday. Shall we say one-o-clock? Please confirm with my secretary."

The new Bishop had only been officially installed the week before but Graham Harper had left no time before pouncing. This stark invitation had given Stephen no choice but to accept. He did play with the idea of refusing but common sense told him that this would only delay the inevitable and make things worse. Better to get it over with quickly, once and for all, then he could relax and get on with what he was best at. With a heavy heart he directed his secretary to reply in the affirmative. A few days later, with Bishop Anthony's words echoing in his brain, Bishop Stephen's car drove up the newly gravelled driveway of Coates Norton School.

Chapter Four

Graham had just completed a circuit of the campus and returned to the front steps just as the Bishop's car pulled up outside the front of the school building. He straightened his gown, and with thumbs elegantly placed in his lapels, he hurried across to greet his eminent visitor as the car came to a halt, crunching on the deep gravel as the driver manoeuvred the vehicle on the driveway. Graham grabbed the door handle and pulled the car door open even before the driver had applied the handbrake. This unnerving approach startled the Bishop and he jumped as a large hand thrust itself into his face.

"My Lord, so good of you to come. Luncheon will be served in my private dining room in ten minutes. I do hope you will be able to stay for a tour of the school afterwards."

The Bishop caught the eye of his driver in the rear view mirror, and they exchanged a wry grin. His driver had been here before and knew exactly what his boss would experience. Bishop Stephen emerged from the car, flustered by the headmaster's effusive greeting and was rapidly led indoors, the tails of his cassock flying in the late spring breeze. He was led past an empty reception desk, now vacated by Frances, and through the Inner Hall, which smelled delightfully of newly laid lavender polish. He just had time to appreciate that this was a beautiful room and wanted to stop and take in his surroundings, but the headmaster's grip on his elbow was relentless so he didn't stand a chance. The Bishop skidded slightly on the highly polished floor and struggled to maintain his balance, grasped as he was by Graham's hand. He groaned. Surely, this was purgatory. Graham seemed not to notice his guest's discomfiture, and bore blithely onwards to the dining room where lunch was laid out in splendid array.

"Allow me to introduce my wife," went on the headmaster, hardly pausing for breath.

In her early fifties, Barbara Harper was non-descript in every way. Her husband had such a strong and powerful demeanour that her mouse-like manner was vastly overshadowed. She was small and dumpy and her clothes were old fashioned. She was dressed in an unbecoming pink floral dress, belted round the middle with a wide, bright red plastic belt, making her look like a rather psychedelic sack of potatoes. Her hair, dyed an unbecoming jet black, clashed with the bright colour of her dress and showed grey at the roots. Her make-up was heavy with lips bright red, an ugly scarlet gash across her face. Her face powder, plastered in layers, did nothing to colour an otherwise pale and blotchy face. She was a necessary appendage to a successful public school headmaster, something Graham had realised a long time ago if he was going to make it to the top. Barbara knew this only too well and gamely accepted her lot in life.

She much preferred her own company, and that of her children, but she was always there at her husband's beck and call for the showy days of the school year: Prize Givings, Speech Days and Parents' Meetings. She was always required for the show of happy marriage, good morals and calming stability put forward by the headmaster. She was not a happy woman, fully realising that she was nothing more than a useful accoutrement for her husband, but she was loyal and bore her place in life stoically and with good grace. The Bishop shook hands with her, sat down gratefully at the table and closed his eyes, glad of a chance to catch his breath. Graham quickly followed suit and misinterpreting the Bishop's closed eyes, launched embarrassingly into Grace. A knock at the door disturbed his ponderous prayers and he scowled as Gerald poked his head round the door.
"So sorry I'm late, Headmaster. I had to return to my office and an important telephone call from the bank delayed me."
The headmaster grunted and peremptorily waved his hand, bidding Gerald to take a seat. With an embarrassment of ritual he again began Grace but to the Bishop's secret delight, this again was interrupted as Brenda appeared with a heavily laden trolley. Grace was abandoned and lunch was served. Somewhat surprisingly, an

amiable and pleasant tranquillity descended on the room. Helped enormously by generous servings of an excellent white wine, Bishop Stephen began to relax and actually started to enjoy his meal. The food was excellent; a beautifully light soup, followed by a tender and very tasty chicken dish. The vegetables were cooked to perfection; cauliflower and carrots just crisp and roast potatoes, light and fluffy. The pudding was delightful; a tangy and tart blackcurrant roulade. The Bishop appreciated good cooking and when Brenda returned to clear the empty dishes, he told her so. Brenda blushed slightly, and left the dining room with her cluttered trolley, feeling uplifted by someone who had actually appreciated her talents. However, the small talk during lunch left a lot to be desired, dominated as it was by the headmaster's egotism, but the Bishop kept hold of the thought that it would all be over soon. He was amused by Barbara's docility and felt sorry for the woman. He had met the type before in his old parish, under-the-thumb wives, totally in the shadow of their extrovert husbands. He tried to engage her in conversation but each time was thwarted as Graham butted in and edged his mouse like wife backed into his shadow and her timidity.

Detective Sergeant Gabriel Dax, known to his friends as Archie, stood gazing out of the window of the CID office at Teigneford police station. Newly promoted and just relaxing into his new post, having made the move from Hereford some weeks back, he was looking forward to Alexis' arrival. The room was situated on the second floor of the building and from his vantage point he could just see the River Teigne, sparkling in the spring sunshine and bubbling gently over the weir as it sped on its way to join the Severn just south of Worcester. A duck flew up from the water, circled slowly above the tumbling rapids off the weir, then settled again to peck hungrily in the long grass which grew by the bank. Two majestic swans, with this year's brood of tiny grey cygnets, swam lazily in the shallows, their slender white necks in sharp contrast to the dark water. Two small children paddled gleefully in the shallows and the scene left Dax feeling rested and peaceful and certainly not in the mood for work. The slight breeze coming through the open window ruffled his almost black hair and as his deep brown eyes surveyed the scene before him, he felt good. He hadn't learned until yesterday that Alexis had reached her next rung of the career ladder too and had rejoiced at the news that she would be joining him at Teigneford. The two officers had been good friends and had worked well together as constable and sergeant. Despite being a man and woman working closely together, there had never been any hint of romanticism. It was sometimes difficult to convince people that there was nothing in that way between them. Dax was happily married, loved his wife Claire and just thought of Alexis as a good friend, nothing more. The six months Alexis had been away on that squad in London, with all its inherent dangers, had felt like a lifetime, never knowing if she would come back. He'd missed her dearly and had been elated when he'd discovered that his new boss at Teigneford would be his old friend. The news of her imminent return to the county filled him with pleasure. Dax turned away from the window and returned to his desk to ready himself for the afternoon briefing.

Alexis reached the front door of the police station, pulled the door towards her and went in. The reception desk was empty, no one in sight. She pulled her old security pass out of her bag that she'd been given during the burglary investigation and hoped that it still worked, otherwise she'd be here for some time. The clock was ticking on and she was due in the office at two, but she'd hoped to be in a little earlier. It was now half past one. Security was as good as ever at the police station and her pass worked perfectly, so letting herself in quietly, she headed for the CID office.
"Morning, ma'am. Good to see you."
Alexis hadn't been looking ahead as the words hit her ears, but she knew that voice and it stopped her in her tracks.
"Archie! What in heaven's name are you doing here?"

"I'm your new DS," he replied, a wide grin on his face. "I knew you were coming and after an early call from the super, I thought I'd beat you to it."

"Oh, Archie, am I glad to see you. No one said. Why didn't you tell me you'd been promoted too?"

"Thought it would be a nice surprise."

"Oh, boy, it's that all right. What a fantastic start."

Apart from the newly promoted Detective Sergeant Dax, the office was empty and Alexis couldn't stop herself. She hurried across to Dax and gave him a huge hug. Hardly professional, but just at that moment, she couldn't care less, so glad was she to see her friend. Pulling back from the embrace, she studied him. It had been a while since they'd last met but he hadn't changed.

"We've got lots to talk about," said Alexis, her face alight with joy. "I've missed you, Archie. No one told me you'd been promoted. You kept that quiet."

Dax grinned, his face, too, alight with the pleasure of seeing his friend and long-time colleague again. Whilst Alexis and Dax chatted, she became aware of others in the office as two desks became occupied.

"Come and say hello," invited Dax. "I'll introduce you."

Alexis knew that her team should comprise of three constables and a detective sergeant, the post now filled by Dax, and that one member of the team was the existing member of the CID office. She idly wondered how her presence would go down with someone who had become a fixture of the office for some time, and who had obviously worked with the outgoing Detective Inspector Redway. This brought back a memory of her first time in the Squad office in London. This was becoming a habit, she thought.

"Afternoon both," said Dax brightly. "Let me introduce you to Detective Inspector Alexis Longbow. Ma'am, let me introduce you to Detective Constable Steve Moss and Detective Constable Mike Evans."

Alexis looked in turn at their faces. The first was an older man, probably in his forties, his eyes brown, his brown hair greying slightly at the temples, his shoulders slightly stooped. Alexis already had a nodding acquaintance with Detective Constable Steve Moss. He was a dour, taciturn sort of chap with whom she had worked at Teigneford on the burglary case a while ago. He'd been in the job for somewhere close to twenty years and she wondered why he'd never sought promotion. He'd been friendly enough but she'd never really got to know him that well. Another man sat at the back of the room. He was much younger, probably in his late twenties, also brown haired but without the grey. Alexis was pleased to see them but also felt a little disappointed. The Assistant Chief Constable had promised her three detective constables and she assumed that the two men who now faced her was it. Two DCs and one DS wouldn't be enough for a burgeoning CID department. She would have to have a word with the superintendent and hope he was amenable to adding the third officer that the ACC had promised. She looked at the small group, and putting her best optimistic face forward she addressed her new team.

"Steve," she said, turning to the older man. "It's good to meet you again."

Steve smiled gently, a little warily Alexis thought but it seemed genuine enough. He stood and shook her hand readily so she felt encouraged. The bond between members of her team would only come as they worked together and got to know each other properly. She turned to the unknown face.

"Mike, was it?" she asked.

"Yes ma'am. It's good to meet you," he replied, his face open and friendly, a grin on his face.

He too stood and shook Alexis' hand. His grasp was strong and firm and Alexis responded in kind. Just as she was about to ask him to tell her a little about himself, the phone on the main office desk rang. Dax picked up the receiver, listened for a second or two, then promptly handed it over to Alexis.

"It's for you, ma'am," he said. "Superintendent Barnes."

Alexis groaned quietly as she reluctantly took the receiver. She wasn't ready for this yet, hardly having had a chance to draw breath all day. The conversation was brief. After a quick 'yes sir', Alexis replaced the phone and turned back to the three men in the office.

"I'm so sorry, everyone. I am summoned to the upper room. Mr Barnes wants a word."

She very quickly picked up the sympathetic murmur that went round the office and felt encouraged.

"Archie!" she went on. "I'm going to have to see Mr Barnes before we go any further, so if you could gather the info on anything that you're all working on so I can get up to speed with you all, we'll have a chat when I get back downstairs."

"Righto, ma'am, will do."

Alexis turned back to the other two people who were sitting quietly at their desks.

"I'm so sorry, both. I promise we'll all have a chance to get to know each other as soon as possible. In the meantime, just shout at me if you need anything, but if in the first instance you can be guided by Sergeant Dax, until I've had a chance to get my feet under the table so to speak, that would be great."

Alexis' informal tone seemed to go down well; she even saw the face of the oldest member of her team, Detective Constable Steve Moss, twitch into a ghost of another smile. Hopefully, that was a good sign. Alexis then left them to it and headed upstairs to introduce herself to Superintendent Barnes. With the warning of the ACC brought back to mind, she tentatively knocked on his open office door.

"Ah, Miss Longbow, do come in."

Alexis groaned inwardly as the rather high pitched tones of the station superintendent, Edward Barnes, greeted her as she walked into his office. Suddenly, she felt truly exhausted after her travels and her legs trembled slightly as she acknowledged the man. Barnes was a short, plump man, only just the regulation height for a police officer. His jacket strained slightly across his chest and his mouse coloured hair, or what was left of it, was combed across his bald pate in a vain attempt to convince others he still had a full head of hair. Alexis had heard a lot about the, man, some of it rather discouraging, but now having to work with him, she would try to respect the superintendent. He was good at his job but he did have a reputation for being condescending to his female workers, be they police or civilian. Alexis just wasn't in the mood but with a stoicism she didn't really feel, she walked up to his desk.

"Take a seat, Miss Longbow," Barnes ordered.

Alexis dutifully sat down in a chair some distance from the superintendent's desk, already feeling at a disadvantage.

"I'll come straight to the point," Barnes said, his voice squeaky and soft. "I was not consulted over your appointment and was sorry to see Inspector Redway take early retirement..." Barnes paused.

Alexis jumped in.

"Any idea as to why he did go early, sir? Very unexpected."

"Family reasons, I gather," replied Barnes rather obliquely, leaving Alexis feeling dissatisfied. That didn't tell her anything. She suspected there was more to the man's rapid departure than Barnes was letting on but she could be patient. Archie would know.

"Yes," Barnes went on, clearing his throat. "As I was saying, I was not consulted over your appointment and you would not have been my choice."

Alexis bit back a sharp retort. She'd been tempted to say, 'thanks very much, sir' but thought better of it. She knew exactly why she hadn't been his choice, she was female. She sighed gently. This was something she would just have to get used to.

"I may call you Miss Longbow, I gather?" he went on pompously.

"I'd prefer Inspector Longbow, sir, or Alexis in private."

Barnes blinked, his mouth opening and shutting like a gasping goldfish. His face coloured slightly and Alexis could see storm clouds gathering. However, Barnes shut his mouth and just grunted.

"I will want a full report of your time in London at your earliest convenience, Miss Longbow."

Alexis was overwhelmed with anger, not just at the refusal to acknowledge her new rank but also his interference in what had been a confidential secondment. Her work was classified. It was really none of his business. Whatever she had done in London had nothing to do with the operational viability of the Teigneford CID office. She gritted her teeth and again bit back the reply she would have loved to have given. Instead she countered with a generality.

"I have given ACC Grainger my full report. I'm sure he would be more than willing to fill you in."

She deliberately kept her tone light and friendly, avoiding any edge to her voice. She wasn't sure if the superintendent was convinced or not. Alexis knew very well that the ACC would do nothing of the kind, so she felt better for having given this answer rather than the one that had immediately sprung to her lips. Barnes twisted away from her gaze, looking out of the window; the atmosphere cooled, the conversation stilled. Alexis wriggled with impatience and surreptitiously glanced at her watch. She felt frustrated at not being able to get on with her new job, but she had no choice but to wait. After a short pause, the superintendent turned back to her and Alexis took her chance.

"Also sir ..." she paused, suddenly tongue tied. The superintendent was not going to like what was coming next. He raised an eyebrow but said nothing.

"The ACC did say that my new CID team would include three DCs, as well as a DS. As I only have two DCs at the moment, I wonder if I could ask if a third has been appointed?"

Superintendent Barnes sat back in his chair and stared at Alexis. He cleared his throat.

"As it happens, I have been in conversation with the ACC on that matter. He did make it clear that was his intention. However, we are a bit thin on the ground at the moment, so the best I can do is a WPC as an attachment."

Alexis sighed. WPC indeed. The 'W' had long gone out of use – so much for equality.

"Sir?" she countered.

"Yes. We have a WPC Hannah Pembridge who has recently joined us from Shrewsbury. She is fairly new to the job but she is out of probation. I know nothing about her, save to say that she has done a

CID attachment during her probation, so she'll know the basic ropes, as it were."

Alexis was secretly pleased. She realised that the superintendent was thinking that a female officer would be a hindrance rather than a help, but having another woman on the team would even the balance. Saying nothing of her thoughts, she went on.

"Thank you, sir. I'm sure she'll be fine. Will you arrange that or shall I?"

Barnes grunted and Alexis wondered if he was disconcerted by her easy acquiescence. However, after a short silence he answered her question.

"I'll arrange that. Leave it with me."

"Thank you, sir."

With that, the superintendent stood and Alexis realised the conversation had ended. Barnes simply waved her away with an ominous farewell.

"We'll speak again, Miss Longbow."

"I'm sure we will, sir. Thank you."

As she went back downstairs to the CID office, thanks were far from her mind. She was fuming at his reluctance to use her proper rank but as she reached the door to the CID office, she stopped, shook herself and put the misogyny out of her mind, for now.

Graham Harper and his guests had just reached the port and Stilton stage, and Bishop Stephen, surreptitiously looking at his watch, wondered if he could make a quick exit. He knew that if he accepted the headmaster's invitation to tour the school, he'd be there all afternoon. Surely now, he could claim another appointment, perhaps an afternoon meeting with the Mothers' Union? However, the good Lord was not looking down on him just at that moment because as the Bishop sipped his coffee from an elegant porcelain cup, an unearthly scream pierced the air.

"What the dickens…" the Bishop exclaimed, startled by the sudden noise, as he dabbed furiously at a small drop of brown liquid, which had spilled onto his immaculate cassock in his surprise. The headmaster's face darkened angrily, his red cheeks suffused with an angry purple as this unwarranted intrusion threatened to spoil what had been a most delightful hour. Wiping his chin on a beautifully laundered napkin, the headmaster turned to his guest.

"Please excuse me, my Lord. I think the school play rehearsals have got a little out of hand."

Leaving the Bishop to finish his port, Graham left the dining room and went in search of the ghastly noise. He looked in the Hall but the stage was empty. No rehearsals there at the moment. Frowning, he turned and retraced his steps, breaking into an undignified run as a second scream filled the warm, dinner scented atmosphere. Just then, Jane Milling, hurtled out from a side corridor. She was sobbing hysterically and her face was as white as a sheet.

"What on earth is the matter, woman? Pull yourself together," the headmaster growled angrily.

Jane pointed vaguely down the corridor, her hand trembling violently in her distress. Her mouth worked frantically as she struggled to speak, but no words came. Her breath came in short, sharp gasps and at last she said one word.

"Mavis!"

Her eyes rolled in their sockets and as her legs folded underneath her body, she collapsed as she fell into a dead faint. Graham Harper caught the woman as she fell and Jane crumpled ungainly in his arms. The disturbance had caught the attention of three sixth formers, who were on their way into lunch. They stopped and stared, giggling at the sight of their pompous headmaster, arm in arm with a dishevelled domestic. Out of the corner of his eye, Graham caught sight of the unwanted onlookers and glared at them.

"Go and find Miss Jarvis, for goodness sake."

The three sixth formers, their grins rapidly dissipating, did as they were bid and ran along the corridor towards the dining hall where Brenda and the kitchen staff were still busy, serving dinner to hungry children.

James Picton was having a quiet ten minutes in the library, snatching a rare moment of calm as he attempted the Times crossword. The room was empty, divested of pupils who by now were tucking into lunch in the main dining hall. He had hoped for a few moments of peace and tranquillity before the mayhem of his own lunch in the dining hall and afternoon lessons thereafter. James was a busy man, not just the music master, but also the organist in the school's chapel and violin teacher to a few of the older pupils and he relished any private moments he could snatch during a long and busy day. The library faced south and the midday sun shone in through the tall glass windows. A feeling of contentment had crept up on him and these precious moments of calm had been just the thing. He had just completed three down and six across of a rather tricky crossword, when he too heard the scream. His gentle calm now irrevocably destroyed, he jumped up in alarm and hurriedly ran from his seat to see what had caused the commotion. Poking his head around the library door, he saw the headmaster more or less arm in arm with one of the domestics, who was by now spread-eagled across the floor. James could hardly suppress a grin, but just about managing to pull his face into some semblance of gravitas, he straightened his jacket and walked out of the library to see if he could help.

The headmaster heard his approach across the tiled floor and looked up in annoyance, hoping to have sorted this out without an audience. He had dispatched the sixth formers but now a member of staff was in attendance. Even in the stress of the moment, Graham realised that this would be the talk of the staff room before too much time had elapsed.

"What do you want, Picton?" he growled ungraciously.

James was not fazed. So long used to the headmaster's temper he simply ignored him.

"Thought you could do with a hand, Headmaster. You look as if you have your hands full," James answered without guile, his face straight.

"Miss Jarvis will be in attendance very soon so I do not need you. You may go."

"Right you are, Headmaster," responded James, who had no intention of doing anything of the sort.

As James lingered, it became very evident that Graham's embarrassment was not to end there. The door from the dining room opened and Bishop Stephen poked his head out. As he glanced at the scene he seemed amused, adding to the headmaster's discomfiture. His long, lean face, a little flushed after good food and wine, broke into a light grin. He couldn't help it. He had swiftly become very aware of his host's pomposity and couldn't but be slightly gratified that the mighty had fallen for a moment. The Bishop checked himself as he caught sight of the Headmaster's angry face and stepped to one side as Mrs Harper joined him at the door. Curiosity had got the better of her, but as she too took in the scene, immediately shrunk back into the room, unwilling to become part of the spectacle. The Bishop fought valiantly to compose his features and bent down to help the stricken woman. As Graham reddened furiously with anger and embarrassment, his tongue let loose.

"My Lord, you may return to the dining room. Matters are under control here. You are not needed."

The Bishop, his gentle mood now dissipated and irritated and annoyed by the Headmaster's abrupt tone, replied curtly.

"It is patently obvious that matters are not under control. The least I can do is try and help the poor woman as much as I can."

Graham had the sense to keep quiet and bit his lip, his face now purple.

The corridor was becoming a little crowded, much to Graham's increasing annoyance as Brenda arrived with Ella shortly behind her. The situation he thought he had firmly under control had escalated into a full blown soap opera, which even he knew would be the talk of not only the staff room, but also the dining room, the boarding houses and probably everyone's home by tea time. He was mildly thankful that the students had disappeared, the sixth formers taking a curious third former in tow as they left, but the adults around him, crowding him and adding to his irritability were increasing by the minute. Brenda arrived to find the Bishop dabbing Jane's face with water from the carafe in the dining room. Jane still lay spread-eagled on the floor, Graham having abandoned her to the cold tiles. She still swooned and seemed incapable of speech as she moaned softly. The headmaster stood to one side, his expression unreadable, his temper rising rapidly.

Jane gasped again, "Mavis".

"What on earth is the woman drivelling about," asked the headmaster roughly. The Bishop looked up, taken aback at his rough tone. Graham looked away, caught out in a show of his usual temper, all signs of pomposity and grandeur gone.

"Mavis is one of my domestics," said Brenda to the Bishop. "She didn't turn up to assist at lunch, but I didn't have time to track her down."

Jane tried to sit up but failed.

"Miss Jarvis," she managed to gasp. "Mavis is down there – I can't wake her up."

Jane swooned again and collapsed into Brenda's arms. Graham Harper rolled his eyes in disgust at this display of apparent feminine weakness which he abhorred and, turning on his heel, disappeared along the corridor away from the disturbing scene and back to his office. He had forgotten all about the Bishop, so intent was he in preserving what was left of his dignity. James eyed the headmaster's retreating back in disgust, then shrugging his shoulders, accepted the inevitable and took control. Leaving the now sobbing domestic in Brenda's very capable hands, he walked slowly down the corridor in the direction of Jane's vague gestures.

The now empty corridor led towards the storeroom and seeing a door left slightly ajar, James gingerly pushed it further open and looked into the room. To start with, he saw nothing untoward. The wooden shelves were lined with neat rows of tins and packets and other dry foodstuffs, each one carefully labelled and dated by Brenda. The light in the windowless room was poor and the one low energy light bulb which hung, shadeless, at the far end of the room gave scant illumination to the cupboard. James stopped and allowed his eyes to adjust to the gloom. He sniffed the air and his nostrils caught the lingering scent of something both sickly sweet and pungent. The smell caught at his throat and he wrinkled his nose in disgust. He could feel his pulse quickening and his heart thumped uncomfortably in his chest as he stepped further into the room, and walking carefully, he made his way up between the shelves, watching where he put his feet as he went. The light improved as he got to the far end of the room, nearer the bulb, and that is where he saw her. A young woman had fallen across a table, placed at the end of the room, and a stool was upended in a pile of overturned toilet rolls. James stopped in his tracks, his eye surveying the ghastly scene, his stomach repelling in the dusty gloom. He realised with a sick certainty that this wasn't going to be as straightforward as he had imagined. The unfortunate domestic, for indeed it was Mavis, had fallen awkwardly on her back. It looked as if she had been sitting on the corner of the table, doing what he had no idea. Her head hung sideways over the edge, her round face suffused with purple, as she had struggled for air in her death throes. The rest of her body lay spread-eagled across the scrubbed boards of the table; one arm hanging limply down by her side, the hand tightly grasping a stained white mug. Her eyes stared unblinkingly into an unseen distance; her mouth hung slack as an unsightly dribble slowly meandered down her chin, leaving in its wake a vicious red mark. A pool of green bile and vomit had formed amongst the bottles of cordials stored under the table. With the feeling of revulsion rising further from the pit of his stomach, James gingerly felt for the dead woman's pulse. There was nothing there, the beat had gone, life snuffed out. She was definitely dead; there was no doubt about that. With trembling fingers, he closed Mavis' eyelids, shutting out the light of life from her once and for all. He could do nothing else, this last tiny act, a small sign of

James' compassion in a violent scene. Her skin still felt warm, the coldness of death still at bay. As he stepped away from the body, Mavis' arm fell further away from the table and the mug she had been holding in her last grasp banged against the leg of the table. James jumped, unnerved by the sudden motion. His stomach clenched as the smell, now so sweet and cloying in the close murky atmosphere of the storeroom, made him feel light-headed. Seeing that the poor woman was beyond any help, he turned and rapidly left the room, carefully locking the door behind him with the key that Jane had left in the lock. This was now a matter for the police.

James returned to where Bishop Stephen was still trying gamefully to console Jane, who was still swooning and moaning slightly. Brenda stood to one side, unsure what to do, content for the moment to let the Bishop take over.

"She won't wake up, she won't wake up," Jane moaned over and over again.

The mantra began to get on James's nerves. He snorted. This was time to be a little brutal if he was to help her.

"For goodness sake woman, Mavis is dead. You will not be able to wake her ever again."

It was a verbal slap in the face but it most certainly had the desired effect. James was not a cruel man by any means but there were times when a sharp word in the right place had more power than any softly softly approach. Jane gulped, startled by the strength of James' voice. A little colour returned to her face and she sat up, her breath coming in quick gasps as she took in what James had said. The shock of what she had just seen was still there, but her composure began to return and she nodded, almost to herself as breathing returned to normal. She seemed to shake herself, as if trying to bring herself together. With her breath now more even, and with tears now falling gently down her pale cheeks, she tried to explain.

"Miss Jarvis asked me to get something from the store room. I couldn't find the key in the kitchen, so I assumed the door was open. I didn't think anything of it at the time. I came down the corridor, and I saw that the door was open."

Jane paused for breath and tried to stand. Bishop Stephen supported her as she stood. She brushed herself down and passed a hand through her dishevelled hair. He led her into the headmaster's dining room closely followed by James and Brenda, who had since dispatched Ella back to the kitchen to carry on with serving dinner to all the children. All were now anxious to escape the scrutiny of passing children, who were still making their way to the dining room, and gain some privacy whilst they tried to fathom out what had happened. Gerald had long since disappeared, anxious to get on with his spreadsheets and unwilling to become part of the spectacle, but Barbara, seemingly incapable of making a decision as the crisis unfolded around her, sat where she had been placed for the Bishop's now long forgotten lunch. Sitting Jane carefully in a chair, the kindly cleric solicitously poured her a glass of water. Although still a little pale, her face damp with tears, she now seemed fully in command of herself as she continued her explanation.

"I thought it a bit strange as the key was in the lock and I couldn't hear anyone inside. Everyone was in the kitchen getting dinner sorted, so I assumed someone had been down earlier and forgotten to lock the door and bring the key back. I went in to get what Miss Jarvis wanted and check that everything was OK. Then I found her ...." Jane tailed off miserably, her new found composure faltering slightly. She sniffed loudly.

James turned to the Bishop and Brenda and briefly explained more of what he had seen and what he now had to do. Brenda blanched but bore the news with remarkable fortitude and, nodding briefly to the two men, she helped Jane out of the chair and led her away for a fortifying cup of tea. James decided that two heads were better than one in such a difficult situation as this one was turning into.

"Bishop," he asked. "Would you be kind enough to just confirm with me what I have seen? I want a bit of back up, just in case."

The Bishop had long since resigned himself to a long afternoon at the school, any thoughts of getting back to his office any time soon, now long gone. He had seen death before. One doesn't rise up through the ranks of pastoral care without seeing a dead body or two, but as far as he could remember, the situation as described briefly by James had never come his way before – accident, sudden death, illness, old age yes, but suspicious circumstances – this was a new one. However, nodding gently, quietly accepting the inevitable, he followed James along the corridor towards the store cupboard.

Graham Harper sat in his study and stared sightlessly out of the big bay windows of his office, his mind on a different horizon. He had been severely shaken by events, which had spiralled out of his control, and had been ridiculed by his sixth formers. He had been found wanting by an honoured guest and his personal equilibrium had been shattered. In fact he had been highly embarrassed and he was extremely angry as he ran over the events in his mind. He sighed heavily and ran his thick stubby fingers through his wiry white hair. A cloud slid quietly across the sun and the colours died in the gloom as it obscured the light. Graham usually loved his office. It was warm and quiet; a sanctuary away from the hustle and bustle of his job, and his wife, but as the room lost its light, so his mood darkened with it. Now he felt abused and out of sorts. He had lost control, a situation that he was unused to and it unnerved him. The sun reappeared and his mood lightened as the light played on the roundels in the large bay windows. The glass split the light as the sun shone and coloured dots of light played fitfully on the plush green carpet, its smooth pile creased and tumbled with his footprints.

He shook himself out of his gloomy reverie and resolved to get a grip. Graham wanted Frances but sensibly realised that now was not the time. He started violently, shaken from his thoughts, as the door suddenly opened. James, accompanied by Bishop Stephen, entered without knocking, the seriousness of the matter taking away the need for elementary pleasantries. The Bishop caught the quick look of annoyance that flitted across the headmaster's face as they entered but ignored it; now was not the time to get angry. Stephen felt sickened and dirty, sullied by the events of the last half hour, and his host's behaviour did nothing to improve this feeling. He was glad to have James around; he felt comforted by the man's presence. He had provided a firm support and he felt secure in the self-control that the music master had already shown. It had been an unpleasant task the two had just shared. Time hadn't improved the scene, but both men stoically took to the task in hand and checked the scene. Mavis still lay where life had abandoned her, her mouth deeply scored by the liquid which still dribbled from her mouth. Her hand still grasped the cup and the single light bulb swung mercilessly to and fro, disturbed by the activity, its gloomy glow casting a malevolent spell over the scene. James stood back a little as the Bishop had approached and hung his head silently as Stephen sketched a cross in the air and spoke a quiet prayer of committal to God.

"Does she need an ambulance?" asked the headmaster, abruptly, as the two men entered without ceremony.

"She needs a hearse", the Bishop replied tartly, as he moved into the room, leaving James to close the door behind them.

The headmaster blanched.

"A hearse! The woman only fainted. I was there, you know," Graham added with sarcasm.

The Bishop snorted, derision giving an edge to his soft voice.

"I wasn't talking about the woman who collapsed, man, she's fine now. It's what, or rather who she found in the storeroom, I'm talking about. One of your kitchen assistants is dead. Either you or I need to call the police. Now!"

Graham Harper coloured angrily. He wasn't used to being spoken to like this, especially in his own study. He stood up and faced the Bishop, height wise half a head taller than Stephen, but his demeanour lessened by his manner. Forgetting for a moment who

Stephen was, Graham thrust what there was of his chin forward and spoke menacingly.

"Let me remind you, I am the headmaster - I make the decisions in this school. I do not think the police need be involved in a simple death. What on earth was the woman doing in the store room in the first place? You'd think she'd have the common decency to find somewhere private to die."

Bishop Anthony's words flitted into Stephen's mind as he faced up to his ill-mannered host. The man was indeed very dislikeable. However, Bishop Stephen did not flinch in the face of the headmaster's anger, but having kept his calm for so long, and under ever increasingly difficult circumstances - he was human after all - he finally lost it. With contempt clearly on his face, he raised his head to meet the Headmaster's eye, rising a couple of inches in his shoes as he did so.

"Mr Harper, I don't think you quite realise the seriousness of the situation. The dead woman has been found in suspicious circumstances. She has not died from natural causes – even an idiot can see that, if they cared to look."

The barb hit home and Graham Harper swallowed nervously, his angry, blood-suffused face paling visibly as he took in the Bishop's words.

"The woman has ingested something which has led to her death," continued the Bishop remorselessly. "I can smell it on her and see the rather unsavoury results. It may very well be an accident, it might not, but it does need to be investigated by the proper authorities," Stephen concluded angrily.

James stood to one side, and without mirth, grinned at Graham's discomfiture. The headmaster had met his match in the Bishop. A pastoral shepherd the man might be, but he was no wimp, that was plain to see. James kept quiet counsel and watched the play unfold.

Stephen sat down rapidly having, at last, run out of steam. He had not wanted to come to the wretched school in the first place; he had suffered Graham's insufferable priggishness; he had come face to face with violent death and he was now very tired. Shock had settled on his system, he wasn't as young as he used to be, and it was now taking its toll. The day had disintegrated into tragic farce and with the delightful effects of a good meal and a glass of wine or two now long gone, he felt exhausted and weak-kneed. The headmaster blinked as the Bishop collapsed in the chair and had the grace to look a little shame-faced as he saw Stephen's grey pallor. At last, Graham realised that due process would have to be invoked so with great reluctance, he reached for the telephone and dialled 999.

The call was brief. Graham didn't labour the point, working on the premise that least said, soonest mended. James realised what the headmaster had tried to do, but grinned to himself as he realised that this was going to be a real trial for the man. Graham Harper, for one of the rare occasions in his life, would have no control whatsoever over what would happen next and James delighted in that prospect. Graham replaced the phone. He swivelled his leather chair and stared out of the window, ignoring his guest. He closed his eyes and drifted away from the horrors of the moment. He needed Frances; he needed her warm lips and her ample bosom; he needed to be caressed and told that everything would be OK. Had it only been an hour since they had last been together? The thought of her firm breasts cradled in his hands brought a small smile to his lips and movement in his trousers. He unconsciously moved his legs – Oh, Frances! Feeling disgusted and embarrassed by the headmaster's complete disregard for normal polite etiquette, James watched as the headmaster absentmindedly adjusted his dress. It sickened him. He leaned across the table and reached for the tray of coffee that Brenda had so thoughtfully provided in the study. There was a gem of a woman and so undervalued, James thought, as he poured coffee for the Bishop, who took the cup, gratitude showing plainly on his face.

Graham's reverie was interrupted as the school bell announced the end of lunchtime. He flushed as he saw the Bishop looking strangely at him, almost as if he could read his thoughts. He shifted in his chair and helped himself to a cup of coffee. Graham drank deeply, the caffeine filling his veins and bringing some colour back to his face. With the cup raised to his lips, his hand shook slightly as a knock came at his door. He ignored it – he didn't need any interruptions right now. The knock came again and this time the door opened and Graham looked in amazement as a small blonde head of a boy peered round the solid oak of the study door.

"I did not give you permission to enter, boy! What are you doing here?"

"Sorry, sir, you asked me to come and see you after lunch," squeaked a little voice.

The headmaster reddened angrily. He didn't like to be caught out, especially by a snivelling first year boy.

"It is not convenient now – go away!"

The door closed rapidly and the child swiftly made his escape, unable to believe his luck.

The clock ticked as an uneasy silence descended on the room. Nothing was said as each man retreated into his own thoughts. Graham Harper was now very keen to be shot of his guest. He had served his purpose, but was now witness to something extremely unpalatable. The headmaster was a control freak, determined to be the master of everything in his school. His teaching staff had long learned that to argue with the man was pointless and ultimately fruitless. Graham turned to his guest at last. To have such an eminent person involved in something so alien to the school was untenable. The Bishop must be allowed to leave. The headmaster stood up and straightened his gown, now crumpled and extremely unkempt. Looking less like the crow and more like the scarecrow, he pompously and overtly formally addressed Bishop Stephen.

"My Lord Bishop, I am so very sorry that you have been exposed to such unsightly scenes here. I am sure you will want to be gone as soon as possible and allow yourself to forget what has happened. I will arrange for your driver to come to the front of the school to collect you. I bid you a fond farewell and hope that we may meet again soon, hopefully under more favourable circumstances."

The headmaster held out his arm to shake the Bishop's hand which the cleric studiously ignored. Stephen allowed himself a small smile, which Graham, had he been more sensitive, would have noticed. However, as the man was so wrapped up in his own problems and oblivious to anyone else's feelings, the smile went completely unseen. It was obvious to the Bishop, that having served his purpose, the headmaster wanted him away before anything else unfavourable should happen, such as visits from the police. The sooner he was away from this ghastly man, the better, he thought, but Bishop Stephen knew that legal wheels would have to be set in motion and he'd better stay whilst they got going. He would not let the headmaster get off so lightly.

"I am sorry, Headmaster, but I really feel that I ought to stay. I have been involved in this very unfortunate event from the start, and as I have viewed the scene, my witness statement will be vital to the police. If I was to leave before they arrive, I do not think it will be looked on favourably. I thank you for your concern, but I regret that I will have to see this through here until I am given the go-ahead by the authorities to leave."

'You're stuck with me whether you like it or not,' the Bishop thought to himself.

Graham visibly sagged, his shoulders dropped and his face paled. He realised he was beaten.

"As you wish," he replied ungraciously.

Leaving the Bishop to telephone his office to inform them of the circumstances, Graham sailed from his office, slamming the door ungraciously behind him. James and the Bishop simultaneously looked at each other. Words were unneeded and probably better left unsaid but each man knew exactly what they were thinking. Maybe James' thoughts were a little less charitable than the Bishop's, but it was probably a close run thing.

Chapter Five

Alexis entered the office and Dax knew straightaway that she was out of sorts.

"How did it go?" he asked solicitously.

"Don't ask!" Alexis replied tersely as she headed for her office. "Right, let's get to work," she said as the moment passed. "What've we got?"

This was the first time she had been in her own office and she wrinkled her nose as she entered, the air stuffy and still smelling of stale cigar smoke. The rules about not smoking in an office had been in operation for quite some time, but it didn't appear as if Colin Redway had taken any notice of them. An ashtray sat to one corner of the desk, grey ash and a stub still very much in evidence.

"Yuk!" exclaimed Alexis as she threw open the window.

Dax followed his new boss into her office and watched as she rapidly consigned the offending dish to a large envelope, then dispatching it to the nearest bin.

"I'm curious, Archie," she asked. "What made Redway go?"

"Long story! I'll reserve that one for when we have a pint in our hands later," replied Dax enigmatically. "Suffice to say it involves trousers and back handers."

"Oooh, interesting, sounds juicy. Yes, definitely one for later. Right, back to business."

Dax handed some papers to Alexis and she took a minute or two to ruffle through them.

"Anything happening I should know about?" she asked.

"Nothing drastic. Nothing very exciting," replied Dax. "Mainly bits and bobs – a criminal damage investigation that's ongoing, just waiting for forensics, and a spate of cycle thefts. Oh, and I've got a court appearance on a rather explosive burglary next week. Promises to be a good one that."

The word 'explosive' sent a frisson of excitement down Alexis' spine, fresh as she was from those she'd experienced in London.

"Explosive? Do tell!"

"Well, you know Ogden's, that big automotive parts factory on the industrial estate..." Dax paused.

"Yes, Archie, I've only been gone six months, senility hasn't quite set in yet," Alexis rejoined.

Dax reddened, momentarily embarrassed. Alexis saw the flush and immediately felt bad.

"Sorry, Archie, shouldn't have said that. It's already been a long day. Haven't had much sleep over the last week and things are catching up with me. Forget I spoke."

Dax relaxed, he knew where he was now. Alexis hadn't changed, she was just shattered.

"Right, well, we had a report of an explosion there a month ago. Night shift went hurtling up there at two in the morning and when they got there, found Stan Briggs minus a hand. You remember ..."

"Yes, who could forget good old Stan," replied Alexis with a wistful smile. "Thought he'd retired long ago, now that safes were getting too sophisticated. He's getting a bit long in the tooth, isn't he?"

"He's sixty, I think; he's been a regular on our books for years. Anyway," went on Dax, "seems the silly bugger was trying to crack the safe with a bit of explosive, and used too much. Went off before he was ready and blew his hand off. He's lucky not to have lost his crown jewels as well. The door blew off and threw his bag against him, which saved him. We found him in a pool of blood, unconscious and minus his mitt."

"How's he doing now?"

"Uniform called the ambulance and they managed to staunch the blood, but the hand was a goner. He came out of hospital a few days ago and he's in court next week. Irony of it was, the safe was empty. He'd missed pay day by twenty four hours."

Alexis laughed, the rather tragic scene forming a comic picture in her mind.

"I think retirement definitely beckons now. He was caught 'bang to rights' without a doubt."

Alexis and Dax both laughed at her pun and then spent the next ten minutes chatting about nothing in particular. Dax returned to his desk and Alexis sat in her new office, reading the various case files which had been finalised and needed a signature before filing. She relaxed; her homecoming had been good, her welcome tentative but promising. London, with all its horrors, was but a distant dream even if people were still trying to blow themselves up in the shires.

As she sat quietly at her desk, Alexis quickly became absorbed in what she was reading and at first didn't hear the tentative knock on her door. She had left the door open, and the gentle chatter in the outer room had soothed her, and become part of the background atmosphere of the office. Alexis looked up as a second tap eventually permeated her thoughts and saw a young woman in uniform, with short black hair and very dark brown eyes, standing in the doorway.

"Good afternoon, ma'am," came a pleasant voice. "I think you might be expecting me?" she finished with a question in her voice.

Alexis quickly made the leap of understanding and stood up with a warm smile on her face, her hand outstretched in welcome.

"You must be Hannah?" said Alexis.

"Yes ma'am. It's good to meet you." greeted Hannah in return.

"It's good to have you on the team. Mr Barnes has worked fast. Come in, take a seat."

Hannah came into the room and sat down opposite Alexis. She wriggled a little nervously in her seat and looked around the office, wrinkling her nose as she too smelled the rather unpleasant scents of Alexis' predecessor. Alexis watched for a brief second and noticed the apprehension but also saw a strong, friendly face and felt encouraged.

"I gather you've done a CID attachment?" Alexis gently probed.

"Yes ma'am, last year. I'm out of probation and would like to follow a CID career. Thanks for having me here. I really appreciate it."

"It's good to have you," Alexis finished with a smile.

Alexis stood up and led Hannah out of the office.

"Archie, this is Hannah. She's joining us. Please could you introduce her to everyone, find her a desk etc. I just need to finish off reading the various reports on my desk, then we'll go from there."

As Dax crossed the room to introduce himself to the newest member of the office, the telephone on Alexis' desk buzzed. She turned to pick up the receiver and as she listened intently, her face turned grim, her previous contentment disappearing as the words sunk in. She replaced the receiver, stood up and went back out to the outer office.

"Archie, I haven't had a chance to get updated on everything that's going on at the moment, but are you sure we haven't anything urgent in the pipeline?"

"No ma'am, nothing that can't wait. Why?"

"We've got something come up at a school, up near the Mynden Hills. They've found a body."

"Nothing like a baptism of fire for you," replied Dax, concern flecking his voice with genuine warmth as he realised that this was not the first day that Alexis needed. "What's happened?"

"Apparently they've found a woman lying dead in a pile of vomit," went on Alexis without holding back.

"Oh, lovely," responded Dax dryly. "Just what I need after lunch."

Alexis laughed.

"Not sure of the circumstances. The headmaster says it's an accident, but I'm not assuming anything yet."

"Righto, ma'am," Dax replied.

"Right, Archie, you're with me. Steve and Hannah - you get forensics alerted and come out with them."

Alexis paused for a brief moment. She had realised in that split second that if they all went to the scene, and including in the number all the forensics personnel, it would all look a bit mob handed so she turned to Mike who sat expectantly watching her, waiting for his own instructions.

"Mike, would you mind staying here, do a bit of research? By the time I get back I'd like to know everything there is to know about the school, its staff members, their history; you know the drill?"

"Yes ma'am. Will do," replied Mike willingly. Secretly he was rather pleased. He loved the computer investigation side of things and a dead body sitting in its own vomit was the last thing he fancied just at that moment.

The staff room at Coates Norton School was agog with excitement. Most people were there as the hour after lunch was a quiet time within the boarding houses, giving the pupils a chance to do a bit of homework under the supervision of the house parents.

"What do you think happened?" asked Margot Preece, her long auburn hair swaying gently around a young and pretty face. Her slight French accent, weathered by English marriage and several years since away from her native France, caught the mood exactly. She looked up excitedly from a pile of French exercise books she was marking, as the conversation buzzed round the room.

"Not absolutely sure, as yet," replied Michael Shepperton, the Biology teacher. "One of the domestics was found dead in the storeroom, not sure which one, domestic I mean, not store room. The room was in a right mess. Apparently, she'd drunk something."

"Bet the headmaster was furious – how dare a mere domestic snuff it in the school," went on, as Andrew Danvers, the Chemistry teacher joined in the conversation. "Any idea who it was?"

"No idea," replied Michael. "Apparently Miss Jarvis was looking for Mavis earlier. Perhaps it was her."

"I heard she'd had a heart attack," said Denise Grant, the English teacher.

"Who told you that?" asked Margot.

"One of the Sixth Formers, George Claret," answered Denise.

"Never believe anything that boy says – he lives in a fantasy world," piped up Mark Hathaway, the Sports Master.

"Perhaps she committed suicide – had enough of serving lunch to 'orrible offspring", went on Michael.

This amiable chit chat was suddenly interrupted by the entrance of the headmaster. No one stood up, all respect long gone. Graham Harper sniffed in disgust at this breach of good manners but sensibly realising that this wasn't the time for argument, made his announcement.

"By now, you will no doubt be aware that a serious mishap has befallen one of the domestics."

"You mean she's dead", exclaimed Mark. "Can't get more serious than that, Headmaster," he added, enjoying the headmaster's discomfiture.

"Mr Hathaway, please refrain from interrupting," Graham Harper retorted.

Mark suppressed a grin.

"The matter has been placed in the hands of the police who will be here shortly. I wish to make it very clear that none of this is to be discussed outside of the school and any statement you make to the police must be cleared through me first."

Michael Shepperton snorted.

"A problem, Mr Shepperton?"

"Headmaster, I think you will find that all statements will be taken in private with no external or other undue influence. I fear that you will have no jurisdiction over our testimonies. We can only say what we saw or heard, which I suspect is precious little anyway. The police won't tolerate any other interference."

Graham Harper came further into the room, his face a dangerous purple, as he digested what Michael had just said.

"If you fall out of line, Shepperton, your job will suffer."

With that, the headmaster turned on his heel, and made an unglamorous exit as his crumpled gown caught on the doorknob. He tore himself free and slammed the door behind him.

"Phew," exclaimed Mark. "The man's a nutcase. What a load of old bollocks."

The tension eased in the staff room as ghoulish talk of suicides and horrible deaths took over the conversation. They were a good bunch in that room, hard-pressed teachers who worked long hours for the good of their charges. The headmaster was rewarded with excellent exam results, which over-inflated his ego. He took all the credit for this success but it was purely and simply down to the goodwill of his staff. The conversation turned at length to sporting fixtures as Mark Hathaway asked if anyone could referee a football match arranged with another school and the demise of the unfortunate domestic disappeared from people's minds. One man, however, who had been standing quietly, unseen in the staff room kitchenette, had heard everything. Alan Rees, the caretaker, had seen something, which at the time had seemed unimportant but now he had it in context. As he washed his hands and dried them on a towel, he thought of the interesting possibilities this brought about.

As Dax drove through the town, then preferring to take the back lanes, rather than the main 'A' road, he turned off onto the country roads which led north towards the Mynden Hills. The day was warm, the landscape beautiful with fields dotted with the white of sheep and their new born lambs and as wild daffodils at the roadside danced in the breeze which was whipped up by the passing car, Alexis relaxed in her seat as the countryside sped by and closed her eyes. Dax looked quickly at her and smiled. This brief spell of rest would do her the world of good. As they got nearer the lane up to the school, which led through a valley bordered by a stream and steep hills, Dax spoke, rousing Alexis from her slumberous day dreams.
"We're here."
Alexis opened her eyes.
"Oh, sorry Archie. Must have dozed off."
"Doesn't matter. Do you good."
Alexis and Dax turned off the road and pulled up at the entrance to the school. Large black ornate iron gates stood open, welcoming

the visitors, their pointed golden tops sparkling in the warm sunshine. The long gravelled drive widened out before their eyes, finishing with a wide sweep at the front of the main school building.

"It's a beautiful building," said Alexis as she paused to take in the view. She hadn't yet noticed the leaning chimneys and the crumbling mortar, the house still glowing in the afternoon sunshine and hiding its dark secrets in shadowy recesses.

"S'pose you're right," answered Dax, his attention more on his driving as he put the car into gear and prepared to negotiate the deep gravel. The car bounced ungainly over the bumps left in the gravel by the morning's traffic and the man-made humps built to slow down cars. Dax swore silently under his breath.

"Bloody speed bumps, they'll knacker the suspension. They're hardly necessary with all this gravel on top of them. Why on earth have they used so much? Feels more like Brighton Beach than a driveway. I can't get much over five miles an hour anyway. Be fun trying though," he finished wickedly.

Alexis turned to Dax.

"We'll introduce ourselves and then after we've seen the body, Archie, I want you to just have a sniff round, pick up the atmosphere; see what lurks in the corners."

"Righto, ma'am. Just give me the nod," replied Dax.

Alexis rang the doorbell and the two officers waited on the doorstep. Frances, fresh from lunch, appeared and after an uneasy double take at the sight of the police, invited them in.

"If you'll sit here for just a moment," she said, indicating a long polished oak bench, "I'll call the headmaster and let him know you are here."

She returned to her seat, her perfume wafting gently in the air as she walked, and as she buzzed through to the headmaster's office, the two officers sat down on the bench. Alexis stared idly round as she waited, taking in the tiredness of the oak panelling with its chip out of here and a knot missing from there. A bulb was out in the chandelier which hung from the ornately plastered ceiling and another was missing, adding to the slightly run down feel. She glanced at Frances, and smiled gently as she summed her up in a word, 'flirt'.

Alexis was unmarried. Not through choice but by the simple fact that the right man had not yet appeared on her horizon. There had been one or two who had come close but not yet her own particular Mr Right. Being only in her early thirties and eminently presentable, there was plenty of time. Sometimes she felt lonely, missing the companionship of a partner, but for now she was happy enough with the situation; no need to rush. She looked at Frances obliquely through half closed eye lids, inactivity bringing on a kind of lassitude. She'd met the sort before and dismissed the show of exposed flesh and bright pink lipstick without a further thought. The phone buzzed on Frances' desk and disturbed her thoughts as the receptionist took the call.

"Please come this way. The headmaster is back in his office and ready to see you."

Frances led Alexis and Dax into the inner hall, and as she knocked gently on the headmaster's office door, Alexis just had time to look around as they waited for entrance. It was a warm, half oak panelled room; huge portraits of long dead headmasters adorning the upper walls. Ornate plaster cornicing graced the ceiling and the glass chandelier glistened in the sunlight, which filtered through leaded windows. A large, black grand piano stood silently in the corner and Alexis itched to get her hands on it. It looked a beautiful instrument and she idly wondered if it got much use. The door to Graham's office suddenly opened and Frances ushered the two officers in. Alexis blinked in surprise as she saw the Bishop sitting on the sofa; she hadn't expected that.

"Stephen, what are you doing here?" she exclaimed in her surprise. "You're the last person I expected to see."

She walked up to the Bishop and embraced him warmly. She hadn't missed the headmaster's expression as she did so.

"It seems that introductions aren't necessary, Miss er…? Graham couldn't disguise his annoyance at this seeming lack of respect for such an eminent man. He turned to Dax.

"Can't you control your officers, Inspector? This behaviour is unbecoming."

Dax grinned.

"Let me introduce you to Detective Inspector Longbow. The Bishop is her sister's father in law. They have known each other for some time. I, by the way, am Detective Sergeant Dax."

Alexis stopped in her tracks. Bishop? This was new. Bishop Stephen saw the mystification pass across Alexis face as she looked at him.

"Tell you later," he mouthed gently.

The last Alexis had heard was that Stephen had been the Dean of Worcester Cathedral. His promotion to Bishop had come as a complete surprise to her.

"We have a lot to catch up on, it seems," she said quietly, her face beaming with pleasure.

Graham looked at Dax as if he couldn't believe what he was hearing. A woman in charge of a man! Unforgiveable! Alexis and Dax watched the headmaster as his eyes swivelled between them. She sighed gently, recognising the familiar misogyny that seemed to proliferate amongst men who thought they were better. This promised to be a tricky investigation if the headmaster harboured such views. Graham swallowed hard and grunted, his expression voluble in its silence. However, he realised that to say nothing was probably the better option and limited himself to introductions.

"Bishop Stephen you obviously already know," he said, his voice hard with distaste. "I am Headmaster Graham Harper, and this is James Picton, my music master."

Alexis shook hands all round. She was keen to get on with things but realised that in such an environment, protocol was important and she didn't want to ruffle anyone's feathers just yet.

"I don't think there will be any need for a major police investigation, officers, it's just a simple accident …."

Alexis interrupted him.

"Thank you, Mr Harper, but I would like to view the scene without any further delay and make my own judgement."

Graham sniffed in annoyance. How he hated being told what to do by a woman. He turned to James and said,

"Mr Picton, I have a lesson now. Would you mind showing these officers to the storeroom?"

In an instant, Alexis recognised the type of man Graham was; bossy, not used to being questioned and more than likely, a bully. This was going to be interesting.

"Just one moment, Mr Harper," interrupted Alexis, as Graham turned to leave.

"I beg your pardon," said the Headmaster, irritated, unused to having his orders countermanded.

"Have you seen the body?" asked Alexis.

"No, I haven't," replied Graham. "Nor do I want to."

"There may be the matter of identification."

Graham's complexion blanched. James grinned. He quickly realised that Alexis was playing the headmaster. However Alexis, having summed the man up very quickly and accepting that the headmaster could add nothing more at that moment, allowed him to leave. She was an excellent judge of people; she'd had plenty of practise in her career and recognised the type immediately; a man with grandiose ideas and rife with misogyny too. Alexis wickedly decided that she would get Hannah to take the headmaster's statement. That should unnerve the man.

"You may go for now, but we will get your statement later."

Having been peremptorily dismissed, like a recalcitrant school boy, Graham was given no choice but to go. He left his office feeling livid, his furious brain seething with anger and humiliation. James, who now had little choice, agreed to take the detectives to the storeroom. He followed the now rapidly departing headmaster out of the office, and going ahead gestured the two officers to follow him. Alexis glanced with a raised eyebrow back at the Bishop, who nodded imperceptibly, guessing the question and agreeing to stay.

As they walked through the hall, passing the gleaming Steinway grand piano tucked into the corner, and under the stern portraits of previous headmasters, James gave them a brief run down on the morning's events. Alexis listened without interruption, preferring to leave decisions and comments until after she had seen the body. They reached the storeroom door, the corridor now deserted and quiet and James took the key from his pocket.

"If I may have the key now, please Mr Picton," Alexis requested. James handed over the key and she unlocked the door.

"Did you lock the door yourself?" asked the inspector.

"Yes, I thought it best to secure the scene. Seen too many CSI programmes on the telly, so know the drill."

"Good for you. Well done," grinned Alexis.

She was impressed by his manner and was glad that she had found at least one member of staff who appeared to have a sensible head on his shoulders. The door swung open and James flinched as the now familiar stench assailed his nostrils. The smell had strengthened as the mustiness and lack of air in the room had added to the odour and he recoiled in disgust. He instinctively stood back, allowing Alexis and Dax to enter the room ahead of him. James had already seen more than enough. It would be a long time before he could dispel the first sight of the unfortunate Mavis lying in her own vomit and showing the vivid signs of a violent and painful death. There was precious little room anyway and three would have been a crowd.

James switched on the light, and as the low energy bulb slowly brightened to its maximum, Alexis and Dax picked their way carefully through the debris of the disturbed store room, pausing as the body came into view. The two officers saw the vomit and the bile on the floor and watched as a trickle of fluid still dripped from Mavis' mouth. Alexis couldn't miss the angry weal it had scored in her chin and winced in disgust. Scenes of death were never pleasant, but after a sleep deprived night, a hectic and emotional morning and with no time for lunch, the bacon sandwich a distant memory, this one felt much worse. Alexis donned vinyl gloves and walked forward, touching nothing to start with but noting everything. She then gently pressed her fingers against Mavis' neck and this initial appraisal confirmed that Mavis was indeed dead, her pulse long gone. She had died violently and in agony. Whatever she had ingested looked caustic, thus causing the red mark on her chin. She saw the domestic's hand hanging loosely down beside her and frowned. The manner of her fingers, slightly curled, didn't look quite right. It looked as if she had been holding something.

"Mr Picton, could you spare a minute, please? Would you mind?" Alexis asked quietly.

James hesitantly entered the room from the corridor. He thought he had seen the last of the awful scene, but picking his way carefully through the upset toilet rolls and overturned bottles of juice, he joined the two detectives with a questioning glance.

"Sorry to put you through this again, sir, but can you tell me if this scene is exactly as you left it, before you locked the room?"

James looked round at the shelves and the floor. He saw the same things, the table and the upturned stool, the dim bulb hanging from the ceiling, the body lying awkwardly at the end of the room. Reluctantly, he pulled his gaze towards Mavis, grimacing at the smell. He pulled a handkerchief from his pocket and held it over his nose as he quickly eyed her up and down. He frowned. Something was missing; there had been something there which had now gone. He shut his eyes for a moment and tried to recall his first sight of the scene. Opening them, he looked again carefully and Alexis waited patiently as James contemplated the scene.

"The mug! She was holding a white mug, but it's gone."

Alexis and Dax raised their eyebrows in question.

"But how can that be? I locked the room and it was there then," finished James."

James was mystified. He bent down to look under the table but restrained gently by Dax he stood up again. Alexis grunted.

"Someone has obviously been in here after you left. Who would have a key?"

James thought.

"Well, the headmaster obviously, and I suppose Gerald - he's the Finance Manager - might have a master key. Miss Jarvis would have her own set of keys as well. I think this is her key here, it was in the lock when I left the room," James finished, pointing to the key, which Alexis now held and which she had used to unlock the room.

"Miss Jarvis?" enquired Dax.

"Yes, she's the Catering Manager. This is her storeroom," replied James.

"Anyone else?" went on Alexis.

"I wouldn't think so, but you'd have to ask the headmaster for confirmation."

"Thank you. If you wouldn't mind going back to the headmaster's study we'll see you back there shortly."

James nodded and gratefully turned on his heel and left.

Alexis eyed the scene for a few moments longer. Suicide? Murder? Accidental death? Could be any one of the three. Post mortem might shed some light on things, but first things first. Get the forensic boys in and see what they turned up. Alexis and Dax left the storeroom, locking it carefully behind them. As a precaution she sealed it with tape. Not having the only key, Alexis knew that the room wasn't totally secure, but the tape should put people off.

"Right, Archie, give the forensic lot a shout. See if they're on their way with Steve and Hannah. Give them a quick rundown before they get here so they know what to expect. Once you've done that, have a wander round and start sniffing."

"Righto, ma'am," replied Dax cheerfully, anxious to sniff fresh air rather than the malodorous stink in the storeroom. His stomach was strong enough but there were limits, especially after rather a full lunch.

Thus giving Dax the nod to get things rolling, Alexis returned to the headmaster's study. She found her way back to the room fairly easily, once more passing under the suspicious eyes of previous headmasters. Alexis eyed them as she walked. She mused that mortality was a great leveller. Once the nemesis of many an unfortunate school boy, these grim faced men were now long dead and gone, mouldering in their graves and pushing up the daisies, as her old grandmother was wont to say about all the people she managed to outlive. Alexis shuddered as she remembered her schooldays. She hadn't enjoyed her time at school. She'd done well, but she had chafed at the bit to get away. Being a bookish sort of girl, she'd never really fitted in with the competitive sporty types at her school, taking refuge each break time in the school library. That had been her sanctuary and a place to relax, away from the sometimes spiteful taunts of the school bullies. She pushed her gloomy thoughts to one side and pushed open the door to Graham's study. The headmaster was nowhere to be seen. Now bereft of the man, the room seemed to have opened up and the atmosphere lightened. Graham's imposing presence put a dampener on any environment. Alexis was pleased that only James sat there with the Bishop, who, now rested, had regained his normal healthy pallor.

Alexis sat down on the chair next to the Bishop.

"Stephen, thank you for staying. I won't keep you long. May I ask why you are here?"

"Can I ask why you are here?" countered the Bishop. "I thought you were in London. This is a wonderful surprise."

Alexis had first met the Bishop six years ago when he was still Dean of Worcester Cathedral and when her sister had married Luke, Stephen's son. The occasion had been glorious. It had taken place in a beautiful country church, four miles outside Teigneford. Alexis and the Bishop shared a passion for music and had soon found themselves chatting away about the latest recording of Bach's Mass on CD. From then on, they had become firm friends.

"Too long to go into detail," replied Alexis with a smile, "But got a call to come back yesterday, interview at Headquarters this morning, promoted by lunchtime, so here I am. Bit of a whirlwind really."

"You must be shattered?" said the Bishop, seeing the lines of tiredness around Alexis' eyes.

"Nothing that a good night's sleep in my own bed tonight won't sort out."

The conversation paused slightly as Alexis collected her thoughts.

"It looks as if you've been promoted too. When did that happen?" She hadn't at first noticed his purple shirt, a change from his usual attire, in her initial greeting.

"Just over a week ago. I'm surprised Georgia didn't say anything."

"Communication has been a bit hit and miss since I've been in London. My fault really. Been so busy and wrapped up in everything. I'm so sorry I missed your installation. Would've loved to have been there," she finished wistfully.

"You didn't miss much. A lot of fuss about nothing," Stephen finished candidly.

Alexis laughed.

"So why are you here now?" she went on, her eyes still alight with the pleasure of seeing her friend.

Bishop Stephen filled Alexis in about the invitation to lunch and gave a brief rundown of the events of the morning. His account was succinct and detailed, and Alexis quickly realised that her friend had little to add that she didn't already know. James concurred with everything the Bishop said, as they had shared the experience of the time from when Jane's scream had pierced the air to when both men had sat down in Graham's study.

"If you don't mind, Bishop," said Alexis reverting to formality and acknowledging his new title, "I will get one of my officers to take a brief statement from you, and then you can be on your way."

The Bishop nodded gratefully and settled down to wait. His ordeal was nearly over; he could leave this ghastly school.

"Mr Picton," said Alexis. "Thank you for all your help this afternoon, I know it wasn't pleasant. Do you have any commitments for the next hour?" she asked.

"No, I have lessons at four, then a short chapel service after tea, but I'm free until then."

"Thank you," said Alexis. "I would be grateful if you wouldn't mind waiting with Bishop Stephen. I can then get both your statements taken together."

James nodded and shook hands with the Detective Inspector. Alexis left the office leaving James and the Bishop to their abandoned coffees, and headed for the staff room.

Hannah and Steve had arrived at the school shortly after Dax's call, rapidly followed by a couple of black vans containing the forensic team. He quickly dispatched the two constables to the staff room and the headmaster's office to take statements and gather as much information as they could, and the forensics team he led round to the store room and left them to it. The attendance in the staff room was sporadic to start with as lessons were in session and teachers were busy, but as the bell sounded for break, the room began to fill and they all had something to say. The two officers worked hard and gained statements from everyone in the room. Alexis stood quietly, preferring to stay in the background. She had long realised that much could be gleaned just by watching people. Body language could be quite eloquent. On the whole, the teachers appeared without guile but one man interested her. Andrew Danvers, on the face of it, had little to offer. He had been in class all morning, then clearing up in the chemistry lab after experiments before lunch. He had been in the dining room when Mavis' body had been found, but he didn't appear relaxed. His eyes flitted from officer to officer, then out of the window. His shoulders seemed tense and his hand shook slightly as he lifted a tea cup to his mouth. Alexis suspected that there was more to this than just the shock of an unexplained death in the school and wondered if the man was hiding something. For now she couldn't think what, but perhaps time would tell. The detective inspector left the room as the statement taking continued and went in search of Dax.

The forensic team dusted, photographed and swabbed the crime scene, the room lighting up with flash as they busied themselves in the small, stifling space. Mavis' poor, lifeless body was eventually removed and the room was sealed. The corridor had been roped off to stop innocent eyes from catching sight of the mess, but curious children still gathered at the end and watched as people came and went. Brenda emerged from the Dining Hall, and shooed them away and then stood herself, watching sadly as Mavis was taken away.

"Strange woman," murmured Brenda to herself. "What had she done to earn this? No one deserves to die like this."

With a deep shame, she realised that she had never got to the bottom of the woman, nor had she really tried. Mavis had proved to be a reasonable worker but seemed to have too many secrets. She had a side to her that Brenda had never been able to penetrate.

Alan Rees was alone. The caretaker's hut was a small, untidy space, full of odds and ends. Dirty papers hung out of equally dirty filing trays. Alan Rees was a good caretaker, conscientious and careful with his work, but he wasn't the world's best book keeper. Still, that didn't matter right now. He had a telephone call to make. He sat at the table with a mug of tea cradled in his hand, the white sides of the cup swathed in black marks from greasy fingers. Steam rose gently from the cup as Rees punched in the number on the phone. The conversation was brief.

"I saw what you did. Didn't make sense at the time but now I know. We need to talk."

After a few brief moments, and a stilted conversation, Alan Rees hung up with a small, satisfied smile on his face. The appointment was made.

As the interviews and the statement taking continued apace inside, Detective Sergeant Dax strolled outside, determined to get the feel of the place. He often did this and Alexis had long realised that an innocent wander around the edge of the crime sometimes produced results. She was content to let Dax disappear and take in the atmosphere. One never knew what might crawl out from under a stone. The spring sunshine still shone and the air felt warm, but as the day lengthened, the breeze cooled too quickly and Dax shivered as he went into the shadows. He wasn't a sensitive man as a rule but today he felt that things weren't quite right, and it wasn't just the sudden death they were investigating. The school felt uneasy with itself. People averted their eyes as he walked past and the usual hubbub of happy children seemed strangely absent. Dax stood in the middle of the quad and looked up at the weather cock perched precariously on a crumbling chimney pot.

"Why do they call you Archie?"

Dax jumped as a small voice came up to him from below. He looked down and saw a small boy peering up at him.

"Pardon", replied Dax, surprised.

"Why do they call you Archie?" repeated the boy stubbornly.

Dax smiled. He'd been asked this question so many times, but this was the first from a child. He must have heard the name when Alexis chatted to him when they had first arrived.

Deciding to humour the lad, Dax replied good naturedly.

"My name's Gabriel."

As the child looked blank, Dax continued.

"You never heard of the Archangel Gabriel?"

"Nope," replied the child, cheekily.

"Archie short for Archangel, get it?" went on Dax, with dogged persistence.

"Nope," answered the child with monotonous repetition. "Is he a pop singer?"

"No, he's in the Bible."

"Uh?" came the response.

The boy looked puzzled and decided to give up. He turned away suddenly and ran off round a corner.

"What on earth do they teach kids these days?" Dax thought grimly as the boy disappeared into the building. "What a waste of money."

Dax wandered off and walked up a path leading to the tennis courts. A wall ran alongside and on it, hidden partly from view by a giant rhododendron bush, Dax saw a young girl sitting with her face in her hands. As he got nearer he saw she was crying, her eyes swollen with tears and her cheeks puffed and red. She didn't seem to be more than twelve or thirteen years old, but her face looked tired and weary, as if she had the world's problems on her shoulders. She looked up at Dax as he approached and got up to run away.

"Hang on a mo. It's OK, I'm a policeman. Here's my ID."

Dax stood at a distance and held out his card. The girl stopped. She stood there, bedraggled with tears and looked dreadful. She was wearing school uniform, and her hair, dark and braided into long plaits, hung limply down her back.

"What's up? Are you OK?" Dax went on, gently.

The girl sniffed noisily and wiped her eyes with the back of her hand, a runny nose wiping itself alongside a grubby blouse cuff.

"Shouldn't you be in class?" Dax went on quietly.

He didn't get too close, neither did he touch. The girl peered mournfully at Dax's ID and sat back down heavily on the wall. Her shoulders slumped, the strength suddenly draining from her, all fight gone. Dax sat down beside her, carefully keeping a distance. He didn't want to alarm her. She sniffed loudly and in a hoarse, strained voice uttered three words.

"He hurt me."

Then suddenly, without another word, she jumped up and was off before Dax could stop her. She disappeared into a large building next to the tennis courts. Dax didn't pursue her, thinking it was probably nothing, maybe just a playground tiff, but it was an item he tucked away into the filing cabinet of his brain, nonetheless.

Dax returned to the main school entrance and bid the Bishop goodbye, as he, at last, was able to leave. He stood as the Bishop's car moved from its parking place up to the front of the building and watched as the car drove back down the driveway and off into the road, carrying its precious cargo back to sanctuary in Hereford.

Chapter Six

Dax was in a world of his own, thinking about the girl he had just seen and wondering idly if the Bishop had enjoyed his lunch when Hannah appeared at his elbow and made him jump.

"I really enjoyed that."

"What's that?" asked Dax.

"Taking Harper's statement. God how he hates women."

"Did he say anything useful?"

"No, nothing really, but it was fun while it lasted."

Dax waited sensing there was more to come. Hannah didn't disappoint.

"I eventually tracked him down in the staff room. He didn't like that. He visibly bridled when I said we'd do it there rather than in his office. He was like a fish out of water. Others came and went and I didn't let him off the hook. He basically said he'd been having lunch, or rather luncheon, get you, and heard a scream. Got up to investigate and found one of the domestics swooning at his feet. I got the impression he was highly embarrassed at having to recount this, especially as his Deputy Head came in at that point. I played him and he didn't half squirm."

Hannah paused as she recalled the interview, a smile on her lips.

"He spoke very unkindly about his female staff, moaning that they were all hormone fuelled idiots. He spoke quite warmly about his receptionist, though. I wonder if there's anything in that." Hannah stopped, musing at the prospect.

"I got the impression from the D.I. that she'd heard Harper was having a fling with the woman. God knows what she sees in him," replied Dax.

"Wonder if Mrs Harper knows anything about this?"

"Shouldn't wonder but probably keeps schtum, for the good of the school, you know. I've met the type before. Docile, pathetic little women who wouldn't say boo to a goose. Can't stand the type," finished Dax.

"Do we know if it's murder or suicide yet, sarge?" asked Hannah.
"Dunno yet," replied Dax. "Have to wait for the P.M. result.
Hopefully, we'll get that tomorrow. Even then it may not be
conclusive. Just have to wait and see. How are you getting on with
the statements?"
"I think we're probably just about there with everyone who's here
today. A few gaps to fill tomorrow, maybe, but I'd like to get back
to the nick and consolidate what we've got."
"Righto, Hannah, you do that. I'll tell the D.I. where you're at.
Well done on jumping in feet first. Probably not the start you had
imagined?"
"No, not really. Been fun though," she grinned happily.
"I'll see you back at the nick later."
"Thanks, sarge. See you then."
Hannah left with her pile of statements and Dax went in search of
Alexis. The afternoon lengthened and the school emptied of its day
pupils. Parents came and went, most oblivious to the day's events;
soon, however to be filled in by excited children who hadn't missed
a trick. Rumour and speculation were rife in the school and the toll
it would take would soon manifest itself. The police team had done
as much as they could for the first day's investigation, so Alexis
decided to call a halt for the time being and have a briefing back at
the nick the following morning. Ignoring Frances, who always
seemed to be in attendance close to the headmaster's study, Alexis
tapped gently on Sarah's office door. Expecting a brief ''come in'
she was surprised when the door opened, held by Sarah herself.
"Come in," she said kindly. "Would you like a cuppa? You look
worn out."
Alexis suddenly realised just how shattered she was and accepted
gratefully. Sarah returned to her desk and put a brief call through to
the kitchen, and before five minutes had passed, Alexis was seated
in a comfortable chair, next to an ornate tiled fireplace, with a cup
of very good coffee in her hand.

"Oh, this is good. Really needed this," Alexis said as she carefully placed the cup back down on the table. "How long have you worked here?" she went on.

"About ten years. God knows how I've stood it so long," she added unexpectedly.

Alexis hid her surprise and waited for the rest. Sarah too was showing signs of a long, hard day and the rest given by the need to sit and chat overwhelmed her.

"You have probably gathered by now that Graham Harper is a very difficult person," went on Sarah candidly. "The previous head, who I started with, was a good man, a true academic who loved the school. He also treated his staff well and the school flourished. Mr Harper took over five years ago and things have gradually gone downhill since."

"In what way?" Alexis asked as Sarah paused to sip her own coffee.

"Well, he demands too much of his staff. He is full of grandiose ideas and the teachers don't have enough time to teach and fulfil his wishes."

"For example?" prompted Alexis.

"He spends a huge amount of time and money going on foreign trips to cultivate parents who might be interested in sending their children to the school. It only ever produces students who can't speak a word of English and this puts a huge burden on the teachers who have precious little spare time as it is. Everyone is expected to do their turn in the boarding houses. He never expects someone to have a home life. We have houseparents who are employed for the job, but the pay is pathetic and he expects so much. He's a bully and he's had not just me in tears on a few occasions."

Sarah finished with a hiccup and spluttered as her coffee found its way down the wrong hole.

"I'm sorry," she apologised. "I've probably said too much. It's been a long day."

"Tell me about it," sympathised Alexis with feeling. "I was up at four this morning." Sarah blinked in surprise as Alexis went on, trying to capitalise on the open mood that Sarah was in.

"It's kind of you to speak so frankly like this. An investigation like this is always enhanced by a bit of background information and I feel that you speak from the heart."

"I love this place," said Sarah, her composure returning. "It deserves better."

Alexis finished her coffee and replaced her cup on the tray and stood up. She made her farewells to Sarah, asking her to inform the headmaster that they would return tomorrow to continue with the statement taking and left her office, leaving Sarah to tidy her desk and finish her day in peace. Alexis met up with Dax, who had returned to Reception, and seeing no sign of Frances, left the building and walked back to their car.

A few hours later, as the day fled and twilight dimmed the streets outside, Dax and Alexis sat in the CID office discussing what they had learned.

"I've read through the teachers' statements, or those we've got anyway." said the detective inspector. "Nothing much there. Just gossip really. Receptionist is having it off with the headmaster, God knows what she sees in him; Chemistry teacher is a bit randy and was seen kissing one of the Sixth form girls by Margot Preece, the French teacher; worth more investigation there, I think. He's definitely hiding something. Mrs Harper is a frightened rabbit – boring Barbara they call her. No one seems to know anything about the dead woman. Seems the headmaster likes to keep a distance between his teaching staff and the domestics, so there wasn't much fraternisation there. The statements from James Picton and the Bishop back each other up; can't see anything coming from that direction. Much the same from Harper himself. God, what a prig that man is. Hannah enjoyed taking his statement. I gave her the nod that he might be a bit misogynistic and she played that up. If that's what they're producing from public schools these days, God help us."

Alexis paused and rocked back on her chair.

"Right. Who've we got left?"

Dax sifted through the statements that Hannah had collated and left on his desk, and consulted the list of gaps he'd made in his pocket book.

"We still need to interview the receptionist, old flirty face herself. Mrs Harper, too, oh and the caretaker", replied Dax. "There are a couple of teachers away on school trips. Those we can catch tomorrow. Other than that, that's about it, I think."

He briefly consulted the staff list in the school book he'd lifted from Reception.

"Seems there's a school chaplain, too, a Dr Ernest Cannerby, MA Oxon. Why are all these clerics MA Oxon. Don't they teach it anywhere else?" Dax finished.

"Probably a good idea to get something from him. He gets to hear and see things others don't. Might be useful unless he claims the secrets of the confessional", went on Alexis.

"Isn't that just the Catholics?" asked Dax.

"God knows."

"He probably does," finished Dax with a laugh.

"I don't think we need to interview any of the children. They would have been in class all morning," Alexis said. "Just keep that option on the back burner, just in case."

"Funny about that missing cup," mused Dax. "Wonder where that went."

"Yes, that is highly suggestive. Someone's got something to hide," agreed Alexis. "Suggests a suspicious death, if nothing else. Why would it disappear otherwise? James Picton said it was one of hundreds in the school. Nothing to set it apart from any other, so we'll never see it again, though. It's long gone. I'll send Hannah and Steve back tomorrow to get statements from those we still need and hopefully, by tomorrow too we'll get the PM results. Do we know anything about the dead woman yet?"

"Not a lot," answered Dax. "She's been at the school for a couple of years, employed as a cleaner and domestic staff in the kitchen. I had a brief chat with Brenda, but the woman seems to be a closed book. Brenda said she had no real complaints about her work, but she was a secretive woman - kept herself to herself, didn't mix much with her colleagues and didn't seem to have any close friends. She got on OK with everyone but didn't open up with any of them. Bit of a mystery, really."

Dax stopped and consulted his notebook.

"Seems she lived close by, in the village. She was married and lived with her husband and her mother, who is disabled. That much I did find out."

"Right," said Alexis, "Tomorrow we'll go and look at Mavis' home. Might glean something there. Anything else about her?"

"One of the other domestics said she came in one day showing off a new dress. She said it cost a lot of money and boasted the fact. When she was asked how she could afford it on her cleaner's pay, she went quiet. Very odd."

"Oh, did she?" Alexis' ears pricked with interest. "That's worth exploring. Anything else?"

"Nothing that stands out as yet. I need to read the statements thoroughly, something might turn up."

"Leave that for now. We've done enough and I'm shattered," said Alexis. "It's been a hell of a day."

"Something I was going to tell you though, but I can't think what it was," finished Dax.

Alexis stood up and pushed her chair back.

"It'll come back to you. Right, there's nothing more we can do tonight, fancy a drink."

"Righto, you're on, mine's a pint."

With that, Dax and Alexis left the office and headed for the pub.

The roads were deserted. The school run and rush hour traffic had dispersed and the evening visitors to the theatre had long since settled in their seats. Teigneford was wrapped in a gentle somnolence as the two officers strolled through the back streets from the police station, passing galleries with large modern paintings lit up by tiny lights and delicatessens, their olives and coffee beans carefully covered, ready for tomorrow's trade. As their path took them over the river, the waters, tumbling over rocks by the bridge, glinted in the streetlight that stood above. Alexis loved the town. It had everything she needed – theatre, music, good food and not so far to go to peaceful countryside, a balm to her nerves whenever she needed it, and so sorely required just at this moment. The pub was still lively, an hour away from closing time, and Alexis and Dax entered. After acknowledging a cheery wave from the landlord, and, less fortunately, the local press reporter, they ordered their drinks. The Strangefellows Arms was a small pub at the edge of town. It was a favourite with Alexis, the closest to her own home, just three miles south of the town and she was keen to enlighten Dax as to its charm. It was only a stone's throw from the police station. It was a good place to unwind after work and share their day before heading off home.

The pub lent itself nicely to private conversation, having as it did nooks and crannies aplenty. The evening was cool, not quite summer, so a fire crackled merrily in the huge inglenook, orange flames reflecting off highly polished horse brasses which hung from blackened sixteenth century beams. Alexis, mindful of the fact that she was very tired and still had to drive home had settled for a glass of low alcohol wine, but Dax sipped thirstily from his pint glass, the rich amber hue of a real ale from the local brewery whetting his whistle. After a while, the warmth of the fire and the comfort of her seat relaxed Alexis and she sat back contentedly in the alcove.

"So what was the squad like?" asked Dax after a while.

"It was tough," replied Alexis after a long pause as she reflected on the question. Did she really want to answer?

"Saw some things I wished I hadn't. But it was an experience I'm glad I had. Puts some things in perspective."

The conversation was quiet, Alexis not wishing to dwell too much on what she'd experienced in London. However, realising that Dax was genuinely interested, she elaborated a little.

"That bus bomb was the worst. I missed the horrors of the Tube explosion, thank God. I was out on another job and couldn't get back."

Alexis felt a brief spasm of guilt as she remembered that day. She would have loved to have been there, to help, but she was stuck out in the suburbs on an enquiry and Commander Nevern had felt she was better used there. Everyone had everything in hand, as best they could under the circumstances, and she'd been ordered to carry on with her enquiry, despite her best efforts to get to the scene. Dax waited patiently, sensing there was more to come and took a sip from his glass as Alexis went on.

"That bus bomb was horrific. I felt so impotent, nothing I could do, other than keep others away. I can still see the scene."

Alexis lapsed into silence as her memory took over but after a while, she continued with his story.

"I felt disgusted, sickened by it all. I can remember the urge I had that day just to be with you, with my friends. I'd had enough by then and wanted to come home. It made me feel guilty. There I was with everything, a good job, a lovely home, friends and a beautiful part of the country to live in. I just wanted to walk away, but I couldn't."

Dax spoke gently, seeing his friend's distress.

"Lexi, you're only human. Who can blame you? You didn't walk away; you stayed and did a brilliant job. You wouldn't be where you are now with two pips on your shoulder if you had walked away, or done a bad job."

"Thanks, Archie. I still felt bad, though."

Alexis paused again and took a large gulp from her glass, her throat dry as she remembered the scene. She suddenly realised that she needed to talk; to vocalise her thoughts; get the scene out in the open and lay some ghosts. She and Archie had been close friends for so long that she couldn't think of anyone better than him to share it with and to help her make some sense of it all.

"The devastation made me feel sick. The bomb went off at exactly twelve, just when it had been promised. We'd only been given five minutes to clear the scene, but it wasn't enough. When I arrived, the bus was standing to one side, its top open to the sky, the roof twisted and torn, wrapped round a large lime tree on the other side of the road, like a ghastly red ribbon. There were walking wounded wandering around, all over the place. I couldn't tell if it was their blood on them or someone else's. They were the lucky ones."

"What did you do?" asked Dax gently.

"Once the area had officially been declared clear, we all went in with the paramedics. I saw at least six people lying still on the ground. I followed one of the paramedics round as he checked each one in turn. Every time, he stood up shaking his head. Everyone was pale with shock, speechless as they realised the death and destruction that had been caused. It was almost an indescribable scene. You think everyone would panic, run screaming around, but there was none of that. The bomb blast itself stopped everyone on the scene in their tracks, some people for ever."

Alexis paused, and her face showed real grief. She'd lost no one special to her, but all the same the loss still felt dreadful.

"Then, weirdly, a deathly calm settled on everyone. There were sounds of moaning, and the odd cry for help, but generally, there was silence. The dust began to settle and those that could ran to help those who couldn't."

Alexis paused and Dax waited. The fire crackled and a log fell into the hearth, sending a shower of sparks into the air. It startled her slightly and she sniffed as she shifted in his seat.

"You don't have to say any more, if you don't want to," said Dax, thoughtfully, realising how difficult it was for his friend to unburden herself like this.

"I must, it's cathartic. Once I've said it, it will fade in my mind. I hope," Alexis added with a rueful grin. "Are you all right listening?" asked Alexis anxiously, as she realised that to some extent she was burdening her friend with images that were probably better left in the shadows. "It's all very well me blithering on like this but you might not want to hear it."

"Listen, Lexi. I've been your friend for, what, how many years, I've lost count. If you can't talk to me and unburden yourself, who can you talk to?"

"Thanks, Archie."

Dax stood and collected the two, by now, empty glasses and went to the bar to get a refill. As Dax got caught in conversation at the bar by the local press reporter, Alexis stared at the flames, seeing pictures and remembering more. It was good to get things out in the open but the effort was costing her a lot. She felt exhausted, not yet had time to go home, unpack and above all rest, but just for now, she was happy where she was. Dax returned with one brimming pint glass and a small glass of the same wine for Alexis. She raised an eyebrow.

"Who was that you were talking to at the bar?"

"Fred Perkins from the local rag. Just fishing. God knows how he'd heard but I didn't tell him much, only more or less what he knew already. Time enough for a press statement when we've got more to tell. He seemed happy enough", replied Dax.

"Did he ask who I was?"

"He did," replied Dax with a grin. "Told him he'd find out all in good time. You want to carry on?"

Alexis nodded.

"It had been a very warm day, sultry with a storm threatening. The sun beat down on the street. The smell of burning flesh and spilled blood, mixed with diesel fumes from the wrecked bus was everywhere. It made me feel sick. At first it had been deathly quiet, everywhere uncannily still after the mayhem of thirty minutes ago. Then, just as if someone had thrown a switch, everything erupted in sound and activity. Ambulances, sirens blaring, screamed away from the street with the obviously wounded and a paramedic and I walked amongst what was left, trying to categorise each victim in turn, morgue or hospital. I realised after a while, that I was just listing bodies. Their humanity had been blasted away and I didn't have time then for emotion. I had a job to do. Even that realisation made me feel guilty. These people, until a few moments ago had been alive, going about their daily lives. They had wives, husbands, brothers and sisters, probably children too. Now they ceased to be people, just a list of bodies and bits and their descriptions, reduced to a sheet of paper and a body bag, and believe me there were lots of bits."

Alexis shuddered but persevered with her tale.

"Once we'd done that, there was little I could do as the medics took charge."

Dax sat still, not willing to move, in case he interrupted the flow. He knew his friend needed this exposure of her thoughts. He saw the tiredness etched on her face, but he could also see the worry lines smoothing themselves away as Alexis talked.

"After that," she went on, "when all the victims had been removed, dead and alive, we started the sift. Each bomb scene has to be painstakingly searched. Even the tiniest piece of evidence can convict a bomber. A careless fingerprint on a part of the mechanism has brought a few to justice. It was just that which we needed to have. I bagged as much as I could. Some of it was still attached to someone's flesh."

Alexis stopped suddenly and shook, her forehead glistening with perspiration, her hair damp and curling across her forehead, as she remembered what she'd had to do.

"At one point, I thought that was it for me. A call came through that another bomb had been found close by. I couldn't leave but to stay was dangerous. I stayed and it was a false alarm, but I had a few anxious moments, I can say."

Alexis picked up her glass and took a large sip. She licked her lips, the horrors she had seen clouding her thoughts and removing her from the present. Dax watched his friend as the expressions flitted across her face, the flickering firelight catching the shadows around Alexis' eyes. He leant over and touched her hand, a gesture full of compassion and long friendship.

"I'm glad you're back. I missed you."

"I'm glad to be back. It's good to be able to talk about these things with you," went on Alexis. "It's just work up there and back down here, you can't really talk about the reality of the situation. People just wouldn't understand. They know where I've been but it's like talking about death, makes people uncomfortable. Thanks for listening, Archie."

"You're welcome," said Dax simply.

"Talking about death," Dax changed the subject. "What do you think about the body at the school?"

Alexis sat up in her seat and stretched her long, boot clad legs nearer the fire. She wriggled in comfort as the warmth permeated her tired muscles, the wine, albeit low alcohol, warming and relaxing her from inside. Her gloomy thoughts receded as the gentle buzz of the pub and the sounds of the crackling fire took over.

"Good question. My gut reaction is that it was either accidental - possible, suicide – unlikely, or murder - most probable. It certainly wasn't a natural death. There are easier ways of doing yourself in. We'd better wait for the post mortem results then go from there. Tomorrow I want to get statements from the floozy on reception; Mrs Harper, who was close to the scene being in the dining room with her husband, and the School Chaplain. If you could interview the caretaker, I'll take care of the rest."

"OK, Lexi, will do," agreed Dax.

The two officers sat back in their chairs and relaxed, putting the horrors of Coates Norton School and bomb ridden London to the back of their minds for the rest of the evening.

As they chatted in the warm, companionable surroundings of the Strangefellows Arms, a few miles north, Coates Norton School sat quietly, enveloped in the dark valleys between the Mynden Hills. An owl hooted in the newly leafed top of a large stately oak tree as the sky lit up with a full moon, reflecting its light down on the silent playing fields. The moon slid fitfully in and out, from behind wispy clouds and cast a silvery sheen across the grass as it came and went. The dew tipped grass glistened in the moonlight. The world was quiet and still. It was close to midnight and someone stood in the shadows, hidden in the dark depths of the large rhododendron bushes which grew alongside the school swimming pool. The water in the pool was cold and deep, but hidden from the world outside by a thick blue cover, pulled out across the water to protect it from falling leaves. The school was tucked up inside various boarding houses and no one was about save for Alan Rees and another. The caretaker walked alongside the tennis courts, unseen by the other, disturbing the owl as he tripped slightly on a lump in the grass. The owl, startled by the soft tread on the grass, took wing and flew away, its long wings stretched out, silhouetted against the full moon. The silence was suddenly interrupted by the harsh bark of a fox and the person in the shadows jumped at the sound, but then tensed as sounds of footsteps were heard. Alan Rees reached the paved path, and appeared by the pool edge, suddenly illuminated in a shaft of bright moonlight. Just as suddenly, the moonlight disappeared and the caretaker's confidence evaporated in the ensuing gloom. He nervously licked his lips as he peered round, seeing shades and shadows in the night shrouded bushes.

"Are you there?" Rees asked, a catch in his voice.

The other person smiled and said nothing, allowing the tension to mount and pervade the night air.

"We need to talk," Rees went on. "You wouldn't want to let anyone else know what you've done," he went on more confidently.

Still nothing stirred, no one moved. Alan Rees turned back towards the pool, away from the shadowy shrubbery. The other saw the chance and moved quickly forward, an arm raised holding a heavy hammer. The rustling bushes forewarned the caretaker as he whirled round startled, but he was too late. He hardly felt the blow, it came so quickly. His head bounced against the pool edge as he hit the ground and his eyes closed. Alan Rees would shortly be departing his mortal world, leaving for life's last adventure, unasked for and, most definitely, unexpected. The murderer stood quietly, looking down at the still form of Alan Rees lying on the ground by the pool edge, not knowing whether death had occurred or whether the unfortunate man was just out like a light. No matter, the murderer thought, the water would do the rest. It was only a simple task to roll the caretaker into the water. The murderer lifted the pool cover slightly and pushed hard with a booted foot. Alan Rees shifted, sliding in his own blood, then with an extra push from the murderer's determined boot, he rolled silently into the pool, oblivious to the cold, chlorinated water. A few bubbles rose, the man not yet dead after all. The owl hooted as the caretaker died, a few more bubbles escaping from the unfortunate man's mouth as he took his last lethal breath, his unconscious lungs expecting air where there was none. The chlorinated water cleansed the blood as it seeped slowly from the man's shattered skull. He was gone. The ripples slowly ceased as the man's body moved gently away from the edge and after carefully rearranging the cover, the murderer moved away, melting quickly back into the shadows. The moon re-emerged and the owl hooted, bringing normality back to the scene. It was as if nothing had happened.

The brief interlude at the Strangefellows Arms last night, and the cathartic effect of unburdening herself had led to a long awaited good night's sleep for Alexis. She awoke the following morning, refreshed and ready to face a new day. The day was bright and breezy and the air in her bedroom was cool and fresh. Her mind was clear and she felt full of energy as she breezed into work. The office was empty; still a little early for most of the team. Alexis had always relished those times when the room was quiet, no distractions from telephone or computer, or chatter from the team. It gave her a chance to catch her breath, put the kettle on and sit quietly with a cup of coffee before the mayhem of the day ensued. However, this morning her peace was quickly shattered as the door flew open and what can only be described as a Viking whirlwind blew in, in the shape of Hamish Magnusson. Hamish was the new pathologist and had taken over just before Alexis left for her stint in London. The previous incumbent, Dr Peter Lane, had retired after a long and successful career as the county's chief pathologist and Hamish had been appointed in his place. Alexis had met Hamish briefly at Hereford the day he'd been appointed but had, as yet, little chance to get to know him. Alexis looked up as the red headed pathologist entered the room, his presence filling the empty space. Hamish, the product of a Scottish mother and an Icelandic father had inherited all the Viking genes; red hair, and a beard to go with it, and shoulders that could have tossed the heaviest caber. His manner was bright and breezy and Alexis guessed that he would be good to work with.

"Morning Hamish. Good to see you again."

"Morning, Alexis. It's good to see you back. We hardly had a chance to get to know each other before you cluttered off to the Metropolis. That has got to change."

Hamish's voice was warm and full of expression and Alexis knew he meant every word. The rank structure didn't affect forensic pathologists, civilians attached to the police service, and Alexis had been quick to acknowledge the difference. She didn't mind. Her name meant more to her than her rank, especially with friends, although she was quick to remind those who didn't show the respect she deserved, something that Superintendent Barnes would come to realise, she thought ruefully. But Hamish was genial, friendly and, from the little that Alexis had already gleaned about him, very good at his job. Alexis stood up from her desk and shook Hamish by the hand.

"Definitely. You must join me for a drink in the not too distant future. Now, business. What have you got for me? Good news I hope."

"I've done the PM."

"Bloody hell, that was quick."

"Well, we haven't had any murders here for a while so business was slack. I always enjoy a good corpse. Something to get my teeth into."

"Not literally, I hope," rejoined Alexis with a grin.

Hamish laughed, a deep throated rumble that emerged from the depths of his enormous chest.

"No, not my idea of a good breakfast, that's for sure."

Hamish handed over a thin file and Alexis flicked quickly through the papers within. The pathologist turned his back on the detective inspector and headed for the kettle as Alexis settled back in her chair and read. The report was brief but to the point and made grim reading. The stomach contents suggested that the woman had recently ingested coffee with milk, no sugar and an extremely strong solution of phenol, more commonly known as carbolic acid, quite possibly in the same cup. Apart from what looked like the remains of a partially digested crumbly biscuit, her stomach was otherwise empty which probably contributed to the efficacy of the poison. It was also noted that the woman had been suffering from a severe head cold and her sense of taste and smell would most likely have been severely affected. Otherwise, she was in good health. All her internal organs were in good condition, other than her stomach and upper bowel which had been affected by the phenol; her bone structure was good and she wasn't and had never been pregnant. Her stomach and oesophagus had been severely scarred by the liquid she had drunk, and her face scored by acidic bile and ejection of the stomach contents. Dual cause of death – asphyxiation by ingestion of phenol affecting breathing capabilities and severe trauma to stomach and digestive system. Hamish returned as Alexis finished reading.

"Not the best way to finish your days. Very painful," he said, as he put his coffee mug down on the desk. Alexis pushed a coaster towards him and Hamish obediently picked up his hot mug and carefully replaced it back down on the proffered coaster. She had a long way to go to make the office truly hers but she had started by clearing the desk, giving it a bit of a polish and furnishing it with a couple of coasters.

"Have a seat, Hamish. Pull up a chair. I'd like to pick your brains." Alexis indicated the chair placed to one side of the room.

"You sure I've got some," replied Hamish with a grin.

"I bloody well hope so, otherwise we're all in the doggy doodahs." Alexis paused as Hamish made himself comfortable.

"Was it a quick death?" she asked, compassion in her tone.

"Death would not have been instantaneous and would have been excruciatingly painful."

"Wouldn't she have stopped at the first sip? Surely she'd have felt the burning action of the phenol?"

"Yes and no. As I said, she had a heavy cold so she wouldn't have at first noticed the taste. If she'd left the coffee until it was nearly cold, she would have drunk a large quantity straight away and not sipped it. That would have been enough to do the damage that killed her. There was a slight puddle and some caustic damage to the floor so she didn't drink the full cup. But she'd drunk enough." Hamish noticed the frown on Alexis' face.

"What's up?"

"It doesn't clear up the question; accident, suicide or murder. The only way it could have been an accident was if the cup and its contents had been intended for someone else, but then that was really murder. Suicide? A hard way to go but if you were that desperate then it wouldn't matter."

Alexis knew that suicide was never that simple. The question asked by those ignorant of mental distress posed the question, 'how could they?' The answer was easy – if a mind was in such turmoil, and the only way out was death, then a peculiar sort of logic takes over. Mental illness can lead to a thought world encompassing hell so what more logical conclusion could a potential suicide come to but to end life bringing release from the torment. Alexis paused in her thinking.

"Somehow, I don't really believe that this was suicide. From what little I've gleaned from Brenda and others working with Mavis, she'd come across as hard working when she chose to and reasonably content with her lot. A little secretive maybe, but this didn't necessarily indicate a mental problem."

Hamish finished his coffee and stood up.

"I'll leave you with your conundrum. I've still got some other toxicology tests to do, so I'll get back to you on those."

"Yes, thanks, Hamish. I'm really grateful for your speediness on this. We must get together for that drink. Mustn't leave it too long."

The two shook hands and the Viking whirlwind left the office, leaving a serene peace in his wake. Alexis sat back down and re-read the post mortem report while the office was still quiet. She'd already sub-consciously ruled out accident and suicide so her only conclusion in her mind was, indeed, murder. But this then led to another question; why was she murdered? What motive could there possibly be? She needed to have a good look round Mavis' home, and speak to her family. Alexis threw down the papers on her desk and stood up. Reaching for her jacket, which she'd slung over the back of the chair, she entered the outer office which had now filled with people and chatter as the day had moved on. The kettle had been busy and Alexis noticed the full mug of steaming coffee on Dax's desk. She faced the people in the outer office and as she cleared her throat gently, they all turned to look at her.

"Right everyone, a quick catch up before Archie and I head off to Mavis' home. Where are you all at? Steve?"

Steve picked up his pocket book and flicked through the pages.

"Hannah and I have got most of the statements – just a few gaps as you know. We're going to pop out to the school again this morning and get as much done as we can."

"That's good. As soon as we've got everyone's statement we can start cross referencing them for things that don't quite add up," said Alexis. "Mike, did you manage to glean anything from your computer trawling yesterday?"

"A fair bit," he replied with a grin. Mike had had a very pleasant afternoon; the office had been quiet, the coffee free flowing and a computer that had actually behaved itself for once. He had been in his element.

"Coates Norton School has been in existence for well over a hundred years. It's an independent school that takes boys and girls, day students and boarders. It's a proper academic establishment, national curriculum et cetera, but they do have an emphasis on outdoor pursuits. I suppose their location in the hills lends itself perfectly to that. They do a lot of Duke of Edinburgh's Award stuff and do sailing and canoeing on the reservoir up there. I've got a complete list of the staff – teachers, domestic, admin etc, so, Steve if you need to cross reference your list with mine, feel free."

"Thanks mate."

"His nibs, AKA Mr Graham Harper, has been in post as headmaster for five years and nothing much has changed in that time," went on Mike. "If anything numbers have fallen slightly so in these penny pinching and belt tightening times I wouldn't mind betting the school might be on the verge of financial difficulties."

"That backs up what I got from his PA," agreed Alexis. "She said that the school had gone downhill over the last few years, since he took over and everyone was fed up with it, but could do nothing. Anything else?"

"I've trawled the police computer to see if anyone has any record. There's precious little. The odd speeding fine, parking ticket, the usual sort of thing. One thing did emerge though … something that was a bit interesting …"

"Go on Mike," ordered Dax. "Don't hold us in suspense."

"Well, Harper left his last post in a bit of a hurry. I found a bit of rumour mongering on the Old Boys website from his last school. Nothing substantiated but it's suggested that he had a bit of a fling with one of the teachers. He was married then but as I say nothing proven, just a rumour."

"Interesting that," said Alexis. "The staff room seems to think he's at it again with the receptionist, what's her name …?"

"Frances Smythe," supplied Hannah helpfully, eager to make her contribution. "I got that impression too. If the headmaster thinks it's all a closely guarded secret then he's got a shock coming."

"Was he asked to leave, Mike?" asked Alexis, her interest piqued.

"No, he just left a bit quick, that's all. Well, at least it looks that way. As I say, nothing substantiated."

The chatter stilled for a minute as everyone drew breath and Alexis collected her thoughts.

"Right, everyone. Steve and Hannah back to the school. Mike, if you could get on to Hamish again and see if the forensic report has been put together, that'd be great. Archie and I are off to see where Mavis lived."

"Is there a PM report yet?" asked Dax.

"Oh sorry, should've said. Yes. Mavis died by ingesting phenol, or carbolic acid as it's better known. Nothing to prove murder or accident as yet. Time will tell, but my gut instinct is murder or, at the very least, manslaughter."

"How was it administered?"

"She drank it with her coffee, Hamish thinks, along with a biscuit."

"Poor woman. Not an easy way to go."

"Right, Archie. Finished your coffee? We need to get out to Mavis' home. Have you got her address?"

"Yup. Got it here. Brenda gave it to me yesterday."

"Right, let's go and see what we can find."

Dax looked longingly at his half full coffee mug, but accepting the inevitable, abandoned it and grabbed his jacket.

"You coming, Fliss? We'll miss the coach."

"Coming, Maz. Just got something in the post. Want to have a quick look."

"Bring it with you, then. We're going to be late."

Felicity Smith and Maisie Bourne, thirteen year old girls in Year Nine at Coates Norton School were getting ready for a two day expedition up onto the Mynden Hills, a preparatory trip for the beginning of their Duke of Edinburgh's Award. Both girls were excited and Maisie was in a hurry to get on the coach.

"It's leaving at nine and it's nearly ten to. Get your finger out, Fliss," urged Maisie, excitement and exasperation in equal measure in her voice.

"Just coming. You go on ahead. I'll catch you up."

Maisie picked up her heavily laden rucksack, slung it over her shoulder and went off downstairs leaving her friend behind with her post. Felicity sat down on the bed, disturbing the neatness of the covers that she had pulled straight that morning. She always looked forward eagerly to the post; she didn't always get something but today was different. Not bothering to inspect the outside of the envelope, she eagerly ripped open the seal and pulled out a small glass bottle with a diffuser top. She looked at it with interest – it looked like a spray perfume bottle. There was no note with it so assuming it was from her rather absent minded mother, who quite regularly sent her little things in the post and quite often forgetting to put a note in with it, and hearing the busy bustle in the quad that filtered through the open bedroom window as the expedition bus started its engine, Felicity put the little glass bottle, which contained a clear liquid, into her cagoule pocket to investigate later. She shouldered her own heavy burden, in the shape of a rather weather beaten rucksack, and hurried off to join her friend. She didn't see the packet flutter to the ground to disappear under the bed.

Chapter Seven

As Alexis and Dax went downstairs and outside to the car park, the promise of a bright and breezy morning disappeared and the sky clouded over leaving in its wake a mean spirited drizzle, which now fell on the town. It felt uncomfortable and chilly so once inside the car, Alexis turned up the heater, hoping for a little warmth. Dax drove off and headed for a small village, just on the outskirts of the Coates Norton estate. As he drove out of the town, the busy roads gave way to country lanes and a brief burst of sunshine lit up the primroses that grew wild at the edge of the road. The road ran alongside a small brook, which tumbled over a short waterfall, its water slightly depleted by a lack of rain over the last couple of weeks. The road ran flat, fields on either side, which on the left soon climbed to where trees grew on the ridge. The distinctive outline of the Mynden Hills came into view and a cap of mist shrouded the tops, lending a dismal look to the landscape, a landscape which only yesterday had been bright and sunny, and alive with birdsong. The road climbed gently, weaving in and out of small villages and eventually they arrived at Lyston, a small village on the outskirts of the small market town of Mynde itself, with a mixture of houses, both old and characterful and new on modern bungalow estates. Dax spotted a small pub at the side of the road and noted it for later, perhaps. As they drove through the village, looking for the house, Alexis turned to Dax.

"When we get there, I want you to do your usual sniff around while I talk to whoever's there. I expect the husband will be out at work, but they live with Mavis' mother. I gather she's housebound, got diabetes in a bad way, so presumably she'll be in."

Dax nodded, not averse to a bit of practical investigation. He was good at interviewing a suspected villain, but sometimes generally chatting to people left him a bit out on a limb. Alexis was good at all that stuff, he wouldn't dare to call it her feminine charm, so he readily agreed to her plan.

"Righto, we'll get in and introduce ourselves, then I'll have a nose around, if I can."

The car turned into a small cul de sac and the house hoved into view. Dax pulled up at kerb and parked the car. He was looking forward to his investigations.

Mavis Greene had lived with her husband Doug and her mother, Mrs Sandra Dale, in a small bungalow on one of the small village estates. It looked quite presentable, with two tubs of spring pansies flowering by the front door, and a small tightly budded climbing rose around the door attempted to impress on any visitor that this was really a country cottage, not one among several bungalows, all looking the same, on a small modern estate. The two officers walked up the driveway and the scent of burgeoning lilac wafted around them from a tree growing in next door's garden as Alexis rang the doorbell. There was a short pause before the door opened, and then an elderly lady sitting in a wheelchair appeared, her face puffy, her blood shot eyes still wet with tears.

"Mrs Dale?" asked Alexis solicitously.

"Yes, that's me. You the police?" she replied in a surprisingly firm voice.

Producing their IDs, Alexis and Dax nodded.

"May we come in?" asked Alexis. "I know this is a bad time for you but we do need to ask some questions and have a look at Mavis' things."

Mrs Dale nodded and wordlessly turned her wheelchair round, beckoning the two police officers to follow her. She wheeled herself expertly up the hallway and the two detectives went in and after closing the door behind them, followed the elderly lady up the hall and into the living room.

"Would you like a cup of tea?" Mrs Dale asked solicitously.

Realising that the tea making would take some considerable time, Alexis declined, preferring to get on with things, and reduce the lady's distress as much as she could.

"That is very kind, but no thank you." she replied.

As Dax hovered in the background, Alexis sat down on an expansive rather dilapidated looking brown faux leather sofa. Its appearance belied its comfort and she relaxed. As Mrs Dale wheeled herself into a better position, whereby she could look at the officers easily, Alexis summed her up. The lady appeared to be well in her seventies, her condition probably exacerbating her aged appearance. Her hair was grey, but arranged carefully into a permed finish. Her clothes were old but clean and tidy. She obviously cared very much for her appearance, not letting her obvious disability get the better of her, but her face was ravaged with grief. Alexis felt sorry for her, understanding her distress, and hastened to get on with things to bring this new ordeal to a quick close. As she settled herself, Dax spoke.

"Do you mind if I have a look at Mavis' room, Mrs Dale? Maybe there are some answers there." Dax asked gently.

Mrs Dale nodded quietly and Dax left the room, leaving Alexis to prise as much information as she could out of the unfortunate lady. Now left on her own, Alexis turned and faced Mavis' mother, who was sitting patiently in her wheel chair.

"Do you have someone to look after you?" Alexis asked kindly.

"Well, Mavis does all the housework and cooks dinner, so I'm OK, oh ..."

Mrs Dale tailed off miserably as she realised what she had just said.

"She won't be doing it any more, will she?" she continued with a huge sniff, her eyes brimming again with tears as realisation dawned once more.

"What about Mavis' husband?" asked Alexis.

"Oh, you mean Doug? He won't help. Bit of a waste of space, really. He means well but we never really see eye to eye. Mavis married beneath her. Still, he does love his gardening, can't fault him on that."

"What will you do now that Mavis has gone?"

"Dunno," the old lady mumbled, her tears spilling over onto an already wet cheek, her fingers tearing at a very soggy handkerchief.

Alexis resolved to have a word with Social Services, gently, without causing alarm to Mrs Dale. In all conscience, she couldn't just leave her to the not so tender mercies of an allegedly useless son in law.

"Mrs Dale, can you give me a bit of background about Mavis?"

"What do you want me to say?"

"Well, what were her interests, things she didn't like? Who were her friends? What she did in her spare time. Was she happy? You know that sort of thing."

"She spent all her free time looking after me," the old lady sniffed and reached for a tissue on the table next to her, her cotton handkerchief now spent and useless. "She didn't have any close friends. She got on OK at work, I think, and she enjoyed her job. She got on with the people she worked with but she did say once that there were some funny goings on at the school, though."

Alexis looked up quickly.

"Funny goings on, what did she mean?"

"Well, she never really went into detail but she said that some of the sixth form girls were a bit randy. That's the trouble with a secluded life like they get at a private school, don't experience life properly and have to experiment within the school, stuck in a weird sort of closeted environment."

This was interesting talk, and Alexis made a mental note to enquire further amongst the Sixth Form.

"I was a teacher once, until this wretched diabetes got the better of me. I worked down south, then had to come up here and be looked after by my daughter. I miss the south, sometimes."

The old lady broke off and stared wistfully out of the window. Somehow, this didn't surprise Alexis. Mrs Dale had come across as articulate and well-spoken, her pride intact but physically brought low by circumstance.

"Is there anything else you can tell me? What were her finances like? Did she get a good wage at the school?"

"Huh, a good wage, what from that old skinflint Harper? She got the very legal basic. Worked her fingers to the bone and for what?"

Mrs Dale exploded. "Don't get me on that one," she finished with a snort. "We did OK, though, we didn't want for anything. Doug works in Teigneford as a mechanic, and I get my benefits, and Mavis' wage was enough to give us the odd luxury now and then. She said she was saving up for a cruise. That would've been nice. Probably won't happen now."

Alexis was intrigued. She knew that Mavis' hours were part time, and if Mrs Dale was correct, how could she afford to save for a cruise. Interesting and definitely worth looking into. Just then the phone rang and Mrs Dale reached across the table to answer it. As she spoke, the short interlude allowed Alexis to look around the room. It was clean and neat, the fire was out but the central heating was on and the room was warm. The furniture looked tired but was also clean, and comfortable, as Alexis had discovered when she'd sat down. On the mantelpiece above the fire, family photos of Mrs Dale and her daughter adorned the shelf. There seemed to be no other family. Doug was noticeable by his absence. No love lost there, thought Alexis. The floor was uncarpeted, but the polished oak boards gleamed in the light. Alexis thought they were a little incongruous in the room but then realised that the carpet had been done away with to ease the wheelchair's motion. However, these boards were solid oak and would have been very expensive to install. On a limited budget, laminate flooring would have been a better idea. How had Mavis and her husband afforded them? The phone call finished, Mrs Dale replaced the phone in its station and turned once again to her visitor.

"I love your floor," Alexis said, when she had her attention. "I love oak and solid wood."

Mrs Dale smiled, "A gift from Mavis, said I deserved it."

"Must have been expensive?"

"She told me she'd had a win on the lottery and wanted to treat me. Anyway, that's none of your business," she concluded with asperity.

"I'm sorry to pry, but when someone meets an unnatural death, uncomfortable questions have to be asked."

Mrs Dale said nothing, only grunted.

"Well, that's what she told me and I have no reason to doubt her."
Alexis filed this titbit away in her mental filing cabinet and in an attempt to mollify Mrs Dale, indulged in less intrusive questioning. Time enough later for probing, probably upsetting questions, once murder had been fully established.

Dax, meanwhile, had been busy. He had no idea where Mavis' room was but the exploration might be useful. He walked up the hallway towards what he thought might be a bedroom. It turned out to be a bathroom and, after donning protective gloves, Dax quickly investigated what there was. A small bathroom cabinet brought no surprises: the usual indigestion powders and aspirin, a half empty bottle of cough mixture and a small pot of cotton buds. A box of plasters completed the entire contents of the little cupboard. There was no sign of any diabetic medication but Dax had a feeling that it had to be kept cool, so it was probably in the fridge in the kitchen. He turned his back on the little room and headed up the hallway. He looked towards the end of the corridor and saw another door. This time he was in luck. Inside he found a double bed, and rightly assumed that this was the room that Mavis shared with her husband, Doug. He went in and shut the door quietly and quickly went across to the dressing table. This was strewn with half used make up and scent bottles. Dax knew that this sad little collection would very rapidly be consigned to a rubbish bin, as Doug moved in and tidied away his late wife's life. Dax began to pull out drawers, carefully examining their contents, but there were no hidden packages, only underwear, T shirts and some long forgotten gym wear, the folds gathering the dust from the corners of the drawers. Dax scanned the two shelves which were screwed to the wall. There was nothing much to write home about here either, just a few dog-eared paper backs. Dax quickly thumbed through the pages of these but apart from a bookmark from a local bookshop, nothing fell out and they told him nothing. Dax turned and faced into the room. The room looked normal with no apparent secrets; a room full of the usual female things. Mr Greene obviously shared the room with her; the double bed was unmade and pillows on both sides were rumpled, but his presence otherwise was fairly non-existent. Dax pulled back the duvet and lifted the pillows. Practised hands felt under the mattress but found nothing. It was a pine bed with a separate mattress and therefore open to the floor underneath. Dax knelt down and peered under the bed, but apart from dust and an empty suitcase, there was nothing. Dax stood up and dusted his knees, sneezing as the debris tickled his nose. He turned to the only other item of furniture in the room - a large, heavy, old fashioned dark wood double wardrobe. This was full of clothes, both his and hers. A short rummage and a prod of pockets again produced no results, no hidden compartments, just clothes and a few shoes on the rail at the bottom. Dax pulled each shoe out in turn and upended them with still the same result – nothing.

Dispirited, Dax left the room and turned his attention to the dining room. Here he had more luck. The old, battered wooden bureau was full of junk and Dax sat himself down on a rickety wooden chair to see if he could find anything interesting. He quickly flicked through the various papers on the desk and coming across some recent bank statements, he read them carefully. There was nothing out of the ordinary: a couple of Direct Debits for insurance and mortgage; some sporadic small credits and two regular monthly credits from the school and a garage in the town; obviously wages for both Mavis and Doug. There were a couple of cheques which had been written and these tallied with the cheque book stubs which Dax found in the same place. A few debit transactions and cash withdrawals completed the picture, but nothing jumped out at him. Putting these to one side, he dug deeper and found some letters. Again, these shed no light on anything; one from someone thanking Mavis for a birthday present, an official one from the Council and a Poll card for the forthcoming local elections. Dax sat back and looked round the room. It was a plain room, slightly dated with a patterned Artex ceiling. It looked a little shabby, the wallpaper faded and stained around the light switch on the wall, where careless fingers had groped for the switch in the dark. A single bulb hung from the light fitting and the brown, tasselled lampshade sported a festoon of thick cobwebs. It was a room little used and probably left to its own devices, Dax thought. There was little furniture in the room apart from the bureau. An old nineteen fifties dining table and four ill matched chairs stood in the middle of the room, and a large plant, its leaves gasping for a drink, sat patiently waiting for its inevitable demise in the middle of the table. Dax stood up and went to the window and looked out. The room looked over the back garden and there he saw where the care and attention had been lavished. Even in the gloom of a dull drizzly day, he could see that someone was a keen gardener. He watched as a large tabby cat ran across the immaculate lawn heading for a favourite spot in the equally immaculate flower bed. He grinned as the cat relieved itself and then proceeded to destroy the groomed surface of the bed. The cat, now having done its business, walked off and settled down under a large cherry tree, its branches heavy with blossom, growing up by the back wall. Turning back from the window, Dax noticed a small side table in the corner of the room. The drawer was sticking out slightly and with his interest piqued, he decided to investigate. He tried to pull the drawer out but it resisted – something was obstructing it. He put his hand under the lip of the drawer and by slightly lifting it, managed to slide the drawer out easily. As he touched the wood, his fingers brushed against something and bending down to see what he had touched, he found a small book taped to the underside of the drawer. Opening it carefully, with gloved fingers, Dax saw that it was a Building Society book. Nothing unusual in that but it was something ordinary in an extraordinary place. He quickly replaced everything as it had been, but kept the Building Society book for himself. Placing it carefully in a plastic evidence bag, he pocketed it and with a last glance back at the room, switched off the light and returned to the living room, where Alexis had been chatting with Mrs Dale. She looked up as Dax entered the room, and a brief nod from him told her that his search had been fruitful. Swiftly wrapping up her conversation with Mrs Dale, Alexis stood up, releasing herself from the enveloping cushions of the old sofa. The two officers made their farewells and left.

After driving a little way out of the village, Dax parked up in a small lay by, next to the church and turned to Alexis.
"What's next?"
"Do you fancy a bite to eat at that pub I saw you eyeing earlier? We can compare notes. Then we'll get back to the nick and see where we're at."
Dax didn't need to be asked twice and agreed eagerly. Twenty minutes later they were comfortable ensconced by the fireside of the White Hart, pint in hand and a very palatable cheese ploughman's sandwich each on their plates. As Dax swallowed the first bite of his food, he started to speak. Alexis held up her hand.
"Eat first, talk later. Let's just enjoy the moment."
With their plates soon cleared, and glasses half full, Alexis then turned to business.
"Right, what've you got?"
"Well, at first I couldn't find anything out of the ordinary. No compromising letters, nothing odd in her bank statements. I even looked in the bathroom cabinet to see what medication she was on. Apart from a few over the counter pills and potions, nothing. No tranquillisers suggesting depression or suicidal thoughts. Nothing in her bedroom either so I had a look in the dining room. I found this."
Dax brought out with a flourish the little passbook and described to Alexis how he'd found it.
"There are some interesting credits and as an effort had been made to conceal the book, I wonder if they're suggestive of something not quite right going on."
Alexis took the book from Dax and examined it. The balance was quite considerable, with a regular monthly amount of £50 going in since September two years previously.

"How long had Mavis been working at that school?" she asked

"I asked Brenda that yesterday. She said just over two years."

"The timing is odd," mused Alexis. "You know me, I don't like coincidences."

"Blackmail payments, perhaps? She saw something at the school and took advantage of it then her blackmailer turned on her and topped   her."

"Hang on," said Alexis laughing. "Let's not get carried away. Two years is a long time to wait to take revenge."

"Well, it is suggestive," said Dax, refusing to be deterred. "Did you find out anything from the old dear?" he asked, returning the book to his jacket pocket.

"No, not really. Mavis is her only daughter, in fact her only child. She will take the loss doubly hard. Mavis married Doug Greene five years ago, who according to Mrs Dale is a waste of space. There are no children. Nor will there be now," mused Alexis. "Mrs Dale has diabetes, as we knew, which has affected her legs, thus the wheelchair. Mavis divided her time between the school and caring for her mother."

"How's she going to cope now?" asked Dax.

"No idea. I wondered about that but didn't ask. It didn't seem polite. Unless Doug can help, I expect the poor old thing will go into a home, unless she can get a home help or something. I'll drop the nod to the Social Services, on the quiet."

Alexis paused, struck by the fates suffered by some people more than others. She shook herself mentally and went on.

"Still, that's not our problem at the moment. We have a suspicious death to sort out."

Alexis and Dax relaxed as they finished the rest of their drinks, comparing notes on their actions of the morning. Just as they drained the last dregs of ale from their glasses, and prepared to leave, Alexis' mobile phone buzzed.

She reached for the phone in her bag.

"D.I. Longbow," she answered.

She listened and the smile on her face quickly disappeared.

"When?" she asked tersely. "We're close by. We'll go there straight away."

She replaced the phone in her bag and turned to face Dax.

"That was Steve. Apparently they've lost their caretaker at the school. I wouldn't normally bother with a missing person – I'd leave that to uniform – but I don't like coincidences."

"How can you lose a caretaker?" Dax asked with a grin. "Sounds like carelessness."

"Dunno. Let's go and have a quick chat with Steve and find out."

Dax eased himself into the driving seat and leaving Alexis with hardly enough time to fasten her seat belt, roared out of the pub car park and headed, once more for Coates Norton School. Inside, they found Frances at her desk for once.

"Right, what's going on? I gather you've mislaid your caretaker." Dax asked her abruptly.

Frances flushed angrily and seemed flustered, her normal suave appearance disappearing as the headmaster made a sudden appearance.

"Officers, my office, if you please!"

Alexis and Dax looked at each other, taken aback by the man's abrupt attitude, but accepting the inevitable, they followed the headmaster in to his office. Frances' perfume lingered in the air and Alexis noted the deep dip in the soft upholstery of the plush sofa. An earring glinted on the cushion, caught in a thread, and Alexis smiled to herself. She would have fun with this.

"Yes, Headmaster, what can we do for you?" Alexis opened.

Graham cleared his throat.

"I have received a call from the caretaker's office. I was here with Miss Smythe, making arrangements for the school play tickets."

Too much information, thought Alexis.

"And?" she encouraged.

"Apparently he's missing."

"Missing?"

"Yes, he was supposed to be getting the course ready for a cross country run tomorrow and hasn't appeared for work. We were just a little concerned."

Alexis wasn't taken in by this false showing of care. Graham Harper didn't care; well, not about people, more about the job not getting done.

"Does he have a habit of 'going missing?" Alexis couldn't hide the sarcasm in her voice.

"No, he does not," replied the headmaster angrily. "He is very conscientious."

"Well, knowing what's been going on in this school recently, we'd better have a look for him, shouldn't you?"

Graham didn't miss the challenge inferred by the change of pronoun.

"I will instigate a search."

"Good, keep me posted," finished Alexis. "I'll leave my two officers here, they're still catching upon statements. I'm going back to the police station. I can be contacted there."

As Alexis turned to leave, she remembered the earring and couldn't resist the temptation.

"Oh, by the way, I think Miss Smythe has left her earring on the cushion. It appears to have got caught on a thread."

Alexis smiled as she saw the headmaster's guilty flush. He was so easy to read. Graham adjusted his gown, and ran a finger round his collar, clearing his throat unnecessarily. Leaving the headmaster to his embarrassment, and feeling slightly lightened by the exchange, she and Dax headed outside. Steve had been hovering in the quad, hoping to catch his boss before she left.

"Hi, Steve. You OK?"

"Yes ma'am. Thanks for popping round. Just wanted to fill you in on the missing caretaker."

"Mr Harper has told me that he didn't turn up for work, which is out of character. You got anything further?"

"No, not really, ma'am. His handyman says he's usually here at the crack of dawn but he didn't turn up this morning."

"I expect he's had the good sense to get out of this infernal place," replied Dax. "Can't say I blame him."

"You're probably right," replied Steve with a grin. "But with everything that's going on, something out of the ordinary becomes extraordinary."

Alexis smiled. She liked his attitude. Never one herself for taking anything for granted she appreciated the same work ethic in her officers.

"Just have a quiet nose round … keep me posted. Thanks Steve."

"Will do, ma'am."

"How are you and Hannah getting on with the remaining statements?"

"Pretty much there, I think. Just about to wrap everything up and get back to town."

"I'll leave you to it."

Alexis and Dax headed for their car and made off, leaving deep tracks on the driveway as Dax negotiated the thick gravel. They'd hardly driven two miles when Alexis' mobile bleeped.

"Is there no peace?" she asked Dax wearily as she wrestled with the seatbelt in the attempt to get her phone out of her pocket.

Recognising the dulcet tones of Hannah Pembridge, her Detective Constable, she listened in silence.

"Bugger," she said to Dax at the end of the call. "Just what we need. You are not going to believe this."

Dax looked across from the driver's seat in expectation.

"Don't tell me we've found the caretaker."

"Yup. Apparently, Mark Hathaway, the Sports teacher has found his body in the swimming pool."

"Well, at least it will save taking his statement," Dax replied with heavy irony.

"You always look on the bright side, don't you," retorted Alexis.

Dax laughed.

Making a quick turn in a layby, Dax rapidly covered the two miles back to the school. He didn't stand on ceremony and with a flurry of gravel under the tyres, pulled up outside the school. Hannah was waiting for them on the driveway.

"Steve's with the body. Thought I'd hang on here and take you up there."

"Lead on," invited Alexis grimly.

"Just one moment, I will tell the headmaster you are here," said Frances who had come up behind them.

"Why has everything got to go by the bloody headmaster?" Dax asked with irritation. "We've really got better things to do than wait for him every time."

Alexis laid a restraining hand on Dax's arm, then turned wearily back to Hannah.

"Get on to Mike, please. Get him to organise Hamish and the SOCOs. I'll meet you back outside."

"Yes ma'am."

Dax, ignoring Alexis' gentle warning, brushed past Frances angrily and went straight to the headmaster's office. Without ceremony, he entered, ignoring Graham's angry flush.

"Right, you'd better take me to it, immediately."

"This way, if you please," the headmaster replied, swallowing his irritation with difficulty.

Mark Hathaway stood forlornly at the side of the pool, the body of Alan Rees still laying where it had been found, face down and now floating on the surface of the water. It appeared that the cover on the pool had been pulled back earlier that morning for a swimming lesson and the body had been discovered. Even from a distance, Alexis could see that the man's head had been savagely beaten, and the hair, dark, damp and curled, still bore traces of blood where his life's force had been viciously spent. The blood spilt from his head in the initial hit, had pooled into a dark, thick congealed lump in the cool of the night, and was obvious by the side of the pool.

"Did you notice the blood," asked Dax with interest.

"Not at first," replied Hathaway. "The cover is rolled back from the end, and I went by the side of the shed, so I didn't see the blood, which was on the other side. It was only when we pulled the cover back and saw the body on the bottom of the pool..." Hathaway paused, his recollections of the morning's discovery making him recoil from the images in his mind.

"Sorry," he faltered.

"That's OK, just take a minute," replied Dax solicitously.

Hathaway coughed and went on.

"We didn't know who it was at first, but then we got hold of him with the long pole we keep at the edge to help the kids. As we pulled him up he rolled in the water. We knew who it was then."

"Did you pull him out?" asked Alexis.

"No. We thought at first he might just have tripped and fallen in. We pulled him to the edge and it was then we saw the blood."

"Was he dead?" asked Dax.

"Well, he wasn't going to get over that bash on his head quickly, that's for sure," replied Hathaway with asperity, brought on by disgust at the memory. "We hadn't seen that to start with, not until we got him close in."

Alexis gently tapped Dax on the arm. She could see that Hathaway was nearing the end of his tether and more questions would be a waste of time. This time, Dax acknowledged the touch.

"Well, thank you, Mr Hathaway. We appreciate your efforts. Go and get yourself a cuppa and we'll have one of our officers take your statement later. We'll catch up with you in the staff room, if that's OK?"

Hathaway nodded, and almost ran away, glad to relieve his eyes from the scene. Graham Harper stood at a distance, distaste and disgust very apparent on his face. The stress of the last few hours was beginning to take its toll and a nervous tic played around his heavy eyelids. An initial cursory investigation showed that Rees had been hit over the head and rolled into the pool under the outstretched cover, tearing it in the process. Graham had noticed the tear, as had Alexis and Dax, and the inevitable cost of repair darkened his already dismal mood. Graham Harper's concerns were financial. Any feelings for his deceased caretaker were either carefully hidden or not there at all. Dax looked at the headmaster in disgust. As the chlorine in the water would have removed all traces of anything worthwhile, Alexis ordered the body's removal from the water. Dax picked up Hathaway's long pole, which had detached itself from the caretaker's body and was now lying in the water at the edge of the pool. Wielding it dangerously, Dax manoeuvred it into place and managed to grab the collar of the unfortunate caretaker, who had floated back out to the middle of the pool and was gradually sinking again. Slowly and carefully, Dax pulled the body and soon it gently swung alongside the pool's edge. Dax and Alexis bent down, and between them managed to haul the lifeless body out of the water. Soon, it lay dripping on the paving stones at the side of the pool. The headmaster turned away in disgust and simply walked away. There was nothing Alexis or Dax could do until Hamish turned up, so they sat on a bench under cover at the side of the pool and waited. Eventually, the air was filled with voices and Hamish turned a corner and greeted them with a smile.

"You're keeping me busy. You've only been here two days and already given me two bodies. Hope it doesn't carry on like this," he finished genially.

"Sorry, Hamish. Could've done without this myself. Not the start I had in mind, either," she replied ruefully.

Due process was set in place, and soon the scene had been meticulously examined, any traces of foreign matter carefully bagged, and the body removed. A thorough search of the shrubbery next to the pool had revealed precious little, although an indentation in the soft leafy undergrowth and a broken branch did suggest that someone had been standing there for a while. The footprints were too indistinct to give an exact indication of foot size, but the imprint suggested a large foot. Casts were made and photos taken for comparison later. Samples of the soft loam were bottled and tagged and the broken branch bagged. You never know, Alexis mused, perhaps they'd be lucky enough to find some pollen

140

from the broken buds on the murderer's clothes. Stranger things had happened. She also realised that if they were lucky enough to find a pair of shoes or boots with the same loam embedded in the tread, they might be able to make an early arrest. Time would tell. Alexis retraced her steps away from the pool side and went in search of Mark Hathaway. She found him, taking refuge in the staff room, his cold hands, still a little shaky, holding a hot cup of tea. He was alone, the school still in class and his eyes looked sunken with shock.

"Are you OK?" Alexis asked, concern in her voice.

"I'll survive," Hathaway replied weakly. "Not the usual start to a day."

"No, it must have been quite a shock."

"You could say that," Hathaway replied bitterly.

"Are you up to giving us a statement?"

"I suppose so. At least I'll get it over and done with."

His statement was short and sweet. The pool had only just been filled, only three days before, and the cover placed to protect the water. It had remained unused until Hathaway went to get it ready that morning, thus making his grim discovery. Other than that, nothing else of value was forthcoming. Leaving the unfortunate Sport's Master to his now cooling tea, Alexis left the staff room and made her way back to the pool where Dax was finishing up activities with Hamish and the forensic team. The man's limbs were beginning to stiffen, suggesting that rigor mortis was setting in and even with his limited scientific knowledge, Dax realised that the caretaker hadn't been dead for long."

"He's only been dead a couple of hours," he whispered to Alexis.

"What makes you say that?" she answered distractedly, her eyes viewing the scene as Rees' body was zipped into a body bag.

"Well, he's beginning to stiffen up."

"Don't be so sure," Alexis warned. "He's been lying in very cold water on what was a very chilly night. Cold temperatures slow down the rate of rigor so he might have been dead longer than we think."

"Oh," replied Dax, chastened by his lack of knowledge.

"Don't worry. Hamish'll give us a better time of death, hopefully. I suspect it was during the night, when nobody was around, but we shall see."

As they watched the mortuary van disappear with its grisly load down the driveway, Alexis and Dax returned to their own car and slowly made their way back to the police station where they sat down together to discuss the day's events.

"We need to pool our thoughts," said Alexis with a grin.

"Oh, love the pun," replied Dax with a laugh.

The body of the unfortunate caretaker had arrived at the mortuary and Hamish had made a very brief initial examination. In a quick call to the D.I's office, he was able to confirm that a condition called primary flaccidity had occurred. He explained that this occurs directly after death, becoming fully present within an hour, where all of the muscles in the corpse's body relax. This had lasted longer than had at first seemed and which had confused Dax. The cold water had indeed delayed the onset of rigor mortis and Hamish was able to estimate that death had occurred some hours earlier, probably around midnight, just as Alexis had predicted but that further tests would confirm this. Even now, rigor only extended to the neck and jaw, so there was a way to go until it had passed completely.

Everyone had now returned from the school so Alexis called her team together. This was still a new experience for her and one she rather enjoyed. Her old boss in Hereford had always had these sorts of meetings but they had always left Alexis feeling frustrated. His approach was dogmatic and one-sided, an occasion when he voiced his own opinion and left no room for anyone else's. He used it as a formal briefing session, never asking for anyone's ideas or opinions, and she had always felt that he was missing a trick. This thought reminded her that she still didn't know why Teigneford's Inspector Redway had left so abruptly and made a mental note to catch up with Dax on that one. Alexis faced her expectant audience. She outlined the facts as they knew them from what she was now considering as two murders. Photos of the two victims were pinned to a board and Dax grimaced as his alighted on the cruelly disfigured face of Mavis. Alan Rees seemed to just be asleep; the damage to his skull hidden by his thick curly hair and the effects of death not obvious on his now serene looking face. Alexis encouraged everyone to chip in. Anything, even if thought to be totally inconsequential could lead to something useful. So often, on the Squad in London such chats had gleaned some useful information and more than one arrest had resulted. However, she was out of luck on this occasion. They simply had no clues. It was a waiting game as the investigation had come to a brief stop. Mavis' post mortem result had established her death was caused by phenol and Alexis was now assuming murder; they were still awaiting Hamish's full report on the unfortunate caretaker so everything was at a standstill. There was nothing left for the time being but to just read and re-evaluate all the statements, which were now complete.

"Have we, by any chance, found Mavis' mobile phone? It wasn't with her at the school," Alexis asked casually.

"It hasn't turned up anywhere in her effects," replied Hannah.

"Interesting! It's normally an item someone keeps with them all the time. I suppose it could be at her home, but we could do with having a look at it, if we can find it."

"I'll have another trip out to Mavis' home," replied Dax. "I'll have another dig."

"Thanks, Arche," replied Alexis.

"Does anyone have any suspicions or opinions about anyone at the school, however slight?" asked Alexis hopefully.

For a moment, silence reigned in the room then Steve spoke up.

"If it's just opinions and feelings you want, I could offer a few although we all probably realise these already."

"Go on!" encouraged Alexis.

"Well, the headmaster is a bully, no one likes him." A murmur of assent went round the room. "He's at best just flirting or, worst, having an affair with that floozy on Reception."

"I think that's pretty common knowledge in the staff room, "agreed Hannah. "I spoke to that James Picton, he didn't hold back. Seems they often go away for weekends, allegedly on educational conferences but they all know it's a hotel somewhere."

"Do you reckon Mrs Harper knows anything about this?" asked Alexis.

"Well, if she doesn't she must have her head in a cloud. It's so bloody obvious."

"Poor woman, she doesn't look very happy," went on Hannah sympathetically.

"Well, would you be with a dolt of a husband like that?" chortled Dax.

"Anything you think might be suspicious," asked Alexis generally of the room.

"The only thing I can think of," replied Dax, "is that chemistry teacher, what's his name…?"

"Andrew Danvers," Hannah replied helpfully.

"That's him," went on Dax. "He just didn't seem comfortable when we were talking to him."

"I agree," said Alexis. "Someone to bear in mind, perhaps? Did we ever establish who had keys to that store room?"

A sort silence ensued broken by Dax.

"The only sets we know of belonged to Miss Jarvis, Mr Leigh and Harper himself. I suppose there could've been an extra set, or even just a copy of that particular key, but there's no way of knowing. It's an old lock, that cupboard has been there for as long as the building has been a school, so there could've been spurious keys knocking around."

Alexis nodded quietly.

"You're right, Archie. If we accept there are only three keys, then we must suspect one of the owners of those keys. If we go with your theory, Archie, then anyone could be a suspect."

She shrugged her shoulders in exasperation.

"Mike, can you do an extra search on their backgrounds, please? Leave it until tomorrow, though. I don't hold out much hope but I s'pose anything's possible"

"No probs, ma'am," agreed Mike.

"Right everyone, time's getting on. There's not much more we can do today. Get off home, all of you, and I'll see you here bright and early tomorrow."

With that final remark, she wound up her briefing and returned to her own office as her three detective constables made a quick exit from the outer room. The silence that ensued was welcome, giving her a brief moment to collect her thoughts. For a few minutes she sat quietly, looking round her own room. It still bore faint traces of its previous occupant and she made a mental note to visit the second hand market next weekend, pick up a picture or two, and maybe a side table on which to put a coffee machine. She wasn't a great one for house plants but she thought a spring bowl of hyacinths might refresh the room with its scent and add a bit of colour. Housekeeping done, she turned to the paperwork on her desk and as ongoing enquiries in the Coates Norton case were stuck until Hamish had done his best with the forensics, she applied her mind to outstanding casework that needed her attention.

Dax had stayed at his desk wanting to contact the Building Society about Mavis' savings book before the day was done. After some initial un-cooperation, miraculously dissipated by the mild threat of a search warrant, and a long chat with the branch's manager, he found himself none the wiser. The regular payments had been made in cash, and not by cheque, and their origins could be anywhere. There had been some withdrawals, now and again, and one tallied with the fitting of the oak floor boards, so that eliminated the puzzle on that. Wherever Mavis was getting the money from was a secret that, for now, she had taken to the grave. Dax himself had suspected, perhaps, that Mavis had been fiddling the benefits system, using her mother's disabilities for an illegal claim, perhaps claiming for a Carer's Allowance for her mother, at the same time working and stashing her ill-gotten gains away in the Building Society, but a quick call to the Department for Work and Pensions local office had disproved this theory. Mrs Dale was receiving her own benefits and Mavis was not claiming anything in her own name. Dax was not satisfied with leaving this enigma alone. The money had come from somewhere and he was convinced that this had led to Mavis' murder. Mrs Dale knew nothing about the money or even the Building Society account itself. She managed her own money. Then Dax had a thought; he suddenly realised they hadn't spoken to Doug Greene yet, Mavis' husband. He mentally kicked himself. This was very remiss. He should have dealt with this at the start. Doug had never even been seen yet, let alone interviewed. Perhaps he had an idea where the money had come from.

Dax looked at his watch; it was now late in the afternoon. His enquiries and the follow up reports had taken some considerable time and now it was too late to visit anyone. Dax decided to go back to Lyston early next morning, before Doug had left for work, and have a chat with the man and have another look at Mavis' room, perhaps find Mavis' missing mobile. There must be something there to explain the payments into the Building Society. Having disproved Benefit Fraud, he still suspected blackmail; it made a lot of sense. Brenda had told him that Mavis had been very secretive. Perhaps this was the secret she had been hiding and it had ultimately proved to be her downfall and led to her death. Still, best to keep an open mind until it could be proved one way or the other, he thought.

As the soft evening light dwindled and turned to night, Andrew Danvers, the Chemistry teacher and Elizabeth Grant, a girl in the Upper Sixth at Coates Norton School, were whiling away a happy hour away from the school. Their occupation was highly questionable but extremely pleasurable to both of them. Andrew had collected Elizabeth after lights out and had driven her to a secluded spot in the woodland. It was now dark and very quiet, and the spot he had chosen was hidden from view by a slight dip in the woodland floor. The ground was covered with soft ferns and the remnants of last year's autumn leaf fall and felt soft. Andrew had laid out the car blanket from his small Corsa, and the last half hour had been highly satisfying, sexually. Andrew had been toying with the idea of getting a larger car, for when the winter nights made al fresco sex not quite such a pleasant experience, but for now the moonlight and the still warm air, which had gathered after the drizzle had ceased and the clouds had passed and the day had been warmed by the sun, made the experience very pleasurable. At last, the two sat up and rearranged their clothing. Elizabeth was flushed and excited, not just by the sexual activity but also by the highly immoral aspect of the adventure. Never one to stay in the background, she had easily brought herself to the notice of the very handsome chemistry teacher, who had quickly become beguiled by her extremely pleasing looks. Neither realised that their secret was common knowledge, but safe in their ignorance, they chatted happily.

"What do you think of that domestic snuffing it?" asked Andrew.

"I knew she died but I didn't get to hear much about it. What happened?" Elizabeth asked.

Andrew then went onto regale his amour with the last couple of days' events and the girl giggled.

"I bet the headmaster liked all that happening. I bet he was insufferable."

"He tore Michael Shepperton off a strip in the staff room when he argued with him," Andrew replied with glee. "Man's an idiot, the headmaster I mean. About time we had a change."

The two stopped their chatter for a while and cuddled contentedly together, Andrew nibbling Elizabeth's luscious ear lobes. A pair of moths danced in the twilight above their heads and Elizabeth watched, relaxed and happy, as she lay in Andrew's arms.

"I'm glad she's gone though," he went on at last.

"Why?" asked Elizabeth, puzzled. "What had she ever done to you?"

"Well, she always gave me such funny looks. I often wondered if she knew about us. She spooked me, always nosing around."

Andrew suddenly stopped speaking, realising that perhaps he had said too much. He had secrets too and didn't want to arouse Elizabeth's suspicions. He was enjoying himself far too much. Elizabeth, feeling too drowsy to notice anything amiss, sighed contentedly and snuggled down in Andrew's strong arms. She dozed quietly on Andrew's shoulders as he stared out on the darkened countryside, his thoughts in a whirl. He was no fool. The events of the last couple of days could lead to difficulties for him. Just for now, he kept his counsel and said nothing.

Chapter Eight

High up on the sharp unforgiving ridge of the Mynden Stones, a small campsite nestled in a hollow. Four bright orange tents snuggled against the rocks as the ancient stones, once at the bottom of a long forgotten sea, glistened in the rising sun, throwing their silhouette in sharp relief against the pale morning sky. The air was fresh, the sun not yet strong enough to bring any warmth, but to Felicity it was heaven. She had crept out of her sleeping bag as Maisie slept, wanting to experience the dawn and the birdsong that went with it. To the east, the sun began to touch the landscape with a gentle pink and although her legs were tired from the long walk she had done yesterday, Felicity looked forward to the second day amongst the spring flowers and wild glacier shaped landscape that the hills offered her. She breathed in the damp air and relaxed, slight tensions easing from her young face as she savoured the new day.

Leaving the tent behind her, which still contained a sleeping Maisie, Felicity walked away from the campsite and headed for a pile of rocks which had been piled up alongside some old mine workings. She didn't go far; she just wanted a few minutes on her own. The area was securely fenced and she stayed well away from the dilapidated buildings which still remained. The area had a kind of stark beauty which suited Felicity's frame of mind. The industrial activity which had maimed the countryside had been weathered by countless winters since the old mines were abandoned, and spring flowers grew in cracked concrete clefts. Broken brick work lent a warm red glow to the scene, which by now was bathed in bright sunlight. Shadows were sharp against the walls of a hut and Felicity smiled as movement in the wild flowers gave away the presence of a tiny rabbit. It was a peaceful scene and as the young girl carefully climbed the rock pile, she relaxed in the gentle spring breeze.

Over the last few weeks she had felt a bit lost; unhappy and missing home and her parents. She longed for the end of term. The little gift she had received from her mother still lay untouched in her pocket but now, as the sun rose above the sharp stones, she pulled it out of her pocket. She held it in her hand, admiring the cut glass of the little bottle. It was beautiful. As she eased the lid off the bright gold diffuser, she pressed the top gently and took a gentle sniff as the scent of lavender filled the air. It caught the back of her throat and made her cough gently, but the scent was glorious so she pressed again and sniffed harder. The birds sang their dawn chorus as Felicity stood up and the sun, now high above the hills in the distance, glowed warmly in the skies above.

Later that morning, Alexis and Dax yet again made their way back to Lyston. Alexis dropped Dax off at Mavis' house, leaving him to have another look round to try and find something that would explain the hidden book with its mysterious payments. Dax still suspected blackmail and as he too knew about the shenanigans with Andrew Danvers and the Sixth Form girl, wondered if that was the source of the money. He had already voiced his suspicions to Alexis and with these thoughts in his mind, she drove off and headed for the school as Dax knocked on the door. This time the door was opened by Mavis' husband, Doug Greene. Dax had not met the man before so he introduced himself and showed his ID. Doug Greene opened the door wider and showed Dax in.

"I'm really sorry to bother you again," Dax opened politely. "But I need to have another look through Mavis' personal effects to see if we can find some answers."

Doug nodded glumly, his unshaven face drawn and haggard in his grief, too tired to argue. Dax felt sorry for the man. An ordinary normal hard working man cut down by the horribly abnormal.

"Do you mind if I leave you to it," asked Doug. "I'm just getting breakfast ready for my mother in law. She's taken it very hard."

"Of course," agreed Dax readily, much preferring it that way. He would have felt at a disadvantage otherwise, unable to move freely, encumbered by the man's presence. Doug disappeared into the kitchen and Dax once more headed for the bedroom. He had found the bank book but nothing else of suspicion in the dining room. This time he wanted to search Mavis' private space more thoroughly. After putting on protective gloves, he began by lifting the mattress and feeling through the bed linen on the bed. Having already investigated the underneath of the pine bed, he gave it just a cursory look. There was still nothing of interest there so finding nothing in the bed itself, Dax stood up and looked round the room. He rifled gently through the dressing table, looking carefully underneath the drawers to ensure that nothing was secreted there, as it had been in the dining room. His search was unsuccessful and Dax became more and more dispirited. He stood up, straightening his aching back. Stooping over the dressing table and clambering under the drawers were not doing him any good at all. With a rueful thought that he wasn't getting any younger, Dax's eyes turned to the wardrobe, a heavy ornamented lump of solid oak. It looked distinctly old fashioned, most unlike more modern light furniture. This time, however, its appearance struck a chord taking Dax back to a time when he was ten years old and his fifteen year old brother had hidden something behind their wardrobe. Dax had been looking for something else and had been amazed when he'd discovered the naughty magazine, as he had called it at the time. He could still remember the row his mother had had with his brother. Dax grinned at the memory. Walking across to the wardrobe, he looked behind but it was too close to the wall to see much at all. He was dimly aware of years of cobwebs, gathered by generations of industrious spiders, and as one brushed his mouth as he leaned close to the wall, he spat suddenly, clearing his lips of the offending trail. Brushing his face with his hand, he put his shoulder against the side of the wardrobe and managed to budge it a little. The heavy wardrobe inched out slowly and there he found it, the answer to his question. Taped to the back of the wardrobe at the bottom, easily accessible by thin fingers with the wardrobe back in its place, if you knew where to look, was a grubby envelope. Withdrawing it gently and with excitement rising, Dax carefully opened the unsealed packet with his gloved hands and pulled out a small colour photograph. He stood up and went to stand under the lamp, which hung from the ceiling, and examined the photo. It was of poor quality and very grainy but it showed two people clearly enough. One appeared to be male, the other a young female, the man lying on top of the girl in a compromising position. Their faces were hidden from the camera, so identification would be tricky, but it was something. This wasn't proof of blackmail, but together with the Building Society book and its regular payments, it was highly suggestive. He carefully replaced the photo in its envelope, and in turn placed that into a plastic forensics bag. After carefully pocketing the packet, he heaved the wardrobe back against the wall and looked around, ensuring that he had left nothing out of place. He returned to the kitchen and found Doug, who had finished breakfast and was now making a sandwich and covering it carefully in cling film, ready for his mother in law's lunch. Mrs Dale was nowhere to be seen.

"Do you mind if I have a quick word, Mr Greene," asked Dax solicitously. "We haven't yet had a chance to chat."

"No, that's fine. I thought you'd want to talk to me sooner or later," replied Doug. "Fancy a cuppa?"

Dax saw the kettle boiling, so thought the cuppa wouldn't take long and it would take away the lingering remains of any dusty cobwebs from his mouth.

"A coffee'd be great. Thanks."

Dax waited as Doug spooned the coffee into two mugs, and poured the water in.

"Milk, sugar?"

"Just milk, thanks," replied Dax.

Doug handed the coffee to Dax and sat down gloomily on the kitchen stool opposite Dax.

"How are you," opened Dax gently.

"Oh, you know…" Doug trailed off.

"I am so sorry for your loss," replied Dax with the cliché that suited but didn't really mean anything.

"Thanks," mumbled Doug, accepting the comment at face value.

"Can you think of any reason why anyone would want to kill Mavis?" went on Dax.

Doug flinched. "No, I haven't got a clue. We were married, and I loved her but she was never one for opening up to anyone, least of all me. I know her Mum never wanted her to marry me but we were happy in our own way."

Dax decided to say nothing of the photo he had just found behind the wardrobe, but thought he would mention the Building Society passbook.

"When I came out here the other day and had a word with Mrs Dale, I found a Building Society passbook. There was a considerable sum of money in the account. Do you know anything about this?"

Doug looked up in surprise, his gloom and despondency momentarily replaced by the thought of unexpected riches.

"No, hadn't a clue. How much is there?"

Dax felt slightly disgusted by Doug's change of mood but understanding the reason why, nevertheless filled him in.

"There was close to a thousand pounds in there."

"Phew," replied Doug, scratching his head in amazement. "The sly old dog. Wonder where she got that from."

"I was hoping you could answer that," replied Dax.

"I'm really sorry, I just don't know. She never told me how much she earned."

"Did you wonder how she managed to pay for the oak flooring?"

"I just thought it was savings. Are you telling me that it wasn't?"

"We just don't know at the moment, enquiries are still ongoing," admitted Dax.

It was obvious to Dax that Doug thought he was in for a little windfall, but if the money proved to be illicitly gained he thought it would be highly unlikely that Doug would benefit from this particular little stash.

"Oh, by the way, is Mavis' phone here?" asked Dax. "We've looked for it at school but it's not there."

"She kept the thing with her all the time, moulded to her fingers, I reckon. She was always Twittering or Facebooking or something, never without it. I assumed you'd got it."

"No, we've not found it. Well, thanks for your help, anyway. We'll keep you posted," finished Dax. "Oh, how's Mrs Dale by the way?" he added as an afterthought.

"Not so good," replied Doug. "I can't give her the care she needs – I work full time, you know - so we've agreed that she'll goes into a nursing home. I'm taking her there tomorrow to try the place out. Real shame, but there you go."

Dax felt slightly disgusted by Doug's apparent lack of care and indecent haste in getting rid of his mother in law, but wisely kept his mouth shut.

"Where is she, by the way?" asked Dax looking round.

"She's in the dining room, finishing her breakfast."

"Oh, well, I hope things work out OK for her."

Making his goodbyes and thanking Doug for the coffee, Dax headed for the car and left, glad to leave the depressing situation behind him. There was always more than one victim in a murder, and unfortunately Doug was making sure it was his mother in law. Dax looked at his watch and after manoeuvring himself carefully out of the cul de sac, swiftly headed for the pub, where he had prearranged to meet his boss.

Alexis, meanwhile, had gone back to the school and begun her investigations in the chemistry laboratory. That phenol must have come from somewhere and the school's chemistry lab was the obvious place to start looking. She had made her way up the steps to the chemistry laboratory and, by chance, found a girl, who she assumed to be the lab technician, tidying up after the morning's experiments.

154

"Good morning," asked Alexis politely, producing her ID. "I'm Detective Inspector Longbow from Teigneford Police. And you are?"

"I'm Rita Chappell, the lab technician for the whole school."

Rita scrutinised Alexis' ID carefully.

"I would like to have a look at your chemical store cupboard, if I may?"

Rita stopped in her tracks. This was her domain and her initial reaction was to bristle at the implied criticism.

"I keep a tidy cupboard, Inspector. You won't find anything wrong in there."

"I'm sure you do," replied Alexis placatingly, "but I have to check everything, as I'm sure you will be aware".

"Why do you need to look in there anyway," Rita asked with an edge to her voice.

Alexis sighed. Why did everyone have to stand in her way? Patiently, she persisted, keeping her voice low and measured.

"I'm sure you're aware of the murder of Mavis Greene?"

"Yes, of course I am. I'm sorry for her family".

"Well," persisted Alexis. "She was poisoned and the substance used was phenol. I have to check any possible sources of the phenol and your chemistry cupboard is an obvious place to start, as I'm sure you will agree."

Alexis paused with a quizzical eyebrow raised, watching Rita carefully as she waited for her reaction.

Rita paled at Alexis' words.

"What a horrible way to die," she whispered.

"Yes, it was," agreed Alexis quietly. "So anything you can tell me that might help to find out who did this, would be helpful. Don't you agree?"

Rita nodded.

"The cupboard is over there, at the back of the room."

Rita led the way to a small cupboard, which Alexis noticed had two strong mortise locks.

"Good security you have here," she said.

"Oh, yes. I insisted on this when I started here. Security was too lax before that. Things used to go missing."

"How long have you been here," asked Alexis hoping she had started after the murders had begun.

"Oh, been quite a while now, going on for ten years."

"Oh," replied Alexis, concealing her disappointment. "Do you keep a record of chemicals kept here?" she went on.

"Of course I do" Rita replied indignantly.

"May I see it?"

Rita unlocked the cupboard and reached inside. She brought down a hard backed ledger, which she handed to Alexis, who opened it and started to read. She was impressed. Each chemical was listed; its purchase date, the supplier, its cost and dates of whenever it was used. Alexis noted that the phenol, or carbolic acid, had been purchased three months previously. It had been used four times since and showed an amount left of 2.5 kilograms.

"May I see the packet, please?" she asked.

Rita turned round and began to peruse the shelves. She soon found what she was looking for and reached up for a white packet, wrapped and sealed firmly and clearly marked phenol.

"What do you use the phenol for," asked Alexis.

"It's one of the oldest antiseptic agents. Apart from the odd experiment, I use it mainly as a disinfectant," Rita replied.

Alexis took the packet from the lab technician and weighed it in her hands.

"Please could you weigh this for me?" she asked.

Rita looked up quizzically but did as she was asked. The scales, accurate to a milligram, wavered and then settled on a fraction over two kilograms.

Rita lifted the packet off the scales and fiddled with the calibration knob at the back of the instrument.

"A problem?" asked Alexis.

"Not sure, it's just a bit odd, that's all."

"How so?"

"There should be another half kilo there. That's what my ledger says. We used it last week for an experiment, and I checked it then. See, here are the dates and my initials."

"Are you sure your scales are accurate."

"They're state of the art. They have to be as I'm dealing with some dangerous chemicals in here. The scales say just over two kilos, so that's what's there, but my book says two and a half. Oh, my god, some of it's been taken," finished Rita, her voice rising in panic as realisation dawned."

Alexis grunted. The packet didn't appear to have been tampered with but there was definitely some missing.

"Who has access to this cupboard?" asked Alexis with a grim face.

Rita looked worried.

"Well, I do, obviously. Both Mr Danvers and I have a key, and I think the headmaster has a spare. Where there's a lock, the headmaster insists on having a spare key. Other than that, no one."

"Do you mind if I take this packet?" asked Alexis, in effect giving Rita no choice.

"No problem," replied Rita, accepting the inevitable.

"Right, that solves one question," Alexis said. "At least I am eliminating possibilities."

"Do you think this packet was used to kill Mavis?" Rita asked, quietly.

"I have no way of knowing exactly, but circumstantially, the evidence is for that supposition. A test will find out for sure."

"What a horrible way to go. It must have been agonising for her. I liked her. She was good at her job."

"It's nice that you think of her that way. So often domestic staff get ignored," went on Alexis.

"Much the same as me," sniffed Rita. "They only know when you're not here and moan then. If you are here and doing your job, then you only get ignored. The kids are good though. I like being with them." Rita smiled.

Alexis bagged the packet of phenol in a plastic forensic bag and sealed it.

"Well, thank you for your co-operation, Miss Chappell. You have been very helpful. I'll have one of my officers get in touch to take a statement from you."

"OK," replied Rita, miserably.

Alexis made her farewell and turning on her heel, left the laboratory, leaving Rita looking pale, and staring dejectedly after her. As she walked back to the car, Alexis suddenly thought about the store cupboard where Mavis had been found. What was she doing there? Thinking of keys to cupboards had reminded her that she hadn't asked. 'Come on girl! You're slipping', she thought. She looked at her watch; there was still time before she was due to meet Dax at the pub, so making her way around the back of the main building and heading towards the kitchen, she hoped to find Brenda Jarvis. She slipped in through the back door and stood for a while in the entrance to the kitchen savouring the delicious smells that emanated from the ovens. She began to feel very hungry. The kitchen was a hive of activity, as lunch was being prepared for two hundred and fifty hungry mouths and Brenda was there, surrounded by her kitchen assistants. She looked hot and bothered, as pans steamed gently on the hob, and ovens roasted red hot as they cooked the meat. As she moved further into the kitchen, Brenda looked up and saw her. She beckoned Alexis to follow her, so moving carefully amongst the steaming pans, tables laden with serving trays and busy kitchen assistants, Alexis weaved her way around the various ovens and sinks, out of the kitchen and down a corridor towards a door set in the wall. Brenda opened it and went ahead. Alexis followed and found herself in a pleasant room, airy and bright with colourful soft furnishings. The sun shone through large picture windows, filling the room with warmth and light. It looked homely and inviting, and Alexis realised that this was where Brenda lived, whilst she was working.

"This is a lovely room," she commented.

"Thank you," Brenda replied simply. "It's my home. I've been here now for thirty years. I love it."

She paused for a few seconds, lost in memories then, pulling herself together, she went on.

"Now, what can I do for you?"

"I'm sorry to have to make you remember, but I need to know what Mavis was doing in the storeroom, and how she gained entrance. I assume you keep the door locked?"

"Yes, I do. After breakfast that morning, I lent my key to my deputy manager, Ella, as she was going to fill up the salt and pepper pots on the dining tables. The morning was so busy, what with the Bishop coming an' all, I forgot about my key, an oversight on my part, I'm afraid, but I have done this many times before. I only saw the key again when your chaps had finished with the room."

"May I have a quick word with Ella, please?" asked Alexis. "I just need to pin down this key business."

"Yes, of course. I'll ring through to the kitchen and ask her to come here, more private. Would you like a cup of coffee or tea?" she asked as an afterthought.

"No, thank you. I don't want to keep you long and I have to be on my way soon."

Alexis sat back in Brenda's comfy sofa and waited as she dialled the kitchen.

"Oh, hello, it's Miss Jarvis here. Could you ask Ella to come along to my room?" She paused, listening. "Thank you."

After replacing the phone, Brenda wiped her hot brow with a hanky and turned to Alexis.

"Are you any further forward with this? Do you know what happened," she asked.

"We have some leads, but I can't go into them just yet. Suffice to say that Mavis ingested phenol and we suspect foul play."

Brenda shivered slightly and sniffed miserably and was about to go on when there was a knock on the door.

"Come in," Brenda invited.

A blonde head poked itself around the door, and a middle aged woman entered. She looked flustered, red with exertion and heat.

"Hello, Miss Jarvis, you asked for me?"

"Yes, Ella, come and sit down."

Brenda introduced Alexis.

"Inspector Longbow here wants to ask you a question or two."

Ella looked at Alexis, her fidgeting hands giving away the fact that she was nervous, an action that Alexis didn't miss.

"I gather, Ella," opened Alexis, "that you had Miss Jarvis' key on the morning of Mavis' death."

"Yes, I did. She lent it to me so I could fill up the salt and peppers."

"What did you do with the key when you had finished with it?"

"I should have given it back to Miss Jarvis, but she'd disappeared, so I kept it with me, for safe keeping."

"Did you lend it to anyone else?" Alexis went on.

Ella shifted uncomfortably in her seat, her eyes first looking at Brenda, then down at the hands in her lap.

"I lent it to Mavis as she wanted to get some more coffee for the staff room ready for break; we keep the spare jars in that storeroom. I forgot about it until I found out what happened to her."

Ella turned to Brenda, her eyes troubled.

"I'm so sorry, Miss Jarvis. I should've said something before, but it completely slipped my mind."

"Don't worry, Ella, these things happen." replied Brenda pragmatically. "What happened to Mavis would probably have happened anyway, if not in the storeroom then somewhere else. It isn't your fault."

Brenda patted her friend gently on the knee and Ella looked back at Alexis.

"I'm so sorry," she said.

"Thank you, Ella. That's explains the key for me, and how she happened to be in the storeroom," replied Alexis gently.

"Is that all, Inspector?" asked Brenda.

"Yes, thank you. I'll let you get on with things. By the way, I wish I could stay, that dinner smells delicious."

Brenda smiled, and after dismissing Ella back to the kitchen, led Alexis back outside. She waved goodbye and disappeared back into the kitchen herself.

Back at the car, Alexis rang the police station and arranged for an officer to come to the school to take a statement from Rita and Andrew Danvers, with particular emphasis on the man's rumoured affair with the school girl. She needed to know if the chemistry teacher was being blackmailed. Pocketing her phone at the end of the call, she drove swiftly down the driveway and made her way back to the village pub, where Dax was sitting waiting, two drinks and a couple of sandwiches already on the table.

"You needn't have waited," said Alexis.

"I couldn't start without you," replied Dax. "How'd you get on?"

"I was going to ask you the same question,"replied Alexis.

"You first," said Dax with a grin.

"Well, I think you were right about blackmail. There's about half a kilo of phenol missing from the lab."

Dax grimaced.

"Did you discover anything?" asked Alexis hopefully.

"I think we might be getting somewhere at last," replied Dax.

"What d'you mean?"

"Well, I found something else back at Mavis' house. It was hidden behind her wardrobe."

With that, Dax produced with a flourish the photo from his inside pocket. Alexis took it and examined it closely.

"This is interesting. Why would Mavis hide this? She must have had some purpose in keeping it hidden," said Alexis, thoughtfully.

She turned the photo over in his hand and saw a date, carefully, printed in black capitals. JULY 2019.

"The fact that this was hidden tends to suggest that this isn't an innocent photograph," replied Dax. "D'you reckon that's Mavis' writing?" he finished.

"I don't know," replied Alexis. "We'll have to get a comparison made by a handwriting expert. It's not very good quality," she added as an afterthought.

"Ah," replied Dax. "I've had a think about that. I reckon she took the pic on her phone and, as a backup, downloaded it to a computer or a laptop and printed up a copy. Sometimes, if you press the wrong setting, you just get a draft print, rather than a best quality. I reckon that's what we've got here, a draft copy."

Alexis stared at the photo again.

"How about this as a hypothesis? This is a photo of someone at the school who shouldn't have been doing this." Alexis waved the photo in the air. "Mavis saw them and photographed them."

"Her husband said she'd kept her phone welded to her hand," said Dax with a grin.

"Are we any closer to finding her phone, by the way?"

"I did ask the husband. He didn't know. It wasn't at their home. He assumed it was with her, as I said, welded to her hand."

"Interesting it's gone missing. I wonder if the murderer took it from her body, along with the cup. Perhaps there was something compromising on it." mused Alexis. She looked at the photograph again.

"I wonder if she'd started to blackmail someone with this. The blackmailer got fed up with shelling out and bumped her off."

"Could be," agreed Dax. "Do you think it's that chemistry teacher? He was spotted kissing a Sixth Form girl. Could be them in the photo."

"Maybe," Alexis agreed. "The evidence is stacking up against him, albeit a bit circumstantial. As phenol is such a specific chemical, it was bound to have come from the obvious place. There is some missing so logic says that the missing chemical is also the murder weapon. This does put the Science teacher in the frame. Rumour has it that he is having it off with a Sixth Form girl, so I thought he might be involved in blackmail, as you said and wanted to do away with the perpetrator, which is why I thought that hidden bank book of Mavis' might have been a clue. She was always snooping around, apparently. I think it's time we had him in for a chat. Rattle his cage a bit. About time we got a bit pro-active, gets people nervous," she finished with a grin.

Alexis picked up her drink. Never being one to stick to feminine stereotypes, a glass of wine or a G & T, she preferred a pint of cider with lunch, in this case a pale cider from a local brewery. It was crisp and tangy and Alexis relished the taste as she sipped. She went quiet and Dax, recognising the signs of concentration in his friend, left her to it. He munched on his own sandwich quietly and followed his own train of thought.

"Oh, I meant to ask," Alexis said, breaking into Dax's own thought processes. "I never did find out why Redway left so early. Trousers and backhanders, I think you said?"

Dax laughed.

"I got this second hand from Steve when I started at Teigneford. Just after you left for London, they had a burglary at that gents' outfitters in the High Street. No one hurt but a lot of posh shirts and suits were nicked."

"Go on," ordered Alexis, puzzled as to where this was leading.

"Well, Redway attended on his own. He convinced the manager to add a couple of suits to the stolen list that didn't actually go missing. The Insurance Company got suspicious, made their own enquiries and the truth came out. Redway got a choice, jump or be pushed. He jumped."

"What a bloody fool," whistled Alexis. "How on earth did the insurance company find out?"

"Well, no one can prove anything but Steve thinks they got a tip off from someone at the nick. He assures me it wasn't him although he did have his suspicions. Redway actually wore one of the suits to work, you see, and he has upset an awful lot of people."

"He didn't. Oh my God, where did he leave his brains? What an absolute fool."

"We actually have a lot to thank him for," went on Dax mysteriously.

"And how do you arrive at that conclusion?"

"His loss, our gain. You!"

Alexis had the grace to blush. That was one thing she hadn't thought of. Lifting her glass, she toasted her predecessor.

"Here's to him. May he have a long and probably unhappy retirement."

"Cheers!" agreed Dax.

As Alexis finished the last drop of cider, her phone rang disturbing the tranquillity of the atmosphere in the pub. She took it from her bag and saw that Hannah was the caller.

"Sorry, to bother you ma'am, but we've had a call from the school. Apparently one of the children has gone awol."

"Oh not another disappearance. What on earth is happening at the school?"

"This one's a bit different. Some of the Year Nines have gone on a camping trip up in the hills – something to do with the D of E Award - and one of the girls has gone missing. Not our problem possibly, but I thought you ought to know."

"Thanks, Hannah. Too many coincidences again. Story of my life," finished Alexis grimly.

Alexis listened carefully to the meagre details that the police had been given, then bearing in mind the coincidence, ordered Mike to get a proper search in motion, then go up to the campsite itself.

"Hannah, you go with him, and get Steve to join us at the school in an hour. We need to get a bit more background. Keep us posted. Fingers crossed she's just wandered off and got lost."

Within ten minutes of Hannah's call, Mike had organised a full search team. Passing it by Superintendent Barnes first, he'd been given the go ahead to get as many uniformed officers, dog handlers and anyone else who was free up to the small campsite in the Mynden Hills. He and Hannah arrived ahead of the main search party and pulled up alongside a white transit van, emblazoned with the school's crest. Michael Shepperton, the Biology teacher, was busy loading rucksacks into the back of the van and looked up as the two officers got out of the car. To one side, Margot Preece the

French teacher stood surrounded by a small group of children, one girl and two boys, and everyone looked miserable.

"We came up here yesterday," started Margot after Mike had introduced themselves. "First day of what should have been a full two days of walking."

"I gather one of the girls has gone missing?" asked Mike, as the first of the search team arrived.

"Yes," replied Margot miserably. "It's Felicity. She vanished this morning. Everyone was here last night. We always do a full head count. We've abandoned today's walk until Felicity turns up."

"She was using one of these tents?" asked Mike, pointing to the small group of orange tents, still erected and yet to be dismantled.

"Yes. She was sharing with another girl."

"Can I have a quick word with her, please?"

Margot gestured towards Maisie, who was sitting on a rock, her expression fearful.

"When did you last see your friend?" asked Mike gently.

Maisie looked apprehensively at the two officers, then shut her eyes briefly as she thought back to the previous evening. Opening them again, and blinking slightly in the sudden sunlight as it came back out from behind a small cloud, she answered.

"Last night. We had supper together, read for a bit until the light faded then got our heads down. We were shattered after the day's walking. I last saw her tucked up in her sleeping bag."

"Did you see her go out this morning?"

"No, I was spark out. I didn't wake up until Miss Preece called us at eight this morning."

"Is there any reason you can think of as to why she should wander off?"

"No, not really. Maybe she just woke early and needed some fresh air. Fliss has been a bit, er …" Maisie tailed off, her throat catching with worry.

"Yes?" asked Hannah, as Maisie went quiet.

"Oh, nothing."

Mike and Hannah looked at Maisie with concern. It was apparent that Maisie had been going to say something but then thought better of it. They didn't push her. Time enough later.

By now, the full search team had arrived, and Mike told them who they were looking for. Everyone tailed off in different directions, and soon the area was quiet. Mike stayed at the campsite to liaise the search and came to a decision.

"I think it best if you get the children back to school now – leave us to it. We'll catch up with you there."

The two teachers rapidly agreed to this plan of action and Michael made short work of dismantling the tents and getting them stowed safely in the van. Within twenty minutes, the site was clear and the two officers stood back and watched as the transit van drove off down the track, heading for the school, its wheels throwing up a cloud of dust as it disappeared out of view.

"Call this in to Inspector Longbow, Hannah, can you?" asked Mike. "We need to keep her updated."

"Do you think we'll find her alive?" Hannah ventured, her face lined with concern.

"Of course we will. The silly girl has just wandered off and got lost. Don't be alarmist."

"There are loads of old mine workings round here. They used to dig up lead."

"I know but they're all fenced off. She'll be fine. She'll turn up safe and sound. Don't worry."

Hannah kept quiet. She too was smitten by the coincidence and didn't share Mike's optimism. Pulling her phone out of her pocket, she started to punch in the number for her boss but just as she went to press the call button, a shout echoed around the hillside. Mike and Hannah looked at each other. He smiled.

"Told you!"

Chapter Nine

Lunch time had taken longer than usual for Alexis and Dax as the two officers used the time to catch up with each other and discuss the next step. Nearly an hour after learning about a missing girl up in the Mynden Hills, Alexis' phone once again disturbed the peace of the pub. A pleasant lunch time came to an abrupt end as Alexis replaced the phone in her pocket. Her face was grim.

"They've found her, Archie."

Dax could tell immediately by the expression on his boss's face that the news wasn't good.

"Is she …?"

"I'm afraid so."

"Bugger."

The two officers lapsed into silence as each digested the news.

"Any idea what happened?" asked Dax.

"Apparently she got up early, before anyone else was awake and wandered off. One of the teachers roused everyone at eight and found the girl was missing. They had a quick look round but when they couldn't find her, called it in to the police station. Mike's search team got up there very quickly. I'll give Mr Barnes credit for that. He doesn't hang about when needs must. A dog sniffed her out. She was found at the bottom of a mine shaft, her neck was broken."

"Oh bloody hell. I thought all the mines up there were mapped and fenced off."

"This one appears to have been missed. Seems the entrance was overgrown and couldn't be seen. It wasn't deep, looks like an exploratory shaft Mike thinks, but deep enough to do the damage."

"Does Hamish know yet?"

"He's on his way. This school is keeping him very busy," finished Alexis drolly.

She paused to think for a minute then went on.

"Archie, I'll drop you off at the school. Give them the news. Steve'll join you there. There's nothing to suggest foul play, just a horrible accident, but the way things are going, I'm not taking anything for granted. I'm going up to the campsite and liaise with Hamish if you could have a word with the houseparents and make a preliminary search of the girl's room. I'm not expecting to find anything, but you never know."

"Right you are. See you later?"

"Yes. I'll join you there with Hannah."

Alexis and Dax headed for the car and quickly got on their way back to the school.

"I'm going to be doing this journey in my sleep before long," said Dax ruefully, as he negotiated again the deep gravel and pulled up outside the front door of the school. Leaving Dax with his instructions, Alexis took over the driver's seat and headed for the hills.

The early morning sun had vanished, leaving in its wake a cloudy sky that promised some afternoon rain. As she drove, Alexis asked herself the question – why was she going up to the hills? They didn't need her there – she didn't need to be there herself, so why? She had two murders on her books now, both needing her immediate attention so why did she feel the need to be with the dead girl? Something niggled her mind but then throwing off the idle thoughts, she negotiated the last mile along the dusty track up in the hills. There she found Hamish, who had just arrived, and Mike. Of the school group there was no sign. Most of the search party had gone too, their unhappy job done, just a dog handler and his dog waited patiently by the group of vehicles that had now gathered under the sharp unforgiving ridge of the Mynden Stones.

"Hi Hamish," greeted Alexis. "What have we got?"

"Not sure yet. Just got here. You want to have a look?"

"Yes please. Who found the body?"

"I did, ma'am," replied the dog handler. "Or rather Raven did here," he went on pointing to a jet black Alsatian dog, who looked

168

with deep brown eyes at Alexis. Alexis wasn't a great dog lover so kept her distance and eyed it warily.

"Can you describe the scene?"

"If it hadn't been for Raven here, we'd never have found her. There is nothing to see on the surface, just rocks overgrown by grass. Raven picked up her scent and found her very quickly."

"Thank you. Well done, Raven."

At the sound of his name, the dog pricked his ears and growled gently. Alexis backed off a foot or two. She felt distinctly uncomfortable when faced with a large dog, particularly a working dog. They had attitude, which was necessary, but not one she appreciated.

"Where's the body now?" she asked Mike.

"She's still in the hole. It isn't deep – you can see her from the surface but I managed to get down to her without any difficulty to see if she was OK. She wasn't," he finished miserably."

"Do you need me now, ma'am?" asked the dog handler."

"No thank you. You did a great job. I'm sorry it had such a sad ending."

The dog handler nodded grimly, and after a gentle tug on its lead, Raven followed his handler obediently, as they both headed for their van. Alexis had lots of questions buzzing round her head but first she needed to be there.

"Lead on, Mike. Hamish needs to get busy."

As Alexis followed Mike along a well-worn track up to the old mine buildings, a spot of rain fell on her face. She looked up to the sky and saw dark clouds gathering in the distance and felt that whatever investigations had to be made should be done without delay. They were in for a deluge but for now, the rain stayed mercifully light and as the far distance disappeared in a haze of drizzle, Alexis saw Hannah standing by the pile of rocks on which Felicity had sat in the dawn sunshine. The young officer jumped up quickly as Alexis walked up to her, pleased to see that Hannah had ditched the uniform, dressed now in smart trousers with a contrasting red jacket under a waterproof coat. Apart from the coat, it wasn't the best or most appropriate gear for a hillside environment but despite the grim surroundings, this made Alexis feel happier; Hannah was now properly part of the team. Seeing her face, however, brought it home to the detective inspector that this was probably the first time the young woman had seen a dead body having missed Mavis' discovery and not seen the caretaker's mortal remains beside the pool. The fact that the body was that of a child would be doubly hard to bear.

"You OK?"

"I'm all right. Had better days but goes with the job, I suppose," replied Hannah, a catch in her voice.

"I'm afraid so," responded Alexis sympathetically.

"Such a shame for a young girl," went on Hannah, her voice stronger now. "These mine workings are so dangerous. Whatever was she doing away from the campsite?"

"We'll probably never know," replied Alexis sadly. "Kids do some daft things sometimes."

As the three officers pondered the workings of an adolescent mind, a shout from Hamish disturbed their thoughts.

"Inspector, can you come over here!"

Alexis turned to see Hamish standing at the top of the shaft, now clearly open and exposed to the damp air.

"What's up?" said Alexis, surprised at the look on Hamish's face. His features were grim, his eyes bleak.

"Her neck is broken but I don't think that killed her. It's only six feet to the bottom of the shaft and if she'd gone in feet first, as you'd assume from a fall, she wouldn't have broken her neck, it would've have been her ankles that would take the first shock. The top of her skull is damaged - she went head first, hence the broken neck. Then there's this."

He held up a handful of broken glass, one small piece still attached to a golden diffuser.

"What is it?" said Alexis, peering at his outstretched hand.

"Not absolutely sure yet, but I found the broken bits under her body. She was still holding some of the bottle; there's some glass embedded in her hand. I think it might be a scent bottle. There's a powerful aroma of lavender, but there's something else. It's a sharp acrid smell …"

A memory broke briefly into Alexis' thoughts.

"You're not saying what I think you're saying…" she asked.

"I'll have to do some tests obviously, but I'll buy you a drink tonight if this isn't phenol."

"Oh bloody hell," swore Alexis. "I knew it. That's why I came up here. I sensed something was wrong. I couldn't work out why in my mind as I drove up here. Now I know."

She turned away from Hamish and saw Hannah, her face bleak, her eyes wet with unshed tears. Alexis didn't mind her team showing emotion, it made them human and it was Hannah's first case after all but she needed to distract her from the situation a little.

"Hannah. I think you and I need to get back to the school. Mike, stay here with Hamish and I'll catch up with you both later."

Hannah nodded miserably, wiping her cheeks with a cold hand as one tear coursed its way down her face and as Hamish prepared to lift Felicity's bruised and broken body from the mine shaft, Alexis led her back to the car and drove off, leaving the hills behind as they succumbed to the threatened deluge.

Dax, meanwhile, had made his way into Graham Harper's study bypassing Frances' empty desk. He had just about had time to inform the headmaster about the discovery of Felicity's body when his phone rang and the grim news as to the unexplained manner of her death came through. Keeping the details to himself for a minute, until they themselves were more certain as to how the poor girl had succumbed, Dax decided to start a search of the girl's room. He made his way back outside, leaving the headmaster sitting miserably in his chair, no doubt wondering how this would impact the school, thought Dax uncharitably. Frances had returned to her desk and sat innocently at her computer, for all the world the busy receptionist she was paid to be. Dax looked at her in undisguised disgust. Frances didn't miss the look and tossed her blonde curls with irritation.

"Where does Felicity Smith live?" he asked tersely.

"In the girls' boarding house," sniped Frances angrily, taking exception to Dax's tone. "It's that big white building next to the art studio."

Dax left Reception and bumped into Steve, who had arrived and now stood outside in the quad, on his phone.

"Forensics," he mouthed gently, he too having received the grim news.

Dax nodded, then leaving him to it, walked rapidly across the quad and over to the house in question. It was easy to find. Despite the dismal weather, the white building stood out against a backdrop of newly leafed beech trees, the fresh green paintwork of the doors and windows matching the shrubbery and adding to the pastoral scene. A small group of girls, probably not much more than twelve or thirteen years of age, hovered outside the front door, misery showing plainly on their small white faces. One of the girls was dressed in expedition gear, her feet still shod in hiking boots and Dax rightly assumed that the expeditionary group had returned to the school and the news of Felicity's disappearance was now common knowledge. Dax had been seen coming and the door opened as he drew close. A tall white haired man waved the girls away, then beckoned him inside, quickly shutting the door against the dismal weather. Dax, at first misled by the white hair, thought the man was elderly, but a closer look showed him to be in his early fifties, just prematurely white. He had a kind face with laughter lines firmly etched into his temples. Standing next to him was a woman, similarly aged with short blonde hair, swept becomingly across her brow. She looked pale, understandable under the circumstances, but her stance was resolute and her handshake warm and firm.

"Let me introduce ourselves," said the man. "I am Charles Davenport and this is my wife, Angela. We are houseparents in this girls' boarding house. We've been here for nearly twenty years. Do you have any news?"

Dax realised that the news of Felicity's death hadn't yet reached his ears, and with a sinking feeling knew he had to be the bearer of bad news.

"We've found Felicity." Dax faltered as he saw immediately the brief ray of joy that flitted across the Davenports' faces, "but I'm afraid it isn't good news."

With a deep breath, he went on to explain that the child had died, in what could be an accident but as yet was unexplained.

"I would like to see her room, if I may?" Dax went on gently.

"This is devastating news. Felicity was a lovely girl, well liked … but I'm wittering on … come this way."

Without waiting for a response, Davenport turned on his heel, leaving his wife standing miserably behind him and led Dax upstairs to the bedrooms. The house was old; he guessed it had once formed part of the original estate. It was a beautiful house with huge sash windows and an elegant oak staircase, which swept majestically up to the first floor. Dax had no time to look in the downstairs rooms as Charles Davenport forged ahead, but the panelled doors and brass doorknobs showed a glimpse of former glory and he could only guess at what lay behind. Upstairs was less beautiful, changed as it had been to accommodate small bedrooms for the girl boarders. Davenport pushed open a door half way along the landing and indicated that the detective should enter. Dax went ahead and found himself in a small two-bedded room.

"Which is Felicity's bed?"

Davenport indicated the bed at the far end of the room against the wall.

"Does Felicity share this room with anyone?" he asked.

"Yes. Maisie Bourne. You saw her outside. She was on the expedition with Felicity. She'll be very worried. Do you want me to tell her?"

"Not just yet. My inspector is on her way. I think it might be better coming from her, if that's OK."

"As you wish," replied Davenport, not sure if he was relieved or not.

"Shall I leave you to it?" he went on.

"Yes please. I'll come back downstairs and have a chat later."

Davenport turned, his shoulders drooping in misery. Dax watched him go, his heart heavy too.

As the sound of Charles Davenport's steps disappeared into the distance, the room fell silent and Dax sat quietly on a chair by the open window at the other end of the room for a minute absorbing the scene. As he reflected on Felicity's untimely death, a clock ticked gently on Maisie's bedside table and birdsong permeated the room through the window. A slight breeze moved the curtain, and soughed through the dormitory bringing with it a sweet smell of damp earth. He looked out of the large bay window that graced the end of the room and the scene almost made him forget why he was there. Little children played in the nursery playground, only a stone's throw from the house. They were oblivious to all the ugly scenes that Dax imagined in his mind, and he rejoiced with them in their innocence. Blue tits clamoured for seed from a bird feeding station that had been placed in the boarding house's gardens; a stream trickled alongside the wall, its gentle babbling sounds soothing and soporific. Dax almost felt rested by the sounds; his tension eased. But the school bell roused him from his reverie and he turned his mind to the job in hand.

At first Dax saw nothing untoward in the room; both beds were separated by wooden panelling to afford a modicum of individual privacy, but he pushed ahead and after donning gloves, headed for Felicity's bed. The room was tidy, each bed made, the duvet and pillow on Maisie's bed neatly arranged, just as she had left them the morning before. Felicity's bed was dishevelled and untidy, the duvet hanging off the edge, where it now hung, a corner touching the floor. The pillow was smooth and the bottom sheet was still in place so Dax assumed that the girl had made the bed that morning, but between then and leaving the room, she had sat down on top,

174

thus disarranging the duvet. He imagine the scene; ready to go up to the hills, rucksack packed, excitement mounting. Just a last minute thing to do which she'd done sitting on the bed, then off in a rush not noticing the duvet on the floor.

He looked at the bedside table and saw small things that made his heart lurch. There was a small teddy bear sitting guarding a photo of two people, a man and a woman, whom Dax assumed were Felicity's parents. They were yet to find out that their daughter, entrusted to the care of a distant school, had died. Sometimes the job got to him. His manner could be brusque and sometimes hard, necessary to deal with the rigours of a police career, but his heart was human and human frailty and death caught him out sometimes, particularly that of a child. Pulling his mind and head together he pulled open the top drawer of the bedside table and found a small pale grey inhaler, the type used by asthmatics, lying in a small box on top of a pile of tissues. He bagged it then moved on to the lower drawer. In this he found a small book, a diary he assumed, and very private, secured as it was by a small gold padlock. He searched for the key, but it wasn't to be found. Making a mental note to ask Hamish to look carefully through Felicity's effects with her body, he bagged the diary and moved on.

There was nothing much else to find. A quick rifle through a small cupboard showed Felicity's clothes; school uniform, PE kit, casual wear for out of school hours. He felt carefully in pockets, shoes and boots but all were empty apart from a small sweet wrapper caught within the folds of a blouse pocket. He bagged it nevertheless. Dax was done, no more to find so he turned away and headed for the door. He stopped suddenly as something made him turn back; a nudge from his subconscious maybe but something had caught his eye. He bent down to lift the duvet that was touching the floor and as he did so, he noticed a packet. It was easy to miss having fallen under the bed and hidden by the folds of the fallen duvet. Turning it over, he noticed it had been addressed to a Miss F Smith. The school's address had been written in full but there was no postmark or stamp. He found it empty but as he handled it, a waft of lavender filled his nostrils. He noticed a damp patch on the inside of the packet and he sniffed it carefully, to check on the source of the smell, but then Dax smelled something else. His mind reeled with unimaginable possibilities as a pungent aroma assailed his nostrils. Shaking his head in disbelief, he slipped it carefully into a plastic evidence bag to preserve any fingerprints that might be on it then jumped slightly as the door to the bedroom opened and Charles Davenport poked his head round.

"Just thought I'd let you know that Maisie is downstairs with my wife. We haven't said anything to her but she knows something's happened to Felicity. News travels fast here," he finished ruefully.

"Right thanks, I'll be down in a mo," replied Dax.

As Charles Davenport turned to leave, Dax called him back, holding out the packet as he spoke.

"Did this come by the ordinary post," he asked.

Davenport fished for his glasses, which were in his jacket breast pocket and settled them on his nose. Taking the packet from the sergeant's outstretched hand, now safely encased in its plastic evidence bag, he peered closely at it.

"I assume so. I never really noticed. I always bring the post in from the post room each morning, and leave it on the hall table here and the girls sort their own mail out from then on."

"How is the post sorted?" asked Dax.

"All the school's post is delivered in a lump by Royal Mail. Usually, Sarah Dixon, the head's PA, sorts it in her office and then puts it into individual pigeon holes for staff to collect. You'll have to ask her if she saw this particular packet." Davenport peered more closely at the packet. "I don't remember this specifically. It hasn't got a stamp so it couldn't have come from Royal Mail, unless they missed it."

"Does anyone have access to the post room, where the post is left?" went on Dax.

"Any member of staff could go in there. The children certainly don't have access to it, and I don't think the domestics normally go in there. Miss Jarvis collects any post for them herself from her own pigeon hole."

"Could anyone have just left it here, bypassing the post room?"

"Possibly. The door is left on the latch for the girls to come and go. I suppose someone could have come in unnoticed."

"Did she suffer from asthma?"

Davenport blinked at the sudden change of subject.

"Er, yes, she did but it was only mild and her inhaler was always sufficient to cope. Oh, by the way, your inspector and her colleague have arrived. They're downstairs too."

"Thanks, I'll join them."

Dax went downstairs with Davenport in search of Alexis. He found her at the bottom of the stairs. Beckoning him outside, away from prying eyes and ears, he followed her and stood against the wall, out of the drizzle which was now turning into a mean, persistent rainfall.

"Found anything?" she asked, her face grim.

Dax showed her the evidence bag containing the stained packet.

"Have a sniff,'" he offered.

"I know what you're going to say," followed Alexis as she too pulled out a small evidence bag.

"This is just a small piece of a glass bottle. Hamish has the rest for analysis. We found this under her body. I'll wager my pension your smell is the same as mine."

Holding the bottle top out under Dax's nose, Alexis went on.

"Smell this but be careful though! Just a gentle sniff, that'll be enough."

Dax sniffed cautiously. The smell of lavender was overpowering but the underlying aroma made him catch his breath.

"This is the same as in that storeroom yesterday," he responded, excitement mounting in his voice. "It's that bloody phenol again. The bottle must have been in the packet and it has leaked slightly."

Alexis took her phone out of her bag.

"I've got a few photos of the campsite area – not calling it a crime scene yet, but my gut feeling is that it is."

Dax flicked through the photos on her phone, some taken by Hamish at the bottom of the shaft, and came across a picture of Felicity's face, her eyes half closed, her face blooded and bruised by her fall. His heart missed a beat and he drew in a sharp intake of hissed breath.

"Damn."

Alexis' looked up in surprise. Dax wasn't usually one to let his emotions get the better of him, even if it was a child who had died.

"What's up?" she asked.

"I knew there was something I wanted to tell you the other day, when we came here the first time, but in the heat of everything that happened, it clean went out of my mind. I saw this girl when I was doing my walkabout. She was sitting up by the tennis courts and crying. I tried to find out what was wrong, but she was too wary of me. All she said was, 'He hurt me'. I assumed she'd had a playground tiff and thought no more of it. Maybe I was wrong. I should have tried to find out more. Shit, shit, shit."

Alexis shook her head.

"You can't blame yourself for this. We're not even sure what happened yet. Don't let your imagination run away with you, Archie."

Dax snorted.

"Maybe you're right." He appeared unconvinced. "This is no bloody accident," he cried angrily, smitten by the coincidence of seeing her alive and well so recently.

Alexis nodded grimly, her suspicions now confirmed.

"That thought had crossed my mind."

"She was asthmatic too. I found an inhaler in her bedside drawer. If she breathed this in, thinking it was perfume, it would've hit her lungs hard."

Alexis replaced the evidence packet in her bag and braving the now heavy rain, went back inside, leaving a very unhappy Dax to seek out Steve and the forensic team.

Alexis found Maisie sitting with Angela Davenport and Hannah in the living room. The girl looked pale, her face crumpled with a frown as she struggled to understand the situation.

"Hello, Maisie," said Alexis gently. "I hope you don't mind, but I would like to ask you about Felicity. I gather she's your friend."

Maisie nodded silently. She had already mentally prepared herself for questions as Hannah had introduced herself. Forbearing to get the ball rolling, Hannah had simply sat with Maisie and tried to relax her. Maisie sat quietly resolute; Alexis saw the strength in the girl's face and was encouraged.

"When did you last see her?" she opened.

Maisie sniffed and tilted her head as she thought.

"Has something happened to Fliss? What's going on?"

Alexis realised that Maisie was an intelligent girl and wasn't going to be fobbed off with platitudes. She was a young adult, beginning to leave childhood behind, and she deserved to be treated as such. She decided to play it straight. The girl would find out sooner or later anyway, and better to come from her with the comforting Mrs Davenport sitting beside her than by ugly rumour and innuendo.

"I'm afraid Felicity has had an accident and has died."

Maisie flinched as the words hit her. Her eyes filled with tears and she gulped noisily.

"How?"

"That's what we want to find out," went on Alexis, her voice soft and gentle. "When did you last see her?" she repeated.

Maisie sat quietly for a few seconds as she came to terms with the situation. She wriggled in her seat and pushed back her hair behind her ears. Mopping her eyes with a tissue readily supplied by Mrs Davenport, she replied.

"Last night, in our tent."

"So you didn't see her go out this morning?"

"No. I was shattered after yesterday. Slept right through until Miss Preece woke me up."

"Did Felicity say anything to you about something she got in the post?"

"I knew she got something in the post yesterday, just before we left."

"Did you see what she got?"

"No, not then. We were in a hurry – the coach was waiting. I told her to hurry up."

Maisie finished with a gulp, her voice catching as tears threatened to overwhelm her as the memory of her friend's delight appeared in her mind. Alexis continued, her manner quiet and gentle. Hannah watched, still and silent as her boss went on.

"You say not then. Did you see anything later? Did Felicity show you anything?"

"Yes, last night, when we in our tent. She'd forgotten about it during the day. She'd put it in her pocket and it fell out as she got into her sleeping bag."

"What happened next, Maisie?"

"She showed me a little glass bottle She said her mum had sent it to her."

"Did you see her use it?"

"No. Just as she showed it to me, Miss Preece said 'lights out' so I think she put it back in her pocket and we both went to sleep. I haven't seen her since. Was she…?

Maisie tailed off miserably and began to cry more forcefully.

"Was she what?" asked Alexis quietly.

"Oh, nothing," sniffed Maisie.

"Is there something you want to say?"

Maisie raised her head, opened her mouth as if to speak, then closed it abruptly, her lips tightly shut. She lowered her head. Alexis realised there was more to come but sensibly realised that now was not the time.

"Thank you Maisie, you've been a huge help. If you think of anything you'd like to tell me, tell Mrs Davenport first and she can give me a ring. Is that OK?"

Maisie nodded dumbly, lost for words and tears overwhelming her eyes once more. Alexis stood up and thanked the two houseparents. Charles Davenport took Maisie back to class, deciding that the mental activity of a Maths lesson would be the best thing to take her mind off Felicity, then returned to the house. Leaving Hannah to get further statements from the two houseparents, Alexis went outside in search of Dax.

A small forensic team had arrived just to make sure there wasn't anything further to be found in the girls' room. Dax told them about the packet then left them to it, for once unsettled by the impersonal nature of their task. He realised that if Felicity had used the spray in her room, and not left it until she'd reached the hills, the scene could have been very different. It was one small silver lining in a very dark cloud. Although he hadn't seen Felicity in death, the photos had brought it home to him. He thought of the child's lifeless body and knew that Hamish would find this one difficult; Dax knew he had a daughter roughly the same age. To Dax, Felicity had been a child, a warm blooded living person who had perhaps needed his help, but which he had failed to give. He came down the ornate staircase and went outside, anxious to get away from the room, needful of clean, spring fresh air. He was soon joined by Alexis who filled him in on the interview, albeit brief, she had just had with Maisie.
"Phew! Good old Miss Preece. Saved Maisie from having witnessed Felicity's death."
"I'm glad about that," replied Alexis with feeling. "If it is that bloody phenol, which I highly suspect it is, Maisie could have been physically affected by it if she'd tried to help her friend. A narrow escape."
"One small consolation amongst this bloody mess, I s'pose." replied Dax, angrily. "It wouldn't have been pleasant. I wonder if it's got anything to do with her crying the other day."
"Maybe, maybe not," replied Alexis. "I think Maisie has more to say, but we shall see."

Alexis looked at Dax's face and saw the stress lines gathering around his eyes.

"You're not still taking this personally, I hope, Archie?"

"Oh, I dunno. Maybe I could have done something if I'd stayed and listened."

"From what you've told me, she ran away before you had a chance."

"Yes, but I could have still done something. I should've done something."

"For God sake, Archie, stop beating yourself up about this. I don't think anything you could have said yesterday would have saved the girl today. You couldn't have stopped a parcel being sent, you couldn't have been with her when she opened it, you couldn't have stopped her using it."

"Yeah, I s'pose your right," finished Dax, although far from convinced by Alexis' argument.

Alexis paused, thinking, then made up her mind.

"I want a room set aside for us in this God forsaken place," she said to Dax. "We'll have all the staff in one by one, and retake their statements. Everyone! Leave no one out. Get the crew in, all of them. This is going to get nasty unless we sort it out quickly. I really hope we haven't got a serial killer and I hope I'm not jumping to conclusions. On face value this could be a simple tragic accident, an asthma attack that she couldn't cope with maybe – we don't know it was phenol yet, but with the domestic's death the day before yesterday, I can't afford to make assumptions. I don't like coincidences."

After a little difficulty from the headmaster, who objected to the police taking over his school, a small room was eventually found for the officers to start making their enquiries. Alexis was anxious to see Sarah again, to see if she could shed any light on the mysterious parcel that Felicity had received the previous morning, so leaving Dax in charge of the statement taking, she headed for Sarah's office and knocked gently on the door. Hearing nothing, she opened the door and poked her head around it. Sarah was busy audio typing, small headphones clinging to her ears. Alexis tapped the open door again and this time the gentle noise permeated the headphones.

"Hi Sarah, can I come in?"

"Of course," said Sarah jumping up from her seat, the headphones falling from her head onto the desk. "Sorry, had my head in one of his nibs' letters. He does go on a bit."

"Sorry to intrude but I've got just a couple of questions, if that's OK," went on Alexis.

"No problem."

Sarah turned her chair to face Alexis who had sat down in a chair by the fireplace. It wasn't a normal office. It looked fully equipped with modern technology, a functional desk in place as Sarah's work station, but this seemed at odds with the room itself. At one time, it had been a reception room in the old house, now converted into the school, and an ornate Victorian tiled fireplace glowed against the starkness of a white emulsioned wall, giving the room colour and vibrancy. Large pine cupboards, set into the alcoves either side of the fireplace, and probably once used to store precious ornaments or tableware, now housed stationery and printing inks. Sarah seemed at home in her office and Alexis noticed the feminine touches that she had introduced; a plant here, a picture there. This reminded Alexis that she still had work to do in her new domain back at the police station, not the least of which was a decent coat of paint.

Sarah looked unhappy, upset by the news of Felicity's death.

"Was it my fault?" she asked miserably.

"Was what your fault," replied Alexis, puzzlement flitting across her eyes.

"Felicity's death."

"How could Felicity's death be your fault, unless there's something you haven't told me?"

"I sent the parcel over."

"Blimey, news travels fast. How did you get to hear about that?"

183

"One of Felicity's friends came into the office a short while ago and said Felicity had been sent a parcel and something in it had killed her. I do the post, therefore, mea culpa, my fault."

"Hey, hang on, slow down," said Alexis, anxious to stop the proliferation of breast beating that seemed to be alive and well that day. "Felicity did get a parcel, and that is what I wanted to ask you about. You couldn't have known what was in it, unless you sent it yourself."

Sarah jumped, angry at the implication.

"Of course I didn't."

"Well, stop feeling sorry for yourself and give me the facts."

Sarah blinked, her cheeks reddening with momentary irritation at Alexis' sharp words and verbal slap. Then she relaxed, realising that she had merely been trying to release her from her self-imposed guilt.

"Sorry," she responded simply.

"Right, let's have the facts. Who is responsible for the incoming post?"

"I am. It comes in a large grey Royal Mail sack, and I simply divide it in my office into various boxes, one for the headmaster for me to sort later, one for Gerald and one for the room where everyone has their pigeon holes."

"Who has a pigeon hole in that room?"

"Each member of staff has their own slot, there's one each for the two boarding houses, one for the boys and one for the girls. That's collected by the houseparents and dished out in their own house. Miss Jarvis has one and I put her mail in that plus anything for any of her domestic staff. There's a hole for the caretaker and his staff as well. I think that's about it."

"Do you remember specifically finding something for Felicity?"

"What did it look like," asked Sarah. "That might give me a better idea. I don't take a lot of notice of envelopes, other than the addressee, but I think I'd remember a parcel."

"It was a white padded envelope, about twenty by thirty centimetres. It was addressed to Miss F Smith, and the address was written in full. There was no stamp."

Sarah sat back and thought for a few seconds.

"I don't think there were any packets like that yesterday. I remember one parcel, quite big and heavy, and there were several large A4 envelopes; they were mainly for Gerald. We sometimes get unstamped mail, the Post Office can't be bothered to ask for the postage, but I honestly can't remember anything like that. I have a habit of looking at stamps; I collect them for charity, so I think I would've noticed something unstamped. I don't think I'm being a lot of help, am I?" she finished apologetically.

"You're doing fine," replied Alexis, encouragingly. "You see where this is leading me, don't you?"

"Well, if it didn't come in the post, then it must have been put in the house itself, or in the boarding house pigeon hole by someone personally."

"Spot on!"

"Perhaps it's got fingerprints on it." Sarah exclaimed with excitement.

"Hang on, that's my job," laughed Alexis. "I had thought of that."

Sarah grinned. Thanking her for her information, Alexis left Sarah to her work and returned to where Dax was conducting the interviews. She entered the room and sat down next to her detective sergeant as he spoke to Mrs Harper. Alexis looked at the lady dispassionately and allowed herself to wonder about her. She appeared dazed, slightly incoherent and dithery. Her appearance seemed little changed from when she had first set eyes on her, at a distance, on the day that Mavis had been killed. She wore a different but equally shapeless dress and her shoes were unpolished and in need of new heels. Her hair, so obviously dyed, had been treated to a new rinse and now sported a bright henna colour, which hadn't mixed well with the original black. She was a stereotype, one that Alexis had met before, a downtrodden wife, permanently in the shadow of her husband and never raising her head above the parapet. Having come up against the forceful nature of Graham Harper, Alexis actually felt sorry for her. She thought of her own situation, a woman in a male world. Superintendent Barnes came to mind; there again a small man in a big position but seemingly completely unable to deal with the women in his life. He was old school; women should know their place, back behind the broom or at the kitchen sink. At that moment, Alexis could see trouble ahead with the man. She was sure of her position and confident in it and definitely no shrinking violet, unlike the poor woman sitting in front of her. Her attention returned to Barbara Harper, who sat quietly, head down, her hands clasped in her lap. There didn't seem to be any signs of irritation or concern; just a quiet acceptance of her lot.

Dax went over Mrs Harper's previous statement, but her recollections brought nothing new to the story of lunch with the Bishop, saying only that she had gone straight home after everyone had left the Dining Room, being only too glad to get away. She rarely came up to the school, preferring to stay in her own domain, relatively happy and comfortable. She had few interests; she loved her garden and her knitting. She had no friends in the school, having been discouraged from mixing by her husband, and apart from a weekly shop, very rarely left the house. She had not known any of the victims personally, never coming into contact independently with either staff or children. She did not participate in anything connected with the school, apart from formal lunches, Speech Days and Prize Giving. As the interview drew to a close, Barbara escaped thankfully and was last seen almost running back down the driveway, like an animal released from captivity, back to the headmaster's house. Alexis stood up and walked across to the large window of the room. She watched Barbara's retreating back, thinking how much she merged into the surroundings, Apart from her grossly coloured hair, and a little too much red lipstick, there was nothing particular to mark her out. She promptly dismissed the headmaster's wife from her thoughts.

186

Next on the list was the Chaplain, Dr Ernest Cannerby. He was an elderly gentleman, probably in his seventies, with a round benign face which smiled easily and Alexis could see how the children would feel comfortable with him. Cannerby confirmed that he knew of Mavis and Felicity. Felicity had been part of his Confirmation class that year, along with three boys. He had spoken clearly and directly, a shrewd man but without any guile.

"Do you ever go into the girls' boarding house?" asked Alexis.

"Occasionally, but never without one of the Davenports."

"Why's that?"

"I am in a special position of trust in my job. I have a purely pastoral role. Children say many things to me that they would never say to another member of staff and I respect their confidences. I am also very aware that a male member of staff talking to girls in such a situation is fraught with difficulties and I am very careful to avoid any situation that could compromise this. If I do have to see a girl on their own, then I will always ask Mrs Davenport to accompany me. She is like a mother to the girls and they trust her implicitly and have no fear talking to me in front of her."

"How do you go about your confirmation classes, then?" asked Alexis.

"There I have safety in numbers, particularly if the genders are mixed."

Cannerby went on to explain the format of his classes. However, other than these and official chapel duties, he had very little input into daily school life. He had his own accommodation in the school and when alone, enjoyed music and reading the classics. He was currently engaged in his own translation of Virgil's Aeneid and was enjoying the challenge. Alexis enjoyed talking to the chaplain, her own interests in music and the classics a source of companionable chat. Reluctantly, the detective inspector drew the interview, or rather a very pleasant conversation, to a close, dismissed Dr Cannerby, and started to collate the statements she had taken.

Dax, who had left Alexis to it, had been busy in the staff room rounding up statements that hadn't been done on the day of Mavis' death. He returned and poked his head round the door just has Alexis stood up to don her jacket. The room had got stuffy, and the lack of oxygen was making her feel light headed. The sudden draught of air through the open door was most welcome.

"Have we got everyone now?" she asked as Dax came into the room.

"Yes. Each member of staff has now been re-interviewed. We've spoken to all those missing from the initial round up, now back from their various trips, and taken their statements. No one's noticed anything out of the ordinary and no one's seen any strangers wandering round the school grounds."

The two officers got up to leave the office and after closing and locking the door behind them, Alexis pocketed the key. They both went outside for some much needed fresh air after the stuffy room and Dax breathed in deeply.

"I don't like this place," he said casually to his boss. "It gives me the creeps. Don't know what it is about it, but I just feel uncomfortable."

"Oh, it's just your inferiority complex," replied Alexis with a grin. "Us state school plebs must know our place."

"Cheers," said Dax ruefully. "That makes me feel heaps better."

They laughed and walked purposefully across the quad towards the car, which was parked outside the imposing frontage of the school's main building.

Chapter Ten

Next morning, Alexis found both Alan Rees' and Felicity's post mortem reports on her desk. Felicity's was very revealing. She read through them, her brow darkening with anger as she read through each meticulous sentence. Hamish had been thorough, nothing left untouched, and Alexis perused each page carefully. The girl had suffered a broken neck and the top of her skull had been broken in two places, indicating that she had fallen head first. However, she had been dead before she hit the ground. Felicity's death had indeed been caused by the ingestion of phenol, but not by swallowing. Hamish deduced that the girl, an asthma sufferer, had received a vaporiser scent bottle filled with a phenol solution, laced with lavender to disguise the smell. Out on the hills, Felicity had used the spray and inhaled a large volume of atomised solution. Her lungs, weakened by the asthma, had reacted strongly to the caustic spray and her tubes had immediately gone into spasm, causing anaphylactic shock, thereby suffocating her. Alexis sat back, picturing the scene. Felicity had left the security of her tent, intending to greet the dawn. If she had been unhappy, then the solace of a peaceful sunrise, miles from anywhere, might have been a welcome balm to the child. Combined with what she thought of as a gift, Felicity would have been happy. That was some small compensation, perhaps, Alexis surmised. There had been no asthmatic's inhaler found at the scene, Dax having found presumably the only one in her bedside drawer, so if she had needed it, Felicity would have been without. Maybe she didn't even have the chance to use an inhaler. Alexis frowned as she read on. This was not all. The report went on, outlining the horrible fact that the girl had been four months pregnant. Alexis linked this in her brain to what the girl had said to Dax in the playground. Alexis just could not bring herself to believe that Felicity had voluntarily offered herself for sex. Thirteen was still young, even by today's standards, so this left only one conclusion; sex had been forced on her. The child had been raped. Dax's words rung in her brain – 'he hurt me', she had said. Alexis read on. Hamish's conclusion was brief. Death was caused by suffocation, brought on by severe irritation of her asthmatic lungs by the phenol. This would have been almost instantaneous and she probably fell as a result of her death throes, unfortunately finding the missing mine entrance in the process. As regards her pregnancy, he had simply said that she was four months pregnant. She may not necessarily have known that she was pregnant, as a girl's periods at that age were notoriously intermittent but Alexis felt instinctively that Felicity had known about her pregnancy, a girl just knows. She'd would probably have been aware of changes in her body, maybe even the onset of morning sickness, the odd dizzy spell, the swelling of her immature breasts. Alexis felt sick for her. Andrew Danvers was engaged in something illicit with a Sixth Form girl. Did his predilections extend to thirteen year old girls as well?

She turned her attention to the caretaker's PM report. Although he had sustained a vicious blow to the head, he had actually drowned in the pool. Hamish surmised that the unfortunate man wouldn't have survived the head injury; it had been deep and brain tissue had been exposed, but he was actually still alive when he had hit the water, just. He had taken one breath, before his brain gave up the ghost, but that one breath had been enough to ensure that a drowning death had preceded a brain death by seconds. It was still murder, however he had died. There was nothing to suggest that the perpetrator was the same as in Mavis' death but Alexis just didn't believe in coincidences.

Alexis suddenly felt very tired. She'd hardly had time to catch up with herself since getting back from London, and being thrown straight into a murder enquiry was taking its toll. She longed to throw down the papers and just go for a walk. Deciding to put the report down carefully, rather than throwing the file to the floor, Alexis stood up and went across to the window. The sunshine was strong and the river in the distance sparkled as the light played on the water as it flowed gently over the weir. She stuck her head outside the office and called to Dax.

"Fancy a stroll, I need a break."

Dax looked up in surprise.

"OK, ma'am. Could do with a break myself."

The two officers grabbed their jackets, Dax, a well-worn hooded black waterproof jacket and Alexis a more refined blue padded jacket with a fur lined hood. Although the weather was sunny again after yesterday's heavy rain, a chill breeze had set up, ruffling the blinds in the office, and with it the warmth of the day had lessened, so the warm coats were much needed. Dax and Alexis said nothing as they headed for the outdoors, and walked slowly down the street, instinctively aiming for the river.

"You OK?" asked Dax anxiously as they reached the weir.

"Yes, I'm fine, just tired. I'm sleeping OK but I haven't really had a chance to catch up with myself. The more I read about this case, the more sickened I feel as to how low humans can reach."

Dax nodded gently.

"You run along with this job, and get inured over the years as to what can happen, but every so often, something jumps out and grabs you and brings you up short."

Dax paused as a duck jumped out from the shallows, and tipped its head down into the sparkling shallows near the edge of the river.

"On the other hand, nature can have a way of restoring the balance," as he smiled at the duck's antics. "Has something specific happened to make you feel like this?" went on Dax.

"Yes, in a way, it has," agreed Alexis. "I've just read the PM report on Felicity. It was as we thought; suffocation due to inhalation of the phenol solution, exacerbated by her weakened asthmatic lungs."

"Well, we guessed that," replied Dax, slightly puzzled as to his boss's reaction.

"That wasn't all." Alexis paused, knowing how Dax would react to the unwelcome news. His reaction to Felicity's death and the personal interest he had adopted for himself was uppermost in Alexis' mind and she wasn't sure how to proceed.

"Go on?" said Dax, puzzled by the delay and Alexis' prevarication. There was no point in stalling. Alexis answered swiftly and brutally.

"Felicity was pregnant."

Dax winced.

"So that's what she meant by 'he hurt me'. I should have stopped her and listened. I never thought it could have been such a terrible thing she was suffering. Do you think it was Danvers? The bastard." he finished angrily.

"The thought did cross my mind," Alexis agreed. "Look, Archie, I know you're taking this personally but there was nothing you could have done. She ran off before you got the chance."

"I should have followed."

"Archie, stop! You can help her now by finding out who did this. It may or may not be Danvers, but we need to know to stop whoever it is before they do it to some other poor kid. Hamish is rushing through a DNA test on the foetus; we can then match it with Danvers. If it doesn't match, we will have to look elsewhere. One step at a time."

Dax didn't look convinced, but said nothing, misery clear on his face.

"Let's go through everything we've got. Here's as good a place as any," said Alexis, sweeping her arm round in front of her.

The path had taken them along the river bank and there they found a seat, tucked into a bend in the river and away from the noise of traffic. The air buzzed with tiny insects, a bumble bee making its presence felt on some riverside balsam plants. The ducks, now more in number, as they realised they had human companions who might have food with them, bustled on the banks below them. A streak of grey and white on the opposite bank revealed the presence of a heron.

"Don't see many of those," exclaimed Alexis, as the bird pounced on the river and emerged with a tiny fish held tightly in its long beak. Dax smiled, his shoulders easing from the pressure.

"Right," said Alexis, returning to the business in hand. "We've got a dead domestic, poisoned with phenol; we've got a dead teenage girl, poisoned again with phenol, but in a slightly different manner. We've also got a dead caretaker, bashed over the head with some blunt instrument and rolled into the water to drown. There will be some kids won't want to go swimming there for a while," she added ruefully as an afterthought.

"What is the connection between them all?" asked Dax, who had his own ideas but wanted Alexis to put them into words.

"Try this! Mavis was murdered, probably by someone she was blackmailing. She picked up the cup from somewhere which had the poison in it, the murderer knowing her comings and goings and deliberately leaving it out for her. It's well known that Mavis had a habit of picking up cups wherever she went, even if they were still full. Some sort of OCD, perhaps. This one was still hot, so she drank it, with disastrous consequences, hence murder number one. Murder number two: the caretaker, a sudden and unplanned murder, a murder borne out of necessity, maybe?" Alexis went on. "The only conclusion I can come to here, if they are connected, is that he saw something and tried to capitalise on it, a bit of blackmail. The murderer met up with him to sort it out, or so Rees thought, but bumped him off instead of handing over any demands."

"Seems logical," agreed Dax.

"It's a working hypothesis, which brings us to murder number three. Felicity Smith, killed maybe when she told her abuser she was pregnant."

Alexis paused as two hikers passed them on the path. They nodded to the two seated on the bench and walked on, leaving Dax and Alexis in peace to resume their analysis.

"It's too much of a coincidence that the same substance was used for two unconnected murders, otherwise why would anyone want to kill an innocent thirteen year old girl. This does tend to put Danvers in the frame," replied Dax.

"I think you're right," agreed Alexis, stretching out her legs in front of her, frightening off a duck that had got just a little too curious.

"The only good thing to come out of Felicity's death is that we now know there's a sexual predator on the loose. The bad thing is, we think it might be Danvers but we can't be sure."

"We will," said Dax quietly, but with steely determination in his voice.

Alexis and Dax continued chatting for a while, neither willing to return to the grind. They pushed ideas one way and another, batting them off each other. Whichever way they went, they couldn't deny that Andrew Danvers fitted the image and, so far, the evidence. They were stilled into silence as the soporific effect of running water and buzzing insects took over. Then with a jump, Alexis pulled herself out of her reverie and stood up, frightening the ever growing and demanding group of ducks that had gathered at their feet.

"Go back to that wretched school and bring in Andrew Danvers. Take Mike with you. Danvers has got some questions to answer, and pretty damn quick."

Dax, looking up in surprise at Alexis' sudden anger, said nothing. He stood up and nodded, grabbed his jacket and was off, leaving Alexis staring at the water. After a while she stood and headed for the riverside café, still wishing to prolong her time out of the office as long as possible, a cup of coffee being an added bonus. The café was quiet and gave Alexis the brief respite she needed away from work. The coffee arrived, hot and frothy, and she savoured the flavour and the caffeine but then, facing the inevitable, she at last stood, paid for her drink and went back to work.

She picked up the papers she had earlier discarded and continued reading the pathologist's reports. Her mood lightened slightly as the report did contain some good news; a partial, if miniscule, fingerprint had been found on one of the shards of glass from the broken scent bottle. The fingerprint experts were working on it to see if they could find a match. Alexis sighed and put down Felicity's file and turned to that of the caretaker. This was simple. The man had drowned in the pool, his head injury sufficiently brutal to bring about deep unconsciousness, but not enough to kill outright. There had been some considerable force behind the blow; the wound was deep, a smallish round blunt hole in the front of the skull, possibly caused by a hammer, indicating that the victim had faced his assailant. The man would not have suffered, other than a brief shaft of blinding pain, no longer than a couple of seconds. He would have been unconscious before he hit the ground. His right side was badly bruised, and his right wrist chipped, consistent with a heavy fall on that side. There was no other forensic, the chlorine in the water had seen to that. The casts of the prints in the soft earth had produced a footprint of a heavy shoe or perhaps a wellington boot. Fairly indistinct but something, nonetheless. At that moment, Dax knocked on Alexis' door, and she looked up in surprise. Hadn't she just sent him out to the school to arrest Andrew Danvers? She looked at her watch and was surprised to see that two hours had elapsed since he'd left. Where had the time gone? Alexis beckoned her Detective Sergeant in and Dax perched himself precariously on the corner of the desk.

"Danvers is in the interview room. I've arrested him on suspicion of misappropriating chemicals from the store cupboard. It'll do to start with," said Dax, as he filled Alexis in on the events of the last couple of hours. "He isn't happy, he's acting stroppy, but I got the impression he was expecting it. He hasn't said anything of value yet, though, just had a good moan."

"Let him stew for a bit, take some of that cockiness out of him, hopefully."

Dax then noticed that Alexis had the PM reports in her hands.

"May I?" Dax asked, holding out his hands.

"Be my guest. Not exactly bedtime reading, but interesting all the same."

Dax picked up the file and went out to the main office, and sat at his desk. For a while he brooded over the sequence of events and kept going over them in his mind. Was there anything he could have done? Followed Felicity and got the truth out of her, perhaps? At last, logic told his overworked brain that he couldn't have prevented Felicity getting pregnant but he was going to find the bastard, if it took him for ever. He got up from his desk and went out to the small kitchen to make himself a cup of coffee. On his way back to his desk, he stopped at Hannah Pembridge's desk and apprised her of the situation. She nodded gently.

"Thanks Archie. Let me know if I can help with anything," she responded.

"Will do," Dax replied.

He returned to his desk and read through the rest of Hamish's report, tucking all the information away for another time.

An hour later, Alexis and Dax made their way down to the interview room. Andrew Danvers looked up as the two officers entered, his face drained and pale. He sat cradling an empty coffee cup in his hands; a triangular packet of sandwiches was on the table, clearly untouched. He acknowledged the officers' existence with a blink of his eyes, but said nothing. Placing the empty cup back on the table, he sat still, clasping his hands together. The room was quiet, insulated from the outside by thick walls and reinforced windows. A clock on the wall silently whiled away the minutes. There was no ornamentation in the room, apart from the recording equipment fixed to the table. The atmosphere was oppressive, filled with unspoken thoughts. Dax sat down and readied the recording machine in preparation for the interview. Danvers watched the activity out of the corner of his eye, but studiously avoided any interaction. Alexis quietly closed the door behind her and paused, standing behind Danvers, looking at the man's back and judging how to go about the interview. She guessed, correctly, that this was a new experience for the teacher and sensed that Danvers was very frightened. Alexis realised that if she spoke gently, without stress and keeping her voice low and unemotional, she would probably get more out of him than if she employed a tough cop attitude. She caught Dax's eye and gently waved her hands, palm down behind the man's back. Dax got the drift and nodded gently. Softly softly.

Dax sat up straight and faced Andrew Danvers. He pressed the start button on the machine and began the preliminaries of caution, time and place. Andrew sat silent and stony faced throughout, avoiding eye contact with his interrogator. Alexis at last sat down next to Dax and began the questioning.
"Do you know why you are here, Mr Danvers?" she opened.
"I know what you arrested me for but that's not why I'm here, is it?" replied Danvers frankly.
Dax looked up in surprise.
"Look, I'm not stupid, nor am I guilty of anything."
"Go on," encouraged Alexis, reluctant to stop the flow. If the man wanted to speak, then let him. He would either incriminate himself with his garrulity or if he spoke the truth, then Alexis would know.
"Rita told me there was phenol missing from the store cupboard. She also told me that this had been used to kill that domestic. Mavis, wasn't it?"
"Yes, that's right," agreed Alexis. "Can you explain the missing phenol?"
"No, I can't. Rita is very careful with all chemicals. There is a rigid protocol for dealing with the stuff. It would be more than my job's worth to buck the system, and I do value my job, in case you're asking."
"Who has keys to the cupboard?" asked Dax. "There are two locks I believe."
"Yes, there are and with different keys. I have keys, of course, and Rita. There are spares which the headmaster has. He has a key to everything. He doesn't need them, but he insists on being in control."

"Yes, I got that impression," Alexis agreed. Dax grinned and Danvers caught the look. He smiled briefly, the tiny release of tension and a glimpse of a shared camaraderie lightening the atmosphere.

Alexis changed tack.

"Did you know Mavis well?" he asked.

"No, not really. I, er …" Danvers paused.

"You …? prompted Dax.

"Oh, nothing."

Danvers slumped back in his chair, his hair damp with sweat, his eyes tired and bloodshot with worry and stress. Alexis was losing patience. She didn't have time for this pointless prevarication, so deciding to play her trump card, she pulled out a photo from the folder in front of her, the one that Dax had found in Mavis' home, now enlarged and of better quality, and turning it round to face Danvers, laid it face up flat on the table

"Do you know who it is in this photo?" she asked.

Danvers turned his head away from the clock, which he was mindlessly watching as the second hand ticked its way inexorably round. He picked up the photo and stared at it, the blood suddenly draining from his face as recognition set in. The sudden pallor highlighted the lines of stress around his face. Even in his distress and realising that identification would probably prove to be impossible, he nevertheless knew he couldn't fool the Detective Inspector. They were two intelligent people facing each other and Danvers was not on the winning side. He seemed to reach a decision, his body language acquiring a strength that hadn't been there before. He put the photo back down on the table and faced his inquisitors. With a renewed strength he cleared his throat and spoke.

"Not a lot of point denying anything is there?" he began.

"No, not really" replied Alexis gently. "Trust me, the truth is always the best and the most believable."

"The photo is of me and a girl. I'd rather keep her name out of it, if I can. It's the one that Mavis has been blackmailing me with. She showed me a copy."

This sudden, rather bleak, statement surprised Alexis. She hadn't expected it to be that easy.

"Go on," she encouraged.

If there were gaps in this testimony, she could ask questions later but for now she was content to let the man talk. Danvers took a deep breath. He had opened the flood gates. There was no stopping now.

"Mavis started at the school just over two years ago. She was a meddler and a bit of a peeping tom. She would pop up in all sorts of places, creep up on you when you thought you were alone. One evening, just under two years ago – it was about 10 o clock in the evening, when all good domestics should have been tucked up in bed, I was engaged in, shall we say, a little light exercise down by the stream at the school. It was a lovely evening, the sun was just setting and it was still light, and the air was warm."

Danvers stopped and smiled at the memory.

"Mavis crept up on us. I think she'd been watching us for a while. Before I knew it she'd snapped us with her mobile. I couldn't do anything, I was somewhat 'in flagrante delicto'; my trousers were down round my ankles."

Dax stifled a grin and Danvers stopped and reddened, embarrassed by his revelations. It all appeared so salacious and grimy now that he was talking about it. It had seemed so innocent and lovely at the time. For the first time, he realised that there would be consequences for his actions.

"This means my job, doesn't it?" he went on.

"That depends on the school, or the headmaster, I would think. Not my decision, fortunately," agreed Alexis, although not without a little sympathy. It took two to tango, and the girl must share the blame, but Danvers was the one who should have had the control, being in a position of responsibility. The chemistry teacher went on.

"It wasn't long after that the bloody woman started blackmailing me, when the autumn term started, if I remember correctly. She didn't want a lot, but £50 a month was still a fair bit. I was so pleased when she was killed."

"Did you kill Mavis Greene?" asked Alexis brutally.

"No, I did not but I'll buy the one who did a pint. They did me a huge favour," he went on viciously.

Alexis tried a different tack. There had been two more bodies.

"Is Miss Grant the only girl you've had sex with?"

Andrew flinched.

"How did you know it was Lizzie?"

"It's common knowledge in the staff room, I'm afraid," grinned Dax. "You were being blackmailed for nothing. A school is a very small place, particularly a boarding school. Everyone knows everyone and everything. I suspect Mr Harper was unaware, lucky for you, otherwise you'd have been sacked long ago."

"Oh shit," groaned Andrew. "I've been a bloody fool."

"I'll repeat my question," went on Alexis. "Is Miss Grant the only girl you've had sex with?"

"Yes," replied Andrew, wearily, all fight gone. He slumped in his chair.

"Are you sure?" Dax joined in.

"Well, I think I'd know," replied Andrew with spirit.

"You haven't been playing with little girls, by any chance?" asked Dax.

Andrew jumped up from his seat, pushing back the table as he stood.

"Of course, I bloody haven't. What sort of man do you think I am?" he responded angrily.

"Sit down, Mr Danvers. From what I've seen so far," Alexis responded mercilessly, "you have shown yourself the sort of man who shirks his responsibilities and engages in an affair with a girl in his care, albeit one of age. We are merely exploring the possibilities that you have shared yourself around."

"Well, I haven't. I don't know what you are suggesting."

"You are aware that a thirteen year old girl died yesterday, also from phenol poisoning. She was pregnant."

Andrew blanched.

"Oh God, that wasn't me. I knew Felicity. She was a bright little thing. I would never do anything like that. I'm a normal, rather hot blooded heterosexual, not a pervert that delights in little girls. I'll admit to sexual relations with Lizzie, and I was being blackmailed by Mavis but I have never killed anyone nor got anyone pregnant."

Andrew sat suddenly, his anger spent. Laying his head down on his hands, he broke down completely and sobbed quietly into his shirt sleeves.

"We'll leave it there for now," said Alexis quietly. "You'll be taken down to a cell and held in custody until we can get things checked out."

"Interview concluded ..." Dax looked at his watch. "Time, 4.15pm." He clicked the switch and the recording machine stopped.

A uniformed officer took Danvers down to the cells and Alexis and Dax left the room.

"Do you believe him?" asked Dax, as they sat together back in Alexis' office.

"Yes, I do. He's been bloody stupid and he knows it but I think that's it. We'll hold him until the various DNA samples are checked, then go from there."

"Righto, ma'am," replied Dax. "I need a coffee. Want one?"

"Yes please," replied Alexis. "That was hard work."

Dax left the office to make the drinks leaving Alexis thinking, her eyes on the distance, nothing in particular. On his return, Dax handed over the mugs and the two of them sat, drinking and chatting about the next step. Alexis looked at her watch.

"Is Maisie a boarder?" she asked suddenly.

"Er, yes, I think she is. Why?" asked Dax.

"There's still time. I want you to take Hannah out to the school and interview Maisie, and her close friends, if they are there. There must be something they know. Girls like that share things."

"Righto, ma'am," replied Dax, glad of the chance to get some fresh air and blow some cobwebs away, albeit ones not clinging to his mouth, even if the task to be undertaken was distasteful. Leaving Alexis in her office, Dax returned to his own desk. He picked up the phone and called Coates Norton School. When the phone was answered, he recognised Frances' sweet tones and grimaced.

"Put me through to Charles Davenport, please," he asked abruptly.

Nothing more was said, no polite response, just a clicking of the phone as the connection was made. Dax had no idea if Davenport would be there at all; did the man teach? But as luck would have it, he had caught the right time and the boarding master was in his room. Dax quickly filled Davenport in on the latest developments and outlined what he wanted. He could almost feel the man's revulsion at the end of the phone when the news of Felicity's pregnancy was revealed. The sharp hiss of an indrawn breath said it all. It had hit him hard.

Half an hour later, Dax and Hannah pulled up outside the main school building. Wishing to distance himself from Frances and her vampish ways, Dax strode out purposefully to the boarding house, without going into Reception, Hannah following in his wake. Charles Davenport, true to his word, had assembled Felicity's two closest friends, both of whom now sat in his office. Angela Davenport stood with the girls, a mother substitute so sorely needed at this time. Each looked miserable and Maisie, in particular, looked tired and drained and her cheeks were wet with tears. Dax motioned to Hannah to start. This, indeed, was going to take some tact and diplomacy and a huge amount of compassion. Dax would normally have wanted to interview the girls individually, but with the subject matter being so intimate, he felt that there would be safety in numbers and as Charles left the office to make way for his wife, Hannah began.

"Now girls, thank you for coming here today. I know it must be very difficult for you to talk to us, but we need to know more about Felicity."

Hannah paused as the girls shifted uncomfortably in their chairs.

"Can you tell me if she had a boyfriend?"

At first, the girls sat silently, looking at each other.

"No, miss," said Emma, a tall, lanky girl with short, bobbed hair. "She didn't like that sort of thing. She was all right, a bit boring, but I liked her."

"Did she ever talk to you about girly things; make up, magazines, babies, you know?" went on Hannah carefully.

"She liked reading our magazines, but she never had any of her own. Her mum wouldn't let her. She..." The girl paused, as if to go on, but then clammed up.

"What were you going to say," asked Hannah, gently.

The girl looked at Maisie, a question in her eye. Maisie nodded, the briefest of movements, but Hannah caught it.

"She started to talk about babies last week, for some reason. She suddenly seemed to be very interested."

"Do you often talk about such things, like sex and contraception?" went on Hannah.

"Sometimes," agreed Emma, reluctantly.

Hannah sat forward, almost conspiratorially.

"I know I used to at school. I never talked about such things with my Mum. She always avoided the subject. I remember asking her once what a love bite was, and she told me I was far too young to know about such things. I was fourteen."

Recognising a sort of kindred spirit, Emma went on.

"Felicity never talked about these things, well not until recently. I think she was worried about something, but she didn't let on, well not to me, anyway."

Hannah looked at Maisie, who turned away. Dax stood at the back of the room and watched. He was excellent at reading body language and the turn of the conversation had definitely made Maisie uncomfortable, and not through embarrassment. There was something extra. Hannah turned and looked at Dax, a question in her eyes. He nodded imperceptibly.

"Did you know that Felicity was pregnant," asked Hannah, clearly and unambiguously to both girls.

Emma gasped, obviously shocked. The information was news to her. Maisie, however, wriggled in her seat and looked down at her feet, a brief suggestion of a guilty knowledge. She knew all right, thought Dax.

"It's very important," went on Hannah. "Did she have a boyfriend after all?"

"No, miss, she didn't," said Maisie as she became animated. "I knew Fliss was worried, she dropped hints but didn't say much. We were only talking about it the other day..." Maisie faltered as she remembered what had happened.

"Do you know who the father could be?" asked Hannah, feeling that she was almost there.

"He's old and dirty," Maisie exclaimed without thinking, then realising she had said more than she had intended, promptly clammed up. Emma opened her mouth as if to speak, but she, too, decided to say nothing. The response was disappointing. The atmosphere was thick with emotion. Hannah waited. Dax shifted his position against the wall and Maisie looked up.

"You must tell the officers, girls, if you know anything. You're not in any trouble." Angela Davenport put her arm round Maisie's shoulders and the girl slumped, her unspent tears welling up in her eyes and coursing down her cheeks. She sobbed and her body shook with the effort.

"I can't," Maisie screamed. "He told me not to." Maisie jumped up and ran out of the room, and rushed upstairs. Hannah and Dax heard the door slam on her bedroom.

"Leave her to me," said Angela sadly. "Let her be for now."

Hannah turned to Emma.

"Do you have any idea who it could be? It's very important we find out before it happens again."

Emma looked numb. She just shook her head. Hannah and Dax sighed. Both felt that Emma knew little, but Maisie definitely knew something, but at the moment she was keeping it to herself. She looked frightened. Maisie's violent outburst of 'he told me not to' made the two officers think that the rapist had threatened her, meaning that Felicity wasn't his only victim. This was worrying, to say the least and Dax, believing his gut instinct, knew they were verging on paedophilia. It was a fearful prospect, but for now they had drawn a blank. Hopefully, the DNA test on the foetus might shed some light. Dax and Hannah thanked Emma and Angela Davenport, and left the girl with her boarding mistress. After making their farewells to Charles Davenport, who had been hovering on the doorstep and heard everything through the door, the two officers asked that the news of Felicity's pregnancy could be kept away from others. He agreed with a silent nod and both officers left the boarding house and drew breath outside, taking in refreshing gulps of the gently warm spring breezes of a late afternoon. Dax noticed that Alexis had arrived, seeing her car parked outside the main building. She was just getting out of the car so Dax and Hannah walked across to meet her.

"How'd it go?" asked Alexis, hopefully.

"We spoke to two of Felicity's closest friends. I don't think Emma knows anything useful, other than a bit of gossip but Maisie is frightened. She knows something. I think this is more than a single rape. I've got a horrible feeling it is someone preying on these girls," replied Dax, with anger in his voice. "We've left them with their housemistress. She's going to have a chat with them and see if she can loosen their tongues."

"One thing did slip out," went on Hannah Pembridge. "Maisie did say that whoever it was, was 'old and dirty'. That lets out Andrew Danvers, he's only in his early thirties."

Alexis grinned.

"I appreciate your kind thoughts, thinking that someone in their early thirties is young, but to a thirteen year old girl, anyone over twenty five is ancient, so I don't think we can rely too much on that statement."

Hannah smiled ruefully.

"I suppose you're right. I'd forgotten what it was like to be a young teenager."

"Never mind," replied Alexis. "We've still got the chance of DNA from the foetus. If we get a name, then we can go back and talk to the girls. Once they know we know, they might open up."

Alexis stood for a moment, looking round her, taking in the view. It all seemed so idyllic. There were sheep grazing on fields in the distance; children's voices could be heard around the corner, as day pupils left and boarders headed for their houses. The school building glowed in the soft sunlight, and the weather cock glinted in the sun's rays. The place should be a haven of peace and security for the children. Instead it was turning into a den of iniquity as each question brought about another, and things crawled out from under the stones as each was overturned by the detectives, releasing their dirty secrets. Alexis shuddered. A kestrel hovered above them, its wide wings gently waving in the breeze. Waiting for a kill, Alexis idly thought. We've had plenty of those round here.

"What made you come out here, ma'am?" asked Dax. "I wasn't expecting you."

"I want a word with the headmaster," went on Alexis, at length. "Archie, you come with me, and Hannah, if you could go back to the nick, and see if they've come up with anything else whilst we've been out. Let me know if anything crops up, would you?" she finished.

"Right-o, ma'am, will do."

Hannah took the car keys from Dax and returned to the car. As the car's brake lights flashed as Hannah negotiated the deep gravelled driveway, Alexis and Dax turned and headed for the main front door.

"Don't mention anything about pregnant pupils yet, Archie," said Alexis.

"I asked the Davenports to keep it to themselves for a while," replied Dax.

"Good. I just want to let the headmaster know that we will be asking for DNA samples, ostensibly in connection with Alan Rees's murder. I don't want to let the cat out of the bag just yet, it'll put the perpetrator on guard, but the sooner we catch this feller, then the safer these kids will be."

"OK, ma'am. I'll keep schtum," agreed Dax.

Alexis and Dax walked across the quad, their feet crunching noisily in the gravel as they reached the front door. The late afternoon sunshine suddenly disappeared behind a cloud, and the air cooled rapidly. Alexis looked out towards the west and saw a large bank of dark cloud heading their way. It promised rain, a repeat of yesterday, and she shivered as the gathering menace, mixing with her feelings about this case, left her feeling despondent and angry. She didn't have children of her own, but had frequently enjoyed the company of her sister's twin daughters. They were lovely children and Alexis was very fond of her two little nieces. She could never imagine anything so dreadful happening to them, so why should it happen to someone else's little girl. She stamped her foot angrily on the step at the injustices of life, a small piece of gravel loosening itself from the tread of her shoe. Dax watched and knew what was going through his boss's mind. He felt just the same.

Alexis still felt angry as she reached the headmaster's office. She was in no mood for the man but he had to be faced. His lack of compassion sickened Alexis and his outright arrogance annoyed her. Frances had not been at her desk when the officers had entered the building, so they had gone straight to Sarah Dixon's office. She voiced a gentle 'come in;' as Alexis knocked on her door, and the two officers found her surrounded by a sea of envelopes as she battled with Speech Day invitations.

"You're working late," remarked Dax sympathetically.

"Speech Day is next week and these are the replies to the invitations. I should have had them sorted by now, Brenda needs numbers, but with all the upsets going on, things have got behind.

If you'll forgive me, I must get on. Unless there is something I can do for you," she added as an afterthought.

"No, we just want to see the headmaster. Is he in?" asked Alexis.

"Yes, I think so. Let me just see," replied Sarah.

She got up from her desk and went across to the internal door which joined the two offices. She knocked gently, and getting no reply, tentatively opened the door to see if Graham was there. He was but not as he would have liked to be found. The door opened suddenly, pushed wider by Dax. Brushing by Sarah, who stood there in shock, the two officers walked into the room and found Graham arm in arm with Frances on the sofa, intimately caressing her. His thick fingers probed the innermost depths of her underwear as she laid back, her legs open. Her blouse was unbuttoned to the waist and her hair was awry as Graham, oblivious to the interruption continued his intimate explorations. Alexis and Dax stared at the scene in utter disbelief. They knew that something had been going on between the two, staff room gossip was usually a good source of the truth, but to be so blatant about it. Alexis coughed discretely and Graham looked up at the sound. Rapidly pulling himself apart from Frances, he stood up hurriedly and brushed himself down, straightening his wayward hair.

"Don't you believe in knocking before you enter a room," snorted Graham angrily.

"We did!" Dax replied uncompromisingly.

"You should have waited for a reply," went on Graham, embarrassment replacing his anger.

"Unfortunately, we don't have time to wait. You do realise that there are three murder investigations going on in this school. I would have thought your priority would have been to assist us in every way, rather than spend your time on peripherals," Alexis retorted, her eye roving over the dishevelled Frances. Frances picked herself up, buttoned up her blouse and walked out of the room with as much dignity as she could muster, which wasn't much under the circumstances. Unseen, Sarah hovered in the background, heard the conversation, and smiled. This was definitely one for the staff room.

"Mr Harper," went on Alexis, uncompromisingly. "We will be arranging a DNA test for all your staff, male and female. We have found some evidence connected with the murder of Alan Rees and wish to corroborate this. This will be a voluntary DNA test but we hope that everyone will co-operate. We will set up tomorrow afternoon. Officers will be here from Teigneford police station at two o clock."

Graham sat at his desk, his red vein-streaked cheeks slowly returning to a more normal grey colour. He shifted uncomfortably on his swivel chair.

"I hardly think this is necessary. Surely you cannot think that one of my staff is responsible for this," he asked indignantly.

"You are aware that we have Andrew Danvers in custody. He is helping us with our enquiries on a separate matter, so yes I do think that one of your staff could be responsible. At the moment, the tests are only for elimination purposes," went on Alexis, silently enjoying the headmaster's discomfiture. "It's standard procedure."

Graham slumped in his chair, knocking several papers from his unruly desk in the process.

"Do I have a choice?" asked the headmaster, rudely.

"Yes, you can say no, but that wouldn't look too good on the crime report, would it?" responded Dax with asperity.

Graham stiffened in his seat, ready to reply angrily. Then he slumped, realising that he was cornered.

"As you wish," he replied dismissively.

"My officers will set up in the staff room, less obtrusive there. As a matter of courtesy, we'll take your sample in this office. Shall we say three o clock tomorrow afternoon for you?" asked Alexis.

The headmaster said nothing. He waved his hand dismissively, swivelled in his chair, turning his back on the officers, and stared out of the window. Alexis smiled. She cocked her head at Dax, indicating that they should leave, and the two officers left by the way they had come, cheerily greeting Sarah as they left. She replied with an apologetic smile, an acknowledgement of the shared embarrassing circumstances in which they had all found themselves. Alexis and Dax walked across the quad, now rapidly filling with children on their way to tea. The smells of cooked food wafted around the playground, and Dax sniffed appreciatively.

"I never thought I'd see the day when I felt hungry for school food. My school days seemed to be filled with limp, tasteless cabbage and lumpy custard," he said.

"Not on the same plate, I hope," grinned Alexis.

"This stuff smells good. Do you think Brenda could find us some tea?"

"Not a good idea, Archie, Not at the moment."

"S'pose you're right," Dax agreed sadly.

Dax and Alexis returned to their car and as they drove the few miles back to town, Dax filled her in more fully on their conversation with Maisie and Emma.

Back at the station, Alexis sat in her office, feeling frustrated. Things were piling up but she felt they were getting nowhere. She looked at the clock, now nearing six o clock, and everyone was still at their desks. Just time for a team briefing, or as Alexis preferred to call it, a general chit chat. She never knew what might crawl out of the woodwork, some small thing that might have been missed. It was worth a go. Better than sitting on her backside moaning about a lack of progress. Jumping up from her seat, she threw open her office door and walked into the outer office, startling everyone as she did so. Then she stopped on the threshold, realising that her need for action was not fair at this late stage of the day.

"Right team, I was going to ask for a meeting but it's getting late and we're all tired. It's been a long day. But, if you don't mind, I'd like you all here bright and early tomorrow morning so we can go through things for the day. If we aim for eight tomorrow morning; would that be OK with you all?"

Everyone nodded, looking at each other. Their new boss was so different from their previous one. She actually cared. A general murmur went round the office.

"No problem, ma'am."

"That's fine."

"Sounds good."

"Right, eight tomorrow morning it is. Just a quick catch up before the morning gets going. Pool our thoughts; see where we're at; see if anyone has any bright ideas. Thanks everyone. See you tomorrow."

With that, chairs scraped and computers were switched off. The general buzz of a busy office ceased. Soon Alexis and Dax were left on their own.

"That means you, too, Archie. Go home to Claire," she said. "There's nothing more we can do tonight. I'm going to take the file home and read it in peace and quiet."

"Righto, Lexi," said Dax, slipping into an easy familiarity as they were on their own. "I won't argue. It's been one of those days."

"See you tomorrow, Archie. Bright and early!"

Dax grabbed his jacket and as the door closed behind him, Alexis listened to his receding footsteps as he went along the corridor towards the stairs. Now on her own, she returned to her office and sat down, exhausted by the day and the fact that she still hadn't really had a chance to rest after her rapid return to Teigneford. As she sat, quietly mulling over the day, a thought crossed her mind. She needed to re-read those statements. A bell had rung in her brain, her sub-conscious had made a connection and it was beginning to communicate itself with her consciousness. She needed time to think. It was late; the office was now empty, she needed to go home, relax, take her own time to go over things. Standing up rapidly, a decision made, she turned off the light over her desk and headed for her car. The working day was over.

Chapter Eleven

As Alexis switched on the ignition, the radio sprang into life and the strains of a Bach cello sonata filled the car. She visibly relaxed as the ordered, almost mathematical, tones of the music surrounded her. She pulled out of the car park and turned towards the town. She stopped off briefly at the local supermarket to stock up on provisions - she'd hardly had time to even buy a pint of milk since she'd been back – but soon she was on her way home. The busy roads of Teigneford soon gave way to the quieter lanes which led to her home, the street lights giving way to a blessed dark. The road took her through the forest, a dark, forbidding place at night but a great place for walks in the day. Alexis had missed these simple pleasures in London, her well-worn and comfortable walking boots languishing in a corner of her cupboard at home, and resolved to take a short break once this case was completed, and recharge her batteries. She lived only a few miles from Teigneford, and the drive home was soon accomplished. Her little stone cottage was old and beamed and stood apart from its neighbours a little, separated on one side by a tall privet hedge and on the other by an ancient stone wall. A small stream ran along the bottom of her garden and separated her from farmland and the lower slopes of the hills and forest through which she had just driven. This was her haven, a safe refuge from work, a place where she could relax and be herself. Although she'd been on secondment in London for several months, she'd kept her house on. Her mother had popped in now and then to collect post and generally keep an eye on the house and Alexis had arranged for a cleaner to come in once a week to keep the dust at bay, but now the house needed a good tidy and a lot of fresh air, and some considerable tender loving care, but time enough for that when this murder investigation had been sorted and she could actually draw breath. She drove onto the driveway, the gravel crunching under the tyres, and turned off the ignition, not bothering to put the car away in the little barn which doubled as a garage. As she got out of the car, an owl hooted, startling her with its sudden noise. The swish of wings made her look up as the owl lifted off from the barn roof, its pale feathers caught in the automatic light which had come on at the front door. Alexis breathed in the still, cold air of the night and watched as the bird disappeared over the tree tops and, as the porch light went out, the evening star twinkled down on her from the moonless inky blackness of the night's sky. The moon was yet to rise and the darkness of the scene comforted her and as she fished for the key in her pocket, she felt, for the first time that resolution had edged a step closer.

Later that evening, feeling satisfyingly full after a meal of steak and chips, and clutching a glass of a good red wine, Alexis retreated to her study. She put a Brahms CD into the player and settled herself at her desk. There she sat, reading over and over again the statements that had been taken from the school staff. They were complete; she had statements from everybody in the school, apart from the unfortunate caretaker, who hadn't lived long enough to make one. If he hadn't succumbed to the lure of blackmail and had lived, mused Alexis, the identity of the murderer might have been made obvious, but life was never that simple. There had to be something in these statements that would give her the clue she so sorely needed. Mavis, she was sure, had been murdered, but unintentionally. The phenol had been destined for someone else; who, she couldn't quite get to grips with just yet and the murderer had tried again. Had the intended victim been Felicity all along? Had her rapist found out she was pregnant and wanted to eliminate the danger to himself. If so, why the coffee cup? Felicity wouldn't have had access to a staff cup in the normal course of events so there wouldn't have been any point in trying to eliminate her by that method. Alexis was pretty sure that Alan Rees' murder had come about because of his greed. The man had seen something, tried a bit of petty blackmail and suffered the inevitable consequences. Alexis was convinced that there was one person responsible for all three murders; to have three separate murderers in a small rural school would have stretched the bounds of credulity and coincidence. There must be a common denominator. As she read, the lamp on her desk casting a warm glow over the papers, she felt her head nodding and her eyelids becoming heavy with tiredness. The Brahms and the wine had had the desired effect, relaxing her stressed muscles, but it was putting her beyond any profitable thought. It had been useful to reread the statements, but her brain was now too tired to take anything in. She knew the clue was there; she just couldn't find it. At last, with a sigh and giving in for her need for bed, Alexis collected the papers, locked them in her study safe, and climbed the stairs for a quick shower and, hopefully, a good night's sleep.

The following morning, Alexis beat her team into the office by a good hour. As the sun streamed in through the office windows and the room was filled with that strange crystal clarity of the early sunshine, shadows were sharp and not yet muted by the turn of the day. She sighed gently. If only everything was as clear. Her brain still refused to let go of that nagging thought; it was still shrouded in the mists of her mind. She retreated to her office and read the various reports that had since been laid on her desk. A few odd things had crept up on her, crimes still happened. Teigneford was reasonably trouble free, but there had been a worrying increase in drug trafficking within the town. That had to be addressed by notching up some surveillance on the known scroats who pushed the stuff. The clock ticked on and slowly the office began to fill. Alexis, now realising the time, pushed the papers to one side and stood up to go out into the outer office. She was stopped in her tracks by the shrill, insistent ring of her desk phone.

"There's something you need to see, Alexis," came Hamish's voice, his tone sombre and grim. "I found it in that diary that Archie found, the one with a padlock. The key was round her neck. I've sent a scan to your email."

Alexis thanked him and clicked open her computer screen, which had gone blank. Quickly scrolling through the huge amount of

214

emails that came her way every day and, more often than not immediately consigned to the bin, she found the one from Hamish. There was no note with it, just an attachment of a scanned letter. It made grim reading. Felicity had known she was pregnant and had torn her heart out with words that cut Alexis to the core. Describing her assailant as father, she accused him of robbing her of her childhood, forcing his attentions on her and making her with child. Sadly it did not name her attacker. It was a heartrending apologia and one which should never have had to be written by a child. Alexis printed up the sad note and added it to the file. It was time for the morning briefing.

"Ready, everyone?"

Everyone turned to look at her, and swivelled their chairs to face the front, where their Detective Inspector stood, the morning's sunshine still pouring in through the window and bathing the office in light.

"Archie, what's your feeling on all of this?"

"I'm not sure I can add anything further as yet."

"I know it might be visiting old ground but it could be useful if you could go through it all again from the beginning, now that we're all here, just to see if we've missed anything."

"Well, Mavis Greene, school domestic, poisoned with phenol. We are now presuming this to be murder as same method used in the death of Felicity Smith. Compromising material, namely a photograph, found in Mrs Greene's bedroom suggests blackmail of someone, now confirmed by Andrew Danvers to be him. Photographed by Mrs Greene in a rather compromising act and subsequently blackmailed to the sum of £50 a month. Danvers in custody, admits to being blackmailed but not to any murders."

Dax paused for breath as Alexis pulled the blind against the sun which was now filling the room with dazzling rays. As the room dimmed slightly, Hannah shuffled in her seat and spoke up.

"We know that Felicity was pregnant ..." Her statement caused a buzz in the office and a gasp went round as up to now this hadn't been common knowledge.

"Yes, that's right," agreed Alexis sombrely.

"I know Maisie said someone 'old' but as you say, that could be anyone over twenty five in the eyes of a thirteen year old. Any chance it could be Danvers?" went on Hannah doggedly.

"He denies it vehemently, and I have to say, I do believe him," answered Alexis. "He's a hot blooded randy bugger and fell for the charms of a very attractive eighteen year old girl. Not the sort of thing a responsible schoolteacher ought to be doing, highly immoral, but nevertheless nothing actually criminal in the act."

"Felicity's predicament was the result of someone far less open, more devious and cruel. We also think Maisie has fallen victim too. That's the bugger I want," responded Dax savagely, still feeling a sense of responsibility for Felicity's fate.

A murmur of agreement filled the office and Alexis moved to quell the emotion and looked at Dax, her expression filled with compassion.

"We'll get him, Archie, don't you worry, but we must get this right. Had any more thoughts on the two girls, Felicity's friends, Hannah?"

"Maisie knows more than she's saying, I'm convinced of that, but the other, Emma, knows little, I'm pretty sure of that."

"We're we at with the forensic results, ma'am?" asked Dax.

"We've had the results of the post mortems on all three victims. Mavis Greene and Felicity by phenol poisoning in some shape or form; the caretaker, Alan Rees by more prosaic means - a hefty blow to the head causing unconsciousness followed by drowning caused by immersion after the head injury. Forensics are still working on the swimming pool crime scene. We've got a partial fingerprint on Felicity's scent bottle which may or may not bring up anything and Hamish is still working on the DNA of the foetus. Until we get that, and until we've got the results of the DNA tests we're carrying out at the school later, we seem to have reached a dead end. Oh, and by the way, we're saying that the DNA tests are for elimination purposes only in relation to the caretaker's murder. I do not want any connection made with Felicity or let it become common knowledge that she was pregnant. That stays in this office, is that clear?"

A general rumble of agreement went round the office, and as the sun's glare finally cleared the office, Alexis raised the blinds.

"Archie, please could you fill everyone in on what's happening this afternoon then come into my office. I've got something to show you."

Alexis retreated to her office and sat thinking, as Dax's measured tones outlined the afternoon's procedures, then leaving his colleagues to their various investigations, headed for Alexis' office, puzzled by her strange request.

"So, what's this you want to show me? I'm all ears," he asked a grin on his face.

Silently, Alexis handed over Hamish's email and sat back as Dax read the sad missive, his grin disappearing in an instant as Felicity's grim words assailed his senses. His face darkened.

"She was thirteen, damn it! These are adult words. Whoever did this robbed her of everything." His voice caught with emotion as he handed the paper back to his boss.

"Don't worry, Archie. We'll get him. We can't save Felicity now, or her baby, but we can save Maisie and as I suspect these aren't his first victims, maybe we can justice for them too."

Dax left the office to organise the logistics for the afternoon's activities and left alone, Alexis began a timetable of events so far. She was a tidy, organised woman and liked everything in its place, even her thoughts had to be ordered. Her mind didn't work if things were left all over the place. She drew a fresh sheet of paper from the drawer and began to write, rather than use the computer. The very act of writing helped her to tumble the facts into place. Her pen raced vigorously over the paper and before she knew it, the morning had gone and although she had a neat list, facts all chronologically sorted, she was no further forward. They were still waiting for the DNA results from the foetus; they were still waiting to see if this matched Andrew Danvers and they were still waiting for a match for the fingerprint on the glass scent bottle. Once she had these, then maybe she could get some answers. Dax poked his head round the door.

"You still at it?" he asked.

"Yes, something's nagging at the back of my brain, and I can't pin it down."

"Time you broke it off. Come and have a pint with me, lubricate the brain cells."

"Good idea," said Alexis, throwing down her pen. "I'm not getting anywhere here."

As she spoke, Hamish pushed his head round the door, the sun behind him creating a halo effect with his red hair.

"Do you need me at the school this afternoon, only I've got a bit of a backlog?"

"No, that's fine, Hamish. You carry on."

Alexis paused as Hamish turned to leave.

"Fancy a bit of lunch with us, Hamish?" she asked. "Archie and I are just off to the pub.

"That'd be great. Thanks. Work can wait for a bit."

The three of them left the police station and headed for the Strangefellows Arms. The weather was unseasonably cold, the early sunshine having vanished as the morning had worn on and the threat of rain hung in the atmosphere. It was at times like these, when a case had stalled, that Alexis felt frustrated. She knew the answer was in those statements but for the life of her, she just couldn't find it. The pub was warm and inviting, the log fire burning cheerily in the inglenook so away from keen ears and prying eyes, Dax and Hamish headed for a table in the corner of the pub as Alexis headed for the bar. She placed an order and then returned to sit with her friends. Cradling their pints as they waited for their lunch, Alexis voiced her thoughts.

"I think Mavis was an unintended victim. I don't think Danvers had anything to do with her death, which means, also, he didn't take the phenol from the chemistry lab. Someone else got access to a key. That phenol was meant for someone else. Assuming it was in the cup of coffee that Mavis drank – we can be pretty certain of that –

it seems highly probable that she picked up the cup from somewhere and walked off with it. She'd hardly have laced her own cup of coffee – we've ruled out suicide." Alexis paused.

Hamish sat quietly, sipping his drink as Dax waited, watching his friend's mental processes being played out. He made a good sounding board; he was used to it and he knew it aided Alexis. It was like pushing an unsolved crossword clue out to someone else. The mere fact of voicing the clue or the question seemed to put Alexis' mind on a different track and the answer came unbidden whereas before it had remained stuck.

"That's it!" Alexis sat up straight in her chair. "I knew it was there somewhere. We'd guessed at it but here's the proof."

Dax smiled, enjoying the moment. Hamish just raised an eyebrow.

"Frances Smythe said something in her statement about a cup of coffee going missing and asking Brenda to make her another one."

"Bloody cheek," replied Dax. "Why couldn't the lazy cow make one herself?"

"Suppose Mavis took that cup. Apparently she was in the habit of 'tidying up' after people, even when they hadn't finished whatever they were using."

"Highly likely," agreed Dax. "That would then seem to suggest that Frances was the intended victim."

"Yes, and that explains the little girl's death. When the murderer realised that he, or she – let's be equal in this - had failed, they had another go only got the name wrong. Instead of Frances Smythe, the label said Miss F Smith. Same initials so simple mistaken identity."

"I think you're onto something there, ma'am. Why would anyone want to kill Frances? I know she's a flirt but she's harmless enough, and the caretaker?"

"We've already suggested that the caretaker saw something and decided to take advantage of it, and got more than he bargained for. As for Frances, only time will tell, I suppose."

"Well, we've got the answer to how and where, but who and why are still a problem," went on Dax, as he took a sip of his beer.

"Let's put all this in order," said Alexis. "I know, done this before, several times, but bear with me. You know how my mind works."

Dax nodded with a grin. Anything they'd ever worked on, both as constables and as constable and sergeant, they'd always talked over between them. Why should new promotion make things any different?

"Talking it through helps me to get things straight in my mind. Simple repetition, but you never know if we've missed something."

Dax doubted that. He'd read the statements through several times himself but stayed silent, nodding in agreement as he humoured his boss. Maybe he had read something that Alexis had missed, and vice versa.

"We have the first murder, Mavis. She was killed, I think by accident. I believe the poison was meant for Frances but don't know why. I initially thought Felicity's murder was connected to her pregnancy, but now I'm pretty sure this was also an accidental murder. The poison was meant for Frances but with the mix up of names, she became collateral damage. We have two crimes – murder and rape stroke paedophilia. The caretaker's demise was deliberate. More than likely he was blackmailing the murderer and was summarily despatched."

Alexis paused.

"Hopefully, we'll get some answers when we get a DNA match from the foetus," piped up Hamish, silent up to now as he'd watched the interaction between his two colleagues. He'd been welcomed by everyone in the office but had yet to feel totally comfortable with everyone. It took time to settle into a new job but he knew that would come, with time.

"Thanks for working so quickly on that, Hamish. I think speed is of the essence here; I just want to nip things in the bud before they get worse, especially where the children are concerned. God knows what sort of arsehole we've got here." Alexis responded quickly.

Hamish smiled. He had yet to get to know Alexis well and being well aware of his own liberality when it came to speech, was rather pleased to hear the Detective Inspector letting her hair down a little.

"My thoughts exactly. I've got a daughter about the same age and the thought of anything like that happening to her fills me with disgust."

Hamish shuddered, his drink slopping slightly in his glass. Alexis didn't miss the action and felt for him. Her own nieces were much younger, but their vulnerability struck a nerve. Hamish appeared to be large and bluff, a mighty presence wherever he went, but Alexis saw a softer side to the man, and was pleased. Anxious for the moment to pass quickly before Dax's thoughts began to resort once more to self-pity, Alexis brought her friends back to the matter in hand.

"We need a match from that partial fingerprint we found on the scent bottle. Any luck on that yet, Hamish?"

"No, not yet. I'm running it through several databases but nothing so far. I'll keep you posted."

"If we're really lucky we'll get a match up with what we get from the school this afternoon. Did you ask for fingerprints as well, Archie?" went on Alexis.

"I thought I might just as well. Kill two birds with one stone, so to speak. I told everyone to stress this as voluntary, don't want any comeback."

"Good. Let's hope it brings some answers," said Alexis.

She paused as their food arrived – a granary ham salad for Alexis, a pie for Hamish and a rather indulgent cheese ploughman's for Dax, then changed the subject.

"How you settling into your new post, Hamish?" she asked conversationally.

"Good thanks. A few changes I'd like to make at the lab but on the whole, OK."

Knowing that the mortuary and forensic lab were brand new, a new extension to the cottage hospital in the town, and pretty much state of the art, Alexis was puzzled.

"Changes? What sort of changes did you have in mind?"

"Mainly operational," Hamish replied. "The lab is great, pretty much everything I need but ..."

"But?"

"Yeah. Not sure if you're the person I need to ask, or if this needs to go higher."

"Try me," replied Alexis, mystified as to Hamish's train of thought.

"Well … when it comes to crime scene investigations, you need more than me."

"Yes, that's why we get the SOCO in," went on Alexis.

Dax had a feeling he knew where this was going, having been more present at the various crime scenes that had presented themselves over the last few days."

"You're short staffed, aren't you?" Dax chipped in.

"Well, not exactly but the time delay is a bother."

Alexis and Dax sat back munching on their food as Hamish elaborated.

"When I get the call to go out on a job, SOCO has to come in from either Hereford or Shrewsbury. This adds to the time taken on an investigation and sometimes getting in quick can produce dividends."

"So how do you propose to solve this conundrum?" asked Alexis with a smile.

"Is it possible to get our own dedicated SOCO team here in Teigneford? We're spoiling the barrel, a bright, brand new lab and mortuary for a ha'porth of tar, i.e. no local forensic officers."

"Ah, I see where you're going with this and I totally agree with you," said Alexis. "When we're done and dusted with these school murders, I'll have a chat with Mr Barnes and see if we can do something about this. Leave it with me. Might take some time, he's not an easy man to convince, but I have my ways," she finished with a sparkle in her eyes.

With that promise, the three sat back, pushing thoughts of murder and schools far from their minds. The fire burned merrily in the grate, releasing a shower of sparks as a log settled in the flames. As they ate, Alexis relaxed and when she had finished eating, started to get sleepy in the warmth. It was tempting to just nod off but she knew that if she did, she'd never make it back to the office. So, deciding to get back to work, she finished her pint, placed the empty glass back on the table and stood up to leave. Dax and Hamish made to stand too.

"No, both of you, stay and finish your pints," Alexis ordered kindly.

"That's a tempting idea, but I ought to get back," answered Hamish, raising his glass and finishing the last dregs of his beer.

"Right you, are. Archie, I'll see you back here in twenty minutes."

"OK, ma'am," replied Dax. "Right you are."

Never one to disobey a favourable order, Dax did as he was told, and settled back down in his chair, and grabbed the forty winks that Alexis had denied herself. She was reluctant to leave the warm comfort of the pub. It was very tempting to just sit there and while away the time, but she needed some time on her own. A short walk was all she could afford just at this moment, but it would have to do. She had long been comfortable in her own company and when she was on her own, it afforded her valuable thinking time. The wind had changed direction and the weather had gently warmed and, again, the sun shone. The sky, blue with fluffy white clouds, reflected this warmth and Alexis breathed in the atmosphere and visibly relaxed. A Chopin ballade played itself out in her thoughts and the music eased her mind. She rounded the corner and saw the river. A willow tree overhung the water, its leaves playing with the surface of the shallow water at the edge, causing ripples to fan out across towards the centre of the river. A fish jumped and splashed back in the water, leaving an even larger circle of ripples as it disappeared once more under the surface. It was a peaceful scene, far away from the horrors of murder and abused children. Alexis often wondered how the world was continually at odds with itself. Mankind could be so cruel, with little compassion. Cruelty in nature could be excused, survival was by instinct and habit, but mankind had no such let out. Freewill led a man to both goodness and evil. Every stone, lying calmly alongside the way, once overturned revealed all kinds of nastiness. But she remembered her chat with Brenda. She had devoted her life to the school and its generations of children. She had shown compassion to her workmate, and this impressed Alexis and restored her faith in humanity. It had been a small act, but one that had truly been appreciated. A waddling duck, pecking in the muddy shallows disturbed her thoughts and she looked up. A path wound alongside the river and out of sight but Alexis contented herself with just standing by the water's edge, her jacket laying between the straps of her bag which hung over her shoulder. The slight breeze ruffled the rippling water, and the sunshine reflected off the boulders which lay just beneath. The scene comforted her and the horrors of the world briefly disappeared. A flash of blue caught her eye as a kingfisher darted down to the water and struck, a hapless fish then caught in its beak. This was a rare sight indeed and Alexis felt uplifted by the moment.

The sound of the water brought back a memory. She was ten years old and on holiday, staying on what had become her most favourite part of the world, Dartmoor. She was paddling in the stream that bundled over huge boulders, the breeze playing in the long grasses of the moor. She'd made a small dam with her sister and she remembered the laughter as the two girls got soaked, her mother gently chiding the pair of them. She remembered the smell of damp earth and mossy bogs, the outline of hard granite outcrops against the sky and the song of the lark on the moorland. They had been happy times. She wasn't unhappy now, perhaps a little lonely now and then and sometimes envied Archie and his wife, Claire. Family life had its ups and downs, she knew that, but it was infinitely preferable to a lifetime on one's own. Perhaps one day the right man would emerge on her own particular scene.

The sun disappeared for an instant behind a cloud and the atmosphere darkened. The change shook Alexis out of her pleasant thoughts. The noisy exhaust of a passing motor bike brought her back to the present and reality and she sighed as she remembered the job in hand. She had been sickened by the depravities to which

Felicity's rapist had sunk and knew that he must be found without delay. Alexis suspected that other girls were at risk, certainly Maisie and maybe even boys, if the rapist had no bias towards which sex he violated. She couldn't act just at that moment, as much as she wanted to; she had no proof. The girl might have been impregnated anywhere. She was sure it was at the school, Felicity had hardly been anywhere else, but until she had something concrete to go on, she would have to bide her time. She sighed and turned away from the river and its delights. She donned her jacket, chilled by the sudden loss of sunshine, and walked back to the Strangefellows Arms. Dax was waiting outside, sitting on a bench, reading through his pocket book and refreshing his memory of the facts he had gleaned.

"Ready?" asked Dax.

"Yes, let's get going," replied Alexis. "Too much thinking is not good for the soul," she grinned. "I reckon it's time to face the staff and get their DNA. Hopefully, the headmaster has played ball and got his staff organised."

"You mean, played with his balls," responded Dax with a laugh.

"No, old flossy flirt face does that," grinned Alexis.

Dax and Alexis returned to their car and drove the few miles north to the school. The deep gravel made Dax swear silently, imagining a fearful and painful death for the person who had put it there. It crunched under the wheels as the car came to a halt and Dax applied the handbrake. The two officers climbed out of the car and headed across to the main door, only to be accosted on the steps by the headmaster himself.

"This way, please," he said. "I wish to do this as discretely as possible. Your co-operation would be appreciated."

"Of course, Mr Harper. We have no wish to make a song and dance over this."

"I have informed my staff what you require. I cannot vouch for their happy acquiescence, but I didn't have any outright denials. You will have to work with what you get," went on Graham petulantly, his eyes burning with suppressed anger.

He loathed this official insurgency into his well-ordered life. His domain was threatened and he didn't like it, but what little he did possess in the way of common sense made him realise that there was nothing, for the moment, that he could do about it. Graham Harper led Dax and Alexis across the highly polished floor of the inner hall, the smell of lavender still present after a polish that morning. James Picton was sitting at the piano, gently playing out a tune. He caught her eye and promptly changed his tune. Alexis caught the drift and grinned slightly, as she recognised the opening bars of the *Dies Irae* from Verdi's requiem. She loved classical music, a passion which she obviously shared with James. She acknowledged the reference with a slight nod and a small grin. Was this to be a 'Day of Anger' for someone? She really hoped so. James smiled. A silent accord had existed between the two from the first day, when James had had to take control. Alexis appreciated the man's honesty and integrity. He would make a much better headmaster than the twit they had got, Alexis thought as she and Dax left the hall. Meeting James had reminded of her the day they had first met, along with the presence of the newly installed Bishop. Bishop Stephen and Alexis had known each other for six years, having first met when her sister had married the Bishop's son, Luke. At first, she had been overawed by the Bishop or, as he then was, the Dean of Worcester, an assistant to the Bishop of the time. They had got chatting at the reception afterwards and had discovered a shared interest in classical music. From this a deep friendship had ensued and Alexis had come to value his advice, both spiritual and secular. She thought it would be nice to pick his brains on her first case as Detective Inspector, particularly as he'd been there from Day One, so to speak. Maybe he could give her an insight into the human aspect of the case; perhaps he'd noted something she'd missed. It would be a good excuse to see him and have a chat, anyway. With that resolve in mind, she walked on and passed through the heavy fire proof door, which connected the inner hall to the corridor. Graham walked ahead of the two officers and as he reached another door, he threw it open, showing a pleasant room inside. It was light and airy and, above all, away from prying eyes and therefore relatively private. Alexis thanked the headmaster.

"Perhaps you would be kind enough to ask your receptionist to show my officers in when they arrive." Alexis looked at her watch. "They should be here any minute."

Graham acknowledged this request with a brief nod and left Dax and Alexis alone. Alexis threw her briefcase down on the desk and waited. Dax looked out of the window and as he saw the forensic team's cars negotiate the driveway, he turned back to his boss.

"They're here," he said.

Within ten minutes, the team had set up their equipment, and an orderly queue of staff began to form outside the room. Dax ticked each name off as they arrived, and before long a large plastic box was full of fingerprint samples and the DNA swabs, each item carefully labelled, safely tucked into protective plastic tubes and packets. Alexis looked at the clock, which ticked away inexorably on the wall above them.

"Archie, it's five to three. I did say I would take the Headmaster's sample in his office at three. Give me a tube and I'll go and do it now. I'll do his fingerprints as well. He won't like that, but tough."

Dax grinned.

"Here you go, ma'am," he said, handing over the necessary equipment. "Enjoy!" he finished with a malicious grin.

"Oh, believe me, I will," answered Alexis.

She knew exactly what the headmaster was like; she'd met the sort many times in her rise through the ranks. Self-important bullies who thought they knew everything, particularly when faced with women. Misogyny was still alive and kicking in the police force, and Alexis suspected that Harper was no different in his world. Alexis unashamedly relished the fact that Graham Harper was due a downfall. If the shame and bad press of murder in his school didn't get him, then his affair with Frances certainly would. Professional confidential conduct and her own integrity meant that she could never reveal this little titbit to the wider world but she sincerely hoped that the secret would make it out into the open before too long. Everyone in the staff room knew about it so it wouldn't stay hidden for ever.

Alexis found her way back to the headmaster's office and knocked smartly on the door. A curt 'come' summoned her in and she opened the door. This time, Frances was nowhere to be seen and Alexis smiled at the memory. Graham sat at his desk, looking very self-important. His suit was immaculate and his hair was brushed neatly. The effect was marred by the unkempt, frayed gown, its fur grimy and moth eaten, that Graham insisted on wearing. He no doubt thought that if he looked the part, then Alexis would be subservient. He was badly mistaken.

"I had expected a male officer, Inspector," he said peevishly. "After all, this is rather a personal exercise."

"Oh don't worry, Mr Harper, we're all equal nowadays and I'm only taking a sample from your mouth."

Alexis laid her case down on the coffee table, resisting the temptation to say, 'not anywhere else'. As Graham watched, apprehension began to show on his face. Alexis donned gloves and carefully extracted the sampling equipment from its tube.

"Mr Harper, would you mind coming over here. There is more light and I don't want to cause you any more discomfort than I have to."

Graham hated being called by his proper name, much preferring the more status giving and important title of headmaster. He stiffened angrily at this peremptory instruction, but nevertheless did as he was bidden. He got up from his seat and crossed the plush carpet, now smooth and unblemished after a last minute vacuum. The promising warm sun of midday had disappeared and the clouds had gathered again. The windows were suddenly lashed with sharp, squally raindrops driven by a strong wind. Alexis smiled to herself and thought that Berlioz' '*March to the Scaffold*' would be very appropriate. Graham seated himself gingerly on the edge of the arm chair and lifted his face. Alexis carefully inserted the sample swab and wiped it gently around the inside of Graham's cheek. When she had finished, Graham snapped his mouth shut as if to reclaim his profaned dignity.

"Now, your fingerprints, Mr Harper, if you please."

"I beg your pardon," retorted Graham angrily.

"It is procedure, Mr Harper," replied Alexis wearily.

"You will do no such thing."

Alexis sighed.

"This, as I have said is entirely voluntary, but your reluctance is suggestive."

Graham grunted angrily.

"You did not say anything about fingerprints."

"My officers are doing exactly the same to all your other staff. It is simply for elimination. You have every right to refuse but if you have done nothing wrong, you have nothing to fear."

Graham stood up, his face red with supressed anger.

"This is an indignity."

"It will not take long and it isn't being done in public, unlike your colleagues."

Graham paused, realising he was beaten. He didn't have anything to hide, but hated the process of proving it. He relented with bad grace and extended his hand to Alexis. The Detective Inspector quickly and efficiently took each of the headmaster's fingers in turn, and rolled them gently but firmly on the fingerprint forms. She helped herself to two palm prints as well. 'Might as well go the whole hog,' thought Alexis with satisfaction. Graham stood, his hands blackened with the dye. He wiped them vigorously on a tissue, but the stain remained. He felt sick and dirty, tainted with the evils that had befallen the school and angered with his inability to do anything about it. Even Frances had deserted him. She had taken the day off, claiming a sick bug. He slumped down in his seat by his desk, his crumpled gown entangling itself in the swivel chair as Graham turned away.

"Thank you, Mr Harper. I am grateful for your co-operation," said Alexis as she tidied up her equipment.

Graham kept silent. He waved his ink stained hand at Alexis, and dismissed her. Alexis, refusing to be rushed, took her time, carefully stowing away her newly acquired samples, and arranging her case. Then, with Graham watching angrily, his mouth a tight line across his grey face, she gathered up her case and walked across the room, scuffing the immaculate carpet as she went. As the door closed behind her, she heard Graham snort with anger and frustration. Alexis grinned. James must be telepathic, she thought. The man was at the piano again and, yes, he had caught the mood exactly. The Berlioz rang out under his fingers and Alexis sighed with satisfaction.

The following morning started badly for Gerald Leigh. He sat at his desk, groaning with his head in his hands. The letter he had just received had destroyed his happy euphoria, surrounded as he was by his beloved spreadsheets. There he'd been, happily poring over his sums, when the post had been unceremoniously dumped on his desk. Most of it was the usual stuff; the odd bill, some junk mail and a cheque or two from the parents. But hidden in the pile had been the one letter that he had hoped never to receive. Gerald picked up the letter opener and gently slit the envelope open. The paper inside was marked ostentatiously with the crest of the school and a letter like that coming from outside could only mean one thing – it was a communication from one of the Governors. And so it proved to be. It made grim reading, at least to Gerald's bleak eyes and guilty thoughts. The letter was brief and succinct, and signed by General, Sir Martin Friend, Chairman of the Governors. He wrote that, following the recent appointment of Mr Michael Chance, a chief accountant from a top London firm to the Governing Body of Coates Norton School, it had been decided that in these present financially trying times, he had agreed to do a full audit of the books. The idea behind this was to see if economies could be made bearing in mind rising costs and falling school numbers. Gerald gulped as he read. It all seemed innocent enough, but he knew very well that his creative accounting would not escape a trained eye. There was nothing he could do, other than replace the money himself, which had been spent on the headmaster's fraudulent activities, and that he could ill afford to do. It amounted to a few thousand pounds over the years. Everything would be revealed. His mood darkened, and not even the promise of imminent lunch could raise his spirits. Should he warn the headmaster or let him wallow in his sins. Working on the premise that least said, soonest mended, Gerald decided to say nothing. He consigned the letter to the deepest depths of his filing tray and left for lunch.

The forensic lab had worked round the clock, testing all the fingerprints and DNA samples taken at the school the previous afternoon. Hamish, realising the urgency of the investigation, with particular regard towards Felicity's pregnancy, had urged his colleagues to work late. There had been no argument, each man and woman sickened by the suspicion of paedophilia. The first results through had been Andrew Danvers' and the foetus' DNA tests. Andrew's earlier arrest had allowed Alexis to take DNA samples and fingerprints, and therefore he had beaten the rush. It was quickly established that he was not the father of Felicity's child, so Alexis, her belief in Danvers' denials vindicated, called him up from the cells. Dax was out of the office that morning, giving evidence in court, so Alexis spoke to Danvers on her own. She entered the interview room and found the erstwhile chemistry teacher sitting forlornly at the table. He looked dishevelled and unshaven after what had probably been a sleepless night. His hands shook as he lifted the coffee cup to his mouth and Alexis, not an uncharitable woman, actually felt sorry for the teacher. She realised that he was no murderer, just a fool who had let his hot blooded sexual antics get the better of him. His punishment had been the blackmail, and now the loss of a career and his professional integrity, but for now there were procedures to go through. Alexis sat down and faced the unfortunate chemistry teacher.

"You'll be pleased to hear that we have your DNA results back," she opened uncompromisingly.

"And?" he asked wearily, his eyes red rimmed through lack of sleep.

"It confirms that you are not the father of Miss Smith's child."

Danvers' head shot up, his cheeks flamed with anger.

"I told you so. I may be a fool, but I'm not a pervert."

Alexis ignored the outburst. She was unshaken by the man's anger and continued relentlessly.

"Let's just put it this way. You have been extremely irresponsible and laid yourself open to suspicion. As a teacher, you are in a position of authority and have many responsibilities, not the least of which is the care of the children you teach."

Andrew reddened, Alexis' meaning very clear. He stayed silent and dropped his eyes as the Detective Inspector continued.

"I accept that it takes two to become involved in a situation such as this, but Miss Grant is nevertheless a pupil at the school, albeit of an age to make decisions for herself. She is entitled to a bit of self-restraint from those 'in loco parentis'. Her parents have entrusted her care to the school and for you to take advantage of a personable young woman in such a way is unforgiveable."

Alexis didn't enjoy the words she was saying, but felt she had a right to make his point. It might prevent such an issue in the future if Danvers could now be sufficiently ashamed by his actions. Andrew, at length, looked up as Alexis fell silent. In the few minutes of quiet that followed, Andrew came to a decision.

"You are right. I've been a bloody fool. I'll resign and go quietly. I let my hot blood get the better of me. But she is lovely…" Andrew tailed off in a moment of self-pity. A door banged in the distance and Andrew came back to his surroundings, both mentally and as he ran his hands through his unruly hair, physically too.

"Can I go now?" he asked, hopefully.

"We are still looking into the disappearance of the chemicals from your lab," went on Alexis. "That is still unexplained…."

She was interrupted as Andrew again lost his temper.

"Don't you get it? I did not steal anything, kill anyone or have sex with a child. You've got nothing on me."

"Miss Grant may not be a child but you can hardly say you haven't had sex."

Andrew slumped in his chair, his exhaustion catching up with him, his fight diminishing.

"I'm sorry," he said simply.

"However," went on Alexis, now having regained the authority of the conversation, "I am going to release you on police bail, pending further enquires. I am not going to charge you with anything as yet but it will mean you returning here at a pre-arranged time and date to 'check in', so to speak."

Danvers looked up.

"Thanks," he replied somewhat ungraciously but his eyes were bright with relief.

"At the moment, the headmaster knows nothing about your shenanigans with Elizabeth Grant. I can't vouch for the rest of the staff room. She is a consenting adult so you have committed no actual crime there, but you were in a position of responsibility. I don't have to tell him but I think your decision to resign, rather than be pushed, is a sensible one. We'll leave it there for now, but please take on board what I have said."

Danvers nodded.

Alexis left the interview room, leaving the exhausted, but somewhat relieved, chemistry teacher in the charge of the Custody Sergeant. It wasn't her job to deal with the bail formalities so she went upstairs and back to the CID office, her throat dry and sore, which she realised was more to do with tiredness and stress than anything else. The kettle was full and didn't take long to boil, so soon Alexis had provided herself with a fortifying mug of coffee. The outer office was empty as like any other normal town, life still went on despite the murder investigation and officers were out investigating the various other crimes on their books. Hannah had been called out to a shoplifting in a supermarket on the edge of town, Dax was still at court and the other officers had started investigations into the newly discovered drug problem which had beset a rather down at heel housing estate in the town. Alexis had the place to herself. The weather had continued its unseasonably cold and wet period and a strong wind howled round the corner of the building. Alexis stood alone in her own office and stared out across the back yard and beyond. From her vantage point, Alexis had a view of the castle and its weathered battlements stood forbiddingly grey and bleak against the stormy sky. Clouds whipped across the skyline, and the distant hills turned black in the gloom. Alexis shivered and turned away, her thoughts morbid and dark. The coffee had reinvigorated her body and lubricated her throat but her mind was still tired. Things had stalled again; she needed a break. Returning to her desk, she sat down and switched on a desk lamp, to offset the gloom of the day outside. It cast a warm, bright glow across her papers and Alexis settled down to read through the file again. As she read, she became more and more convinced that Mavis had been killed by accident, the poison meant for someone else. From what Frances had said about her missing coffee cup, it seemed on the surface that she might have been the intended victim, but why? She was vacuous and empty, a flirt, just a pretty shell, but was that a reason to kill her? Maybe she had upset someone but would any have stooped so low as to murder her? Nothing had come to light so far in their investigations but maybe they ought to dig deeper into her private life. Felicity's death, she was sure had also been an accident. It was too much of a coincidence to think that the two deaths weren't connected by the same person, simply by the use of the same chemical. The pregnancy, Alexis suspected, was only known to Felicity herself and maybe Maisie too if Felicity had indeed confided in her friend. Enough fear had been instilled into the girls by their attacker that she would probably have kept that awful secret to herself, and never in a million years confronted the culprit, but girls talk. So following this reasoning, the murder would not have been committed by the father of her child. Or had it?

Alexis sighed. Still no obvious answers, just speculation. What if? What about? Who's done what? The questions rolled through her tired brain, pushing and shoving against each other and producing no answers. Filled with a negative despondency, she pushed the file away from her and finished the cooling dregs from her coffee mug. Then, coming to a sudden decision, she picked up the phone and dialled the private number she had for the Bishop. She needed some guidance, both human and friendly, and perhaps with a little divine intervention thrown in for good measure.

Chapter Twelve

Alexis replaced the phone. Having made the appointment, she felt more relaxed and although still very tired, she felt ready for the rest of the day. Her peace was not to last as hardly had she pushed the phone away from her, its shrill ring interrupted her train of thought. The call informed her that she had a visitor, Chairman of the Governors of Coates Norton School, no less.

"Please could you show him up?" asked Alexis of the caller.

Puzzled, she rapidly tidied her desk as she waited the few minutes before General Sir Martin Friend was shown into her office. Alexis wondered as to the nature of the man's visit. Obviously it would be about the events at the school but the man would have to realise that the police couldn't release any information that wasn't already in the public domain. A gentle tap on her door alerted Alexis to the General's arrival, so she stood up, shook hands with her visitor and invited him to sit down.

"Good morning," she opened pleasantly. "What can I do for you?"

Sir Martin sat uncomfortably on the chair facing Alexis. He seemed a little tongue tied to start with, and fiddled with his tie.

"A word, ma'am, if you don't mind," asked Sir Martin.

"If I can be of help …." Alexis paused and waited.

"This is not going to be easy," Sir Martin continued, wriggling in his seat.

"Take your time," invited Alexis courteously. "Can I offer you a cup of coffee?"

"Yes, that would be most acceptable, thank you," agreed Sir Martin, feeling that a dose of caffeine could be very beneficial at this very moment. Leaving the man seated in her office, giving him time to collect his thoughts and composure, Alexis headed for the outer office and the coffee machine. As she passed Hannah, who had now returned from out of town and was now sitting thumbing through some papers on her desk, she whispered with a nod towards Alexis' office.

"What's he want?"

"Don't know yet. The poor man seems very flustered so he obviously wants to get something off his chest."

"Hmm! Interesting."

"Don't count your chickens yet," she laughed gently. "I can't see him as the murderer or as the father of Felicity's child."

"P'raps not," agreed Hannah with an answering grin.

The coffee made, and with two steaming mugs in her hand Alexis returned to her office and put one mug carefully down on her desk in front of the General, who now seemed a little more relaxed. Sir Martin cleared his throat as Alexis waited patiently.

"I have heard through Chinese whispers that the headmaster is having an affair with the receptionist. Can you confirm?"

Alexis looked down at her desk, stifling a smile, and shifted a few papers. She hadn't expected this question and didn't really know where to begin.

"Rumour has it that it has been going on for quite some time…" Sir Martin tailed off in an embarrassed silence.

The silence was deafening as Alexis struggled with her thoughts. Sir Martin tried again.

"I realise this is a delicate and rather awkward question, and I'm sorry to put you in this position, being as you are a …."

Sir Martin froze, suddenly supremely conscious of the delicacy of the situation, bearing in mind who sat in front of him. Alexis saw the man's discomfort, and realising that he was old school and perhaps a little out of his depth when it came to modern male/female equality in the workplace, rather than take him to task over his slightly old-fashioned attitude, instead took pity on him. She made up her mind and looked up, facing Sir Martin squarely.

"You will forgive me if I say that I couldn't possibly comment," went on Alexis with a slight smile.

"No, of course not, shouldn't have asked. Please forgive me."

"No, no, not at all, it's just …." This time Alexis tailed off as she ran out of words.

"Thank you for your time," went on Sir Martin. "I'll take my leave."

The poor man was used to the regulation of army life but here he was definitely outside his comfort zone. Sir Martin stood up to leave, knocking the chair over in his haste. Alexis jumped up to help the stricken man.

"Sir Martin, please sit down," said Alexis, helping her guest back to his seat. "I repeat what I said about not being able to say anything as obviously our enquiries are confidential. However, may I suggest that a discreet enquiry in the staff room at the school might be beneficial and could be quite revealing?"

"Oh, I say, yes, thank you, er, thank you, yes, I'll do that," spluttered Sir Martin as the import of what Alexis had said filtered through the general's confused brain.

Regaining his control and demeanour, Sir Martin went on.

"There have been some unfortunate things happening at my school. Could I ask if you are getting anywhere with your investigations?"

"We have several lines of enquiry at present, and a little further forward as to where and how, but we are still following up leads and waiting for DNA test results to come through," replied Alexis, without committing herself.

"Yes, quite," said Sir Martin.

"I will, of course, keep you informed."

"Thank you, much obliged, ma'am."

Alexis smiled gently at the formality, the army training showing through, stiff and unbending. She actually felt a little gratified that he had acknowledged her rank – more than her own superintendent had. Sir Martin finished his coffee and stood up to leave.

"Thank you for seeing me. I appreciate that you are not at liberty to divulge anything sensitive and confidential, but I do thank you for your suggestions. I have a feeling that I might need to make some changes at the school."

Sir Martin relaxed enough to wink conspiratorially at Alexis. She blinked, surprised at the sudden informality. She cordially shook hands with her guest and then showed Sir Martin out to the front door. The heavens had opened and the yard was awash. The wind howled and Sir Martin made a dash for his car, getting soaked in the process. Alexis watched as the sleek limousine left the yard, Dax's car taking its place.

"Was that who I think it was?" asked Dax as he slipped off his wet jacket by his desk, having followed his boss up the stairs.

"Yes, it was,"

"What did he want?"

"Wanted to know if the headmaster was having it off with old flirty face."

"What did you say?" asked Dax, laughing.

"I told him to look in the staff room."

"Good advice," agreed Dax.

"How'd it go this morning?" asked Alexis, conversationally.

"Banged up for ten years, thank God. He was a nasty bugger. That burglary was nasty, gave the householder a nasty fright. Still, good old DNA. That scar on his face where he cut himself on the window as he left has done nothing for his sex appeal," grinned Dax delightedly.

"That reminds me," went on Alexis. "The DNA results came back for Andrew Danvers. He wasn't the father so I've bailed him, pending further enquiries."

"Righto. Hope he left a forwarding address. He won't want to show his face back at the school."

"Oh, yes," said Alexis with emphasis. "I suggested he might like to resign rather than get the sack."

"Shrewd move," agreed Dax. "Wonder if he will?"

"Be a fool if he doesn't. Might salvage something of his career if he goes quietly," finished Alexis.

The two officers moved off, sharing the events of the morning and headed for the canteen. Lunch beckoned.

Andrew Danvers, now released from custody and having given the necessary sureties to the Custody Sergeant, stood on the steps of Teigneford Police Station and pondered his next move. His options were limited. Other than go back to collect his personal stuff, he couldn't return to the school. For one thing, he couldn't face his colleagues knowing that they knew everything. How could he have been so stupid? He'd been so careful but he should have known; there were no secrets in a school, particular one as insular and enclosed as a boarding school. Elizabeth, he knew, would soon move on to someone else. There was that new geography teacher who'd just started – he'd seen her eye wandering. She wouldn't miss him one little bit. He put on his jacket, and wandered off down the road and soon found himself in the local coffee shop, nursing a large Americano and a rather nice piece of their rather delicious chocolate cake. He'd missed breakfast and hunger gnawed at his stomach. As he sat and relaxed, enjoying his coffee, his mood lightened. Money might be a bit of a problem for the long term, but thanks to an inheritance from his grandfather, he owned his own place, a small studio flat above one of the nicer shops in town, and he had some savings which would see him through for a bit. Perhaps it was time to let out his flat, do a bit of travel, take a gap year, do some voluntary service overseas or something. He had skills, not to mention his chemistry degree and the ability to speak fluent German. He knew that a possible charge of misappropriating chemicals from the school still hung over him, and he couldn't do anything until that was resolved, but he knew he'd done nothing wrong there and was confident that the charge would be dropped. The Detective Inspector had seemed a fair person, albeit she'd given him a hard time, but logic told him he had been fair game; there was so much circumstantial evidence against him. He'd be OK. On that optimistic thought, he stood up and helped himself to one of the newspapers so thoughtfully provided by the café. He browsed the job pages as he munched on his cake. There were one or two job offers going, but nothing that really took his fancy. There was time, he thought, I'll find something. With a lighter heart and a fuller stomach he grabbed his jacket and walked back to his flat.

It didn't take him long to write his resignation letter, deciding to brazen it out and just state family reasons for his decision. Everyone would know the real reason, but why commit it to paper. Having been brought from Coates Norton, on his arrest, by police transport his own car was sitting back at the school so he had no choice but to fork out for a taxi. He now had every intention of getting away from the school as soon as possible, away from any aggravation. He fully realised he had been a fool and had the grace to feel ashamed of his actions. After a short taxi ride, he arrived at the school and made haste to collect his belongings. Everyone was at lessons so his arrival had gone unnoticed, for which he was immensely relieved. With the resignation letter quickly consigned to the headmaster's pigeon hole and with hardly a backward look, Andrew ran out of the school, now eager to put as much distance as possible between it and himself. He ran to his car and after negotiating the gravel, left his career behind him. By chance, Elizabeth saw him go. She'd been on her way to the medical room, having felt a bit sick that morning - must have been that curry she'd had last night – and saw Andrew leave in his car as she crossed the quad. She'd heard of his arrest and this had made her feel uncomfortable. She had no idea that their sordid activities were common knowledge in the staff room and was oblivious to the chit chat in the boarding houses. A school was a great place for gossip and Coates Norton was no exception. A slight pang filled her stomach as she watched Andrew disappear as he turned into the main road. It had been fun but with a light tread she headed for the medical room, her head filled with the delights of the morning's geography lesson to come. It was time for pastures new.

Back in her office after lunch, Alexis found some more test results, which Hamish had hurried through but which, unfortunately, had not proved to be very helpful. There was too little of the print found on the scent bottle to provide anything close to a reliable match. She found Dax at his desk and shared the information with him. "Well, that doesn't help us much," said Dax despondently.

"Well, it'll give us something to match against if we do get anything more useful."

"Anything else?" went on Dax.

"There's a report on the footprint we found next to the swimming pool. Seems it was a man's size 11, and highly likely to be a wellington boot. The tread print matches one of those posh types of boot, you know, the ones with straps."

Dax laughed. "You're an inverted snob."

Alexis replied with a grin. "No not really, mine are just bog standard black things. You don't need fashion to keep dry and warm. There's also a suggestion that the impression, although a size 11 may have been formed by someone with a smaller foot."

"How so?" asked Dax, puzzled.

"Well, the pressure points of the imprint aren't even, that is someone standing level with the foot filling the boot. The top of the footprint is less clear than the heel of the foot which means that more pressure was applied at the back of the boot, suggesting possibly that the wearer was someone with a smaller foot. This isn't an exact science. The imprint isn't wonderfully clear but it's worth bearing in mind."

"Do we have any idea as to what size it could be, pin it down a bit more?" asked Dax hopefully.

"Well, not an exact measurement but if we follow this as a scenario, then we could extrapolate that someone with a foot size of anything between 6 and 9 is a possibility. As I say, not wonderfully helpful but something to play with."

"So, could be male or female. Not many men with a size 6 foot."

"Worth bearing in mind," agreed Alexis. She paused. "I've had a thought. Let's get a search warrant and see if we can find the things."

"You're joking," replied Dax with amazement. "There'll be loads of wellies at the school."

"Yes, but not necessarily size 11s, and not all with loam from the flower bed stuck in the tread, if we're lucky."

Dax didn't look convinced. Alexis grinned as she saw the doubt on her friend's face.

"If it'll make you feel any better, there might even be the outside chance of a bit of blood on the boots. The caretaker didn't fall into the water, he was probably pushed by a foot, otherwise there wouldn't be any blood on the flagstones by the side of the pool."

Dax brightened. "You've got a point there. OK, I'll get on to it now."

"Ta."

Alexis left Dax to it, and returned to her office to find an email from the forensic team on her laptop. They'd been busy and a list of the first ten DNA results had come through, with a promise of more later that day. Alexis scanned them eagerly but her enthusiasm soon waned as ten minutes later, she realised that, as yet nothing concrete had been discovered. Felicity's attacker was still a mystery, the foetus' paternity still unknown. Alexis sighed. It was going to be a long and very frustrating wait.

Frances Smythe sat at her desk, trying to look busy in the job she was supposed to do, but in reality working hard at her very lucrative sideline. Her Ebay account was flourishing and it was quite time consuming keeping up with the sales. She had a very profitable little business going, selling vintage garden tools, and today was no exception. She should have been collating the replies to the Speech Day invitations, but a large Ebay order had just come in and Frances was working hard, in the school's time of course, fulfilling the order and checking her stock. She would have a bit of packing to do when she got home. A few months previously, her father had died, her only remaining parent, and he'd left her a shedful of old tools and garden implements. Her first thought had been to ditch the lot, but her neighbour, a local farmer, had told her that the stuff was probably worth a bit, being vintage and collectable as it was. Following some market research and Google searches she had realised the truth in this and began selling the stuff on Ebay. Sales had gone well and Frances had made a tidy sum.

Only trouble was, stocks had soon dwindled and sales began to peter out. She soon realised that without new stock her profitable little business would end with the last item from her father's shed. Shortly after coming to this unhappy conclusion, and after wondering what to do next to raise a spare penny or two, one of Frances' rare unselfish acts had led to her offering a helping hand to a friend, who was herself trying to raise a bit of money by selling a few bits at a local car boot sale. In a dull moment, Frances had left her friend to it and wandered round the sale ground. As she reached the last boot, Frances found the answer to her own stock problem. There, looking rusty and very damp in the drizzle that had caught up with the day, was a pile of old tools, looking decidedly worse for wear but salvageable with a little tender loving care. Never one to miss a trick, Frances decided, there and then, to invest in these few rusty old tools and see what she could do with them. Carting them home in a tatty old cardboard box, she got to work with wire wool and oil and within a week had a large boxful of new stock. Her investments had proved to be sound and she hadn't looked back. With summer now more or less upon her, sales were brisk and she needed as much time as she could to keep up with the transactions. Today was no exception and as she buried her head in the computer, studiously ignoring the pile of work in her in-tray, she didn't at first notice the little box that someone had left on the edge of her desk. She had vaguely been aware of someone drifting past, but as they neither stopped nor engaged her in conversation, she ignored them, her head down and wrapped up in Ebay and before she knew it, the bell sounded for the end of the school day. The insistent tones brought Frances out of her other world and back to where she should be, seeing parents as they collected their various offspring and being the elegant front of Coates Norton School. She stood up and stretched her aching back, stiff from two hours of being crouched in one position over her computer keyboard. It was then she noticed the little box, small, pink and wrapped in red ribbon. Her interest piqued, she picked it up and read the message typed in black ink, 'Dearest Frances, from a friend xx'. Smiling knowingly - of course she knew who 'a friend' was - she untied the ribbon and began to unwrap the little box. She lifted the lid and there inside were four little chocolates, nestling delicately against pink tissue paper. She pulled one out, the most delicious looking; a cherry wrapped in the most succulent looking dark chocolate and began to put it to her mouth.

"Miss Smythe, just the person I want to see." The voice made her jump and the chocolate slipped from her hand and caught the edge of the box as it fell to the table.

"Ah, Mrs Logan-James, how good to see you," replied Frances as she collected her wits, recognising the parent of one of the day scholars. "What can I do for you?" she asked patiently, her natural suavity and front of house demeanour kicking in.

"Just to let you know my husband and I will be here for Speech Day next week."

"That's good. I will add you to my list. Let's hope it's a sunny day. Thank you for taking the trouble to let me know."

Frances paused as she realised she had lost eye contact with the ebullient mother, the woman now appearing to look as if she'd seen a ghost. Following Mrs Logan-James' glance, Frances looked down at her desk and saw to her horror that the chocolate, which had almost made its way into her mouth and then dropped, now seemed to be sitting in a pool of liquid, a pungent smell now emanating from the desk where the confectionery had fallen. Instinctively, without thinking, Frances quickly reached down and picked up the chocolate, dropping it just as swiftly with a scream. It had burned her fingers. "I'm not sure what was in that chocolate, but I wouldn't eat it, if I were you," said Mrs Logan-James. "I'd complain to the factory where they made it."

Frances, cradling her sore fingers in a tissue grabbed from the box on her desk, managed to regain her sense of decorum and nodded.

"Excuse me, Mrs Logan-James. I think I need to clear this mess up."

"Well, I'll leave you to it," replied Mrs Logan-James, who rapidly and very thankfully made an exit, leaving Frances with her sticky problem. Frances was not given to panic, and this was no exception, but she soon realised what had just happened and its seriousness. With the events of the last few days firmly in her mind, she drew the inevitable conclusions. With her uninjured hand she grabbed the phone and within a few minutes she was connected to Dax, who was still perusing reports at his desk in the police station. He listened to Frances' now over-excited and rather frantic account of the incident with patience, her equilibrium now deserted her as the pain to her hand overwhelmed her and shock set in. After advising her to seek medical help as soon as possible, he replaced the telephone thoughtfully. This was no accident. After making a few brief notes of his conversation with Frances, he stood up and made his way to Alexis' office.

"Sorry to interrupt, ma'am, but thought you ought to know that I've just had a call from a rather frantic and very upset Frances Smythe."

He then went on to reveal the gist of his conversation, leaving Alexis stroking her chin, as she realised the importance of what had just occurred. It reinforced her notion that Frances was the true victim and the murderer had tried again. Perhaps the perpetrator had made a mistake and this was the break they needed. Without any delay, she had a small team from forensics gathered, the team still working at Hamish's lab on the DNA swabs and, with Dax and Hannah, made her way quickly to the school. Frances met them at the main front door and, for once, Alexis felt sorry for her. Frances' right hand was now treated and heavily bandaged by the school nurse and her face showed signs of stress, her cheeks pale and her eyes wide with delayed shock. All her airs and graces had vanished, her own conclusions drawn from the incident.

"Someone wanted to kill me. That chocolate has been doctored."

This was enough to reduce Frances to tears and sinking into a chair, she dissolved into heavy sobs.

"What on earth is going on here," boomed a loud voice. The stentorian tones of Graham Harper echoed above Frances' cries as he stormed across the hallway. Not, at first, noticing the police standing by the doorway he went on remorselessly.

"For goodness sake woman, pull yourself together. What on earth has got into you?"

Frances looked up at the headmaster, her tear soaked cheeks now regaining a little colour.

"You ... chocolates ...," she sobbed. Hannah moved across to comfort Frances and then Graham noticed Alexis and Dax standing to one side. He stopped in his tracks, brought up short by the presence of three officers back at his school again.

"Why the blazes are you lot here again? What the hell is going on here," he blustered angrily.

Frances opened her mouth, trying to speak again, but Alexis held up her hand and she stopped in mid breath.

"Mr Harper, it appears that Miss Smythe has met with an unfortunate incident. It needs exploration, so I can't say anything further at the moment. I will keep you informed."

Graham reddened, then blanched as he saw the sticky mess, now uncovered on the desk in front of him.

"What the hell..."

Frances held up her bandaged hand. Graham paled even further, his red cheeks fading rapidly to a pallid grey. He was no fool. He could see what had happened. His head spun, his legs suddenly feeling weak.

"Did you give me these chocolates?" Frances moaned quietly.

"Of course I bloody didn't. Why on earth would I give you chocolates, you stupid woman," Graham blustered.

Frances recoiled in shock and sobbed again as Graham's harsh words hit home. Turning sharply, the headmaster returned rapidly to his office before he lost his self-control, what was left of it, leaving Frances to sort out her own problems.

"Hannah, can you take Miss Smythe to somewhere a little less public, and get a statement? Make sure her hand is OK. Get her to hospital if necessary. We'll clear up here," Alexis asked gently.

Hannah nodded and putting an arm under Frances' elbow, lifted her gently from her seat and helped her away from the glare of a group of gathered parents. They, in turn, then drifted away, tutting and muttering. Alexis and Dax stared at the desk, the chocolate now fully dissolved in its own puddle of caustic liquid.

"The same bloody phenol," said Dax grimly. "I'd recognise that smell anywhere by now."

Alexis directed her forensic colleagues to gather as much of the confectionary as they could and once the remainder of the chocolates and their pretty pink box had been removed, and photographs had been taken, Alexis surveyed the damage to the table. The puddle of melted chocolate had caused the wood to almost shrivel, leaving a small crater in the polished surface.

"That's a real concentrated dose to cause that sort of damage so quickly. Someone knows their stuff with this bloody chemical," exclaimed Dax

Alexis nodded heavily.

"I feel bad about this. We should have guessed the murderer would try again once we suspected who the real victim should've been in all this."

"We haven't really had time," answered Dax. "We've only just reached that conclusion ourselves."

"Miss Smythe has been very lucky. If she'd eaten that chocolate …" Alexis trailed off, her brow creasing with the realisation of how close they'd all come. Shaking herself, both mentally and physically, she suddenly turned on her heel and, followed by Dax, returned to her car to make her way back to the police station. Once back there, Alexis collected a message from Hannah, left just as they reached the office. She reported that Frances' hand was hurting badly under its bandage, so she'd taken the receptionist to the local hospital, had the hand treated and dressed again, and taken the woman home. She'd be back in half an hour. Hannah returned as promised, saying she had got a rough verbal account of what had happened but would go out and get a formal statement tomorrow. The three officers sat together in the Detective Inspector's office and with coffee cups in their hands, mulled over what the day had brought.

"Whoever's doing this is getting desperate. We need to keep a close eye on Miss Smythe until we get the bastard."

"I'll get Steve Moss onto some sort of protection for a while," said Dax.

"Try and convince her to stay at home for a while, at least until her hand is better. She'd be safer there," agreed Alexis, standing up. "Right, tomorrow's another day. Go home, get some rest, have a good think and we'll regroup in the morning, eight thirty sharp. Hopefully, we'll have the rest of the DNA results to get us going again and the search warrant. God, do we need a break. This has been going on for too long."

Shooing her colleagues out of the office, Alexis soon followed them. She felt dispirited and tired. She felt so close but not close enough. She sent up a silent prayer for a bit of divine intervention. The end of the week was upon them, today was Saturday. Alexis felt dispirited. She felt the answer was so close, but there were too many loose ends to form a full picture.

Leaving the now empty office behind her, Alexis headed for her car and instead of turning for home, she headed south towards Hereford, and her appointment with the Bishop. She'd been looking forward to seeing her friend again, it had been too long. They had a lot to catch up on. Stephen was waiting for her, the traffic into the city had been heavy at the end of the day and Alexis was running late as a result. He saw the tiredness lines showing heavily around Alexis' face and welcomed her straight into his private rooms, away from the work of his day and into a cosy, almost snug like room where his wife had laid a small table with sandwiches and cake, and instead of a coffee pot, a beautiful white china tea pot sat, wrapped in a hand knitted cosy, with steam gently floating upwards from its spout. Alexis smiled, the scene before her easing the strain from her shoulders at a glance.

"Come, sit by the fire, my dear," the Bishop invited. "Not to put too fine a point on it, you look shattered."

Alexis sank gratefully into a well-worn but exceedingly comfortable upholstered chair, dropping her briefcase down beside her. The small log fire in the grate crackled gently and Alexis found herself relaxing too much. The Bishop busied himself with pouring tea. After handing her the cup, and a small side plate to go with it, he then proffered the plate of sandwiches. Lunch had seemed an age ago and with dinner too far in the future even to think about, Alexis accepted a sandwich eagerly. The tea revived her and before long, the Bishop and his guest were chatting as only friends can.

"So, Alexis my dear, what have you been up to? That is, if you're allowed to say. London must have been very trying."

Alexis allowed herself to ramble on, telling the Bishop about her work in London, relieving herself yet again of the strain she had been under. Talking to Dax had been hard, the first time she'd had the chance to talk freely about the events which had transpired in London during her stay there. Now, the second time with the Bishop, she found it easier. Even the few days she'd been home had been enough to push events into a kind of past, a slot in her memory which could be accessed whenever she chose but one that didn't cause any horrors of remembering. Bishop Stephen let her talk, a man used to listening, realising the cathartic advantages that talking had. Alexis came to a stop, the tea in her hand cooling nicely and the sandwiches having made a satisfying dent in her hunger.

"So, why are you really here?" asked the Bishop with a gentle smile.

"Am I that transparent?" Alexis replied with a lopsided grin.

"It is so good to see you, and we still have so much to catch upon, but I know you're frantically busy with the murder at that confounded school, so I'm surprised you've got the time."

"I haven't' really," agreed Alexis, "but as it's murders now ..."

"Murders? Plural?" exclaimed the Bishop.

"Fraid so," replied Alexis. Leaving out the specific details of the evidence they had gleaned, but knowing she could trust his confidentiality, she went on to fill the Bishop in on events that had transpired since his visit, including Felicity's pregnancy. He visibly paled at the news.

"That poor girl. I see all sorts of humanity in my profession. Some wonderful, some so low it beats comprehension. Is there anything I can do?"

"Well, that's why I'm here, really. I just wanted to get your impression of the school; anyone you met, anyone you spoke to. Anything you thought might be odd or out of place."

"Well," the Bishop pondered. "I wasn't really there for very long but I'll do my best."

"Who did you actually meet?"

"The first person I met was the headmaster, a jumped up 'little' man in my opinion, not short of his own high opinion of himself. No fan of women, I got the impression, particularly how he dealt with that domestic woman who fainted. A disgraceful show."

"Don't hold back, Stephen," Alexis laughed.

"Well, I can speak plainly with you," replied the Bishop ruefully. "I know it won't go anywhere. Graham Harper is an out and out bully, and has completely lost any respect in the staff room. I've met the sort before. A man without any confidence, which is a shame, but who makes up for it by being bombastic and loud."

"I agree. He certainly put my back up but being who I was he couldn't lord it over me. Who else?" Alexis encouraged.

"There were only four of us at dinner; the headmaster, his finance chap and his wife... poor woman ..." The Bishop paused, relapsing into thought.

"Why do you say that?"

"She's typical of a lot of women in that situation - no fire, no backbone, completely under the thumb. She's in the all-consuming shadow of her husband. A woman completely out of depth when it comes to socialising. Mind you, maybe still waters run deep. She'll do one of three thing: put up with her lot, which I suspect is highly probable, she's too far gone; or just walk out one day or perhaps just turn and tell him his fortune - face up to him. You never know."

Alexis sipped her tea, mulling over the Bishop's comments.

"What about the finance chappie, Gerald Leigh?"

"He didn't say a lot at dinner. Mind you, he never really got the chance. I got the impression that he was a decent sort but again overshadowed by the headmaster. I think he's in a very difficult position. Being in charge of finances is a huge responsibility but if the headmaster clicked his fingers, the poor man would have to do what he was told to do. I'm not suggesting there is any financial impropriety going on but if there was, I suspect Mr Leigh is not at fault."

"Interesting. I get the feeling that whatever happens over these murders, then the headmaster is in for a rude awakening."

Bishop Stephen raised an eyebrow. "How come?"

Alexis sat back and relaxed further into her chair, lulled into a feeling of ease by her company, the food and the effects of a warm fire. She spent the next few minutes relating the visit she'd had from the Chairman of Governors. When she'd finished, the Bishop chuckled, a deep warm throaty laugh that was infectious.

"Oh, how I'd love to be a fly on the wall if that day comes," said the Bishop.

"Watch this space. I'll keep you posted, but if he does get the push, it'll be all over the local news and in the papers. Interesting times ahead."

"Are you getting anywhere with the case?"

"Slowly. Can't go into too many details, but we've got some interesting results and we're working through those at the moment. Hopefully, not too long."

The Bishop realised that Alexis couldn't go into too much operational detail about the case she was working on and he accepted that. So, with a top up of tea in their hands, and a piece of cake to go with it, the Bishop and Alexis spent a very enjoyable hour chatting about the things that interested them both, mainly music and the comings and goings of Luke and Georgia, son and sister respectively. But, all good things had to come to an end as a phone call interrupted their tea.

"Sorry, Alexis, I've got to go. Small emergency in the cathedral."

"Nothing serious, I hope?"

"No, just the organist has called in sick for tonight's Evensong so got to find someone else or go without. You don't want to play, do you?" asked the Bishop hopefully.

Alexis was sorely tempted but after a brief quandary she declined.

"I'm happy to twiddle away on my piano in private at home, but the cathedral organ is a step too far. Tempted though," finished Alexis wistfully.

"Come and have a private play, sometime," the Bishop invited cordially.

"Now, that I could do but not tonight. I'm sorry. I hope you find someone."

The Bishop patted Alexis affectionately on her arm.

"Don't worry. I'll find someone."

With that final gesture, and a swift kiss goodbye, Alexis was on her way home, the road north now less crowded after the rush hour.

She spent a restless night, her dreams punctured by images of burnt chocolates and bodies lying across tables. She woke the following morning with a pounding headache and the beginnings of a summer cold. Her throat was sore, her eyes ran with the effect of her sniffles and her nose was stuffed up. She could have done with the day off, just to recharge her batteries and clear her head, but there was too much to do. She threw herself out of bed and thought about the day ahead. If the DNA results were back, there might be a clue there. She desperately hoped for Felicity's sake, or rather that of her friends as Felicity was beyond help now, that there was a match with the foetus. If she could only clear that up, it would be a major step forward. Alexis was convinced that this was a separate crime to the murders, there seemed no link between them. They were looking for two perpetrators. After a shower, the hot steam of

253

which at least helped to clear her stuffy nose, she finished dressing and headed downstairs for breakfast. As she passed the dining room, she quickly glanced at her piano. Music was her passion and kept her sane and playing the piano was a particular pleasure. Since returning from London, she hadn't even had a chance to lift the lid but she promised herself, particularly after her conversation with the Bishop yesterday, that she'd get back into practice. The promise of a twiddle on the cathedral organ was too good a chance to pass up. She sighed as she realised that she'd promised herself a lot of things since coming back from London but, first things first, she had some murders to solve.

The day was dull and gloomy, the sky overcast with clouds that again promised rain. The smell of fresh coffee and warm toast did little to revive her spirits, and it was with a heavy tread that she made her way outside to the car. The blossom of a large May tree danced in the wind, its pretty dark pink flowers heralding something brighter, and its appearance lightened Alexis' mood. She settled in her car, turned up the heater, slipped a Bach CD into the player and headed for work. She reached the office just before Dax, who walked in behind her.

"You don't look so good, ma'am," said Dax with concern.

"No, I've got a lousy cold starting. Don't get too close; don't want the whole office down with it."

"If I'm going to get something, Claire will give it to me," replied Dax with a grin. "She always seems to get things first."

As the two officers headed for their respective desks, Dax went on.

"Are we getting anywhere? I notice there's a pile of files on your desk. Hopefully, they're the DNA results."

Alexis turned and looked through the glass door to her office. There was, indeed, a pile of reports waiting for her inspection.

"Let's hope we've got an answer there," said Alexis, with a heavy sniffle. "This has dragged on a bit. I'd like to get things wrapped up as soon as I can."

Alexis pushed open the door to her office, walked in and slumped in her chair, her head heavy with cold. She looked up as Hannah walked in with a mug in her hands.

"Thought you'd like a cuppa, ma'am."

"Thanks Hannah, you're a star. It'll lubricate my throat."

Alexis took the cup from Hannah, who turned and left the office shutting the door quietly behind her, and pulled the various reports towards her; the first a very preliminary report about the chocolate poisoning. Hamish had concluded that, indeed, Frances had had a very narrow escape. If it hadn't been for a tiny puddle of coffee on the desk, that had melted the chocolate and activated the phenol crystals as they fell, letting off their causticity, Frances would never have known how lethal the chocolate was until she had eaten it. The end result could have been very different. She could have survived with quick treatment, but the crystals inside the other chocolates were highly toxic and would have been very painful, if ingested. Putting that to one side, Alexis pulled a fatter file towards him. Again, this was a report from the pathologist.

'Poor Hamish,' mused Alexis to her coffee cup. 'He's had a busy time.'

She started to read. As she did so, her mood lightened considerably. At last, a breakthrough. She jumped up from her chair, threw the door open and shouted.

"Archie!"

Dax looked up in surprise. He'd been going through the statements, looking for something, a small clue, but seeing the look on his boss' face, he knew he needn't bother.

"What's up, ma'am?" he asked.

"We've got him," replied Alexis with energy in her voice.

"Who?" asked Dax, hoping it was the answer he was looking for.

He still felt bad about Felicity's death, wondering yet if there had been anything he could have done to avoid it. His head told him no but his heart visited a different story on him. All evidence seemed to point to a case of mistaken identity, but he felt responsible, just the same.

"Felicity's rapist," came the jubilant reply.

"Fantastic," replied Dax, the answer rapidly followed by a cheer from the rest of the office.

Dax took the report from the pathologist and briefly scanned the first page. He whistled in disbelief but felt relief, too, as he realised that they'd nailed him.

"I want you to take Hannah, Steve and Mike out to the school with you," went on Alexis. "Arrest the bastard and, now armed with this knowledge, have another chat with Maisie. Corroboration is always useful and maybe this time she'll spill the beans."

Chapter Thirteen

Dax wasted no time. He returned to his desk, grabbed his jacket and was soon on his way out of the office, Hannah and the other two detective constables following rapidly in his wake. Hannah and Dax took to one car and the drive to the school took less time than it should, Hannah hanging onto her seat for dear life as Dax pushed the car to its limit, round the dizzying bends that lay in the valley between Teigneford and the outer villages. Mike and Steve followed in another car behind, having no trouble in keeping up. They arrived at the school in a whirl of gravel, as the cars came to a rapid halt. Dax grinned at the gouge marks he'd left in the pristine stone.

"That was fun," said Steve, as he emerged rather breathless from the second car. Hannah ignored the banter, and with a slight nod towards Dax, headed for the boarding house where Maisie and her friends lived. Dax slammed the car door, locked it and headed for Reception. He bounded up the stone steps, and found Reception empty, Frances obviously still away, nursing her hand. Wasting no time, he headed through the Inner Hall's connecting door and banged on Sarah's door. Within seconds, she opened it. Seeing Dax standing there, obviously in hurry, she wasted no time with pleasantries.

"What's up?" she asked.

"I need to see the Chaplain now. Where is he?"

"I think he's actually in the staff room", replied Sarah. "It's break time. He usually goes in there at this time."

"Good!" replied Dax.

"Why?" asked Sarah.

Dax ignored her, and turning on his heel quickly, headed through reception and into the staff room. He went in without knocking and found the room buzzing, lively with conversation and clinking tea and coffee cups. His dramatic entrance brought the room to a halt and a sudden silence enveloped all who were there. Everyone

257

looked up in surprise at the sudden interruption. Dax looked quickly round the room. At first glance his quarry seemed absent. Dax wasted no time.

"Please could you tell me if the Chaplain is in here, Dr Ernest Cannerby?" he asked without prevarication.

"I am he," came the quiet reply, as a small man poked his head around the door from the adjoining kitchenette. Dax turned and looked at Dr Cannerby. He was a round faced man, in his later middle years. Grey haired and balding and slightly overweight, he seemed a fairly non-descript sort of person, his benign features belying the depravities to which he had sunk. Thick round glasses hid weak, watery blue eyes. He seemed mildly taken aback but as yet no guilt showed on his face, merely surprise.

"What can I do for you?" he went on.

Dax wasted no time.

"Dr Ernest Cannerby, I am arresting you on suspicion of rape and child abuse. You do not have to say anything, but it may harm your defence, if you fail to mention, when questioned, something which you may later rely on in court. Anything you do say, may be given in evidence. Do you understand?"

The Chaplain paled visibly, and his podgy hands began to shake. An audible gasp went round the staff room, a tea cup rattled in its saucer. Without exception, each member of staff first looked at the chaplain in amazement, then Dax in bewilderment.

"Do you understand?" repeated Dax.

The Chaplain swallowed.

"Yes, I do, but I think there's been a terrible mistake. I love children."

"A little too much, I think," replied Dax with asperity.

"What is going on here?" boomed a loud voice suddenly, making Dax jump.

Graham Harper had entered the room unseen by anyone, so rapt were they on the situation playing out before them. The headmaster's crow like presence towered menacingly over the assembled crowd.

"I know manners seem to have gone to the wall with the police these days, but the courtesy of informing me of your presence in the school would have been appreciated."

Dax turned and faced the headmaster. He'd had enough of the man's pomposity.

"Shut up!" said Dax peremptorily.

Graham blinked. "I beg your pardon."

Dax sighed. "If you wish to know, Mr Harper," said Dax, emphasising the Mr and relishing the grimace that Graham showed briefly on his face. "I have just arrested your chaplain for child abuse and rape. He will be taken to the police station and questioned. That is what is going on here. Now if you will excuse me."

Dax smartly handcuffed the chaplain and led him from the room leaving Graham staring in disbelief at his departing back, speechless, robbed of words for once. As the door slammed in front of him, Graham slumped in a chair, his face blanched, all colour draining from his face. He'd just remembered the warning he'd had from someone when he had started at the school. It all came back to him in stark clarity now as he heard the retreating steps of his chaplain and the detective sergeant. He'd refused to believe the warnings from an ex student, saying how she had been touched by the chaplain, in intimate places, all those years ago. Wanderings of a vindictive mind, he had thought at the time. Now he wished he had listened.

Dax handed over Cannerby into the custody of his two detective constables, instructing them to return to the police station, go through the formalities of the arrest and bang him up in a cell to await questioning later. Dax then watched contentedly as the car disappeared down the drive. Felicity could now rest in peace, his duty to her done. A sudden shower of spring rain covered his face as he stood on the gravel. He felt clean again as the droplets trickled down his cheeks. He turned back towards the school and headed for Maisie's boarding house. The rain stopped as suddenly as it had started and his tension eased further as the clouds parted and the sun reappeared, drying the dampness on his face. Birds began to sing as the clouds lifted, raising Dax's spirits even further as they sang. The quad had filled with children as break time got under way and life went on as usual. There was still murder to sort out, but the vileness of child abuse was washed away with the rain. The departing shower produced a brilliant rainbow, its colours vivid against a dark sky as it appeared in a large arc across the horizon. A promise? Dax wondered.

The drive back to the police station gave Cannerby a chance to collect his thoughts. The arrest had severely shaken him, not the least of which was the embarrassment he had endured in front of his colleagues. It was unforgivable of the police to have done what they did and he would complain in the strongest terms possible to the detective inspector's superiors. His mind wandered back over his life in education. He had enjoyed it. He loved being with the children and hoped that this little upset he was now experiencing wouldn't jeopardize his future and the fun he had had with the girls. He had had a long and successful career. He was past the normal retirement age but he'd stayed on, his presence and pastoral duties welcomed by the headmaster. It didn't occur to him for one moment that his career was over. This was just a small upset and everything would carry on as normal once things had been sorted out and explained. He settled easily back into his seat, and watched as the countryside sped by. He'd seen the rainbow too and knew that God's promise held as good for him as it did for anyone else. It would encompass him. He was a good Christian man, devout in his pastoral duties. He had done nothing wrong. He had cared for the children; loved them; treated them with a special attention he'd given to no one else. He had enjoyed the secrecy and the games that he had played. He had seen their fear but this had only aroused his sexual desires even more. As he thought about this, his legs stirred and his trousers moved. He shifted to make himself more comfortable and began to think carefully over what he would say when he was back at the police station. He knew that any evidence the police had was entirely circumstantial; there would be nothing physical and Maisie would say nothing. There was no evidence to link him to Felicity. It was all hearsay and easily refutable. A good barrister, if it came to court, would tear any child to shreds. He had no worries.

He had just reached the conclusion that this was a storm in a tea cup and it would all blow over before nightfall when the car pulled into the back of Teigneford police station and he was bundled unceremoniously in through the back door and into the tender loving care of Sergeant Philip Greenford, the Custody Sergeant. His handcuffs were removed and he was fingerprinted, a DNA swab taken and then led through the formalities. It worried him to start with but then, content in the knowledge that the police had nothing on him, he relaxed as Philip Greenford finished filling in his forms. It would soon be over and he'd be back home for tea. He idly wondered if he'd have time for his confirmation lesson with Maisie. As he thought about this, a smile played with his lips, and he ran his tongue along his slightly protruding teeth as he pondered the possibilities of his evening's entertainment. He was bought out of his pleasant mental ramblings by the stern voice of the sergeant.
"Right, mate!" said the sergeant uncompromisingly. "We're done here, you're off to the cells."
The Custody Sergeant knew exactly why the chaplain was where he was and felt sickened. He was a grizzled, grey haired old-school copper, on the verge of retirement. Throughout his long service he'd met all sorts - murderers, thieves, vicious attackers and, yes, rapists, but this was a first, a child abuser and rapist. He felt sullied and disgusted as he led the chaplain down to the cells. He moved with professionalism but it took a lot of restraint not to wield a fist when they reached the silence and isolation of the cell block. His fingers itched to pan the man. Nevertheless, he contented himself with a curt instruction to remove his tie and his shoes, then with just a little energy, not too much, he pushed the chaplain into his

cell and slammed the door behind him. Shaking himself, both physically and mentally, Sergeant Greenford turned on his heel, leaving Cannerby alone, with time to think. The silence was absolute, the walls too thick to admit noise of any kind. The small window in the door had been slammed closed too so Cannerby had nothing to contemplate other than four scuffed and grey walls in his cell. A ledge under the high window gave him little comfort, the blue plastic mattress hard and without any comfort and far too low under the window to allow any sightings of the outside world. He sat alone, uncomfortable, cold and hungry but still he knew, with a false confidence that he would soon be home.

Hannah, meanwhile, had made contact with Charles Davenport. As they had arrived at break time and, as luck would have it, the children were in their boarding house, returned there after classes to collect their post. Hannah had no trouble tracking down the Davenports. She had rapidly given him an update, and he immediately looked for Maisie. He brought her downstairs from her room and ushered her into his own rooms. His wife was there, making coffee for them both and looked up in expectation as Hannah and Davenport entered, Maisie walking in front of him. Angela lifted an elegantly plucked eyebrow in question, as Hannah made eye contact. Hannah nodded briefly, and Angela visibly relaxed. Maisie stood there, miserably wondering what was going on.

"Maisie," said Hannah gently. "Sit down here, next to me. I have some news."

Maisie did as she was told, without a murmur, and sat quietly next to Hannah, her hands clasped tightly in her lap. Her cheeks were pale with tension, waiting for the inevitable questions.

"We have just arrested the man who made Felicity pregnant. I thought you'd like to know," said Hannah quietly.

Maisie looked up suddenly, a light in her eyes. Her whole face changed as realisation dawned and a new strength seemed to fill her small frame.

"Do you want to tell me what happened?" asked Hannah.

"I can now, can't I?" replied Maisie in a small voice. "He can't hurt me anymore, can he?"

"No, he can't. He is safely locked up in one of our cells, waiting for us to talk to him."

Maisie visibly relaxed and slumped back in her chair. She sat quietly for a minute, thinking, then the floodgates opened.

"Felicity and me ..."

Charles automatically opened his mouth to correct the child's incorrect grammar, but as quickly shut it. Now was not the time.

"We went to Confirmation Classes with Dr Cannerby every week. There were some boys as well but he didn't touch them, well at least I don't think so. When the classes were over, he'd ask either Felicity or me to stay behind, just to go over something, he said, but he never meant it. He used to take us back to his room..." Maisie faltered as she remembered. "The first time he did it, it really hurt. He took me into his bedroom, I knew it was wrong, but he was so strong. He pushed me onto his bed, and I just shut my eyes."

Maisie broke down and sobbed, her tension welling up and escaping with the tears as the memory returned to haunt her. Angela came over and sat beside her on the sofa and hugged her, wiping her tears away with a clean tissue, her disgust apparent and so visible on her face.

"He really hurt me. I felt so dirty. I didn't know what to do."

Maisie sat up and wiped her eyes with another tissue.

"He told me never to tell anyone or I would be expelled. Mum would never forgive me. It was all my fault."

"No, it wasn't your fault, none of it is," said Hannah firmly. "He was a dirty old man who took advantage of you. There was nothing you could have done."

"If I'd said something, maybe Felicity would have been alive now."

"No, we think Felicity was killed by someone else. Her death had nothing to do with the chaplain so whether you had said something or not, it wouldn't have made any difference."

Maisie sniffed, slightly mollified, but her distress was palpable.

"I found out later that he took it in turns with Felicity and me. She used to come back from classes crying her eyes out, and I guessed, but she never said anything. She told me a few days before she died that she thought she was pregnant. The morning after Felicity died, I went to Confirmation Classes. Dr Cannerby told me that he had me all to himself now. I was so frightened."

"When was the last time Dr Cannerby attacked you?" asked Hannah, gently.

"The week before last, Wednesday evening," came the instant reply, as Maisie remembered the torture, still so vivid in her mind. "It was our last lesson. It was my turn."

Hannah realised that any chance of DNA samples from Maisie would be long gone, so at least the child was spared that humiliation.

"Maisie, I am going to ask you a very serious question and I want you to think about it very carefully," went on Hannah.

Maisie nodded quietly, waiting expectantly.

"We will take Dr Cannerby to court. Would you be willing to give evidence against him, tell the judge what he did to you? It would all be done very gently, and only the judge will be able to see you. No one will know it is you."

Maisie paled noticeably and gulped. She was an intelligent girl and the ramifications weren't lost on her.

"Will it stop him from doing it again?" she asked in a tight, quiet voice.

"Oh, yes, definitely. He won't be able to get at you ever again," replied Hannah with emphasis.

"Mum and Dad will have to know, won't they?" Maisie asked miserably.

"Yes they will because you are going to need some help. They will know it was not your fault. They will be upset, yes, but not against you. They love you and want the best for you."

Maisie thought for a moment and Hannah waited. She knew the evidence was strong enough with the DNA results, but personal corroboration would make a conviction inevitable and the emotional impact of Maisie's testimony in court would hold a great sway over the jury. It had to be up to Maisie though.

"OK, I'll do it," said Maisie with determination. "What do I have to do?"

"Thank you, Maisie," said Hannah. "That was a very brave decision. I will take a statement from you now, while we are together and Mrs Davenport is here to help you. Then I think you ought to go home. Mrs Davenport and your Mum and Dad can talk with me whenever they like about getting any help for you. You've been through a lot and you might need some help to sort things out in your mind."

Maisie nodded. She felt numb and emotionless, but relieved that it was all over. She had been through hell, the horror of it all still raw in her mind. She knew her journey wasn't quite finished, but she was alive and she was going home. She would be safe. Hannah spent the next hour, slowly and painfully drawing out from Maisie all the horrible, explicit details making sure that the girl knew exactly what she was saying and that she understood everything. Charles Davenport then took Maisie away so that Hannah could talk more freely with his wife. Angela Davenport had sat and watched, her heart aching for the child in her care. She had let Maisie and Felicity down, and who knows how many other girls in the confirmation classes down the years. The thoughts ashamed her and made her feel very uncomfortable. Hannah looked up and watched the conflicting emotions chasing across Angela's face and understood. She leant over and touched her hand. Tears appeared in Angela's eyes.

"It wasn't your fault. You can't guess the unknown. If a child won't confide then there is little you can do."

"I should have seen the signs," replied Angela miserably.

"What were the signs? Tears, discomfort, silence?" asked Hannah.

"All things that could easily be put down to homesickness, periods, boy problems. The trouble with this sort of thing is that it is so secretive. The perpetrator bullies his victims into silence, Maisie has testified to that."

Angela nodded.

"I know, but it doesn't make it any easier."

"Now is the time you can help. It is highly likely that Cannerby has had his way with a succession of girls over the years, so are you able to give me a list of female confirmation candidates for the past few years?"

Angela nodded dumbly.

"Thanks. I'll leave you to tell Maisie's parents. I didn't want to say this in front of Maisie but she will need a pregnancy test as well, just in case. The swine has obviously proved himself very fertile. Here's my card if her parents want to contact me. I assume you will need to tell the headmaster, although he already knows of the chaplain's arrest?" went on Hannah.

Angela nodded again, bereft of speech. Then shaking herself, realising that self-pity wasn't going to help anyone at the moment, raised her head and with a new resolution, stood and faced Hannah.

"Do you need me for anything further? I'd like to get back to Maisie."

"No, thank you," Hannah acknowledged. "I'll be in touch if we need anything else."

Angela left the room in a hurry and Hannah headed outside for some much needed air. Dax was waiting, sitting on the wall that ran round the garden. He looked up as Hannah approached and saw the tension still vivid in her eyes.

"Phew!" she exclaimed. "Glad that's over."

"Did you get anything?" he asked anxiously.

"Yes, the whole damn lot. Cannerby was at it with Maisie and Felicity alternate weeks, the bastard. Maisie has made a statement, and at the moment is willing to give evidence. That willingness may change when she has time to think about it, but I doubt it. She's a tough cookie and she was great friends with Felicity. I think she'll do it for her, if anything."

"Thank God for that," replied Dax with feeling.

"Do you think we need to tell the headmaster, you know how he's always banging on about courtesy," asked Hannah.

"Stuff him," replied Dax with feeling. "Whenever has he ever shown us any courtesy? He knows I've had Cannerby arrested for alleged rape and child abuse so I don't owe him any favours just now. Besides, Maisie's predicament is none of his business at the moment, not at least until her parents have been told. That'll come hard. Anyway, he's not stupid. He can put two and two together."

Dax stopped, feeling sullied and disgusted all in one moment as he realised how one thing had led to another. At least the man had been stopped, but how many other paedophiles were there out there? He shrugged. He couldn't fix all the world's problems, just try hard to fix those he could locally.

"Yup, you're right," agreed Hannah.

"Cannerby's been taken to the station with Steve and Mike. They'll get him sorted with Phil in the custody suite, then we'll have a nice little chat with him. I'm looking forward to that," he finished with relish.

Dax and Hannah headed back across the quad, now quiet and empty of children. Dax noticed heads bent down in the chemistry lab hard at work and wondered who was taking the lesson, the school now bereft of its chemistry teacher. He had lost touch with that side of the investigation, his mind so full of Felicity's demise, and wondered if they were any closer to a conclusion. This place was getting to him and he wanted to see the back of it as soon as he could. They drove off back down the driveway, slowly negotiating the gravel, grateful to put the troubled school and its bully of a headmaster behind them for the time being. The rain had cleared completely and the sky was blue and amazingly cloudless.

"Oh," said Hannah suddenly, as they got close to the school gates.

Dax had been miles away, lost in his own thoughts and Hannah's exclamation had made him jump.

"You OK?" asked Dax with concern.

"Yes, I'm fine."

"What's up then?"

"Dunno, maybe nothing. Just thought I saw someone I recognised. Can't be though."

Hannah lapsed into silence, her brow creased with the concentration of driving. Dax looked at her but said nothing.

Back at the station, they went their separate ways. Dax headed for the canteen where he found Alexis having a quick cuppa and a sandwich.

"How'd you get on?" she asked, as Dax sat down beside her, a tray laden with food in front of him. "Hungry?" she went on with a grin.

"Too right. Breakfast seems ages ago."

"Did you get anywhere?" went on Alexis leaning forward, her elbows on the table, a half-eaten sandwich on a plate in front of her, a mug in her clasped hands.

"I haven't read the statement yet, but Hannah told me she got everything. Once Maisie realised that Cannerby wasn't a threat to her anymore, she opened up. She identified Cannerby as her abuser, and confirmed that Felicity had been similarly abused. Apparently, Maisie found out a few days before Felicity died, that she, Felicity, thought she was pregnant and discovered that Cannerby had attacked them both."

"Does she realise that this will have to go to court?"

"Yes, she does. She's an intelligent girl."

"Will she want to give evidence?" asked Alexis, ever aware of 'the more the better'.

"At the moment, yes," replied Dax. "Time will tell if she's still keen when the time comes, but Hannah thinks she will be. She's not daft. She knows what she'll be letting herself in for, but she'll get all the help she needs. The next problem she's going to have is when Mum and Dad find out."

"Hopefully they'll be sympathetic."

"Well, they ain't going to like it, that's for sure," replied Dax with feeling. "What parent would?"

Dax sat back and tucked into his sausage and chips, his face grim as he sat in silence. Alexis sat quietly, eating her own sandwich, and watched her friend, knowing exactly what Dax was thinking. She could see the emotions flitting across Dax's face as he filtered the morning's events through his mind. Alexis thought of her two little nieces, her sister Georgia's children. She loved them as her own, and hoped one day to have her own family. That day had not yet come but she could still imagine how she would feel if they had been attacked, like Felicity and Maisie. Alexis felt sick at the thought and tried to dismiss it from her mind. Dax picked up his cup of coffee.

"Oh, by the way, Hannah had a sort of eureka moment when we were on our way back," he said.

"What do you mean?" asked Alexis, her interest piqued.

"I don't really know. We were half way down the drive on our way out of the school, said 'Oh', and said she thought she saw someone or something she recognised, then changed her mind. She didn't say anything else but was quite thoughtful all the way back here."

"Wonder what it was?"

"Dunno."

"She'll tell us if and when it comes to her."

The clock ticked round to two o clock and the two officers finished their lunch.

"Right, let's go and talk to the bastard," said Dax, as he returned his tray to the trolley.

Dr Ernest Cannerby had been brought up from the cells and now sat in the interview room. He felt slightly nervous, never having been in this situation before; it was a new experience, but he didn't feel unduly worried. He knew they had no evidence and the girl wouldn't talk. He'd made sure of that. He sat back comfortably, watching the clock as it ticked round. The sun shone through the heavy reinforced windows, little rainbows dancing on the table as the thick glass cut the light into pieces. The door suddenly opened making Cannerby jump out of his thoughts. Dax walked in determinedly, followed rapidly by Alexis and the two officers sat down at the table, facing the school chaplain. Dax set up the recording machine and the little red light blinked, waiting for Dax to press the start button. Cannerby was cautioned again.

"Do you understand?" Dax asked. "This is now your best chance to come clean."

Cannerby nodded but stayed silent. He had little to say.

"Do you know why you are here?" asked Dax.

"Yes, your numbskulls have arrested me for child abuse and rape, I believe. I have never heard such nonsense," replied Cannerby petulantly. "I object to the manner in which you did it, in front of my friends and colleagues."

Alexis smiled. So that's how it was going to be, was it? She sat back and listened.

"Dr Cannerby, these are grave charges," went on Dax. "We wouldn't have acted without evidence."

Cannerby blinked but held his composure. He knew they were playing him.

"You've got nothing. You're bluffing. I have done nothing," Cannerby reiterated.

Dax held his tongue, not wishing to give too much away at the start. He wanted to keep the man guessing, keep him on his toes. He might let slip something that way. Dax decided to play with him.

"How long have you been at Coates Norton School?"

Cannerby relaxed, unaware of the traps being set.

"Oh, let me think," replied Cannerby, pausing, playing for time and leaning back in his chair, his podgy hands clasped behind his head. "About thirty years now, I believe."

"Where were you before that?" asked Dax.

"I was at a small school in Staffordshire. I taught R.I. there."

"R.I?" asked Dax.

"Yes, Religious Instruction."

"Oh, I see," said Dax. "What school was that?"

"It was Bishop's Mitre School, just outside Stafford."

"Why did you leave?"

"This position came up, and brought accommodation with it, so I applied and was successful."

Alexis stood up and left the room, Dax noting the fact on the recording. He vaguely wondered what his boss was up to, but carried on with the interview. Alexis headed for the CID office and found Hannah there, writing up her notes.

"Oh, hello ma'am," she said. "Have you got a moment, I need to discuss something with you."

"Sorry Hannah, can it wait?" asked Alexis. "I'm in the interview room with Sergeant Dax and the chaplain, cocky bastard," she finished with anger in her voice. "I came up to ask you to do something for me as soon as you can."

"OK, don't let me forget. I think there's some urgency but it can wait until you've done. What can I do for you?"

Alexis pushed a piece of paper across to Hannah.

"Can you look up anything untoward happening at this school about thirty years ago? Anything, however small, particularly in relation to Cannerby?"

Hannah looked at the paper and saw the name of the school that Cannerby had previously worked at.

"OK. I'll pop down to the interview room if I come up with anything."

"Thanks and we'll have that chat later. Don't let me forget."

Alexis left the office and headed back down to the interview room. She entered, and with a brief nod to Dax, sat back in her seat and resumed her previous position. She found Dax almost enjoying himself and Cannerby was beginning to look a little flushed and flustered.

"Dr Cannerby, do you teach the children now?"

"Not as such," came the rather ambiguous reply. "I gave up teaching about five years ago. I am just employed for chaplaincy duties now. I preach on Sundays in chapel, and I am available for pastoral duties."

God help the kids, thought Alexis.

"What do you mean by, 'not as such'? Either you do or you don't." Dax rejoined with impatience.

Dr Cannerby faltered.

"I, er …"

"Yes?" asked Dax.

We're getting to it, now, thought Alexis with quiet and private relish.

"I give weekly confirmation classes in the spring and summer terms."

"Are you giving classes at the moment?"

"Yes, I am."

"When are they expected to finish. Presumably there is a service at some point?" interrupted Alexis.

"The appointment of the new Bishop has delayed things a little, but the service will be in the cathedral during October."

"To whom are you giving them," asked Dax patiently. God, this was like drawing blood from a stone, he thought.

"Three boys and two girls, well at least one girl now."

"Why what happened to the second girl," said Dax leadingly.

"She died." Cannerby paused and sweat began to form on his brow.

"She died? Why what happened?" asked Dax innocently.

"You know what happened," replied Cannerby sharply, losing his temper slightly. "It was Felicity Smith."

"Oh, I see. And who was the other girl?"

"It was Maisie Bourne."

Dax turned to Alexis and raised an eyebrow. Alexis nodded.

"Did you ever ask the girls to stay after the classes?" asked Alexis as she took over the questioning.

"No, er, why would I do that?" asked Cannerby nervously, realisation beginning to dawn.

"You tell us," replied Alexis.

"I don't know what you are talking about. I may have asked Felicity to come back to collect some books from my room, once, but that's all."

"That's all?" asked Alexis innocently.

"Yes, why what else could there be?"

Cannerby was, by now, looking increasingly nervous. Little globules of greasy sweat were beginning to form on the top of his upper lip, and his hair, long strands of which were combed unbecomingly across a significant bald patch, slipped, revealing an equally glistening scalp. In for the kill, thought Alexis.

"Did you know that Felicity was pregnant?"

Cannerby collapsed, his face draining as the bright red of stress dissipated rapidly into a ghostly pallor.

"No, I did not," he managed to stumble out, words faltering on his lips, his mouth suddenly dry.

"Did you know that we can discover the identity of the father from foetal remains?"

Cannerby swallowed noisily, his Adam's apple jumping up and down.

"Did you know that we have been able to identify the father?" went on Alexis remorselessly.

Cannerby shook his head wordlessly, his previous arrogance and superciliousness vanishing, reducing the man to a shivering lump of jelly. Dax and Alexis looked on without compassion. The atmosphere was electric. A heavy shower of rain suddenly spat on the thick windows, sufficiently powerful to penetrate the well-insulated room, the drumming sounding like a thunderstorm in the silent room. The Chaplain suddenly collapsed, all attempt at bravado gone in a second. He dropped to the table, his head resting on his arms. His body shook as realisation dawned once and for all. His head lolled on the table top and Alexis jumped up in alarm.

"Give him some water, Archie! Don't want this to end with another corpse."

Dax filled a tumbler from the carafe that stood to one side and helped Cannerby to take a sip. His ghostly pallor receded slightly and he was able to sit upright again. Phew! thought Alexis. Giving the man a few minutes to regain his composure, Alexis went on, her voice emotionless.

"Dr Cannerby, we have DNA evidence that proves you impregnated Felicity Smith. You are charged with the rape of Felicity Smith. We also have corroborative evidence that you have indulged in underage sex with minors, children for whom you had responsibility. You are also charged with child abuse and having sex with minors."

"You are just going to love prison. They do all sorts of things to people like you in there," said Dax viciously, his anger suddenly apparent and obvious."

Cannerby ignored him, seemingly shrinking further within himself, lost in his own self-pity. Dax and Alexis drew him back into the present and began the long, tedious task of taking a statement from him. With all resistance and pretence gone, Cannerby made no attempt to further prevaricate and the statement and confession with it was soon safely tucked up on paper. At last they were finished, so Alexis had Cannerby taken away to the cells, to be remanded in custody to await a court appearance. Dax watched as the man was led away from the interview room.

"Thank God that's over. Some justice for Felicity at last."

Alexis nodded in agreement.

By the time the interview was over, Alexis had had enough. Her head thumped and her throat ached with the effort of talking. She decided to call it a day, go home and nurse her cold. She told Dax what she was going to do, returned to an empty office, grabbed her coat and left the building, thinking vaguely that there was something she had forgotten, but her head spun so much she just couldn't pin it down. She sighed. Whatever it was it would have to wait. The drive home took little time, the roads were clear and after garaging the car neatly in the little barn, Alexis took a moment to stroll round the garden convincing herself that the fresh air would do her good. She felt guilty at leaving work early, but there were limits to anyone's endurance. The large apple tree was now in full blossom and the garden was alive with the sound of buzzing bees. The daffodils were almost spent but a large clump of bright red tulips, a present from Georgia last year, brightened up the garden, cheering Alexis in turn. The grass needed a good cut and the hedge could do with a trim, but that would have to wait until the nesting season was over, or at least, that was her excuse. Leaving the garden behind her, Alexis headed for the door and let herself in, breathing deeply of its warm atmosphere, or as much as her stuffed nose would allow. This house was her haven and sanctuary with her music, her piano and her books. As lonely as she could be at times, she briefly wondered if she could ever bring herself to share all this with someone, or even leave it behind. Deciding to cross that bridge if and when she had to, Alexis headed for the kitchen and put the kettle on. Settling herself down in the lounge with the day's paper and a cup of tea, Alexis at last allowed herself to relax. Her eyes grew heavy, she nodded off and the tea grew cold.

Back at the police station, Dax made his way back upstairs to the CID office, having seen Cannerby safely locked up in a cell. As he entered, Hannah looked up from her desk, to where she had returned from her investigation regarding Cannerby's previous school. .
"Is the boss with you?" she asked.
"No, she went home. I think her cold's caught up with her. Why, did you want her?"
"Yes, I wanted a quick chat. Still, never mind. It can wait."
"Anything I can do?" asked Dax helpfully.
"Well, there were two things actually. I've got a bit of info about Cannerby's last school."
"Let's have a look."
Hannah handed Dax the results of her investigations. It was a scanned copy of an old report, typed up on an old typewriter and dated thirty years ago. Hannah had been in touch with the Staffordshire Police and they had quickly investigated their old files and come up with the goods, and emailed it through. Dax read quickly and discovered that Cannerby had left his previous school under a bit of a cloud. Nothing had been proved but there had been

a report that he had fiddled with a little girl in the Prep School. No action had been taken, an eight year old's word against an established and presumably honourable school master, but he had, nevertheless, been asked to leave. He had evidently covered up this taint when he had applied to Coates Norton School. This was not provable, but it was all grist to the mill.

"What was the other thing you wanted to chat about?" asked Dax.

"Do you mind if I leave that to see Inspector Longbow first. It's just a whim and I'd rather pass it by her first. Do you mind?" asked Hannah anxiously.

"Not at all," replied Dax, airily.

One less thing for him to worry about just yet. Dax returned to his desk and found an envelope from the court. Rightly guessing what it was, Dax opened the envelope and withdrew the search warrant asked for. Dax was reluctant to bother his boss, knowing she'd gone home to get some much needed rest, but he really had no option. He knew Alexis would want to know it had arrived and action it as soon as she could. He picked up his phone and dialled the familiar number. The phone rang and rang and Dax felt it was just about to cut into the answerphone, but then Alexis answered, her voice harsh and croaky.

"Really sorry to bother you, ma'am," said Dax with sympathy in his voice, "but I thought you'd like to know that the search warrant has come."

"Oh, don't worry, thanks for letting me know," replied Alexis, enthusiasm warming her tired voice. "Sorry I took so long to answer the phone. I'd nodded off over a cup of tea. Tea's stone cold now…" Alexis tailed off.

"Oh, that's OK, ma'am. Don't worry. Felt bad ringing you."

The phone went silent and Dax could visualise his boss looking at the clock and thinking things through.

"Look, time's ticking on now. Won't be long before it's too dark to see anything. How about we make a really early start tomorrow? Let's meet at 6am at the nick and go from there. Get old Harper out of bed if necessary."

"Sounds good. I like the sound of that." agreed Dax readily. "Are you going to be up to it? You looked pretty done in when you left today."

"Oh, I'll be all right," replied Alexis wearily. "You know me."

"Hmm," was all Dax trusted himself with.

Alexis laughed. "You know me too well, Archie."

Deciding to change the subject Dax went on.

"Do you want me to alert the team?"

"Yes, please do. We'll need as many as you can muster. The school campus is quite large and there are lots of outbuildings, not to mention the houses and the school itself."

"Are we going to raid the headmaster's house, too?" asked Dax hopefully.

"Too right we are," agreed Alexis. Dax could almost hear the grin on her face.

"Right, I'm off for a hot cup of tea and an early night. Hopefully, I'll feel less like shit in the morning."

"Sweet dreams," said Dax with a laugh.

"Thanks."

Dax hung up and gathered the team together. He spent the next half hour priming them of tomorrow's early activity. There were no dissenters, everyone keen to hopefully draw the investigation to a close. It would be a long day so Dax advised everyone to go home, get some rest and hope that the following day would bring results.

Chapter Fourteen

Monday breezed in with a gale and an early summer storm. Alexis woke early, having set her alarm for 5am and groaned as the curtains, now blowing frantically in and out, dislodging a picture she had on the window sill in the process, informed her without doubt that the day was going to be difficult with the wind and rain. It didn't exactly help a detailed search but they had no choice. Throwing herself rapidly out of bed to rescue the picture frame and close the window against the encroaching rain, Alexis then headed for the bathroom. She still felt muzzle headed and stuffed in her nose, but her throat was less sore and a good night's sleep had helped to restore her energy levels. After a hot shower and a quick cup of black coffee and a slice of buttered toast, she headed for the front door. As she opened it, a brief gust took the open door and threatened to wrench it out of her fingers. She just managed to pull it shut quickly behind her. A scene of mild devastation met her eyes, nothing catastrophic but she was so glad she'd had the presence of mind to garage the car the night before. The driveway was littered with twigs and small branches. Even a small twig thrown at the polished surface of her car in a strong wind could have caused a nasty scratch. She looked anxiously at the roof of her house, knowing there was a loose tile at the edge. The tile was still in place but that would be the last thing she needed right now, a loose tile taken by the wind and thrown at something, if not her, then possibly the car. Alexis resolved to get it fixed before anything did happen.

There was a momentary lull in the ferocity of the weather as the wind abated slightly, allowing Alexis to get the car out of the garage without any mishap, and hoping against hope that her drive through the forest would be a safe one. As she headed for work, the wind did indeed lessen considerably, ensuring a safe drive, but leaving in its wake torrential rain. Soon the ditches and gullies alongside the country road filled with raging, frothy brown water and Alexis had to negotiate the floodwaters with care, knowing that a careless manoeuvre would compromise her car's catalytic converter. A small brook, which usually meandered peacefully over a small weir had become a raging torrent and a small river cascaded over the road. God, what a day, thought Alexis, thinking she might need those wellies if she found them. Ten minutes later, and with catalytic converter unscathed, Alexis arrived at work, a brief lull in the torrential rain at least allowing her a dry, albeit hasty, run into the office. Making for the coffee machine as a first port of call, Alexis then headed for the main office, unsurprised to see she wasn't the first person in. Dax and Hannah had beaten her to it, but they did live in the town, she comforted himself with.

"How are you feeling, ma'am" asked Hannah solicitously.

"Better than yesterday, thanks. A bit heavy headed but otherwise intact."

Then Alexis remembered what she had forgotten yesterday as she was leaving the office. Hannah had wanted a word, but with her head aching so much and wanting only to go home and rest, all thoughts of work had vanished. Before she had a chance to say anything, Hannah beat her to it.

"Oh, ma'am. Have you got time now for a quick chat, before we head out? There's something I wanted to pass by you."

"I'm really sorry, Hannah, do you mind if we leave it until later. I want to get this search out of the way first. If we leave it any later, we'll lose any element of surprise and I want to disconcert the headmaster."

"Righto, no problem. Probably nothing anyway."

The team collected their equipment, gloves, overalls and shoe covers included, and with Alexis ensuring she had the search warrant tucked safely in her inner coat pocket, three cars and a forensic van headed out to Coates Norton School. The gale of the night before had wreaked havoc on the countryside; a tree had blown across the road and a small band of workmen was working hard to clear the debris. The small convoy of vehicles was momentarily held up and Alexis tapped the steering wheel in frustration. However, within ten minutes the blockage was cleared, and after showing her warrant card, the team was waved through, albeit with advice to go carefully. The river in the valley below the winding road had turned into a raging torrent as the rain had returned with a vengeance. The sky was heavy with dark cloud and there seemed no let-up in the awful weather. Alexis fervently wished that there would be no serious flooding. She vividly remembered the time that a small bridge over a country lane had been washed away a couple of years before, in a sustained period of incredibly heavy rain. That had caused chaos, she remembered ruefully, the bridge being the only way out of the village. Just then, as if in answer to a prayer, the clouds parted for an instant, and sunlight flooded through, the bright light made all the stronger by the surrounding dark clouds. In her rear view mirror, Alexis saw the beginnings of a rainbow. Her fervent wishes had been heard.

As the cars and the van negotiated the school gates and the gravel, the early morning gloom lifted and the rain stopped altogether. The storm was spent. The hour was still very early and there was little life to be seen at the school. Alexis directed Dax to pull up outside the headmaster's house, realising at such an early hour that the man would still be at home and probably still in bed.

"Quietly, Archie. Let's not give Harper too much warning."

Dax pulled gently onto the headmaster's driveway and Alexis emerged. After a quick word to the other officers to hang fire until she'd had a word with Harper, she approached the front door. Then with not a little pleasure and a great deal of relish, she banged the ornate iron knocker heavily on the front door. To start with there was no answer but after another loud rap, Graham Harper opened the door, looking dishevelled in a rapidly donned and rather tatty dressing gown.

"What the blazes are you thinking of?" demanded Graham angrily, his face red with indignation. "Do you know what bloody time it is? Is there to be no consideration?"

"Mr Harper," answered Alexis with asperity, "I have a warrant to search the school and I am starting with your private accommodation. You will allow my officers access to all buildings, sheds, classrooms, laboratories, houses or anywhere they think fit to investigate. We will leave the boarding houses until last to save upsetting the children, but that may become necessary."

Alexis wasn't sure how the headmaster would react; bluster, indignation, downright fury, so she was surprised at the actual response. Harper merely stood aside, ignoring the officers and went into his kitchen to start breakfast. His drooped shoulders said it all - he'd given up. Alexis followed him inside.

"Is your wife at home? She will need to know that we are in the house."

"No, she is not," replied Harper. "She is away at her mother's. She will be here tomorrow for Speech Day. I will not tell her you have been here. There is no need for her to get worried."

"That is your prerogative."

"I assume you will be as careful as you can. I am entitled to some consideration."

"Of course. We will start outside and move inside if we need to. Hopefully, there will be no need."

"What are you looking for?" asked Harper dejectedly.

"I cannot divulge that, sir. You must appreciate that."

Harper merely shrugged and crossed the room to the kettle that had just boiled. He was hardly awake, although the night had not been as fruitful in sleep as he would have wished. His whole manner relied on being top dog; he was a bully although he would have been the last to accept that fact, but now he felt exhausted, beaten, his whole world turned upside down. Frances had been absent since her injury and he missed her warmth and her body. He thought fleetingly of his wife as he poured the hot water into a mug and shrugged. He had a mild fondness for her but she annoyed him; her drab demeanour, her attempts at making herself acceptable to her husband pathetic. He felt soiled, worn out and wished he was miles away.

Alexis returned to the front driveway, closing the front door behind her and spoke to her team.

"Right, everyone, you know what we're looking for. If you do find anything, let me know but keep schtum otherwise. Just tuck it away on the van. I don't want to give anything away at this point. Leave the boarding houses to the last. I don't want to disturb the children any more than I have to. I hope it won't come to that, but we'll have to see."

Dax and Hannah headed for the headmaster's garage, and after negotiating the car with its rather presumptuous private number plate, began searching all the nooks and crannies. The building was full of rubbish, the headmaster not known for his tidiness and five years of accumulated clutter took up a lot of space. The search was thorough to say the least and it produced little of value. There were boxes of odds and ends, old tins of paint, a pile of old newspapers going brown and curling at the edges, a bucket of old spent engine oil and some rusty old tools. Having heard of Frances Smythe's Ebay sales, Hannah thought she'd have a field day in here. As the woman's name came to her mind, Hannah thought guiltily, must find out how she is.

They spent the next hour searching all the outbuildings of all the main buildings. They found nothing of value at the headmaster's house and had moved onto the areas surrounding the Sports Hall, the art studio and the gymnasium. They searched again the housing containing the mechanisms for chlorinating the swimming pool, although this had been searched at the time of the discovery of the caretaker's body. This too produced a blank. At last they turned to the various sheds in the grounds, approaching first a gardening hut in the grounds of the boys' boarding house. This didn't amount to much and didn't look as if it had been used in ages. The padlock on the door hung useless and rusty and the hinges creaked as Dax pulled the door open. Damp wood-rot infested what was left of a window frame, and the glass, cracked at the corner, hung by a sliver of old grey putty. The whole shed was covered in filthy cobwebs and remembering his experience at Mavis' house and his brush with arachnoid festoons in his search, he was careful to avoid the grey swathes of feathery fly traps. The shed was barely big enough to accommodate both officers but both Dax and Hannah entered the gloomy depths and began a search. The building held no promise whatsoever.

"No one's been here in ages," said Dax gloomily. "We're not having much luck."

However, they dutifully searched the small space and before much time had passed Dax was about to give up when Hannah gave a shout.

"Here, look what I've found."

Dax wheeled round, banging his head on a spade, which was hanging on the wall by a nail, in the process and saw Hannah brandishing a hammer, its wooden handle old and battered, but its round tip clean and shiny. The edge on one side was damaged having obviously hit one too many nails in its life and although some attempt had been made to clean it, its shininess testament to that, a suggestion of a brown discolouration was embedded in the rough metal, and Dax would swear his pension that this discolouration wasn't just rust.

"Fantastic," he exclaimed with satisfaction. "If this isn't the murder weapon used on the caretaker, I'll eat my hat, if I had one. Where d'you find it."

Hannah laughed. "Under that pile of old sacking."

She bagged the hammer and took it carefully out to the van. Harper and Alexis were nowhere to be seen. Just as well, thought Hannah, in the case of the headmaster. Whilst Hannah was gone, Dax thought he'd have a poke in the shed's depths. It wasn't long before he, too, struck gold. The floor of the shed was almost non-existent, only the joists remained, and both officers had had to tread carefully, but it was there, in a corner that Dax came across some recently turned earth. Standing up, he searched the shed for something to dig with, the spade being too long for the cramped space under what remained of the floor. He found an old shovel, its handle long splintered and rotted away. Carefully stooping down, he gingerly scraped the earth back and slowly unearthed a large black bin liner. He pulled gently and extracted it from its earthy grave without spilling its contents. Carrying it carefully, Dax went outside for not only some much needed fresh air away from the dust and cobwebs, but also some light. Taking care not to be seen, as the campus was slowly coming to life, Dax opened the bag and to his delight saw inside a pair of dark blue wellington boots with straps, a small canvas bag which felt soft to the touch and a mobile phone. This was it, the search was over. Without touching the items, he folded the top of the bin liner over and headed in pursuit of Hannah. She was still at the forensics van, having a quick chat with Alexis who had reappeared. Seeing the expression on Dax's face, Alexis broke off her conversation and turned to her detective sergeant.

"What've you got, Archie? You look as if you found the Holy Grail."

"In a manner of speaking, I think I have."

Holding the top of the bin liner open, he allowed Alexis to peer in. She grinned with satisfaction.

"I'll bet you a week's wages that whatever is in that canvas bag bears a close resemblance to phenol."

"Definitely a safe bet," agreed Dax.

"I also wouldn't mind betting that that phone belongs to Mavis. We never did find it. Wonder what goodies we'll find on that?" Alexis straightened up, her mental energy restored even if her body still had a bit of catching up to do.

"Right, that's it. Call the team in and let's get back to the nick. No need to let the headmaster know that we're going. I saw him heading up to his office a while ago. Funnily enough, he totally ignored me."

After pulling the front door of the house shut, which the headmaster had obligingly left open, Alexis and the team left the school grounds smartly, and headed back to town, the road now thankfully clear of fallen trees. Once they had returned, and the items left with the forensic laboratory with a request to pull out all the stops, Alexis and Dax headed for the canteen for a much needed lunch. Breakfast had been scant and hurried that morning and her stomach was reminding her that it needed sustenance.

"Do you fancy a jacket potato, Archie?" asked Alexis.

"That would be great, beans for me. Thanks."

With lunch ordered and a large mug of coffee in front of them both, Alexis outlined to Dax the specific instructions she had left with forensics.

"I've asked them to look for blood on the hammer and the wellies, any mud deposits in the wellie treads, and if there are any, do they match the earth at the scene of Rees' murder, a chemical analysis of the bag's contents and anything within or on the boots that could tell us who was wearing them."

"Well, surely someone with size 11 feet. They were size 11s weren't they?" asked Dax. He'd actually forgotten to check, he realised with shame.

"They were 11s, but anyone with a smaller foot could wear them. Don't forget I said that forensics might be able to get something from the depth of the impression in the earth."

Dax looked chastened. "Forgot that."

"Well you don't get to my exalted position without having a good memory," commented Alexis.

Dax looked up in surprise, but seeing the grin on Alexis' face, realised that he was the butt of his superior's rather droll sense of humour.

"Thank you kindly," said Dax with a smile.

"I've also asked the lab to download any photos from the phone. I hope there isn't a password on it."

"Oh, that's on the file. When I asked Mr Greene if he'd seen the phone, he did actually give me her password just in case we found it."

"Can you buzz that through to the lab, as soon as poss?"

"Will do."

Dax whisked his own phone out of his pocket and after a quick call to the lab, and having passed over information, settled down to his food. The jacket potatoes had arrived and the two officers relaxed, enjoying their lunch and relishing the brief opportunity for a break. The case had turned on its head; they were getting somewhere and, hopefully, before the day was out, there would be a definitive breakthrough.

Lunch over, Alexis returned to her office hoping there would be some answers from forensics, but she was disappointed. A bit too soon, she thought. Just then there was a knock on her office door and Hannah poked her head round.

"You got time for that chat, ma'am? Sorry to nag but it might be important."

"Yes, Hannah, by all means. I'm sorry I forgot yesterday. My brain wasn't functioning. Come on in."

Once both officers were comfortably settled, Hannah opened a file on her lap. Alexis waited expectantly.

"Ma'am, you know that shoplifter I was dealing with the other day …?" Hannah paused.

"Vaguely," Alexis answered. "Why, is there a problem?"

"I'm not sure," Hannah continued. "She gave her name as Michelle Hook. She had stolen a couple of small things, she said by accident. She was in her middle fifties and looked a bit dopey, and as she had no record, and it could have been an accident, the store agreed to take no action as long as she paid for the things. They didn't press charges as the woman paid up there and then, claiming a lapse of memory. We gave her the benefit of the doubt."

"Did you just let her go?"

"No, I gave her an official caution, but that was the end of it."

"So, what's the problem?" asked Alexis puzzled.

"Well, when I was up at Coates Norton School the other day with Archie, I saw her again, well, I thought I did. It seemed odd; it didn't seem to fit."

"What do you mean, didn't fit."

"I saw someone like her wandering round outside the headmaster's house. The woman I saw had black hair and Hook had blonde hair, but the resemblance was uncanny. I wondered then what she was doing there. It looked a bit odd but with everything else going on, I didn't really pay a lot of attention. I didn't think much of it at the time."

Hannah paused, thinking ahead of her words. Alexis waited.

"Anyway," she went on. "I came back to the nick and just out of idle curiosity, I ran her name, Michelle Hook, through the database. I hadn't bothered before as it was just a small shoplifting offence and it turns out she had got form, another minor shoplifting offence three years ago. She was arrested, fingerprinted etc but not charged as, again, the store didn't press charges. She paid up claiming a lapse of memory.

"She's on a roll, this woman," interjected Alexis.

"Anyway, I did a search on the fingerprints and came up with a match, but a different name."

Alexis sat up, her gut tingling in anticipation. This was going somewhere; she could feel it in her aching bones.

"Go on, don't keep me in suspense."

"The match came up with a Dawn Jones. She was arrested 30 years ago as a 26 year old for shoplifting and assaulting a police officer in the process of arrest. She was given three years, did a year, then after release, disappeared into the ether and all traces lost."

"I want all the information about this Michelle Hook and Dawn Jones on my desk in ten minutes. Can you do that?" Alexis asked, her face alive with excitement.

"It's right here," said Hannah, puzzled as she handed over her file.

Alexis briefly perused the data that the file held, her eyes resting briefly on the two photographs, one of Dawn and one of Michelle. She looked back up at Hannah, her eyes alight with excitement.

"Right, I want you to get onto the fingerprint department as a matter of right now, and get them to compare that partial we found on the scent bottle with this Hook woman. See if there is any way we've got a match. Once you've done that, go find Archie for me, will you? When you find him, I want both of you in here, pronto."

Hannah got up and left the office and rang through to the fingerprint department, then spoke to Dax.

"Hey, sarge, the boss wants us both in her office, now."

"OK," said Dax. "What's the rush?"

"Dunno, your guess is as good as mine. I showed her the file of my shoplifter and she's suddenly got a bee in her bonnet."

Alexis looked up from the file as Dax and Hannah entered her office. She looked at Dax.

"Right, Archie, describe Mrs Harper to me."

"Well, she's in her late 50s, I guess, shortish, podgy, a bit old fashioned. Her hair's a horrible dyed black colour, I think, not natural anyway."

"But that's…" interrupted Hannah.

"Hang on," warned Alexis. "Archie, can we get that photo of Dawn Jones morphed to show how she'd look now."

"Yes, I've got some software on my computer that can do that."

"Go and do it now," ordered Alexis, her face grave.

Dax stood up and left the office in a hurry. Hannah stayed in her chair and said nothing. Alexis stared into space, her mind rushing ahead. Her fingers tingled and her pulse throbbed in her temples as adrenalin overtook her fatigue and cold symptoms. A few minutes passed as Dax uploaded the photo of the young Dawn Jones into his software. Back in her office, Alexis swivelled her chair round and stared out of the window. Time seemed to stand still as she waited. The sun flitted in and out of small, fluffy white clouds, intermittently casting a shadow over the office. She heard sounds of traffic below her office window as the world went about its business. If she was right, someone's life was about to come crashing down about their ears.

"Got it here, ma'am," said Dax as he rushed back into the office. "You're gonna love this."

Alexis took the photograph's printout from Dax and smiled. Turning the photo over on the desk in front of Hannah, she grinned as Hannah gasped.

"But that's …" she spluttered.

"Yes, Michelle Hook," confirmed Alexis. "It appears that our long lost friend Dawn Jones has been reincarnated as both Michelle Hook and if I'm right…" Alexis paused. "Swap the blonde hair for the rather off-putting black and who've you got?"

"Well, I'm blowed," whistled Dax. "The headmaster's gonna love this," he added with glee.

"Hang on, we only have a partial fingerprint. Has anyone been able to make a match yet?" warned Alexis.

Just then the phone on Alexis' desk rang, breaking into their excited conversation. She listened in silence, grinning as she realised the result.

"We've got her," she declared with satisfaction.

"Who?" chorused Hannah and Dax in unison.

"Mrs Barbara Harper, alias Michelle Hook, alias Dawn Jones. Forensics have found the mud in the wellies matches the earth found at the scene of the caretaker's murder; they've also found Rees' blood on the hammer and the wellies, proving that the hammer is the murder weapon and the wellies were worn at the scene. The blood probably got there when the murderer pushed Alan Rees' unconscious body into the water."

"Is that enough to convict Mrs Harper?" asked Dax anxiously.

"Wait, there's more," went on Alexis.

"The partial fingerprint on the scent bottle, although not enough to convict on its own, does fit with Mrs Harper's full set. It's an index finger on her right hand and …" Alexis paused for effect.

"Yes, cried Dax and Hannah together, with exasperation.

"Forensics say that whoever wore the boots wasn't a size 11 as the impression shows a distribution of weight which represents a smaller foot. They also found a fingerprint on the strap of the right boot, which, although the boots had been sort of cleaned, the murderer missed. It matches, without any prevarication, Mrs

Barbara Harper. Hooray for posh wellies," Alexis grinned. "I reckon that, as she was wearing boots several sizes too big for her she had to do up the straps to keep the boots on. She couldn't do it wearing gloves so in the stress of the moment, she forget about fingerprints and just did what came naturally. Oh, and by the way, the chemical signature of the bag's contents matches exactly the phenol used in the murders. It's a full house."

Alexis sat back in satisfaction, her stress lines around her tired eyes smoothing out as she relaxed.

"But why did she feel the need to kill all these people." asked Dax. "She's a shoplifter. Murder's a whole different league."

"She's got previous for assault, don't forget," reminded Alexis. "Perhaps we'll find out when we arrest her."

"I think she was jealous," said Hannah, her face thoughtful.

"How's that?" rejoined Alexis.

"Well, I reckon she must have known about her husband's affair with Frances. The school is rife with gossip and although she didn't spend a lot of time in the school, she must have heard and seen things. We now accept that Frances was the original intended victim. Hell hath no fury, as they say," finished Hannah.

Just then the phone on Alexis' desk again buzzed. She lifted the receiver and listened quietly to the caller. Again her face lit up.

"This gets better", she said with glee. "What were we saying?"

"Mrs Harper was jealous?" replied Hannah.

"Yes, that's it. She had guessed about the affair between her husband and old flirty face and planned murder. The lab has just told me there was only one photo on Mavis' phone and it's a juicy one. It shows in lurid detail the sexual antics of one headmaster and his receptionist. There can be no doubt."

"Hang on a minute," cautioned Dax.

"Why, what's the problem?" asked Alexis.

"Well, we're assuming Mavis had her phone with her all the time and that it was taken when she was murdered along with the coffee cup. How would Mrs Harper be that certain about the affair to plan murder without the photo? She'd killed Mavis before she had the phone. The timeline is all wrong."

"That's a good question, Archie. We'll just have to ask her, won't we?" finished Alexis with a grin.

"Right," she went on, "we've got enough evidence to arrest Mrs Harper on suspicion of murder. We know she's away today and won't be back until late. Let's be civilised. We'll turn up tomorrow to arrest her and hope she'll provide the rest of the evidence herself."

"It's Speech Day tomorrow," said Dax.

"That'll be fun," said Alexis with a wicked grin. "If the murders haven't completely ruined the reputation of the school, then this will certainly finish it off."

"I feel sorry for all the innocents, the staff, children etc," said Hannah.

"It'll recover. May take some time, but it will," said Alexis.

"Right, it's getting late. I want you all here for nine o clock tomorrow. I'll run through how we're going to do this then and aim to get to the school by half ten. I think Speech Day itself starts at eleven so please be prompt. Oh, and wear something reasonably smart, no trainers, T shirts or jeans. We'll be mixing with the county's hoi polloi so I don't want them to get the wrong idea that Teigneford police are a load of scruffs," she added as an afterthought."

"Blooming cheek," cried Dax, good humouredly. "I'm always smart."

"Yeah, right," rejoined his boss with a laugh.

Gerald Leigh was not having a good day. Following the letter sent by the Chairman of the Governors, the new Governor, Michael Chance, had turned up unannounced that morning and by-passing the headmaster, had made his way directly to Gerald's office.

"Morning, Leigh. My name is Michael Chance, I think you're expecting me."

It took all of Gerald's self-control not to groan. He had been expecting it but not just yet. He'd only just started on a final clean up and, hopefully credible subterfuge on the headmaster's spurious expense claims.

"Good morning, Mr Chance," replied Gerald as smoothly as he could, extending his hand. "So good to meet you."

Gerald grimaced slightly as the new Governor's handshake threatened to maim Gerald for life.

"I am sure everything is in order," went on Chance, "but as Sir Martin and I said, the idea behind this audit is to see if economies could be made bearing in mind rising costs and falling school numbers. You know the drill."

"Oh, absolutely, sir," replied Gerald without much enthusiasm, knowing what was about to happen. His life flashed before his eyes as professional suicide threatened.

"I want all the books, ledgers, spreadsheets and anything else you have on the finances of the school. I have my own laptop so I won't trouble you for computer access. I'll just need a desk and a quiet corner. You won't even know I'm here."

Fat chance, thought Gerald gloomily as he obligingly handed over everything that was asked for. He knew his days as Finance Manager of the school were numbered, the new governor was bound to find everything out. The man oozed capability and acumen. The morning wore on with an inexorable pulse. Chance said nothing, other than the odd grunt, but his body language said a million things. At one point, Chance looked up and caught Gerald's eye. Gerald looked away, his cheeks flushed. A very faint smile played on Chance's lips. Lunchtime loomed and Gerald could bear the pressure no more.

"If you don't mind, I'm off to lunch. Would you like to join me?"

"That is very kind, but I have brought my own lunch. I'd rather just get on with things. The day will run away with me, otherwise."

"OK," said Gerald. "Would you like a tray of coffee? I could get Miss Jarvis to get one across for you."

"That would be nice. Thank you."

Gerald escaped outside, grateful to leave behind the oppressive atmosphere in his office. The day had turned blowy bright, the storm and its rain were long gone and the wind had abated into a stiff breeze, but it was still enough to make the new catkins dance madly on the trees which grew alongside the small stream that ran around the perimeter of the school grounds next to Gerald's office. Lunch was still fifteen minutes away so he decided to take a stroll around the grounds he loved so much and where he had spent most of his professional life. He walked past the Music Suite and stopped to listen to a piano being played. He had no idea what the music was, but it sounded good and something decent in this mad untidy world. He had been a fixture of the school, more or less since his university days, and he was an extremely efficient accountant. He knew, without a doubt, that Chance would discover the anomalies in the accounts and he would get the sack. God knows how he'd tell his wife. Bloody headmaster, how he loathed the man. It was all his fault. He headed for the school dining room and, after giving Brenda the order for the coffee tray, lined up in the queue, eager for lunch and a chance to forget his woes. He collected his lunch and settled himself at a table. He wanted to be alone without any company but even that small thing was to be denied him.

"Hi, Gerald, what's going on round here? The place was crawling with fuzz bottles earlier today."

Gerald grimaced at the rather coarse tones of the sports teacher, Mark Hathaway and tried to make a non-committal answer.

"Haven't got a clue, been wrapped up with the auditor all morning."

Mark grinned. "God help you."

Gerald looked up in annoyance, "What on earth do you mean."

"Well, we all know the headmaster has been on the fiddle for years, all those so-called seminar trips indeed. More like dirty weekends with Frances."

"How on ..." Gerald went to continue then stopped.

"This place is too small for everyone not to know everyone else's business. God knows how you've put up with it all these years. Your creative accountancy must be brilliant."

"Don't want to talk about it, thanks," said Gerald grimly.

"OK, no problem." agreed Mark obligingly. "If you need a character reference, I'm sure there'll be someone here to give you one."

"Huh!" replied Gerald ungratefully. He shifted in his seat and continued with his lunch, which now had lost its savour. As the dining room filled rapidly with noisy children, Gerald pushed away his half eaten dinner, his appetite gone. Feeling the need for his own company and some peace and quiet, he left the room and headed outside. Pulling his rather thin cardigan around his shoulders and bracing himself against the breeze, he strolled along the path which led to the back exit of the school, passing the boarding house where poor Felicity had received her fateful gift. He walked out into the road, which soon petered out into a track, and Gerald followed this as it weaved its way up and through the trees where it met with the higher reaches of the stream. The early morning's rain had swollen the brook and the bridge that the track took to cross the stream looked perilously close to the raging waters. Gerald stopped and stared in fascination at the brown, foaming torrent. He loved this spot and quite often walked up here to catch his breath and rid himself of the headmaster's overbearance. A sudden brilliant shaft of sunshine filtered through the trees and caught the foaming tops of the raging water. The scene was violent, but in all its moods, the water never failed to ease his tension. A small mudslide, loosened by the water, fell into the stream, throwing up a shower of spume and as it did so, the sunlight shone through the spray causing a beautiful rainbow to arch across the stream. Gerald was not, by any means, a fanciful man, but even he took a little comfort from this colourful array. He was surely in need of some comfort, and this tiny episode gave him that small grain. A squirrel ran up the trunk of the large oak tree that grew a few feet from the bridge and Gerald stared at it, marvelling at its agility. Had the squirrel put something away for a rainy day, a nice collection of beech nuts perhaps? Gerald wished heartily that he had done the same. His own particular rainy day was upon him. His moment of comfort passed and so with a sinking heart, he left the scene, its violence perfectly in tune with his tortured mind, and returned to the office to face his nemesis.

Michael Chance was waiting for him, the time on his own during Gerald's absence had given him the quiet and solitude he needed to finalise his opinions. He wasn't an unkind man, and rightly suspected that there were more to his conclusions than just dishonesty on Gerald's part.
"We need to talk, Mr Leigh," greeted Gerald's ears as he walked in through the door.
"I know," Gerald sighed with resignation.

Having dismissed her team to an early end for the day, Alexis couldn't do the same for herself. The rest of the afternoon passed slowly for her. She had the answers she needed but was unable to carry out the arrest she so desperately wanted until the following day. So, she spent the time tidying up her case notes, making sure that everything was ready for the following day. She then actually allowed herself a chance to breathe. Getting up out of her seat, she walked across to the window and looked out across the scene in front of her. It was peaceful, traffic eased after the lunchtime rush, the late afternoon sun shining on the foaming tops of the mad rush of the river. The last few days had happened at a breakneck pace. Her cold was probably the result of pure exhaustion brought about by stress, lack of sleep and rest and her immune system had taken a dive, but the promised action for the morrow and the brief rest she'd allowed herself invigorated her, despite her frustration at having to wait.

Alexis tidied the last of the papers and updated her pocket book, then turned back from the window and looked round at what was now her office. It still held the signs of its previous occupant, Alexis hardly having the time or opportunity to change anything. She'd basically walked into it with a possible murder ringing in her ears and time had stood still since. The filing cabinet and the shelves were a fixture, and the desk, having been divested of her predecessor's rubbish, was rather a nice piece of furniture which Alexis didn't want to change. She guessed that it was a hangover from a long since retired officer – it didn't look as if Redway would have chosen such a lovely piece for himself. Alexis stroked her hands over the now tidied surface of the desk and admired the soft tones of the wood, which looked like pine. It could do with a good polish but apart from that still looked a fine piece. However, the ornamentation of the room left a lot to be desired. A rather garish picture of three elephants adorned the wall. Alexis loved elephants, either in their own natural habitat or as a soft toy sitting on her bed, but they were hardly the right sort of subject for a picture in a modern CID office. She resolved to change this, at the first opportunity for a nice photo of the town. She'd seen some lovely photographs of the castle taken from the hill behind it and resolved to get that sorted as quickly as she could. Also a CD player for those times when she had the office to herself and she could indulge her love of music, and definitely a coffee maker, perhaps one of those with little pods that would make a nice selection of coffees. With these pleasant thoughts running through her mind, she threw in the towel, packed away all the papers she would need for the morning in her briefcase and headed home.

Chapter Fifteen

The following day breezed in with a lovely morning. The clouds and rain of the last few days had cleared and yesterday's storm was but a distant memory. The streams had divested themselves of their excess water and once again, the countryside murmured gently and contentedly in the early summer sunshine. Graham Harper was in his element. He stood on the steps of the school, looking remarkably smart in a newly cleaned and pressed, if rather worn gown, the fur hood brushed to within an inch of its life. He sniffed the air and breathed in the warmth. The troubles of the last few days he had simply pushed to the darkest recesses of his mind; today nothing must mar the climax of the year, Speech Day. Today, he could preen his feathers and show off all the hard work that he had done. He conveniently forgot that any success was due to the dedication of his staff and the hard work of the children. It was still early, just nine o clock. Visitors would start arriving about ten, with Speech Day due to begin at eleven. Lunch was at twelve thirty, and as far as most people were concerned, the highlight of the day. Brenda's special buffet lunches were famous, renowned for their variety, wonderful cooking and plenty of it. Everyone was prepared to put up with the boring speeches from the headmaster, the Chairman of Governors and any other hanger on who happened to be passing by, just for the food.

The sun's warmth had increased as the clock moved forward so taking advantage of a spare moment, Graham sauntered along the path, enjoying the sunshine and the clement weather as he walked. Eventually, he headed towards the Hall, ready for an inspection. He had left clear instructions that all was to be in place by now and woe betide anyone who hadn't danced to his tune. He wasn't disappointed, perhaps a chair or two to be tweaked, but the Hall looked resplendent in the sunshine. Large floral arrangements adorned the stage, the long dark blue curtains were hanging straight and clean, and the Hall was packed with every chair available. Everything looked good and, just for once, Graham felt content and in good humour. He continued his stroll around the school, checking that all was well elsewhere. Preparations were well in hand in the kitchen and the domestic staff were well ahead with their lunch activities. The Prep school classrooms were ablaze with colour with children's pictures and paintings pinned to the walls; the swimming pool, now clean and unbloodied, which awaited the gala and display later, sparkled in the sunlight and the place buzzed with animated activity. He checked his watch, half an hour before the governors were due to take coffee with the headmaster, his wife and honoured guests in the Library, just time to return to his office and check his speech, a chance to rehearse it in his mind. Graham was definitely a happy man.

The sunshine fell on Teigneford too as Alexis mobilised her team. She felt much restored in heath, just a suggestion of a tickly cough, but nothing to hold her back. She felt invigorated as she knew that today should bring a conclusion to the distressing events at the school. After a quick team briefing, at which Alexis was pleased to see that her colleagues had been good to her word as all were dressed smartly but appropriately for the work that had to be done, Alexis, Dax, Hannah and the two other detective constables were on their way to Coates Norton School. As they arrived, they saw the activity as the school hummed with the buzz of people. The car park was jammed packed with a wide assortment of cars, everything from the humble Mini to a rather ostentatious Bentley, and children and parents sauntered in the sunshine around the quad towards the entrance of the Hall.

"Phew," whistled Alexis as a silver grey Rolls Royce, having newly negotiated the speed humps, came to a stately halt in the last space left on the front quad, "there's some money here." She looked at her watch.

"Right everyone, proceedings begin at eleven, it's now half past ten, so hopefully the headmaster will be in his study, and probably his wife will be with him. Let's head for that."

The five officers entered the building. Reception was empty but the doors to the Inner Hall stood wide open. Alexis knocked on the headmaster's door but receiving no answer she turned round and saw James Picton heading in her direction.

"If it's himself you're after, he's in the Library having coffee with the Governors. I'm just on my way there myself," said James.

"Thanks, Mr Picton, lead on," said Alexis cheerfully.

Leaving Steve and Mike, the two detective constables, in Reception, thinking five would be a crowd, unless things turned nasty, Alexis followed James as he went ahead, crossing the carefully polished floor, past the portraits of previous headmasters and into the Library. It was an elegant room with an imposing stone fireplace, topped by an intricately carved wooden mantelpiece. Under the ornately plastered ceiling, a small gathering of people stood, ladies dressed in large hats and pretty dresses, the Governors smart in lounge suits, teaching staff in their gowns, colourful hoods adding to the brightness of the scene. The headmaster stood to one side, balancing a coffee cup in his left hand as he waved the other hand imperiously in the air. Alexis saw he was enjoying himself and grinned as she knew what was to come. It was then she saw Mrs Harper. She had made an attempt to smarten herself up; her hat was rather ostentatious with a large flower attached to the side and her dress matched in colour but in sharp contrast to the smartness of the other guests, she looked dowdy. She noted with pleasure the slight look of alarm that passed swiftly across Mrs Harper's face, the brim of her hat not quite sufficient to hide her features. Alexis made eye contact and Barbara looked down, seeming to shrink into the shadows, as she was so used to doing.

"I'm sorry, Detective Inspector, but I do not think you were invited," Graham said sharply. "This room is for honoured guests only."

Alexis ignored him and headed straight for Barbara.

"Mrs Barbara Harper, also known as Michelle Hook and Dawn Jones, I am arresting you on suspicion of murder."

The rest of her caution was drowned by the sharp intake of breath that swept round the room and the headmaster's audible gasp.

"I beg your pardon. Is this some kind of joke?" snapped Graham, his cheeks suffusing with an angry purple.

"It most certainly is not a joke, headmaster. Murder is never a joke," replied Alexis with asperity.

"Surely you cannot think my wife has had anything to do with any of this. Look at her! She's …."

Graham paused, lost for the appropriate words, suddenly aware that this was not the place to pour scorn on his wife.

"We have evidence to suggest that Mrs Harper is guilty of murdering Miss Felicity Smith. We also believe that she is guilty of the murder of Mavis Greene. She has questions to be answered, too, about the murder of Alan Rees and the attack on Miss Smythe."

Dax had gone across to Barbara and stood beside. She appeared grey and lifeless, her face pale and ashen, the bright red lipstick doing nothing for her appearance.

"Don't be ridiculous, woman," snapped Graham, losing his temper and throwing caution to the winds. "My wife is feeble and slow witted; she couldn't murder a fly, let alone a fellow human being."

Alexis, ignoring the rather misogynistic use of the word 'woman', noticed that for once Graham had acknowledged that Mavis was a human being, albeit condemning his wife as a halfwit in the process. For a moment there was absolute silence, no one daring to move or say a word. Graham stood, shaking with anger, his fists clenched. Then the room erupted with sound as Barbara turned on her husband with a totally unexpected violence. She was no longer the weak dormouse standing quietly beside Dax. Her husband's taunt awoke something in her; she came to life with a vengeance. As she turned on her husband and screamed, Alexis remembered Bishop Stephen's words.

"You never saw me as anything other than a necessary evil, did you Graham my dearest," she snapped with venom, her spittle showering her husband. "I was nothing more than a useful appendage for a so called successful headmaster. You ignored me, except when it suited you. Don't you think I knew all about your goings on with Frances? Do you think I'm blind?" she screamed hysterically.

Advancing threateningly on her husband, she went on, "When I found that phone and saw that picture, I knew for sure, you bastard."

Dax pulled the frantic woman back slightly. Barbara struggled slightly but the action poured cold water on her hatred and she went on in a calmer voice, edged with steel.

"I wish I'd got her as I intended, that wretched domestic woman and the girl were accidents."

Alexis relaxed slightly. Any doubts as to the evidence they did have had flown to the four winds; her confession in front of a load of people had damned her. Graham reddened, acutely embarrassed. Dax looked to the edge of the room as a sudden movement caught his eye. He smiled as Frances, who had reappeared from sick leave albeit with her hand still bandaged, now adorned for the day in a bright pink suit and matching large hat, slowly edged herself out of the room and disappeared. Barbara moved swiftly out of Dax's hold, taking him by surprise, and struck her husband full in the face. His lip caught against his front teeth, and blood spurted down his shirt front. He staggered back, shaken by the onslaught, his coffee cup flying into the air, casting its contents across the floor. Barbara stood back and collapsed into a chair, all anger and hatred spent in that final act of violence.

"What do you intend to do now, Inspector," asked Sir Martin, the Chairman of the Governors. "Quite clearly we have a situation here now, and for the sake of the school I would like as much discretion as possible."

"Yes, Sir Martin, I agree," replied Alexis. "We'll take Mrs Harper away with us as quietly as possible. It's up to you how you handle the rest of the occasion. Is there a back way out which will avoid your guests?"

Sir Martin nodded.

"Mr Picton, would you be kind enough to show Inspector Longbow and her team out of the back and away from the Main Hall?"

James nodded and Alexis hung back with Dax and Hannah, Barbara now quiescent and calm. Sir Martin turned to Graham Harper.

"Headmaster, I think under the circumstances, that you should stay in your study. I will lead the Speech Day and explain that Mrs Harper has been taken ill and you are staying with her."

Graham bristled angrily but then realising that he had no choice, nodded unhappily. He was shaken by the events, and could hardly think straight. Realisation hadn't yet dawned that this would probably mean the end of his headmastership, if not his career.

"You will stay in your study until all our guests have left. I will have lunch brought to you," ordered Sir Martin. "Then I will discuss with you how we move forward."

Graham shook himself, and quickly left the room without a backward glance at his wife. He skidded slightly on the polished floor, and threw himself into his study, slamming the door soundly behind him. A group of parents, passing at that moment with their children, looked up at the sound in surprise, but pulled along by their eager sons and daughters, kept going, heading for the main hall. Sir Martin addressed the Library guests, inviting them to follow him. Still shaken by the events they had seen unfold, they agreed and quietly followed the General, heading for the Hall.

Once the Library was emptied of people, James beckoned Alexis to follow him. Mrs Harper made no attempt to argue or resist, all her strength gone in that final outburst. As Alexis and her two colleagues along with their prisoner, left the Library, the hall now thankfully empty of guests, Dax left them and slipped out to Reception, where Mike Evans and Steve Moss had remained, and asked them to bring the car round to the back entrance. They disappeared rapidly and Dax quickly returned to the Inner Hall and caught up with the rapidly disappearing Alexis. They followed James on what seemed an endless path, passing empty classrooms and down long corridors. Eventually, they reached the back door, having passed through the kitchen where the kitchen staff looked on in amazement. Brenda was there, red faced and harassed as she prepared for the Speech Day lunch, but as Alexis passed she caught her eye with a question on her face. Alexis said nothing, just nodded. Brenda smiled.

"I'll leave you here, Inspector, if you don't mind," said James as they reached the back gate, where Mike and Steve were now waiting for them with the car. "I've got to dash back to the hall. It's time for the school song and the National Anthem. No day would be complete without them," he finished with a wry grin.

"Yes, thank you, Mr Picton, and thank you for all your help, from the start. It has been very much appreciated."

With a cheery wave, James turned on his feet, and at a half run, disappeared back into the grounds, heading for the Hall.

Graham sat dejectedly on one of the sofa chairs in his study. His gown lay in a crumpled heap on the floor, thrown there at the height of his anger and humiliation, but with his temper now abated he sat, a grey and shrunken man. His shirt front was still bloodied, his hair awry and his lip swollen. He sat overcome by the stress of the morning, his comfortable mood having dissipated in an instant with the slap. Now he just felt exhausted. A knock on the door pulled him out of his mindlessness. The door opened without an invitation, and Brenda walked in, pushing a small trolley laden with selected delights from the buffet table. The headmaster had lain in his slough of despond without realising the passage of time; Speech Day had finished and now it was lunchtime. He had the grace to thank Brenda, but she left with just a nod. What was there she could say? Graham looked at the food, but felt no appetite. The vol-au-vents, the delicate sandwiches and the cold meat platter were destined to remain uneaten. Realisation had dawned and with it a total loss of appetite. He was a dreadful man, full of his own self-importance but he wasn't stupid. He knew what was going to happen, but with a final act of defiance, he vowed to fight to the last. He had had no idea that Barbara knew about his affair. He should have realised and been far more circumspect. Had Frances been worth it? Now, with events taking over, he seriously doubted it.

Teigneford police station had been basking quietly in the somnolent warmth of the early summer sunshine but as the small convoy of cars pulled up in the back yard, the building woke up and became a hive of activity. Barbara was led through the back door and quickly processed by the Custody Sergeant and then left in an interview room awaiting Alexis and Dax. It had been a trying morning, so before starting her interrogation, Alexis went to her office where Dax joined her. She needed the stimulus of a cup of coffee and something to eat wouldn't go amiss either.
"How do you want to do this?" asked Dax.
"Well, first I need food. Could you pop down to the canteen and grab a sandwich for both of us. It's going to be a long afternoon, I think."
Dax swiftly disappeared, and Alexis sat at her desk, marshalling her thoughts. She felt pretty satisfied that everything was in place; she had the evidence, both DNA and the more tangible; she had Mrs Harper's confession, but remembering that something said in the heat of the moment could be retracted in the calmer environment of an interview room, wasn't taking that for granted. It had been said under caution, so was admissible, but Alexis would prefer to get it all down on paper. As she went through the morning's events in her mind, she was interrupted by the welcome sight of a cup of coffee and a chicken salad sandwich. Dax sat down opposite her and the office fell silent, as they both ate their lunch, quiet in their own thoughts.

Eventually, the time came, and with plates cleared and cups emptied, Alexis and Dax headed for the interview room. As they entered, Barbara sat in the chair, her back bolt upright, and her eyes unseeing and dull as she stared into the middle distance. As the two officers seated themselves on the other side of the table, Barbara shifted in her seat and lowered her eyes. She looked grey and exhausted, but Alexis sensed that she was relieved at the outcome and was fighting tears as the shock of her arrest had worn off. After the legal preliminaries were taken care of, Alexis began.

"Do you want to tell me all about it?" she asked, gently to start, no point in rushing headlong into things.

Barbara sniffed loudly and pulled a soggy tissue from her pocket. Her already dowdy dress looked even worse for wear, sporting a spot of bright red blood which had spurted from her husband's lip. Her hair, dyed black but showing grey roots, was awry, forming spiky shapes above her eyes. It almost looked comical, thought Dax, if it wasn't so serious.

"My life's been shit from the word go. No one has ever wanted me," she began.

Alexis sensed that there was no self-pity in this bald statement, just a long acceptance of what life had thrown at her.

"I was dumped in a ladies loo about two days after I was born, then I spent all my childhood being pushed from pillar to post. I never had any family, or anywhere that I could call home. I never even knew my real name, if I ever had one. I drifted into crime, I got in with the wrong crowd. No one cared." Barbara paused, memories crowding back as she spoke.

"Yes," replied Alexis. "We know about the time when you were known as Dawn Jones. What happened after you were released? You seemed to disappear."

"I found work in the office of a chemical firm. I changed my name to Barbara Edwards. I started as an assistant in the office and worked my way up to office manager. I did evening classes and got some science qualifications. I really thought I was going somewhere. Then I was made redundant, just as life was starting

305

for me. It knocked me back but I managed to get a job as a lab technician, you know like Rita, at a large private school. There wasn't any of this criminal records check stuff then. No one ever knew about my past. That's how I know about chemicals. I met Graham there – he was teaching History."

Barbara stopped and sighed, a tear forming a tiny furrow in her heavy make-up. Dax reached up and pulled down a box of tissues from the windowsill and pushed it across to Barbara. She pulled a clean tissue from the box gratefully, and made a better job of wiping her tears and blowing her nose. Alexis waited patiently for Barbara to compose herself and then encouraged her to go on.

"What happened after that?"

"At first I was really happy. Graham was kind and attentive. He was quite a catch. He became a senior master at the school, still young, a bit of a flyer really. Soon I had two children, they became my life. Then Graham got another job and things changed."

Barbara stopped and seemed lost for a while in her memories, her eyes closing in anguish as she remembered the time when she first knew she had lost Graham. Alexis idly wondered if Mrs Harper had known about why her husband had had to leave his previous post in a hurry. She decided to leave that little titbit out; no point in winding the woman up unnecessarily.

"He came to Coates Norton. God knows how he got the job of headmaster, he wasn't really ready for the responsibility, but he's always been a good con man, saying things that people want to hear. He obviously managed to convince the Governors, and they believed him. We moved to this God forsaken place, in the middle of nowhere, and I had nothing."

Barbara sobbed, her voice catching in her throat. She pulled another tissue from the box on the table and tried to collect herself. Alexis waited patiently. There was no need to intervene, no need to rush, the flow still came and Barbara seemed relieved to unburden herself. She realised with a shock that this was probably the first time for a long time that anyone had taken any notice of the woman. She felt a stab of sympathy, then remembered Felicity and Mavis.

"I'd left all my friends, even my children were at a different school. I had no one. Then Frances turned up. I knew from the start that Graham was hooked. I hated her; I loathed her every time I saw her. She seemed so sweet and nice on the surface, but underneath I knew she was cruel and calculating, so manipulative. It just got too much for me and I told myself she had to go."

Here Barbara stopped, gulping for air as the enormity of what she had done suddenly overwhelmed her. She slumped in her chair, her eyes closing in misery as a grey pallor swept over her tear stained face. Alexis felt a moment of alarm; she didn't want the woman pegging out in front of her. However, Barbara rallied.

"Would you like a cup of tea?" asked Dax, picking up on his boss' alarm.

Barbara raised her red rimmed eyes.

"Yes, thank you. That would be nice."

"Get something for her to eat as well," chipped in Alexis. "She's missed lunch. Would you like a sandwich or something?"

"Thank you," came the simple reply.

Dax left the office to see to the refreshments and Alexis went on with gentle questioning.

"What did you decide to do?" she asked.

"By chance I came across that domestic's phone. She'd left it in the staff room kitchen the day before I laced that coffee. I got curious. I found that photo of the two of them together. It was disgusting. My husband and that unspeakable woman, tight in each other's arms, their tongues finding each other's tonsils, I bet. I felt sick. It was then I decided to kill her."

The bald statement, recorded for posterity on the machine, silenced Barbara for a minute. The door opened and Dax walked in carrying a tray which he placed in front of the headmaster's wife. Barbara looked at it and reached for the cup, her hand shaking slightly. After a sip of the coffee, the caffeine revived her a little and she went on.

"I left the phone where I'd found it. I'd seen all I wanted to see. She had to go. I had no choice if I was going to reclaim my husband."

"How did you decide to do it?"

Barbara replaced the cup back on the tray, as if not trusting herself to hold it.

"I knew about chemicals, and I did a bit of research on the Internet. I just helped myself to a bit of that carbolic acid stuff from the chemistry lab. I didn't think they'd miss it."

"I'm afraid Miss Chappell is very thorough in her record keeping," replied Alexis.

"Yes, I gathered that when I knew you'd been talking to her. You'll find the rest of the stuff hidden in the garden shed near the boys' boarding house."

"Tell me about Mavis," encouraged Alexis, declining to enlighten Barbara that the stuff had already been found.

"I feel really bad about her and Felicity. I didn't mean that to happen. I slipped into the staff room and made a cup of coffee for Frances. I stirred some of the stuff into the cup and just left it on her table. I didn't even dream that Mavis would clear it up. Frances wasn't there at the time, but I saw her come back just after."

"Mavis, apparently, had a penchant for clearing things away. She had done it a few times before," said Alexis.

Barbara nodded.

"I knew as soon as that other domestic found Mavis in the store room what had happened. My stomach was churning and not just with the most awful lunch I'd had with Graham and the Bishop; Graham is so ingratiating, he makes me squirm. I stayed in the dining room whilst the fuss was going on, then when everyone had gone, I slipped into the storeroom."

"How did you get in? I know that Mr Picton had locked the room."

Barbara smiled.

"I had a spare set of keys made up from Graham's own set. I borrowed them one day, when he was in hospital for a minor operation, oh, a couple of years ago. I thought they might come in handy one day, one never knew. I had keys to everywhere. If Graham had known, he'd have gone ballistic but he never found out."

Barbara giggled, a little hysterically.

"When everyone had disappeared - I know Graham had gone back to his office with the Bishop - I went into the store room and saw Mavis, the smell was ghastly. I felt sick but I had to get that mug. It would have given me away. I had forgotten about fingerprints. I took it, locked the door, and went back to the staff room, washed it up and put it back with the others in the cupboard. I didn't think anyone was in there, but I found out later that the caretaker was in the toilet mending something. He saw me."

"Ah yes, the caretaker," responded Alexis.

"He tried to blackmail me. I didn't have any money of my own so I was desperate. He had to go. He contacted me and we arranged to meet by the swimming pool. I stayed hidden in the bushes, then bashed him on the head. I managed to roll him into the water. I knew that if I hadn't finished him off with the bang on the head, the water would do the rest."

Barbara's voice went hard and brittle and Alexis felt a sharp feeling of distaste. Any sympathy she'd had for the woman vanished as she recounted the demise of Alan Rees.

"So you admit the murder of Mavis?" asked Dax.

"Yes, although I didn't mean it," replied Barbara.

"It's still murder," affirmed Alexis.

Barbara dropped her eyes.

"And you admit the murder of Alan Rees," went on Dax.

"Yes, he deserved it," answered Barbara viciously.

"And Felicity?" asked Dax.

"Another mistake. I tried again when I failed the first time with Frances. I thought I couldn't fail this time. But I forgot that Frances is a Smythe not a Smith. That's where I went wrong. That was a real shame. I am sorry for that."

Barbara paused and pulled another tissue from the box in front of her as another tear rolled down her make-up packed cheeks.

"I tried again with Frances. I bought some luxury chocolates from that posh shop in the town. I doctored them and just left them on her table. She never even noticed me pass by. Got that wrong too." Barbara sniffed miserably.

Dax felt disgusted, tired and sullied by the woman's lack of feeling. Alexis realised they now had everything they needed, there was no need to prolong the misery any further, so with the admissions safely recorded, and the statement signed and carefully stored, the two officers brought the interview to an end. Barbara was led away and placed in a cell, awaiting committal proceedings in court.

"Well, that's that then, all done," said Dax as he sat in the Strangefellows Arms that evening with Alexis, carefully nursing a pint of strong local bitter in his hands.

"Thank God for it. This was a nasty case. At least we got that bastard Cannerby banged up as a result. That might have gone unnoticed if Felicity hadn't died."

"She paid a heavy price," said Dax ruefully. "I can still see her face, tear stained as she sat on that wall."

The two officers lapsed into silence, each in their own thoughts.

"Come on, this won't do," said Alexis after a while. "It's all worked out OK, we've closed the case and Mrs Harper won't be going anywhere for a long while. How about a game of darts?"

"Do you mind if we don't," said Dax. "I told Claire we'd sorted the case and she's done a celebratory meal for me. I'd like to get home, if that's OK."

"No problem," replied Alexis, hiding a sudden stab of loneliness. "We'll catch up tomorrow in the office."

"Thanks."

Alexis was very fond of both Dax and Claire, and had shared many an evening with them, but this evening wasn't to be one of them. As Dax left the pub, with a cheery wave, Alexis cheered herself up by remembering there was a very nice bottle of Chilean Merlot awaiting her at home, and she was sure there was some nice chicken and chips to go with it in the freezer.

A few days later, Sir Martin sat in his own front room, a pleasant space filled with a lifetime's memories, some sad, some happy but none quite like the memories that had been made on that appalling day. As he sat back in his chair, as the early morning sunshine streamed in through the large windows, his thoughts took him back to that ghastly morning when he had had to make all kinds of excuses on Speech Day. He had explained that Mrs Harper had been taken ill and that the headmaster was caring for her, but even to his ears the explanation as to the pair's absence on the stage had sounded lame but it was the best he could have done, under the circumstances. As he stood there, congratulating the children on their achievements and thanking both staff and parents for their support, his practised eye swept round the crowded hall. He caught the whisperings, growing in intensity amongst the gathered throng as they realised the formalities were nearly over. Sir Martin was under no illusion that he would not be able to contain the gossip, and knew with a dreadful certainty that it would have a negative effect on the school. The three murders themselves had led to ten children being removed by their parents and the subsequent proceedings would inevitably lead to more. The presence of the police, and the spat between husband and wife in the Library had not gone unnoticed, and as the school was a very close knit community, the word had spread like wild fire. He knew he hadn't fooled anyone. After the speeches and presentations, happy parents and their offspring removed themselves from the Hall to the enjoyment of Brenda's delicious buffet lunch and Sir Martin headed for the kitchen to ask Brenda to lay a tray for the headmaster, and then take it to the headmaster's office. Sir Martin, this small task, accomplished, then headed for the buffet himself and tried to forget what he would have to do later.

Two hours later, with the Hall and dining room now empty and with afternoon activities by the pool well under way, Sir Martin whispered to his wife as to where he would be for the next hour. She nodded gently, a grave expression on her face. He headed for the headmaster's study and opened the door. The room was in a terrible mess. The desk was covered with untidy piles of exercise books and various letters and papers; bookshelves were similarly adorned with piles of papers stuffed in between books, nothing filed or stored neatly. Sir Martin shuddered. How on earth could anyone work in this chaos? He pitied the headmaster's secretary, what was her name, Sarah something. The man had to go, but he couldn't sack him. Other than a rather injudicious affair with Frances - he had gleaned all the gory details from the staff room with people there more than willing to spill the beans - the man had done nothing wrong. Could he get rid of him for bringing the school into disrepute? Hardly criminal but a possibility. His judicious exploration in the staff room had soon proved that there was no love lost between the headmaster and his staff. Sir Martin cursed himself. He should have seen this, kept a firmer eye on things but he had been content to take the glory and none of the responsibilities. He realised, with a sigh that the buck was now stopping firmly with him.

Sir Martin had entered the room without ceremony and saw the untouched lunch tray. Graham glanced up with a brief look of annoyance. The headmaster's expression changed in an instance as he rearranged his features into what he hoped would show an outward display of horror, grief and disgust as to what his wife had done. Sir Martin wasn't fooled. He hadn't spent a lifetime in the army, with countless soldiers in his charge, to not know how a man worked. Graham was no mystery to him; now he had to be dealt with. Sir Martin found the headmaster sitting immobile, blank faced and grey, the blood still bright on his shirt front. The conversation had not been an easy one. At first, Graham had blustered, trying to maintain some sense of status.
"You'll no doubt want to be with your wife," offered Sir Martin at first.
"Her!" Graham almost spat out the word. "I don't need her. I'm washing my hands of her completely. I gave her everything she

could have possibly wanted; status, a good home, financial security, what more could she have wanted?"

"You perhaps". Sir Martin couldn't stop himself.

"I have no idea what you mean," contended the headmaster, a little wariness entering his voice. "Surely you don't believe what she said in the Library."

Graham shuddered at the thought and nursed his split lip.

"It isn't her word I'm taking, although there was some meaning behind that punch. I'm afraid your secret became open gossip within a few weeks of Miss Smythe starting at the school."

Graham blanched and said nothing. Sir Martin took his opportunity. Having brought Graham to a standstill, he gently suggested, although with an air that didn't expect any argument, that the headmaster should take some leave. It was half term so he wouldn't be missed. The Deputy Head could take over for a while. Graham had eventually acquiesced, albeit unwillingly, but realising the inevitable, had agreed. Making no further comment, he just stood and left the room, leaving his gown crumpled on the floor. Sir Martin stared at his retreating back and then at the tray of food, which Brenda had delivered to the headmaster's study. This had included a rather nice bottle of Chablis, still chill in its cooler. Sir Martin couldn't help himself. The interview had shaken him so he helped himself to a small glass and sat back, happy in his own company for a while as he gathered his thoughts and sipped gratefully on the very agreeable white wine. He'd then left the headmaster's study, to find the building almost empty. Parents and children had left for the half term holiday, leaving the place quiet and its empty corridors unnaturally still.

Now back in his own home, away from the horrors of the school, the door opened, and his wife interrupted his reverie with a welcome cup of tea, bringing him back in his mind to his own front room. As he sipped the welcome liquid, wondering what on earth he could do next, a heavy thud on the door mat announced the arrival of the post. He heaved himself out of his chair and went to

313

collect what had been delivered. Before he opened the large brown envelope which he placed on his desk - he knew roughly what it would contain - he sat back down, his mind disturbed, the moment sullied by recent events and decisions he would have to make. When he had been appointed, first as an ordinary Governor of the school, then three years ago, as its Chairman, he had no idea that the post would lead to such onerous duties. This hadn't been in the job description, he thought ruefully. Sir Martin got up and went over to his desk. He picked up the envelope and removed the report prepared by his fellow Governor, Michael Chance. It contained startling news which unsettled him, but also gave him the answer he was looking for. The events at the school had shaken him to the core; after all, Mrs Harper had been part of the package that had prompted the Governors to appoint Graham Harper in the first place. Sir Martin was not a man of fashion, so had not seen the frumpy appearance, or the badly dyed hair. He had seen a quietly spoken woman, proud of her husband and obviously a caring person. All in all, it had sat well with him and his fellow interviewers. How wrong could a man be?

So now, sitting in his own room, re-reading Michael Chance's words, he had the answer he wanted. The report was very thorough. The man's years of experience in the city had made him a ruthless financial investigator and he hadn't missed a trick. He had come to the school and had eventually spent three days examining the books, much to Gerald's dismay. Michael had worked his way through all Gerald's precious spreadsheets, grunting every now and then, making notes in red pen in the margins, making copies of everything that interested him. It hadn't taken long for him to see the carefully hidden discrepancies in Gerald's creative accounting. The headmaster's peccadilloes became painfully obvious, and Gerald had readily admitted the cover ups. Michael had been very fair in his report; nothing had been left out but had emphasised the mitigating circumstances. He had made it quite clear that Gerald had been under enormous pressure from the headmaster; Harper

314

had been very manipulative and had really left Gerald little choice but to do what he wanted. The report went on to point out that since Harper's appointment, the school roll had diminished quite dramatically, as parent after parent became disillusioned with Harper's management, but Gerald Leigh's accountancy skills had actually made a bad job significantly better than it could have been with very careful husbandry of the available finances, notwithstanding the headmaster's fiddling. Chance advised against disciplinary measures against Gerald, but recommended a change of leadership and a careful monthly audit of the finances, until such time as the school had recovered its fortunes. He suggested that the school needed a new broom, time to sweep away the dross and start again. A relaunch for the autumn term with a new headmaster was what was needed. With a sustained advertising campaign over the next few weeks, numbers would hopefully begin to pick up again and the school's fortunes would be reversed. Sir Martin decided that he now had good reasons to dismiss the headmaster for his fraud, definitely a criminal offence. He decided against a criminal action if Harper went quietly. He would even give him the benefit of choice; either go quietly by resignation or be sacked with the full force of the law against him. He knew what he would do. Frances would also be asked to resign. If she didn't go willingly she would be sacked too, for gross misconduct in a public office. Sir Martin looked in his diary and saw that the week ahead was empty. He lost no time and made arrangements to visit the school.

Graham had ignored Sir Martin's instructions and had returned to the school. Sarah couldn't believe her eyes when he had walked in, bold as brass, and carried on as before.

"Is there something the matter, Miss Dixon?" he asked as Sarah looked up in amazement.

"No, headmaster. It's just that I didn't expect to see you here today."

"And why not, may I ask?" replied the headmaster. "I have done nothing wrong. My place is here, at the helm, guiding the school, through what will be difficult times ahead."

Sarah didn't trust herself to speak. She bowed her head, and Graham, eyeing her suspiciously, left her office and disappeared through the connecting door into his own. Sarah lost herself in her work, tidying up after a very demanding and quite disturbing half term. The summer term was always her busiest and there was much to do. As the clock ticked by, she became so engrossed in her office housekeeping that she hardly noticed as her door opened and a tall, grey haired man walked in. A gentle cough made her look up and she smiled as she recognised him immediately as Sir Martin.

"Is he here?" he asked without preamble.

"Yes, Sir Martin. He hasn't left his desk all morning. I've left him to it."

"Wise woman," smiled Sir Martin.

Sarah smiled in return and returned to her work as Sir Martin, annoyed at having his orders ignored, entered the headmaster's office without knocking. She couldn't help but overhear the heated argument that came from the other side of the door, the blustering coming from Graham himself. Half an hour later, she heard the outer door of the headmaster's study slam with a violent bang and Sir Martin re-entered her office.

"I know I shouldn't say this but I really enjoyed that. I have sent the headmaster home. He will be leaving the school with immediate effect. I have given him a month to vacate his house. I have dismissed him for financial irregularities and bringing the school into disrepute. This is in confidence, well as much as in confidence as it can be in this place. I'm sure the staff room will get to hear about it sooner or later."

"Frances?" asked Sarah.

"She's next. Need I say more?" replied Sir Martin candidly. "I'll see her in Mr Harper's study."

"Do you need me?" Sarah asked. "I thought I might have a coffee in the staff room."

"No, you clutter off. I know where you are if I need you."

Sir Martin winked conspiratorially. Sarah smiled.

As Sarah got up from her seat and prepared to vacate her office, Sir Martin went on.

"I will be informing the Deputy Head of my decision, and he will take over until a replacement head can be appointed. I trust you will support him and me in these rather unfortunate times?"

"Of course, Sir Martin, you can rely on me."

"Good girl. Thank you. Please ask Miss Smythe to come in, would you?"

"Of course."

Sarah left her office, feeling bemused and amused. The future looked bright. As she passed through Reception, she passed on Sir Martin's summons, changing the wording slightly to say that the headmaster wanted to see her in his office rather than letting the cat out of the bag too soon. Frances smiled knowingly and after collecting her cardigan from the back of her chair, swiftly made her way into the headmaster's study. Sarah paused, imagining the look on Frances' face as Sir Martin opened his conversation.

Sarah opened the door to the staff room and found it lively with animated conversation. The atmosphere seemed light and cheery, a feeling she hadn't felt in the room for such a long time. Although the school had emptied of its charges for a week, the staff stayed on, making good use of the peace and quiet to catch up with lesson planning and administrative work so often required of teachers.

"Well, that's it then," said James, as Sarah entered.

"Well, that's what then?" asked Sarah innocently.

"The head's going."

"Blimey, that was quick. I thought I'd be telling you all the news."

"I was in the hall, sorting out some piano music. I couldn't fail to hear the conversation, or should I say argument, coming from the head's study. We've just seen his nibs fairly flying down the driveway, looking like a deranged harpy in that excuse for a gown. Hoo, bloody, ray! About time too."

Sarah spent a pleasant twenty minutes discussing all the possibilities and left the staff room feeling light hearted and happy. On her way back to the office, she bumped into Frances who appeared suddenly from that direction, her cheeks damp with tears and her make up smudged. She saw Sarah and sniffed. Sarah watched her back as Frances headed for Reception, and looked on in amazement as Frances collected her coat and bag and stomped out the front door. She never looked back. Sarah walked to the front step and watched happily as Frances slammed herself into her car, and screeched off, negotiating the loose gravel down the driveway at break neck speed. The staff room had also witnessed this rather dramatic exit and cheered in unison. Sarah returned to her office to find both it and the headmaster's study empty. Sir Martin had left.

After making his way to the office of Nicholas Broughton, the Deputy Head, and apprising the man of the morning's events, Nicholas having already been warned of the expected outcome, a way ahead was discussed for the future of the school. Nicholas was invited to apply for the post but warned that the application process would be open and above board and he could expect no favours. Following a cheerful half hour in the now Acting Head's office, Sir Martin headed for Gerald Leigh's office. He knocked gently and went in without further preamble.

"Good morning, Mr Leigh," he opened cheerily.

Gerald couldn't respond in the same manner. He knew just what was coming. He almost started to reach for his coat, knowing there could only be one outcome to this interview. The end result was inevitable.

"No, sit, Gerald. I just want a chat."

Gerald slowly lowered himself back into his chair, confused as to the man's tone. This didn't sound like a man who was sounding his death knell. His heart fluttered slightly, hope daring to rise.

"As you know, Mr Chance has made a thorough examination of the school's finances," opened Sir Martin quietly.

Gerald's hope was squashed back into the depths. It was all very confusing.

"Yes," replied Gerald gingerly, not wishing to commit himself to any comment, one way or the other, or influence the tide of the conversation, just yet.

"It makes disturbing reading, as you can imagine."

"Yes, it would. I'm ….."

Gerald was stopped in his tracks.

"I know what you're thinking," went on Sir Martin imperturbably. "We are fully aware of what Mr Harper has been up to and also that you have had a hand in the deceit."

Gerald squirmed. This wasn't going well.

"However, Mr Chance and I are fully aware that you were put into an intolerable position and probably had no choice but to acquiesce in the headmaster's demands."

Sir Martin paused and Gerald held his breath, not daring to hope.

"We are also aware that the school's finances are in a perilous situation but also that they would have been even more dire had it not been for your careful husbandry of the school's finances, notwithstanding the headmaster's fraud."

Gerald slumped in his chair. Could he hope?

"With that in mind we have decided on the following action."

The Chairman of the Governors then went on to explain what had been decided and that Gerald would not face any disciplinary action. After a long conversation, when all the nuts and bolts of the decision making had been discussed, Sir Martin stood, shook Gerald's hand and left in a flurry of activity. Gerald just sat and stared out of the window, He had been dreading this interview knowing it had to happen. Now he felt considerably happier if not a little chastened. He'd had a really narrow escape.

Epilogue

Two weeks later, Alexis sat at her desk, drinking a mug of coffee from her new coffee machine. A beautiful picture of the castle now adorned the wall and a small pot of geraniums on the desk danced happily in the summer breeze that came through the open window. She had arrived early that morning, now fully recovered from her head cold and eager to get on with the day. On the way in, she had bought a local paper, much out of habit more than anything, but this morning the paper proved to be very interesting. The headlines glared out at her and she read them with mounting glee. Then, jumping up from her desk she went out into the main office.

"Hey everyone, stop everything and listen to this."

All eyes turned to Alexis who stood holding the newspaper out in front of her.

"Mr Graham Harper, the headmaster of Coates Norton School, has resigned from his post with immediate effect. This newspaper has learned that following the arrest of his wife, he has been offered early retirement. It is also reported that Miss Frances Smythe, the school's receptionist has also resigned."

Alexis paused for effect and was not disappointed. A loud cheer went up round the room.

"Never did like that man", said Dax. "Nothing about financial irregularities then or naughty goings on."

"I suspect Sir Martin took the best line he could for the good of the school."

"Seems sensible," replied Dax.

"He got what was coming to him," said Hannah.

The buzz in the office stopped as Alexis resumed.

"Readers will know that a series of murders was carried out at the school, and officers from Teigneford Police, led by Detective Inspector Alexis Longbow, arrested Mrs Harper, the headmaster's wife, on suspicion of murder. She is now awaiting trial at Crown Court for these offences."

"How the mighty are fallen," went on Dax. "Harper must be feeling humiliated beyond measure. Wonder what he's doing now."

"Don't know," replied Alexis. "The grape vine has it that he was asked to leave and given a month to vacate his house."

"Pity the new incumbent," said Hannah. "If the house is anything like the garage, it'll be a right state, particularly as Mrs Harper hasn't been there to keep things tidy. I bet it's gone to the dogs."

Alexis laughed and returned to her office, leaving the paper on Dax's desk for everyone to pore over. She went to the window and looked out, taking advantage of the summer sunshine. The world carried on as normal; the street below her was busy with people coming and going, intent on their own lives. The scene presented a normality which was comforting, but she was not fooled. The crimes still happened, both petty and more serious. She would never be without a job. As she turned back to her desk, her phone rang. Picking it up, she recognised the husky tones of Phil Greenford, the Custody Sergeant.

"Someone to see you, ma'am. Parents of that young lass out at that school."

"Thanks, Phil. Can you show them up?"

Alexis went to the outer door and greeted Mr and Mrs Bourne, Maisie's parents, as they reached the office. After making them comfortable in her office, and after they declined a cup of tea, she sat quietly facing them and waited for them to speak. She had no idea what to expect. Mrs Bourne sat quietly in her seat as Mr Bourne spoke.

"We just wanted to come and see you, just to say thank you."

Alexis blinked in surprise. She hadn't expected a thank you. For once, she was lost for words. What could she say that didn't sound trite? Their daughter had suffered a terrible blow, something which would take a long time to come to terms with, if ever she did, so why did her parents want to say thank you. Pulling herself together, she spoke a simple question.

"How is Maisie?"

"Doing better than we could ever have expected, thank you. The way you and your officers treated her was so kind."

"Maisie still has to endure the trial. Is she still up for that?"

"Oh, yes," replied Mr Bourne fervently. "We did try to warn her about what she would be expected to face, but she's a feisty lass and she's determined. Wants to do it for Fliss, she said."

"She's a very brave girl …" Alexis paused, wanting to ask a question but not knowing how to phrase it without causing offence. Mrs Bourne lifted her head and smiled.

"I know what you want to ask and no, she isn't, thank goodness."

Alexis relaxed. What had befallen Felicity had been spared Maisie.

"I'm glad," she replied simply.

"Anyway, we won't keep you," went on Maisie's father. "Just wanted to say hello and thank you."

"I'm glad Maisie is OK," replied Alexis gently. "Give her our love."

"Thank you. We will."

"I'll keep you posted on court arrangements; it'll probably be within the next couple of months or so, but if there's anything we can do for Maisie or you in the meantime, then just let me know."

Mr and Mrs Bourne stood to leave, and Alexis led them back downstairs. As she watched their retreating backs, she sighed gently. Felicity had paid a huge price but her death had not been in vain. Maisie lived and so would other girls in the future, spared from an evil man and his vile predilections. She went back upstairs, her mind thoughtful, and returned to her office. It was then she noticed a long slim cream envelope in her in-tray, marked with the Coates Norton School crest. She picked it up and slightly puzzled, slit the envelope open carefully with a long thin paper knife and read the contents. Alexis smiled.

'Dear Detective Inspector Longbow

I write to thank you and your team for the discretion and care you observed during your recent investigation into the unfortunate events which took place at the school. This matter was handled with the utmost attention and your discrete action has minimised the damage which could otherwise have been occasioned.

You will no doubt be aware that the headmaster and the receptionist have been dismissed and I thank you for your observations in this matter.

Yours sincerely

General, Sir Martin Friend

Chairman to the Governing Board, Coates Norton School.'

Alexis slid the letter back in its envelope and sighed with satisfaction. Her first case as a detective inspector had been a tricky one, but the end result was all that she could have wished for. Mavis, Felicity and Alan Rees could now rest in peace and the school could move forward. A job well done. The phone on her desk broke through her thoughts. Picking it up, she recognised the rather high pitched tones of Superintendent Edward Barnes. Summoning her to his office, and leaving her with no choice, Alexis put on her jacket and made her way gloomily upstairs. Once seated in front of Barnes' desk, she waited for him to speak.

"Miss Longbow…" he started. Alexis groaned inwardly. "I apologise, force of habit, Inspector Longbow, if I may?"

"Thank you, sir. I'd appreciate that," replied Alexis. Perhaps this wasn't going to be so bad after all.

"I have kept myself fully up to date with events surrounding the recent murders at the school and I congratulate you on a successful outcome." Barnes paused and Alexis held her breath.

"I admit I had grave reservations about your appointment at this station, as head of CID. I was rather upset that I hadn't been consulted over this appointment. However, you have acquitted yourself well and I am now satisfied that your appointment was justified."

"Well, thank you sir. I appreciate your kind words." Alexis found herself echoing the superintendent's rather old fashioned way of speaking. Barnes didn't seem to notice. He stood up and Alexis realised that the interview was over. She stood and shook the superintendent's outstretched hand, noticing as she did so a similar long slim cream envelope emblazoned with a distinctive crest sitting opened on his desk. She smiled. Sir Martin had obviously sung her praises and the superintendent had reacted accordingly. Leaving the office, her heart swelled with pride, and she headed back to her office and her team with a light step. It was a good day.

Printed in Great Britain
by Amazon